Amanda Stevens is an  fifty novels, including t... Graveyard Queen. Her b... eerie and atmospheric and ... the classic ghost story.' Born and raised in the rural South, she now resides in Houston, Texas, where she enjoys binge-watching, bike riding and the occasional margarita.

Rachel Lee was hooked on writing by the age of twelve and practised her craft as she moved from place to place all over the United States. This *New York Times* bestselling author now resides in Florida and has the joy of writing full-time.

Also by Amanda Stevens

Pine Lake
Whispering Springs
Digging Deeper
The Secret of Shutter Lake
The Killer Next Door

A Procedural Crime Story
Little Girl Gone
John Doe Cold Case
Looks That Kill

Also by Rachel Lee

Conard County: The Next Generation
Conard County Revenge
Conard County Watch
Hunted in Conard County
Conard County Conspiracy
Conard County Protector
Stalked in Conard County
Conard County: Killer in the Storm
Conard County: Murderous Intent
Conard County: Covert Avenger

Discover more at millsandboon.co.uk

THE SECRETS SHE HID

AMANDA STEVENS

CONARD COUNTY SECRETS

RACHEL LEE

MILLS & BOON

All rights reserved including the right of reproduction in whole or in part in any form. This edition is published by arrangement with Harlequin Enterprises ULC.

This is a work of fiction. Names, characters, places, locations and incidents are purely fictional and bear no relationship to any real life individuals, living or dead, or to any actual places, business establishments, locations, events or incidents. Any resemblance is entirely coincidental.

This book is sold subject to the condition that it shall not, by way of trade or otherwise, be lent, resold, hired out or otherwise circulated without the prior consent of the publisher in any form of binding or cover other than that in which it is published and without a similar condition including this condition being imposed on the subsequent purchaser.

® and ™ are trademarks owned and used by the trademark owner and/or its licensee. Trademarks marked with ® are registered with the United Kingdom Patent Office and/or the Office for Harmonisation in the Internal Market and in other countries.

First Published in Great Britain 2025
by Mills & Boon, an imprint of HarperCollins*Publishers* Ltd
1 London Bridge Street, London, SE1 9GF

www.harpercollins.co.uk

HarperCollins*Publishers*
Macken House, 39/40 Mayor Street Upper,
Dublin 1, D01 C9W8, Ireland

The Secrets She Hid © 2025 Marilyn Medlock Amann
Conard County Secrets © 2025 Susan Civil-Brown

ISBN: 978-0-263-39713-0

0525

This book contains FSC™ certified paper and other controlled sources to ensure responsible forest management.

For more information visit: www.harpercollins.co.uk/green

Printed and Bound in the UK using 100% Renewable Electricity at
CPI Group (UK) Ltd, Croydon, CR0 4YY

THE SECRETS SHE HID

AMANDA STEVENS

Chapter One

The ringtone pealed persistently. With a muttered oath, Veda Campion snaked an arm from beneath the covers to grope for the phone on the nightstand. Shoving aside the quilt, she glanced at the screen. Her brother's name shocked her awake, and she sprang up in bed.

"Nate? What's wrong? Has something happened to Mom?"

His voice boomed back reassuringly. "Relax. She's fine as far as I know. I had dinner with her early last evening."

"Thank God." They were all still on edge since their mother's heart attack six months ago. Veda leaned back against the headboard and swiped tangles from her face as she frowned into the darkness. "Then, why are you calling at two in morning?"

"Did you forget you're the acting coroner until Dr. Bader gets back from vacation?"

"No, of course I didn't forget. I'm still half-asleep, is all." Actually, her temporary position really had slipped her mind. She blamed the memory lapse on exhaustion and a lingering irritation that she'd been so easily manipulated by her former mentor. Dr. Bader had been persistent about his future plans for her despite her objections to the contrary. She had no interest in returning to her hometown on a permanent basis. Yet somehow her unpaid leave from the Orleans Parish Coroner's Office had turned into a resignation, and the next thing she knew she'd signed a short-term lease on a furnished bungalow in Milton, Mississippi, while she contemplated her next career move.

"Veda? You still with me?"

The question dragged her back into the conversation. "Yes, I'm here. What's going on?"

"A body was found in Cedarville Cemetery earlier tonight. A group of partying teenagers called it in." His tone subtly shifted as tension hardened his delivery. He was no longer her older brother but instead a seasoned police detective following protocol. "We can't finish processing the scene until you come out here and take charge of the body."

She swung her legs over the side of the bed, adrenaline already starting to pump. "You've kept the area clean?"

"Relatively speaking. The first responders set up a perimeter and established an entry point, and we've limited the number of personnel we're letting through the gates. Even so, forensics is going to be a bear on this one. Those kids left footprints all over the damn place. The more time goes by, the greater the chance for contamination."

"Did they touch the body?"

"They swear they didn't, but those footprints tell a different story. I wouldn't be surprised if they texted close-ups of the victim to some of their friends. We'll be damn lucky if the images don't turn up on social media."

Veda nodded absently as she rose. With the phone pressed to her ear, she strode across the room and started pulling clothes from her closet with one hand. "You think it's a homicide?"

"Officially, that's for you to determine, but we've got a male Caucasian shot in the back of the head. So yeah, I'd say we're definitely dealing with a homicide." Nate lowered his voice as if wary of being overheard. "Brace yourself. The victim is Tony Redmond."

Veda froze, one hand still grasping the phone, the other a clean pair of jeans. She let the jeans fall to the floor. "Are you sure?"

"Pretty damn sure, even though he's lying facedown in the dirt."

She closed her eyes and said on a breath, "My God, Nate."

"I know. I wasn't expecting to start my week like this."

"Start your week?"

"Check the calendar. It's officially Monday morning."

"You say he was found prone?" Veda took a moment to collect her composure before asking the obvious questions. "*You* didn't touch him, did you? You didn't roll him over?"

"Didn't have to. I recognized his tattoos."

She went back over to the bed and sat down on the edge as she tried to wrap her head around the news. Her sister's killer shot dead in the same cemetery where Lily had been laid to rest seventeen years ago. Veda didn't know how to react. She had an odd sense of relief—a lightness—that left her feeling ashamed. They were talking about a human being, after all. A son, a brother.

Then dread descended. Justice might have been served, but by whom?

Her heart started to pound, and her mouth went suddenly dry. She swallowed and tried to calm her racing pulse. "You haven't been alone with the body, have you, Nate?"

He sounded annoyed. "Do you even need to ask that question? Give me some credit."

"I know. I know. I just don't want anything coming back on you. On any of us. This is tricky, given our history with Tony Redmond."

"You don't need to worry about me. The officers who responded to the call were still on the scene when I arrived. As soon as I recognized the victim, I alerted the chief. He's already assigned another detective to take lead."

She noted his use of their uncle's title rather than his first name. Probably her brother's way of trying to subvert any notion of favoritism within the police department. He wouldn't like having his credentials called into question. "That's for the best, I suppose, though I doubt the gesture will appease the Redmonds. Conflict of interest in this town goes all the way to the top. None of us should be anywhere near this case. You, me or Marcus."

"It is what it is," Nate said. "We're small-town law enforcement. Our resources and manpower are limited. We don't have the luxury of picking and choosing our cases. You're the only coroner we've got until Dr. Bader returns from his trip."

"He'll be back first thing in the morning. *This* morning. You couldn't have waited a few hours?" she added with a note of sarcasm.

"You'll have to talk to the killer about his timing. If it's any consolation, I did try Dr. Bader's number. He's not picking up."

Veda took another breath, still with that anvil of dread hanging over her head. Her hand slipped to her throat as unwelcome images streamed from a dark corner of her subconscious. She didn't want to think such thoughts, but she couldn't seem to shut off the spigot. "Has his family been notified?"

"Not yet. We're waiting for the official death pronouncement."

She turned on the bed so that she could stare out the window. She had a sudden notion of red eyes watching her from the darkness. Nothing but fantasy, of course. There were no demons in downtown Milton, Mississippi. Only murderers.

"What a sad and sordid ending to Tony Redmond's story," she murmured. "He's been out of prison for only a few weeks, and now this. In spite of everything, I can't help feeling sorry for his mother. She finally got her son back only to lose him for good this time. I can only imagine how hard his death will hit her."

"You and I don't have to imagine, do we?" Rather than an angry comeback, Nate's response seemed measured. "We saw what Lily's murder did to our own mother. She'll never get over it. None of us will."

Veda frowned at his tone. He sounded calm, yet she knew his emotions had to be in turmoil like hers. Lily's killer dead after all these years. Shot in the back of the head by an as-yet unknown assailant. Was it justice or revenge? Or completely unrelated to their sister's murder, as Veda fervently hoped? For some reason, Nate's low-key delivery only deepened her unease.

"Are you okay?" she asked.

"Why wouldn't I be?"

She was reluctant to explain her concern. "You're saying all the right things, but you sound…odd. Almost too cool under the circumstances."

She could imagine his shrug on the other end. "What do you expect? I've been doing this job for a long time. I know how to handle myself. I'm not about to let my emotions or personal animus toward the victim and his family get in the way of doing what has to be done. I'm better than that."

"I know you are."

"But between us? Between you and me?" He paused for a long moment as if debating on how much he would allow to slip through the cracks. "I won't be losing any sleep over what happened out here tonight. As far as I'm concerned, Tony Redmond got what was coming to him."

"You probably shouldn't say that, even to me," she cautioned. "The Redmonds will be looking for any excuse to point fingers."

"I said what we're both thinking. As for his family, they moved heaven and earth to get that creep out of prison. Jon Redmond became an attorney for the sole purpose of working on his brother's appeal. Then he had the nerve to come back here and run for DA so that he could make sure the charges wouldn't be refiled once he got Tony released. He played the long game, and it backfired on him tonight. I bet he'll wish in hindsight he'd left well enough alone. If Tony had been behind bars where he belonged, he'd still be alive."

"That's harsh, Nate."

"It's the truth. Isn't that what you wanted to hear?"

"Maybe, but let's be honest. Would either of us have done any different in Jon Redmond's shoes?"

"Luckily, we don't need to wonder because our brother didn't kill anyone."

Veda found herself shivering despite the summer heat. She tried to ignore the suffocating chill, but an ugly premonition had been slithering closer and closer from the moment she'd answered Nate's call.

She fell silent, loath to give credence to the terrible thoughts running through her head. But she needed to be candid with Nate so that he could dispel her doubts. "Speaking of our brother, when was the last time you spoke with Owen?"

Nate's voice sharpened. "Why?"

"When did you last see him?" she pressed.

"Don't go there," he warned.

She tightened her grip on the phone. "I don't want to, but how can I not after everything that's happened?"

"Damn it, Veda Louise."

"Don't *Veda Louise* me. Whether you want to admit it or not, Owen could be in big trouble."

"For what? It was a scuffle. Stop trying to make a mountain out of a molehill."

"Trust me, I'm not. You've only heard Owen's version of the fight, and he downplayed what happened for Mom's sake. But I was there, and I'm telling you it was vicious. You should have seen the way he and Tony went after each other. I thought one of them would end up dead on the street, and there wasn't a damn thing I could do to stop them. It took four grown men to pull them apart."

"What's your point, Veda?"

"I'm not the only one who saw Owen throw the first punch. Even after it was over, he couldn't keep his mouth shut. He told Tony Redmond if he ever came near anyone in his family again, he'd kill him."

Nate swore.

"You see why I'm worried? I don't want to say it. I don't want to even think it—"

"Then, don't," Nate said. "Owen is home in bed asleep."

"You know that for a fact?"

"I've no reason to believe otherwise, and neither do you."

"We can't just wish this away, Nate. Too many people saw and heard what Owen did. Once those witnesses come forward, our little brother could find himself at the top of the suspect list."

She heard Nate draw a breath. "I'll be the first to admit Owen's behavior does him no favors. He's always been a hothead. I've wanted to throttle him myself more times than I can count. But he's not a killer. Remember that before you go borrowing trouble. For now, focus on your job, and let the police worry about suspects."

If only she could let it go that easily. The public confrontation—undoubtedly captured by at least one cell phone—was enough to trigger suspicion. Unless Owen had an airtight alibi for the time of death, no one would be able to protect him. Not Nate. Not their uncle. Certainly not Veda. She prayed he was home in bed asleep, but even then, unless he had a companion, he'd have no way of verifying his whereabouts.

Earlier, she'd been sympathetic about how the news would affect Theresa Redmond, but what about her own mother? The investigation would take a toll on both families, just as it had seventeen years ago. She could still hear the dread in her mother's voice when she learned of Owen's clash with Tony Redmond.

Promise me you won't go near that man again. I'm serious, Owen. If he decides to press charges, you could end up in jail. I couldn't take that. You behind bars, and Lily's killer free to do as he pleases. I couldn't bear to lose another child.

I'm not going to jail, and you're not going to lose me. You're not going to lose any of us. Right, Nate? Right, Veda? We have each other's backs no matter what.

No matter what.

"Veda?"

"Still here."

"How soon can you get to the scene?"

She shook off the memory and stood. "Fifteen minutes. Front or back entrance?"

"Front. You'll see the lights. And Veda?"

"What?"

"Just do what has to be done tonight and then back off. Dr. Bader will be back on the job in a few hours. Let him handle the postmortem. No reason for you to be involved beyond the death pronouncement."

Just do what has to be done tonight and then back off.

She told herself not to dwell on the implication as she pulled on jeans and a plain white T-shirt. No reason to speculate as to why her big brother seemed so eager to isolate her from the investigation. Not yet, at least.

JON REDMOND YAWNED as he glanced at the time on his phone. It was just after two in the morning and he'd yet to close his eyes. He was too wired to sleep. Too anxious about what his brother might be up to tonight. Instead of going to bed, he'd been sitting on the balcony of his second-story apartment for the past three hours willing his phone to ring. He told himself for the umpteenth time that he was overreacting. Letting his imagination get the better of him. Tony had only been incommunicado for a few hours. No need to anticipate the worst. But coming on the heels of their recent blowout, his brother's silence worried Jon. A lot.

Sipping the bourbon he'd been nursing for hours, he went back over everything that had happened earlier in the evening in case he'd missed a clue. He'd left the office around nine and swung by their mother's place hoping to find Tony in the small guesthouse where he'd been staying since his release from prison. The two brothers had unfinished business to discuss, and Jon had been determined to keep his cool this time. No easy feat, considering everything that had gone down between them during their last confrontation.

Ever since an ex-con named Clay Stipes had hit town, the whole family had been on edge. Stipes posed a myriad of potential problems for Tony and now for Jon. In hindsight, his career as the Webber County DA—not to mention his peace of mind—might have been better served by remaining in the dark, but too late for that now. He'd demanded the truth, and now he found himself embroiled in a mess that could have far-reaching consequences. The sooner he and Tony hashed out a plan to deal with Clay Stipes, the sooner they could send him on his way and put his threats behind them.

But the windows in the guesthouse had been dark, and the front door locked. Jon's knock had gone unanswered as had his text messages and voice mails. He'd left the property without stopping by to see his mother. He didn't want to worry her or his younger sister Gabby unless it became absolutely necessary to bring them into the loop. Having Tony home from prison after seventeen years was a big enough adjustment. No need to exacerbate an already stressful situation.

Instead, Jon had driven around town for a couple of hours checking the parking lots of local bars and watering holes. He'd gone inside a few of the places he knew Tony had recently frequented to see if anyone remembered seeing him that night, either alone or with a companion. No such luck.

Finally, he'd given up the search and gone home. Tony was a grown man. He'd survived nearly two decades in a maximum-security prison. Jon reminded himself that if anyone knew how to take care of himself, it was his brother.

Yet here he sat drinking and brooding when there wasn't a damn thing he could do about the situation until the bank opened at nine. He already had an appointment. All he had to do was go in and apply for a loan. He and the bank manager had gone to high school together. They'd played on the same baseball team. That should count for something. He had good credit, a decent salary and a small piece of land that could be used for collateral. He should be able to get his hands on a significant amount of money without too much effort. Once the funds were transferred into his account, he and Tony could figure out their next move.

He finished the remainder of his drink in one quick gulp. The burn of the alcohol did little to alleviate his unease. Another drink might have helped, but he resisted the temptation. *Stay calm, keep a clear head.* Clay Stipes was a dangerous man. Not just an ex-con but a former cop who'd killed his partner. That he'd gotten out after serving ten years was a testament to the weaknesses and loopholes in the judicial system. But then, he supposed there were those who thought the same about Tony's release.

Bottom line, neither brother could afford to let down his guard until Stipes agreed to leave town. Maybe not even then. Trusting a blackmailer to keep his word was asking for trouble, but Jon didn't see any other way out. Stipes had the upper hand. As long as Marcus Campion remained chief of police, going to the cops wasn't an option.

As the minutes continued to tick by, he grew more and more restless. He reconsidered calling his mother, but she would be fast asleep at this hour, and a phone call would only panic her. He could text Gabby instead. College had turned his little sister into a night owl. He had a feeling she'd still be up, and she had a view of the backyard from her bedroom window. He could at least ask her to check to see if the lights were on in the guesthouse or if Tony's truck was in the driveway. Still, he hesitated. Once he sounded the alarm, there would be no going back.

Then go to bed. What the hell do you hope to accomplish by sitting out here all night?

He got up, but instead of going inside, he moved to the balcony railing and peered down into the manicured grounds of his apartment complex. He was so tense that for a moment he imagined Clay Stipes in the park across the street staring up at his apartment. In the next instant, he realized the sinister shadow was a bush. Not a good sign when he started conjuring bad guys from shrubbery.

Not a good sign and not at all like him. During the seventeen years of his brother's incarceration, he'd managed to keep a level head even in the darkest of times. Compartmentalization was the key. He'd learned how to shut down his racing thoughts the moment his head hit the pillow. It was the only way he'd been able to survive all those years of burning the candle at both ends. He supposed it was ironic and more than a little unsettling that he hadn't had a decent night's sleep since his brother's release.

There'd been a moment, however, as he'd watched his brother walk through the prison gates a free man when the weight of the world seemed to lift from his shoulders. Everything he'd worked so hard for his entire adult life had come to fruition, and his family finally had a chance to heal and be whole again.

The elation had faded almost at once because his brother's physical appearance outside the prison walls was shocking. Looking back, Jon wasn't sure why he'd reacted so viscerally. After all, he'd witnessed firsthand Tony's transformation over the years. The wavy hair that had once made high-school girls swoon had grown down his back, and he wore it pulled back in a scraggly, dull ponytail. Then came the crazy patchwork of tattoos all up and down his arms and around his neck. The boyish swagger of a high-school football star was replaced by the surly wariness of a convict.

He'd bulked up because prison was about nothing if not survival of the fittest.

During his first few days of freedom, Tony had spent most of his time sitting in the sun with his face tipped to the sky. By the end of the second week, he'd begun to open up a little about his time in prison and to even crack a smile now and then. He started to talk about getting a job and maybe going back to school. His plans for the future thrilled their mother. Jon hadn't seen her so happy in years. Everything seemed to be working out until Clay Stipes blew into town with a murder-for-hire scheme that threatened to ensnare the whole Redmond family.

The peal of the ringtone startled him from a deep reverie. He picked up the phone and answered anxiously. "Tony? Where the hell have you been all night?"

The caller hesitated before identifying himself. "This is Marcus Campion." Another pause. "I'm afraid I have some bad news about your brother."

A FEW MINUTES after Nate's call, Veda headed to the garage to check her kit and the supplies she kept in the back of her SUV. A jolt of caffeine would have helped clear the cobwebs, but no time for coffee. She still had a few things to do before she set out for the cemetery. Besides, adrenaline had already made her jittery. Experience had taught her that she was better off sipping water and practicing relaxation techniques on her way to a crime scene.

Her forensic kit included everything from vials and syringes for collecting samples to paper jumpsuits, gloves and shoe covers to protect the crime scene. In a separate bag, she kept rubber boots, sneakers and an extra set of clothing. If the body hadn't yet decomposed, she wouldn't need to change at the scene, but better to be safe than sorry. She'd learned the hard way that the smell of death was nearly impossible to remove from a vehicle once the stench had penetrated the carpet fibers and circulated through the air vents.

She opened the garage door and stepped outside. Drawing in the night air, she stood with eyes closed and tried to ground herself. Images of Lily flitted through her mind. She could almost hear her sister's voice repeating her brother's warning.

Don't borrow trouble, Veda. Be patient and let the answers come to you. You've always been the clever sister. You'll know what to do.

If only that was true, but Veda had never been as shrewd as Lily had made her out to be. She hadn't been blessed with the same powerful combination of beauty and brains that her sister had possessed. Before that fateful night, everyone in town would have sworn Lily Campion had a brilliant future ahead of her. Veda was known as the quiet sister. Smart enough and pretty enough, but never Lily's equal, and she'd always been fine with the comparison. As she grew older, she'd become comfortable in her sister's shadow. With all the attention focused on Lily, Veda could pretty much do as she pleased.

But her sister's murder had changed everything. The once-playful camaraderie between the Campion siblings vanished overnight. Easygoing Nate had morphed into a control freak. Owen, the wild child, became rebellious and reckless. Veda retreated inward. For too many years, they'd remained virtual strangers. Their mother's heart attack had brought them closer, but even now, Veda couldn't say she knew her brothers any more than they knew her. She had no idea what either of them were capable of these days. Tony Redmond's release from prison had pushed a lot of dangerous buttons.

She watched the clouds for a moment longer before climbing into her vehicle and backing down the driveway. Leaving her neighborhood behind, she sped through the deserted streets. As she neared the destination, she began to mentally gear up for the task at hand.

Cedarville Cemetery was located within the city limits, giving the Milton Police Department jurisdiction over the crime scene. The historic graveyard was surrounded on three sides by a forest that cast deep shadows even on the sunniest of days. The place had once fascinated Veda. Some of the interments dated back to the Civil War era, and as a kid, she'd spent many Sunday afternoons with her grandmother wandering through the headstones and monuments.

Like her grandmother, Veda had always sought out quiet little corners, and it could be argued that she still preferred the company of the dead to the living. Not for the first time, she wondered what Lily would think of her profession. Her family had never understood her decision to specialize in forensic pathology, even Nate who knew better than most the value of a skilled medical examiner in the autopsy room. Her brothers found her professional choices strange and her solitary lifestyle puzzling, and she was okay with that, too.

She pulled her SUV to the curb and parked behind the coroner's van, relieved to note that the movers had already arrived on the scene. She would need one of them to video her examination of the body while the other took photographs. The county morgue was a small office. Everyone pitched in where needed.

The wind was up, and she could see flickers of lightning

in the distance. Goose bumps rose at the base of her neck and along her bare arms. She had a bad feeling about the weather.

Climbing into the paper jumpsuit, she grabbed her kit and then followed the voices she heard on the other side of the fence. The sound echoed eerily in the dark, and she found herself shivering again as she approached the gate. Her brother met her just inside. A point of entry had been established using wooden stakes and crime-scene tape. A portable floodlight had been set up near the body, casting a harsh glare over the immediate area. With the backdrop of monuments and mausoleums, the scene struck Veda as surreal.

If she peered beyond the illumination, she could still picture the silhouette of the old stone angel that loomed over the other headstones. She'd once loved the romantic legend behind the crumbling statue, but for a time after Lily's death, Veda could have sworn the angel took on her sister's features. The perceived likeness had unsettled her because rather than emanating a heavenly aura, the marble face seemed icy and judgmental. Rationally, Veda knew the accusatory visage had been born out of her guilt. She wasn't responsible for her sister's murder, and she knew Lily would never have blamed her. Yet how many sleepless nights had she spent agonizing over what she could have said or done to stop her sister from leaving the house that night?

She remained outwardly composed as she tightened her grip on her case.

Nate said quietly at her side, "When was the last time you were here?"

"To Cedarville? Years ago." She glanced around the shadowy landscape. "Hard to believe I used to find this place peaceful. Almost spiritual in a way. Now it just seems sad and oppressive."

"The reason you're here may have something to do with that perception," he said.

"True."

She fell silent, her gaze fixed on the prone outline of her sister's killer. She tried to stay focused, but memories continued to assail her. Lily daydreaming in the backyard hammock. Picking flowers from their mother's garden. In a yellow sundress waving goodbye through the open window of Tony Redmond's truck.

Lily keeping secrets.

Who was he, Lily? The man you fell for that summer. Why wouldn't you tell me his name? And why did he never come forward after you died?

At the back of Veda's mind, a tiny doubt had been flickering for seventeen years. Had the wrong man been sent to prison?

Chapter Two

Veda was jolted back to the present when her uncle came up beside her. He placed his hand lightly on her shoulder. "You made good time getting out here."

She tried to shake off the foreboding that still gripped her as she turned to greet him, but the circumstances and her surroundings made that impossible. "No traffic at this hour. The streets were completely deserted." She suppressed a shiver. "Almost too quiet if you ask me."

"Not for long," he warned. "Only a matter of time before all hell breaks loose."

In his late fifties, Marcus Campion was still lean and rugged with deep lines around his mouth and eyes and a thick head of hair cut military-short. He wasn't in uniform tonight but instead had dressed in jeans, boots and a plaid shirt rolled up to his elbows. His causal attire made him seem more approachable, but his grim expression and ramrod posture were still intimidating.

"We need to talk about what to expect while we're still out of earshot of the others," he said.

"Can it wait until after I've seen the body?" Veda asked. "The weather could change at any minute."

He cast a quick glance at the sky. "Storm's miles away. Besides, this won't take long, and it's important."

She wanted to remind him that the sooner she did her job, the sooner his people could do theirs, but she intuited from the stubborn set of his mouth and jawline that he intended to say his piece, regardless.

Tamping down her impatience, she nodded.

He kept his voice low as he took a step forward to close the circle. "Once word gets out about Redmond's death, the press will be all over this thing. I wouldn't be surprised if we get national attention, considering what happened seventeen years ago. They'll dredge up every sordid detail of Lily's murder and then some. You need to prepare yourselves for the spectacle. And we all need to try and shield your mother from the worst of it. She's only six months out from her heart attack. The doctors said no stress. The last thing she needs right now is to have her dead daughter's name dragged through the mud again."

"We'll do what we can, of course," Veda said. "But this is the information age. It won't be as simple as turning off the TV."

"She's right," Nate said. "Tony Redmond's murder will be all anyone in this town talks about for months."

Marcus put up a hand and said impatiently, "I don't want to hear any excuses. Just find a way to protect her. After everything she's been through, she deserves a little peace."

Veda wanted to point out that her mother's health was the main reason she'd come back to Milton, but instead she folded her arms and waited.

"Both of you need to keep a low profile until the worst blows over," Marcus said. "That shouldn't be hard. I've assigned the case to Garrett Calloway. He's relatively new in town and doesn't have any connection to either family. He'll pick his own team to work the investigation so your involvement should be minimal, Nate. That goes for you, too, Veda. Dr. Bader will be back in the morgue sometime this morning. Let him handle the postmortem. Keep your distance, and be careful what you say and do in public. Everybody and their dog will be watching. If a reporter corners you, your only comment is *No comment*."

"To that point, should you even be here?" Veda asked. "Wouldn't you and your office be better served if you also kept a low profile? Why not let your lead detective handle the press?"

"Nothing I'd like more," Marcus said. "But I'm the chief of police. I can't palm off my duties and obligations on a subordinate just because I find myself in an uncomfortable position. The public needs to know I'm on the job and that I'll treat this case as I would any other."

"What about Nate?" Veda asked.

Her brother glared at her. "What about me?"

"This isn't your case. There's no reason for you to be here."

"That's not your call."

"Keep it together," Marcus scolded in a hushed voice. He glanced around as a man Veda didn't recognize broke away from a group of cops and approached their huddle. Marcus stepped back to allow the man into their circle. "Veda, this is Detective Garrett Calloway. Garrett, my niece, Veda Campion. She's the acting coroner in Dr. Bader's absence."

Veda extended her hand, and they shook. Calloway looked to be around Nate's age, making him somewhere in his mid- to late thirties. Veda remembered her brother mentioning that the detective had been with the Memphis Police Department before moving back to rural Mississippi after a shooting. According to Nate, Calloway was lucky to be alive. His manner seemed straightforward, his handshake firm, and his gaze direct. Veda liked him at once. An outsider with no preconceived opinions and biases seemed a good choice to take lead on Tony Redmond's murder case.

"I've heard a lot about you, Dr. Campion. Webber County is lucky to have you."

"Thank you, but as my uncle said, I'm only here temporarily until Dr. Bader returns."

"I'm trying to talk her into a more permanent arrangement," Marcus said. "But that's for another day. Nate, could I have a word?"

The two wandered off leaving Veda alone with Calloway. She got right down to business. "Anything I need to know before I exam the body, Detective?"

"Only that this looks to be a bad one, though maybe not too shocking for you. Coming from New Orleans, you probably saw this kind of thing on a regular basis. I know we got our share in Memphis."

"I saw a lot of things that I hope to never get used to," she said. "What do you mean by *a bad one*? Can you be more specific?"

He gave her a look she couldn't define in the dark. "It's been my experience since moving down here that the homicides in this county are almost always drug-related or else a domestic dispute that gets out of hand. Or both. This one appears to be a professional hit. Deliberately planned and carried out in cold blood."

She tried not to outwardly react but instead casually lifted a hand to tuck back strands of hair that had blown loose in the breeze. "I would agree that a gunshot wound to the back of the head hardly seems random or impulsive."

"Take a close look at his wrists. Do they look banged-up to you?"

"Ligature marks?"

He nodded. "Which means he was likely restrained before he was shot."

"Even if he was, that doesn't preclude a drug deal gone bad." Veda's gaze flitted to a shadowy corner of the cemetery where her uncle and brother watched from a distance. Why had Nate not told her about the marks when he called earlier?

"I'm not ruling anything out at this point," Calloway said. "What I do know is that Tony Redmond was a big guy. An ex-jock from what I'm told. A local football hero."

"That was a long time ago."

"Looks like he kept himself in shape. I remember seeing him in town a few days after his release and thinking his biceps looked to be the size of small hams. Apparently, he spent a good deal of his time in prison pumping iron. Given his strength and size, he wouldn't have been easy to take down or tie up unless he was first subdued. I'm betting he was either drugged or ambushed from behind. Look for signs of blunt force trauma."

"Given the poor lighting and the amount of blood I see on the ground, that determination might have to be made after we get him cleaned up."

The detective gave another brief nod. "The postmortem will be critical in this case. The sooner we get that report, the better."

"One step at a time," Veda said. "Right now, I need to examine the body, and my team needs room to photograph and video the process."

"In other words, you want my team to back off. I get it. You have your investigation, and we have ours."

"Cooperative but independent," she agreed. "It's the only way to ensure that nothing comes back on either office. No loopholes for a clever defense attorney to exploit regarding methods and techniques."

He said approvingly, "That's an admirable goal, considering the history your family has with the deceased."

She glanced at him in surprise. "You know about that?"

He shrugged. "I used to spend summers down here with my grandparents. People talked back then, and they talk now. From what I can tell, camps are still divided. Some think he did it, a few still swear by his innocence. We may never know the truth now." He glanced back at the body. "One thing I do know. If I were in your shoes, I might find objectivity a little hard to come by."

She echoed her uncle's sentiment. "You don't need to worry about that. This case will be treated as any other."

"Then, the scene is yours, Dr. Campion."

At some point while she'd stood conversing with Detective Calloway, her brother and uncle had gone their separate ways. She thought at first Nate had taken her advice and left the scene altogether. No such luck. He'd only retreated deeper into the shadows. She could see him just beyond the reach of the portable light. She couldn't make out his expression, but she sensed the intensity of his stare. Her scalp prickled a warning. Earlier, she'd been worried about Owen's alibi, but now she was starting to wonder about Nate's.

She shifted her gaze away from her brother and reminded herself to focus. *Just do what has to be done.*

Gripping the handle of her case, she approached the deceased as Detective Calloway observed from the perimeter.

Blood had pooled on the ground beneath the body, and the sight gave her pause even though she was no stranger to crime scenes. This was different. The victim's identity challenged her concentration. Her mind kept wandering back to Lily. How could it not? She was only human, after all.

Her uncle was right. Given the circumstances, this would be a big case for Webber County. Lots of speculation, lots of media attention. The role she and her family played in the investigation would likely come under intense scrutiny. It was imperative that she remain in control of her emotions and perform her duties to the best of her abilities. No mistakes. No lapse in judgment. Not a single shred of evidence could be overlooked because of carelessness or lack of focus.

She set her case on the ground and snapped on a pair of latex gloves as she nodded to the two waiting morgue attendants. "Ready?"

First, she stated her name and credentials for the video, followed by the date, time and location. She took a few moments to draw a verbal sketch of the immediate scene and the condition of the body. Her voice shook a bit in the beginning. She didn't think anyone else would notice, but she cleared her throat and started over.

Don't think about the victim's name. Don't think about what he did. Forget, momentarily, the last images you have of Lily. This is a crime scene like any other. You know what to do. Take readings. Collect samples. Protect the hands. Fill out the paperwork and you're finished.

She continued the commentary for the video as she felt for a pulse, a routine precaution regardless of the mortal wound at the back of his head. Then she checked for rigor mortis, lividity and insect infestation, all of which would help establish time of death and determine whether or not the body had been moved. She took measurements and the body temperature, collected blood and gun residue samples and examined the bruises and abrasions around the victim's wrists. Then she covered his hands with paper bags to preserve evidence that might be trapped on the skin or beneath the nails.

Before she closed her kit and turned the scene over to Detective Calloway, she filled out the forms and tags that would be secured inside the body bag during transport to the morgue. *No mistakes. Everything by the book.*

She nodded to Detective Calloway, who moved in eager to discuss her findings. She waited for her uncle to join them so that she didn't have to repeat her conclusions.

"He hasn't been out here long," she said. "The body is still flaccid. Cooling but not cold, and the blowflies haven't yet found him. I'd say two to three hours at the most."

"That would put time of death around midnight," Calloway said. "The kids who discovered the body called 9-1-1 just after. They were partying on the other side of the cemetery for a couple of hours before they decided to drive around to the front. They must have been here at the same time as the killer."

"They didn't hear a gunshot?" Veda asked.

"I've talked to them. They claim they had the music turned up too loud."

"It's also possible the shooter used a silencer," Marcus offered.

"Unlikely," Calloway said. "The location is remote. Why go to the trouble of obtaining a noise suppressor?"

"That's interesting," Veda mused. "They didn't hear the killer, but if the music was turned up that loud, he must have heard them."

Calloway looked interested. "Meaning?"

"Why would he take the time to remove the restraints around the victim's wrists?"

"That's a damn good question, Dr. Campion."

"No one noticed a vehicle parked in the area or leaving the cemetery?" she asked.

"They came in through the rear gate. The suspect would have been long gone by the time they circled around to the front gate. That's when they spotted the victim. They got out of the car to see if he was still alive."

"Can you isolate their footprints from any other fresh prints?" Veda asked.

Her uncle answered the question. "Even if we could, it wouldn't help much. People are in and out of this cemetery all the time. There was a memorial service here just this afternoon." He nodded in the direction of a fresh grave. "Lots of people, lots of footprints. A procession of cars in and out of both gates."

"Do you think the killer was aware of the recent foot traffic?" Veda asked. "Maybe that's why he picked this spot."

"I have a couple of theories about the location," Calloway said, but he didn't elaborate as he turned back to the deceased. "I'll let you know when you can remove the body."

She nodded and stepped away from the immediate area to give the detective and his team room to work. Nate sauntered over as she and her uncle watched silently from the sidelines. He looked tense and pale in the harsh glow from the portable lights. "What did you find?"

"Time of death was likely around midnight," her uncle interjected.

"That's not what I mean." His gaze was still on Veda. "You kept focusing on his hands. What were you looking for?"

"I was trying to get a better look at the marks around his wrists," she explained.

He looked surprised. "What marks?"

"You didn't see them earlier?"

"Would I be asking for clarification if I had?"

She hesitated. "Weren't you the one who told me to do what needed to be done and then back off? Shouldn't you take your own advice?"

"Just answer the question, Veda."

"No, she's right," Marcus said. "You need to get the hell out of here and let Garrett do his job."

"How am I stopping him?" Nate demanded as he turned his back to the scene. "What marks, Veda?"

She glanced at her uncle who gave an exasperated sigh before he nodded. "He has what looks to be ligature marks around his wrists."

"Ligature marks?" Nate sounded incredulous. "As in, someone tied him up?"

"Detective Calloway thinks Tony was somehow incapacitated—possibly drugged or from a blow to the head—before he was brought out here."

"Did you see any other marks or wounds on the body that would corroborate his theory?" Nate asked.

"Not yet. We'll have a better idea of what happened once we get him cleaned up and on the slab."

"Let's go with Garrett's theory for a moment," Marcus said. "Someone knocked Redmond out, tied him up and brought him all the way out here to kill him. Before leaving the cemetery and with a bunch of kids partying within earshot, he then took the time to remove whatever had been used to restrain the victim's hands. Why?"

"Maybe he was worried about leaving something traceable behind," Nate suggested.

"That was my thought, too," Veda agreed. "We may be able to determine the nature of the bindings once we get those bruises under a magnifier."

"Will you let me know what you find out?" Nate asked.

Marcus cut in impatiently. "Plenty of time to worry about that later. Right now, someone needs to go and see your mother. We won't be able to keep this under wraps for long, and I'd hate like hell for her to hear about the shooting on the news."

"What about Tony Redmond's next of kin?" Veda asked.

"I'll handle the official notifications. You stay with the body, and Nate, you go talk to your mother."

Before Nate could protest, a car door slammed out on the street, and they turned in unison toward the sound.

"Let's hope someone hasn't already blabbed to the press," Marcus muttered.

But it wasn't a reporter who walked through the cemetery gates. Veda caught her breath as the newcomer strode down the designated path, pausing as he caught sight of the body illuminated by the floodlight.

Jon Redmond. The man who had worked tirelessly for nearly two decades to free her sister's killer.

Chapter Three

Veda tried to remember the last time her path had crossed with Jon Redmond other than from a distance. If memory served, their final confrontation had been outside the courtroom at his brother's trial. He'd only been twenty at the time, barely four years older than she, but the hard set of his stare and the harshness of his words had sent a chill straight through her heart.

She felt a similar sensation now as she stared at him in the dark with thunder rumbling in the distance and his murdered brother's body mere feet away. The years melted until she was back in that courthouse. She could still hear the raw anguish in his voice when he'd confronted her in the hallway, demanding to know why she'd lied on the witness stand. The accusation had shocked her, and she'd found herself responding with equal fire.

"I didn't lie! Everything I said in there was the truth."

"But not the whole truth. You said Lily confided in you that she was seeing someone behind my brother's back. But she never mentioned a name? She never even hinted at his identity? Come on, Veda. You must have some idea who he is."

"I don't. She wouldn't tell me. She said..."

"Don't stop now. What did she say?"

"The timing had to be right because a lot of people could be hurt by the truth. Especially Tony. She was worried about how he would react when he found out."

That's not what you said under oath. You said she was afraid of how he would react. Words matter, Veda. There's a difference between fear and worry. What else did you get wrong?

"Now you're just trying to confuse me."

"No. I'm just trying to get at the truth. It never occurred to you that Lily's secret lover could have killed her?"

"Then, why was the murder weapon found in Tony's truck?"

"Someone could easily have planted it. All I know for certain is that he would never have hurt Lily in a million years. He's been in love with her since ninth grade. My brother isn't a killer, and if it takes the rest of my life, I'll find a way to prove it."

Owen had been standing nearby that day, and he'd leaped to Veda's defense as the conversation had grown more heated. He'd shoved Jon aside and threatened to punch him in the face if he ever so much as looked at his sister the wrong way. Even at fourteen, her kid brother had been a firebrand. Loyal to a fault, quick to temper and never one to shy away from a fight. That was Owen. Luckily, Nate was used to cleaning up their younger brother's messes. He'd dragged Owen from the courthouse to cool him off, but not before a handful of onlookers had gotten an earful.

The episode in the hallway was only one of many clashes that summer. The whole town became divided over the outcome of the trial. Everyone had an opinion and a theory. Despite the damning evidence presented at trial, Tony Redmond retained his share of ardent defenders, those vocal few who refused to see him as anything other than the local golden boy destined for greatness. A once-in-a-generation football hero with enough talent and star power to put Milton, Mississippi, on the map.

After Veda's testimony, rumors began to surface about her sister. Whispers of drug use and promiscuity. Veda blamed herself for the attack on Lily's character. Her testimony about a secret relationship had stoked a firestorm of speculation that threatened to taint the memories she had of her beautiful, brilliant, complicated sister. Lily had been no angel. She'd had her flaws and foibles just like everyone else. To the outside world, she was a beauty queen and an honor student, as dazzling in her own way as Tony Redmond. But to those closest to her, she could be emotionally distant and prone to dark moods that sometimes lasted for days. And her fear of thunderstorms bordered on the neurotic. In other words, her sister had been human.

Veda took a long breath as she let those memories and her cursory knowledge of Jon Redmond wash over her. After his brother's conviction, he'd returned to Ole Miss to finish his undergraduate studies and later his law degree. Veda could remember seeing him in town only a handful of times after Tony's incarceration. On those rare occasions, they never spoke or so much as acknowledged the other's presence. That wasn't unusual considering their history. They hadn't been friends even before the murder. He'd graduated the year before she entered high school. Like most people in Milton, Veda had known him as Tony Redmond's older brother.

Now a few other things came back to her about Jon Redmond. He'd been smart, reserved and a talented athlete in his own right, but his sport had been baseball in a state where football reigned supreme. He'd never been flashy or popular like Tony. However, from what Veda could tell in the dark, he'd aged into his classical good looks. She felt an odd prickle at the base of her spine. She and Jon Redmond had never been anything more than acquaintances, and yet their lives had been irrevocably entwined since Lily's murder.

He walked over to the deceased and crouched. The cops that had been milling about gave him space. It seemed to Veda that the night had grown preternaturally silent. Where were the crickets and the nightbirds? Even the CSI team worked with quiet efficiency in the background.

Head bowed, he remained motionless for the longest time beside his brother's body. Veda might have thought he was deep in prayer, but there was something about the rigid way he held himself that seemed at odds with a spiritual invocation. She couldn't help wondering what he was thinking. What he was feeling. If, as Nate had suggested earlier, he regretted his part in getting his brother released from prison. Veda was no stranger to guilt. She knew only too well the destructive nature of self-blame and second-guessing.

As if sensing her scrutiny, he glanced up. She could have sworn their gazes locked before he rose and nodded to Detective Calloway.

Marcus muttered something under his breath.

Veda frowned. "What did you say?"

"I didn't expect him to get out here so quickly. I'd hoped the body would be moved before he arrived."

"You called him?" Nate asked incredulously.

"No way around it. I had to."

"You could have gone to see Theresa Redmond instead," Nate said. "At the very least, you could have discouraged a visit to the crime scene. It's distracting having him here."

Distracting was an understatement, Veda thought.

"Look, son." Marcus put a hand on Nate's shoulder. "I know how you feel about Jon Redmond. I don't like what he did any more than you do, but he's not just the victim's brother, he's also the DA. He has a right to be here. Which is why I'm going to go over there and talk to him. It's my duty, and it's also the decent thing to do. You two stay here and keep quiet. Let me handle Jon Redmond."

"What do you think?" Nate asked as Marcus stepped away.

She turned to study his profile. He was staring after their uncle, his expression inscrutable. "About Marcus calling Jon Redmond?"

"About all of this," he said with a shrug. "Like it or not, it takes you back to that summer."

"I know. Lily's been on my mind ever since you called." She wrapped her arms around her middle and shivered at the distant growl of thunder. "Remember how frightened she was of storms? Earlier in the evening, there wasn't a cloud in the sky, and now this. It's like she's trying to tell us something."

He gave her a troubled look. "You don't really believe that, do you?"

She sighed. "Not really. As much as I'd like to think our loved ones can send messages from beyond, I'm too pragmatic. When you're dead, you're dead. But that doesn't stop me from missing her."

"I miss her, too." He let down his guard for a moment and a note of melancholy slipped in. "Not a day goes by that I don't think about her. I still have spells where the murder keeps me up at night. I'll lie in bed and wonder what her last moments must have been like. How scared she must have been. I was her big brother. I should have protected her."

"We all wish we could have protected her." Veda put her hand on his arm but only for a moment. Neither of them was comfortable with demonstrative gestures. "I'm the one with a reason to feel guilty. All those terrible things that were said about her were because of me. I broke her confidence. I betrayed her trust."

"You told the truth under oath. No one can fault you for that. Besides, who cares what people said? Most of them didn't even know her. As for blame, the only person truly responsible for what happened to our sister was Tony Redmond. We both need to remember that. And tonight, he got what was coming to him."

Veda couldn't help but flinch at his brutal summation. "Do you ever wonder...?" Her gaze flicked away.

"Wonder what?" Nate demanded.

She regretted almost instantly her train of thought. Tony Redmond killed her sister. No one else. The evidence against him may have been circumstantial, but it was overwhelming. He slit her throat with a utility knife he used for work, and afterward he threw the bloody weapon in the back of his truck, either unconcerned about being caught or still out of his mind with rage. Then he drove to the nearest railroad crossing, parked across the tracks and waited. A passerby saw his truck on the tracks and found him slumped over the steering wheel. Unable to rouse him to unlock the door, the man managed to push the vehicle to safety in the nick of time. The police concluded it was a murder–suicide gone wrong. Two wasted lives, and all because Lily had told Tony Redmond she didn't love him anymore.

"Do you ever wonder what her life would have been like if it hadn't been cut short?" Veda improvised. "I like to think she would have found happiness, but those dark periods took a toll. And those nightmares she had. They started after we lost Dad, and she never outgrew them. I loved her dearly, but sometimes I wonder if I ever really knew her."

"People are complicated. She was always Dad's favorite," he said without rancor. "His accident was bound to have had a profound effect. As for the moods…sometimes there's no rhyme or reason. Maybe it was just the way she was wired."

"I guess." Veda's gaze strayed back to Jon Redmond. He was still conversing with their uncle, but his attention seemed to be elsewhere. He wasn't looking at Marcus or his brother's body. Instead, his head slowly turned as his gaze raked the cemetery, probing corners and shadows as if he sensed something amiss or an unwanted presence. For some reason the notion made Veda uneasy. "I wonder what they're talking about."

"His brother was shot dead tonight. What do you think they're talking about?" Nate paused. "Don't look now, but you're being summoned."

Her uncle motioned her over as he called out her name. "Veda? A word?"

She closed her eyes briefly before squaring her shoulders. Speaking with the bereaved was the hardest part of her job. Speaking to Jon Redmond would be even more difficult.

"Just be cool," Nate said. "And for God's sake, don't say anything about the fight, even if Redmond brings it up."

"Why would I? Owen is home in bed asleep. No reason to believe otherwise."

Nate gave her a long stare as she repeated his earlier assertion. "That's right. Now, you better go. Marcus looks like he could use backup."

She joined her uncle and Jon Redmond reluctantly.

"Jon, you remember my niece, Veda Campion. Tonight, she's Dr. Campion."

Jon met her gaze straight on. "Of course I remember you."

His voice had deepened since they'd last met, and there was a note of something that might have been disdain around the edges. Possibly her imagination. Their history would naturally influence her perception. One thing she knew for sure: the stare was the same. The intensity caught her off guard, and for a moment she found herself back on the witness stand.

During her testimony, she'd wanted to look her sister's killer straight in the eyes, make him flinch or glance away in guilt. Instead, her attention had strayed to the first row of spectators directly behind the defense table. Jon Redmond had leaned across the railing to whisper something in his brother's ear, but his gaze never left her. She'd been struck by the electric blue of his eyes and for a moment had floundered helplessly until the prosecutor came to her rescue and repeated the question. Later, he told her that she'd done fine on the stand, particularly for someone her age, but until the guilty verdict came back, she'd been certain that her lapse had cost her credibility with the jury.

She wasn't that same nervous sixteen-year-old now. Jon Redmond's blue eyes had no power over her. She'd been called to testify on numerous occasions during her time with the Orleans Parish Coroner's Office, and she'd quickly learned to control her nerves and hone her poise. A penetrating glare couldn't faze her.

Still, she was relieved when he didn't offer his hand. She stood with her arms at her sides as she nodded a greeting. "I know how difficult this must be for you. I'm sorry for your family's loss."

A retort leaped to the tip of his tongue—she was almost certain of it. His mouth thinned, and his jaw hardened a split second before he glanced toward his brother's body and then closed his eyes on a shudder.

In that fleeting moment, the world seemed to stop for Veda. The voices in the background faded, the harsh floodlight dimmed, and a rush of emotion took her by surprise. She was suddenly keenly aware of Jon Redmond's grief, punctuated by the scent of the cemetery roses that grew along the fence. She had the strangest urge to touch his hand, to weave her fingers through his in an illogical gesture of solidarity, but the impulse passed quickly. When his gaze returned to Veda, still with that glare, she wondered if she'd imagined his vulnerability.

"I understand you've already examined the body and come to a conclusion regarding time of death."

"Midnight," Marcus stated conclusively.

Veda was a little less absolute. "Going by how little the body has cooled—as well as other factors—I'd put time *since* death no more than two hours. Three at the most."

"What are those others factors?"

She shot a glance at her uncle, but he remained passive, arms folded, rocking back slightly on his heels. She turned back to Jon. "Pale but flaccid skin, clouded corneas, rigor mortis in the small muscles of the face that hasn't yet progressed to the limbs. We'll know more after the autopsy. Stomach content can be especially helpful—" She stopped herself from getting too graphic. They were talking about his brother, after all. "I'm sure as DA you're aware of the various tests and procedures that will be performed during the postmortem."

"Yes, I get the picture." He was silent for a moment. "My

brother was shot in the back of the head. Here." He lifted a finger to his crown.

"Approximately," she agreed.

"Point-blank range, would you say?" His voice was carefully controlled, though she thought she detected a slight tremor now and then.

"I noticed what might be singeing and muzzle burn around the entrance wound, but it's difficult to say for certain until the body is examined under better conditions. If I'm right, that would certainly indicate contact or near-contact. You should also know that he has bruises and inflammation around both wrists."

He gave a brief nod. "Detective Calloway mentioned the marks. Was my brother on his knees?"

The question caught Veda by surprise, though she supposed it was a logical conclusion. "I'm sorry?"

"He was shot at close range with his hands likely bound behind his back. Was my brother forced to his knees before he was executed?"

Executed. The word hung between them for the longest moment until Veda broke the tension. "It's possible. We'll know more about trajectory, velocity, caliber and ballistics after the autopsy."

"When will that be?"

"Dr. Bader will be back sometime tomorrow…today. I'm sure he'll make this case a priority. You could have a preliminary report by early afternoon. Toxicology will take longer, possibly a few days depending on the backup at the lab."

Again, he nodded absently, his thoughts apparently elsewhere. "The tox screen needs to be comprehensive, not just a routine check for blood-alcohol content. Look for traces of GHB, Rohypnol or ketamine, to name a few."

"Knockout drugs," Marcus said. "Any reason in particular you think someone dosed him?"

"My brother was a fit man. He was strong, and he knew how to fight. He couldn't have been taken down under normal circumstances."

"Detective Calloway reached the same conclusion," Veda said. "Although, he thinks Tony might have been ambushed from behind."

Marcus shot her a look as if warning her not to say too much. She was reminded again of the fight between her brother and Tony Redmond. Tony had been bigger, but Owen was quicker. He'd more than held his own.

"Did your brother have any enemies?" Marcus said. "I'm sure Detective Calloway has already been over this with you, but I'm asking again. Can you think of anyone who wanted Tony dead?"

"You mean other than a Campion?"

There it is, Veda thought. He was already making assumptions about her family.

Marcus said in a tense voice, "I wouldn't go throwing around accusations until we have all the facts."

"Everybody in town knows Owen attacked my brother without provocation." His gaze shifted to Veda as if he expected her to come to her brother's defense. She wanted to, but under the circumstances she thought it best to keep her mouth shut. "However, I'm not accusing anyone…yet. My brother was behind bars for a long time. You don't survive nearly two decades in a maximum-security prison without making both friends and enemies."

"You have someone specific in mind?" Marcus pressed.

"No." But a slight hesitation made Veda think he wasn't being altogether forthright.

Marcus shot her another glance before he continued. "Word has it someone was in town a few days ago asking questions about Tony. A guy by the name of Clay Stipes. I made some inquiries. He lives over in Kerrville. Turns out he served time with Tony up at the farm. You know anything about him?"

"I know the name," Jon said. "They were cellmates for a few months after my brother's incarceration."

"No idea why he came to town looking for Tony?"

"All I know about him is what my brother told me."

"Which is?"

"He's a convicted cop-killer," Jon said.

Marcus looked grim. "I heard that, too. I also heard he's hiring himself out as a PI, which is probably a front for any kind of service his client is willing to pay for."

"A private detective?" Jon sounded genuinely surprise. "How was he able to get a license?"

"Anyone willing to hire a cop-killer wouldn't care about a license. This guy…he's not someone you want hanging out around your family, particularly with your little sister home from college for the summer. She and your mother are out there all alone in that big house. I'd advise taking some precautions."

Jon's mouth tightened. "I'll watch out for them."

"You might want to watch out for yourself while you're at it. Stipes wasn't just looking for Tony. I hear he was asking around about you, too. You don't know anything about that, either, I suppose."

"I've never even met the man," Jon said.

"A guy like that can be unpredictable. Who knows what he's after? Like I said, you best take some precautions. You own a gun, by chance?"

"I don't need a gun to take care of myself," Jon said. "But thank you for your concern."

Was that a note of sarcasm? Veda wondered.

He gave her a curt nod before he turned and left the cemetery.

Veda watched him until he was out of sight. "That was uncomfortable."

"For him, too, I suspect."

"What was all that business about the ex-con? You think he had something to do with Tony's murder?"

Marcus shrugged. "Could be. The sheriff over in Kerrville says the guy's bad news. I doubt he came to town for a friendly reunion." He rubbed his chin as he stared down the path where Jon Redmond had disappeared. "I'd bet a month's pay he knows more than he's willing to say about Clay Stipes."

"I got that impression, too," she agreed.

Nate said behind her, "He's going to be trouble."

She hadn't heard him approach and whirled in surprise. "Who, Stipes?"

"Did you hear what I said?" He sounded tense.

Veda started to answer, then realized he was addressing their uncle. The two men exchanged a look that, for whatever reason, made her blood run cold.

Marcus said in a resolved voice, "If there's trouble, I'll deal with it. Now, go home and keep your mouths shut until I say otherwise."

Chapter Four

Jon sat in his car unnoticed as the morgue attendants carried his brother's body through the gates on a stretcher. Veda Campion followed, but Nate and Marcus remained in the cemetery. Garrett Calloway hadn't come out yet, either. He'd identified himself as lead detective, but Marcus Campion had done most of the talking. Calloway might be the public face of the investigation, but Jon was under no delusions about who would be running things behind the scenes. For that reason, he needed to speak to Veda alone. He had no idea how she would react to his request, given the bad blood between the two families. If she was amenable, his proposal might provide a little healing, but he knew he was asking a lot.

He ran a hand over his eyes. Exhaustion and grief bore down heavily, and he wanted nothing so much as to retreat back to his apartment and sit alone in the dark with a good, stiff drink. But that would have to come later. Right now, he had to keep it together for a little while longer. His mother and sister didn't yet know about Tony, and that would be the toughest visit of his life.

He scrubbed his face and tried to think back to happier times before the incarceration. Sometimes those memories seemed more like dreams. His brother had been sent away for so long that he'd become a stranger to his own family, and in some ways his return had made all their lives more difficult. The adjustment hadn't been as smooth as any of them would have liked. Tony came out of prison a completely different person. He'd been a scared eighteen-year-old kid when he'd been sent up, and he'd walked out the gates a hard-scrubbed man who'd learned to survive in the oldest and cruelest penitentiary in Mississippi.

There had been times—more than a few—over the years when Jon had wanted to wash his hands of his brother's troubles. Just walk away and live his own life. But the one thing that had never changed was the certainty of his brother's innocence. He'd made a promise to Tony and to himself that if it was the last thing he ever did, he'd clear his brother's name.

He shook off the cloying cloud of despair and tried to focus. The morgue van was getting ready to leave. Veda handed a clipboard through the window before stepping aside to allow the driver to make a U-turn. Then she retreated to the back of an SUV, presumably to store her gear. The light came on when she opened the lift gate, and Jon took that as his cue.

He got out of his car and started down the road toward her vehicle. He didn't call out as he approached because he didn't want to attract unwanted attention. She was leaning into the cargo space and didn't seem to hear the crunch of his footsteps on gravel. Too late Jon realized that he'd caught her in a state of undress. She'd already discarded the paper jumpsuit along with her white T-shirt, and now she stood rummaging through a duffel bag in her jeans and bra.

She glanced around when he cleared his throat, then froze in the glare of the interior light. Their gazes collided for a moment before she whirled back to the duffel bag and grabbed a shirt. With a muttered oath, she jerked it over her head and down over her bra.

"Sorry," he murmured as he tried to gauge her reaction. He'd only had a glimpse of her expression before she turned away, but he thought she looked more surprised than angry.

She cut him a look over her shoulder. "What do you think you're doing?"

No, he was wrong. He heard plenty of anger in her voice now and no small amount of contempt. He tried to fix the situation with another apology. "I'm sorry. I didn't mean to catch you off guard."

"Then, you shouldn't sneak up on me in the dark," she snapped, as she tugged the tail of her shirt down over her jeans and then reached up to adjust her ponytail. Only then did she turn to face him.

She was taller than Jon remembered. Or maybe her rigid posture only made her seem so. She was also more attractive than he remembered. Not the bombshell her sister had been even at eighteen, but he had no doubt Veda Campion turned more than a few heads. Under other circumstances and without their history, he might have had a greater appreciation for her good looks, but his brother had been murdered only a few hours ago. At the moment, he didn't give a damn about anyone or anything else. He tried to tell himself he was only searching for answers, but the simmering rage that boiled just below the surface spoke to a baser need that might have been revenge.

He took a deep breath and tried to calm his racing thoughts. He was here for a reason. Confronting Veda Campion with old wounds and unwarranted suspicions would only drive her away.

"I thought you left." She sounded calmer now, but she

was still yanking at the hem of her T-shirt as if worried she might remain exposed.

He told her the truth. "I came out here to wait for you."

That got her attention. "Why?"

"I was hoping we could have a moment alone." He could see her clearly in the glow from the interior light. Her eyes widened in surprise, followed by a quick frown of disapproval.

"Shouldn't you be with your family?"

He felt a stab of guilt at her query. She knew how to cut to the quick. "I'm on my way there now." He paused to take a breath. "First, I need to talk to you about something. It's important."

She lowered the lift gate so the light wasn't shining in their faces. He wondered if she'd put them in the dark on purpose because he couldn't read her at all now.

"I already told you everything I know. Dr. Bader will meet with you after the autopsy. He'll be able to answer your questions more thoroughly."

"The autopsy is what I want to talk to you about."

"I don't understand." Then revelation seemed to dawn, and she said in a crisp voice, "Oh, I see. You're worried about my involvement. Well, you needn't be. As I mentioned earlier, Dr. Bader will handle the postmortem. This is my last night on the job. As soon as he clocks in, I'll be officially unemployed."

"You won't stay on to assist? Or at least to observe?"

"There's no reason for me to." She opened the lift gate again and began to fiddle with her bags and equipment, undoubtedly hoping to draw the conversation to a close now that she'd put his concern to rest.

He said carefully, "You misunderstand me. I'm asking you to be present."

"At the autopsy? Why?"

"I have my reasons."

"I'm sure you do." She kept her back to him as she finished her tasks. He couldn't see her expression, yet the disbelief and suspicion in her voice confirmed what he already knew: this wasn't going to be easy. "Why do I get the feeling you're working up to something that I'm not going to like? What's this really about?"

"Two pairs of trained eyes and hands are better than one," he said with a shrug.

She gave him a sidelong glance. "That's all there is to it?"

He hesitated. "Dr. Bader's ability to perform a conscientious exam worries me. He's not as sharp as he used to be. He misses things. Cuts corners. His carelessness has caused problems in a few of my cases. I don't want to take a chance that something gets overlooked or forgotten during my brother's autopsy."

She leaped to her colleague's defense as he figured she would. "I think you're selling the man short. I've known Dr. Bader for years, and early on in my career I considered him a mentor. He's always been a skilled pathologist."

"How long has it been since you observed his work firsthand?" Jon kept his tone even. He didn't want to push back too hard and drive her away before he'd laid all his cards on the table. "He should have retired years ago, yet he continues to overextend himself. Are you aware that several surrounding counties have contracts with the Webber County Coroner's Office to perform a certain number of autopsies per month?"

"No, but I'm not surprised. We did the same in Orleans

Parish. Coroners in smaller and poorer counties and parishes don't always have the necessary facilities or training to perform postmortems."

"Dr. Bader also conducts a fair number of private autopsies. Families pay him out of pocket when state law doesn't require a postmortem."

"Also not unusual. Even if death is from natural causes, loved ones need answers and a measure of closure," she said. "Performing private autopsies is neither illegal nor unethical. It's part of the job. Unless you're suggesting that Dr. Bader is somehow getting kickbacks. In which case, where's your proof?"

"I don't have any," he admitted. "All I know is what I see, and his work has gotten sloppy. I need someone in that autopsy room I can trust."

"And you trust me?" She sounded shocked.

He answered without hesitation. "I do. Despite past scandals in the Orleans Parish Coroner's Office, you left with your reputation intact."

"How would you know that?"

He had to feel his way through what could turn out to be a minefield. At that moment, he was all too aware of their history. All too cognizant of the fact that one wrong word could bring the conversation to an abrupt end and crush any chance he had of enlisting her help. "It might surprise you to learn that I've followed your career from time to time."

Wrong tact. She all but physically recoiled. *"Why?"*

"Not for nefarious purposes," he was quick to assure her. "Although, I can see why you might jump to the wrong conclusion given our last meeting."

"You mean the one where you accused me of lying under oath?"

"I shouldn't have done that," he said. "I've long since regretted it."

She waved aside his concession. "I'm over it. Besides, let's not get distracted. Tell me why you, of all people, would be inclined to follow my career?"

"Long story short, the law firm I worked for in Atlanta before I came here had an office in New Orleans. I was sent down to do background research on a murder case. You were on the witness list. I was surprised when I read your name. I didn't think there could be two Veda Campions, so I did some digging."

"I'm sure you did."

He managed a smile. "You wouldn't have done the same?"

She merely shrugged.

"I found out you were a highly respected pathologist in Orleans Parish. And after I watched you take the stand in that case, I understood why. You were not only poised and knowledgeable but also relatable. You explained everything in terms the jury could understand without talking down to them. That's not easy. Everyone on my team was impressed."

"That's odd," she said. "Because I'm pretty sure I would have remembered seeing you."

"I was only there to observe, so I sat at the back. I didn't come up to you afterward because… You know how it is."

She lifted her chin. "Yes, I do know how it is. Which is why I find this whole conversation so puzzling. From accusations of lying to singing my praises. I can't help but wonder why."

"I told you. I want you to assist or at the very least observe my brother's autopsy."

"Still not buying it," she said bluntly. "There has to be more to it than that."

"I'm being straight with you. I intend to do everything in my power to find my brother's killer and bring him to justice, and I'm asking for your help."

"There's just one problem with that request." She folded her arms. "What makes you think I'd want to help you?"

"Because I believe the person who killed my brother also killed your sister."

JON REDMOND'S RIDICULOUS claim kept playing over and over in Veda's head as she left the cemetery and drove to the morgue. All these years after her sister's murder, he was still trying to proclaim Tony's innocence. She wanted to be compassionate enough to give him quarter on the night of his brother's murder, but this was nothing new. From the first, his insistence that Tony had been framed had been so convincing that even Veda had found herself playing the what-if game from time to time. She'd always been able to talk herself down by remembering certain facts. Tony Redmond had been found with the murder weapon in his truck and Lily's blood all over his hands. The right man had been sent to prison, and earlier tonight, justice had been cruelly served.

Dread welled inside Veda as she clutched the steering wheel. She took deep breaths and told herself to get control of her emotions. She was preoccupied and driving too fast. The streets were empty, but that was no excuse. Easing up on the gas, she glanced in the rearview mirror, almost expecting to find Jon Redmond in hot pursuit.

Had he really thought she would agree to help him? After the pain and grief his family had caused hers? She'd been so flabbergasted by his suggestion that she'd stood tongue-tied and flushed with indignation. Finally, she'd sputtered, "You can't be serious!"

To which he'd replied, "I'm dead serious. Your sister's killer is still out there somewhere. Tonight, he murdered my brother to cover his tracks. I won't rest until I bring this person to justice."

"What tracks? Lily was murdered a long time ago. If someone else was involved, the evidence would have come to light by now."

"You know that isn't true. Has her mystery man ever been identified?"

She'd gaped at him in outrage. "Are you still dwelling on that?"

He'd gone silent as if realizing he needed to back off and regroup. "I know this has come as a shock—"

"Not so much shock as utter disbelief. You're living in a fantasyland. You're grasping at straws, trying to make sense of what happened tonight, and I get that. But leave me out of it."

"I can't. You're the only one who can help uncover the truth. You knew Lily better than anyone."

"I'm not sure that's true," she murmured.

"Look." He ran a hand through his hair. "I realize this isn't the time or place. You still have work to do, and I need to be with my family. But I'd like to talk to you again. Soon. Alone. Can we meet somewhere?"

"I don't think so. I'm sorry for your family's loss, and I'm truly saddened for what you all are about to go through. But I can't help you. This crusade of yours... I don't want any part of it. You're right about one thing, though. I still have work to do, and it's already been a long night. So goodbye, Jon."

Not *Good night* but *Goodbye*. She wanted to believe the finality of her farewell would be the end of it, but she didn't think getting rid of Jon Redmond would be that simple. Obviously, he wasn't a man easily dissuaded. *You don't devote seventeen years of your life to a cause only to take* no *for an answer.*

No matter his resolve, he couldn't force her to help him. She wasn't worried about holding her own against him or anyone else, for that matter, but she was more than a little curious about his ulterior motive. He wasn't telling her everything about his intentions just as he hadn't come clean about Clay Stipes. There was more going on than met the eye, and now that her assignment at the coroner's office was coming to an end, she would have plenty of free time on her hands to do some digging.

Not that she'd ever throw in her lot with Jon Redmond. That would never work. The past would always color their individual perspectives, making consensus impossible. However, nothing prevented her from conducting her own investigation. She was good at piecing together puzzles. She did it every day at work.

As Jon had been so quick to remind her, the man Lily had been involved with that summer had never been identified. Veda had always wondered about him, about why he hadn't even showed up to the funeral or the graveside service to pay his respects. But maybe he had. Maybe Lily's secret lover was someone familiar, someone whose behavior and demeanor hadn't given him away even in the face of a tragic loss. Someone closer than Veda could ever have imagined with secrets of his own to protect. And with the kind of insight into Lily that no other living person on the planet could offer. He was still out there somewhere, still keeping his secret. Maybe it was high time he came out of the shadows.

A shiver trailed down Veda's spine, mostly from excitement but with a measure of trepidation. Digging up the past might come with a cost. The possibility of physical danger seemed remote and didn't particularly worry her. The real fear came from the things she might uncover about her sister that would change her perception forever.

She pulled into her temporary parking spot at the morgue and got out. Using her key card to enter the bleak facility, she signed in at the desk and then checked to make sure the decedent had been properly processed. She compared the name and number on the cold cabinet with the corresponding paperwork she'd filled out at the scene. Satisfied that everything was in order, she signed back out and left.

Outside the facility, she stood for a moment searching the sky. The storm seemed to have fizzled into nothing more than distant and sporadic flickers of lightning.

Hey, Lily. If you were trying to tell me something earlier, I missed the clue.

She folded her arms around her middle and shivered. The clouds were starting to thin, but the breeze that blew through the live oaks still felt charged. Maybe the storm hadn't passed after all. Maybe it had stalled in the distance, building strength.

Climbing into her vehicle, she stared absently into the darkness before she shook off her mood and started the engine. She didn't go straight home but instead turned in the opposite direction from her bungalow.

The square of blocks east of downtown—recently redubbed the Warehouse District—had once been a bustling industrial area. Most of the factories and warehouses had been shuttered for decades, but a few had been converted into lofts and apartments, a real estate venture that had once seemed like a pie-in-the-sky scheme. With the influx of newcomers to the area, the district had become more urbanized and desirable, though with a seedy edge that put Veda on guard as she drove through the narrow streets still lined with deserted buildings.

She pulled to the curb across from a brick-and-sheet-metal monstrosity that had once been a shirt factory. Owen lived on the third floor in the corner unit. The windows in his place were dark, but that wasn't unusual at this hour. She would have been more concerned if all the lights had been blazing.

Fishing her phone from her bag, she punched in his number and waited. She expected to see a light go on the moment her call went through, but her brother's windows remained dark, and he didn't answer until the fourth ring.

"Veda? What's wrong? What's happened? Is it Mom?"

He'd jumped to the same conclusion she had earlier, and she was quick to put his mind at ease. "She's fine. So is Nate. This isn't about the family."

"Thank God." She heard him let out a heavy sigh of relief. "What's up?"

"Something's happened. Let me say again the family is fine. But we need to talk. It's important."

He sounded puzzled and mildly annoyed. "Okay, but do you have any idea what time it is?"

"A little after four in the morning."

"And you couldn't wait until a more decent hour?"

"This won't take long. I'm parked across the street from your building. Can I come up?" He hesitated for so long, she wondered if the call had dropped. "Owen? Are you there?"

"I'm here, but I'm not there." His tone had altered slightly, though Veda acknowledged the shift might be her imagination. She hadn't noticed that cautious note when he first answered.

Even so, her fingers curled around the phone in consternation. "Where are you?"

"I'm at Ashley's."

Ashley Duquesne had been his on-again, off-again girlfriend since high school. Veda had once chastised him for stringing her along for so many years, unwilling to make a long-term commitment. *Not that it's any of your business, but what makes you think I'm the one dragging my feet?* She'd made a point to stay out of his personal life after that.

"Have you been with her all night?"

Another hesitation. "She's working the graveyard shift at the hospital. I'm here alone at her place."

Veda wondered why he hadn't gone home to his apartment. "What time did she go in?"

"Her car is in the shop, so I dropped her off around nine. Her shift didn't start until ten, but she wanted to go in early and get a jump start on paperwork. What's this about anyway— Wait a minute. You said this wasn't about family. Ash—"

"This isn't about her, either. She's fine as far as I know." Veda heard a door open and close. "Are you alone?"

"I just told you. Ashley's at work."

"That didn't answer my question."

"I stepped out on the balcony for a minute. What the hell is going on, Veda? You wake me up at four in the morning to find out if I'm alone?"

She drummed her fingers on the steering wheel as she stared out the windshield at a car parked up street. For whatever reason, she took note that it was a dark colored sedan. "I know it doesn't make sense yet, but there's a reason for all these questions. I need to see you in person, Owen. Does

Ashley still live in the apartment complex off Holcomb? I can be there in five minutes. Meet me outside."

"Veda—"

"Meet me outside, Owen."

She severed the call before he could protest. Throwing the phone onto the passenger seat, she started the engine, but her hand froze on the gearshift. She initially assumed the car down the street belonged to someone in the building. No one had come in or out while she sat there, yet now she could have sworn she detected a silhouette through the tinted glass.

Probably my imagination. It was still dark and she was more than a little on edge. It wasn't every day she was called to a crime scene to examine the body of her sister's killer. Not to mention the conversation she'd had with the killer's brother. She was tempted to drive slowly past the vehicle and peer through the driver's window, but instead she turned around in the street and headed the other way.

She kept track of the car in her rearview mirror. The sedan pulled away from the curb and fell in behind her, but the lights never came on. That definitely wasn't her imagination. She was being followed, and another unnerving thought occurred to her. Had the person behind her been watching her brother's apartment? Was she leading him straight to Owen?

At the next intersection, she turned right at the last minute. The vehicle behind her kept going straight, still without lights. She wanted to believe it was only a coincidence that the sedan had left at the same time as she. Maybe the driver had forgotten to turn on the lights. It happened. But she wasn't taking any chances. She took a circuitous route to meet Owen, keeping her eye on the rearview and peering down side streets.

Satisfied that she'd lost the tail—if she had indeed been followed—she pulled into the apartment complex and parked at the back of the lot. When Owen came out of the building a few minutes later, she flashed her lights. He answered with a wave, then wove his way through the parked cars to climb inside her vehicle. He was fully dressed but his hair was unkempt, and his shirt looked like he'd slept in it. That wasn't so unusual for Owen. For a handsome guy, he didn't put a lot of emphasis on appearance.

Unlike Jon Redmond. His image popped into her head for no good reason. Despite the late hour and the circumstances, he'd been well-dressed and groomed at the cemetery except for a thick stubble. He'd looked exhausted but pulled-together.

She forced her attention back to Owen. Apart from the gauze he'd wrapped around his banged-up knuckles, he appeared to be fine. She was relieved to note that he didn't seem particularly stressed or wired but instead looked puzzled and more than a little aggravated.

He slammed the door and turned. "What the hell, Veda?"

She killed her engine and shut off the lights. "I'll explain everything. Just give me a minute." She adjusted the rearview mirror so that she could see the entrance to the parking lot. No one came in or out. She scanned the rows of parked cars. Nothing amiss there, either. Her brother might not be nervous, but she certainly was.

Leaning back against the seat, she tried to relax. It would be dawn soon. She wondered about Jon Redmond and whether or not he'd broken the news to his family yet.

"What are you looking for?" Owen demanded.

"Just checking to make sure I wasn't followed."

He looked at her as if she'd taken leave of her senses. "Are you okay?"

"It's been a strange night."

"Apparently so. Okay, I'm game. What makes you think you're being followed?"

She glanced out her side window. "I may be overreacting, but when I was at your place just now, I noticed a car parked at the curb across from your building. A black or possibly dark blue sedan. The driver pulled out behind me when I left, but he didn't turn on his headlights."

"Probably someone looking to score drugs," he said without much concern. "That area isn't nearly as safe as the developers and real estate agents would have you believe."

"And something tells me you're okay with that."

He gave her a little smirk. "I've never minded a few rough edges. Gives me an excuse to keep up with my target practice."

She sincerely hoped he was joking. "Can I ask you a question?"

"Why stop now?"

"Did you come straight back here after you dropped Ashley at the hospital? You said around nine, right? That's early for you."

"That used to be early for me, but fine. I'll answer your question when you tell me what the hell is going on."

"I'm getting to that. Just humor me, okay?"

He dropped his head to the back of the seat with a heavy sigh. "Let's see. I stopped and got gas at a corner store. Bought some breath mints while I was there. You know, the kind that comes in the little pink tins they keep near the register. Then I dropped by a sports bar and had a beer—domestic—while I caught the last few innings of the game. The

Braves won, in case that was going to be your next question. I left around ten thirty and came back here."

She ignored his sarcasm. "Did you run into any acquaintances at the bar? Anyone who might have noticed what time you left?"

"It was Sunday night so the place was pretty empty." He checked his side window as if her nerves had rubbed off on him.

"Did anyone see you when you came back here? Someone in the parking lot, maybe."

"I have no idea." He turned to stare at her expectantly. "Your turn now."

She nodded and got right to the point. "Tony Redmond was murdered earlier tonight. His body was found in Cedarville Cemetery a few hours ago."

He sat in silence for a moment. "You know this for a fact?"

"I was called to the crime scene. I just signed his body into the morgue. Yes, I know this for a fact."

Another moment of dead silence. Then he said, "Do the cops have any idea who shot him?"

A cold chill went through Veda. She returned her brother's stare for the longest moment before she said in a hushed voice, "I never said he was shot."

"I think you did."

"No, I didn't."

Owen shrugged. "Well, that's what I heard. Besides, it's the logical end to a guy like Tony Redmond."

He'd done his best to gloss over the slip, but Veda wasn't buying it. Her heart started to thud as a dark thought poked and prodded. "Tell me the truth, Owen. How did you know he'd been shot?"

He gave her an enigmatic look. "How do you think I knew?"

Her fingers curled around the edge of the seat. "You didn't just take a wild guess. You seemed too sure."

"So, that's why you're here." He studied his bandaged knuckles. "That explains the third degree. You think I did it, don't you?"

"I don't know what to think. Just tell me how you knew about the shooting."

He turned to meet her gaze, a sly smile curling the corners of his mouth. "Nate called while you were on the way over here. He told me about Redmond."

She reached over and punched his arm. "You jerk. Why didn't you say so?"

"Ouch! I wanted to know what you were building up to with all those questions. Admit it. I had you going. You already had me tried and convicted there for a minute."

"That was cruel, Owen."

"If it's any consolation, you scared the hell out of me when you called. You're good at this interrogation business. A little too good."

"I'm just asking the same questions the police will likely ask if and when they come knocking on your door."

His good humor vanished. "Why would the cops want to question me? I've been here all night. I didn't have anything to do with Tony Redmond's murder."

"Don't be naive," she scolded. "You had a very public and very vicious altercation with Tony just a few days ago. You're still wearing a bandage on your knuckles from that fight. There were witnesses besides me who heard you threaten to kill him."

"That was in the heat of the moment," he protested. "It didn't mean anything."

"The police may not see it that way. Given our history

with Redmond, they could take that threat very seriously. It doesn't help that no one can vouch for your whereabouts at the time of the murder."

"You're forgetting something pretty important," he countered. "Our brother is a detective, and our uncle is the chief of police."

"The case has been assigned to another detective. Nate's been shut out. As for Marcus, he can't do anything that so much as hints at meddling or a cover-up without risking his reputation and maybe even his job."

"They'll have my back." He sounded so sure of himself, she wanted to punch him again. He trailed his finger through a fine layer of dust on the dashboard. "Don't you ever clean this thing?"

"Don't change the subject." She grabbed his hand and examined the bandage. Fresh blood oozed through the gauze. "Owen, you're bleeding."

He pulled free and rested his hands on his thighs. "I keep knocking the scabs off at work. The damn things won't heal."

"You should wear gloves. Or hire some help." Her brother was in the landscape business. He and his partner still did most of the manual labor themselves. "Soil contains a lot of bacteria. Tetanus, salmonella and E. coli, to name a few. You don't want to risk an infection."

"Ash gave me an ointment and a week's worth of antibiotics. I'll be fine."

"Prescribed antibiotics?"

She could almost hear his eyes rolling. "Jeez, Veda. Now you're the pill police?"

"I'm just trying to help."

"I appreciate it but ease up a little. You're starting to sound like Nate. He lives to pick at every little thing I do."

"Why? What did he say when he called?"

"Pretty much what you did. He told me about Tony, and then he said I should lie low for a few days. But I can't do that. I have a job."

"Hopefully, an arrest will be made soon, and you won't have to worry," Veda said. "Until then, Nate's right. You need to keep your head down. And maybe think about talking to an attorney. You don't want to get caught by surprise and blurt out something that could be used against you."

He gaped at her.

"Okay, maybe an attorney is overkill at this point," she conceded. "But you know what they say. *Hope for the best and prepare for the worst.*"

"Wouldn't hiring an attorney just make me look guilty?"

"The police will try to make you think it does, but you shouldn't let that influence your decision. A good attorney can guide you through an interrogation and keep you from saying anything incriminating."

He stared at her in disbelief. "You're serious about this."

She shrugged. "Take it with a grain of salt. According to Nate, I have a tendency to make mountains out of molehills. I sincerely hope that's what I'm doing, but I have a bad feeling about this." She thought about her conversation with Jon Redmond and wondered about his true motivation for trying to enlist her help. If he could get her to let down her guard, maybe he thought she would say or do something that could be used against her family.

"It's your decision," she told Owen. "And Nate could be right. Maybe all you need to do is lie low until this all blows over."

"Ash's brother-in-law is a lawyer. I guess I could run it by him. Get his take."

"That sounds like a good idea."

"Thanks, Veda."

She said in surprise, "For what?"

"For the advice. For coming over here. For having my back."

"Did you think I wouldn't?"

He seemed to consider his answer. "You've been gone for a long time, and you haven't been all that great at keeping in touch. I guess I wondered if you were still one of us."

"Phones work both ways," she said. "So does the interstate. How many times did you visit me in New Orleans?"

His sly look returned. "There was that one time during Mardi Gras."

"You mean the time you and your friends trashed my apartment while I was at work, and I saw you all of five minutes the whole weekend?"

"Yep, that time." He got out of the vehicle, then turned to say through the open door, "It's good to have you home. I hope you decide to stick around for a while. Maybe you can help Nate keep me in line."

"That's a big job. I don't know that I'm up to the challenge," she teased. "Get some rest. We'll talk later."

She drove away from the apartment complex wishing she felt better about their conversation. They'd ended on a light note, but something unpleasant still simmered beneath the good-natured banter. Owen had been able to set her mind at ease about his prior knowledge of the shooting and the fresh blood on his bandage, but there was no glossing over the fact that he didn't have an alibi for the time in question.

Veda didn't want to think the worst of her brother, but no matter how many times she reassured herself that he wasn't a killer, the fight with Tony Redmond kept rearing its ugly head. She'd never witnessed anything like it. The savagery in her brother's eyes had shocked her. In the space of a heartbeat, he'd morphed into a stranger, one who seemed only too capable of taking a human life.

Chapter Five

Dr. Bader agreed to meet with Jon late that afternoon to present his preliminary findings from the postmortem. All the way to the morgue, Jon wondered if he would run into Veda. If by some miracle she'd changed her mind about helping him. But he didn't see her SUV in the lot when he pulled up, nor did she show up for the meeting. Not that he had expected her presence. The Webber County Coroner's Office was very much Dr. Bader's domain.

However, even a brief appearance in the hallway would have signaled that she was at least willing to hear him out. Unfortunately for him, her absence also sent a message. He liked to think it was just a matter of timing. She'd been adamant that her assignment ended with Dr. Bader's return. Maybe she hadn't wanted to step on the elder pathologist's toes.

Or maybe he was grasping at straws again. He'd done that a lot over the years when all hope seemed lost. Sometimes clinging to a lifeline, no matter how fragile, was the only thing left to do.

As much as he'd wanted a second set of eyes in the autopsy room, he had to admit Dr. Bader's summation was clear and concise. He'd answered all of Jon's questions and had seemed in no hurry to usher him out. Despite the coroner's thoroughness, however, little surfaced in the preliminary report that Jon didn't already know or at least suspect.

The downward trajectory of the bullet from the entrance wound corroborated his theory that Tony had been forced to his knees before he'd been shot at close range with a 9 mm weapon. The marks around his wrists had been made by a plastic strap, possibly a heavy-duty zip tie. Law enforcement often used self-locking zip or flex ties instead of standard handcuffs when making mass arrests because they were easy to carry and disposable. But there were dozens of everyday uses, everything from bundling wires and cables to staking tomato plants, and they could be bought over the internet or in any hardware or big-box store.

Dr. Bader's preliminary report was just that—an abbreviated rundown of the findings from the autopsy. Additional information such as ballistics and toxicology could take days.

Jon left the building with a nagging headache and an unpleasant hollowness in his chest. He'd been up since seven the previous morning—thirty-three hours straight—with little more than coffee and a piece of dry toast to keep him going. He felt strung out from exhaustion. A shower and shave might have boosted his morale, but he didn't have time to swing by his apartment. Not yet. There was still too much to do. People to call. Arrangements to be made. If he could close his eyes for even a minute, he might feel like a new man when he awakened, but he couldn't allow himself even that small luxury.

At four in the afternoon, the sun still beat down relentlessly on the asphalt parking lot. As he strode toward his car, he wondered if he should take the time to at least stop somewhere for a quick bite. He couldn't keep going for much longer on caffeine and resolve, but the thought of food left him queasy. He needed to get back to his mother and sister anyway. The news of Tony's death had been devastating, as he'd known it would be. His mother had tried to put on a brave face for Gabby's benefit, but Jon was worried about her. How much grief and heartache could one person suffer before something had to break?

Earlier when he'd left the house for his appointment with Dr. Bader, she'd walked him out to the porch and placed a hand on his arm. "Do you have any idea who did this?"

"No, but I'm going to find out."

Her fingers had tightened around his arm, and her voice quivered with emotion. "Jonny, please be careful."

She hadn't used his nickname since he was a kid. He'd hugged her tight for a very long time, trying to offer comfort and reassurance while secretly relieved that he had somewhere to go, a purpose that allowed him to escape the heavy oppression of grief in the house for even a few hours.

The headache throbbed as he approached his vehicle. He'd managed to snag a space in the shade, which would make climbing inside the hot car only a little less hellish. As he unlocked the door, he automatically scanned his surroundings. Tony wasn't the only one who had enemies. DAs couldn't be too careful these days.

He felt a warning prickle at the back of his neck a split second before he saw someone standing beneath the heavy limbs of the same live oak that shaded his car. The man appeared to be watching him, but his faded jeans and gray T-shirt camouflaged him so well that for a moment, Jon thought the afterimages in his eyes from the glaring sun might be playing tricks on him. Then the man called out his name.

"Jon Redmond?"

He relocked his car and checked his periphery as he walked toward the stranger. "Can I help you?"

The man made no move toward him but instead allowed Jon to come to him. "Do you know who I am?" he drawled.

Jon paused in the deep shade as his gaze raked over the stranger. "I have a pretty good idea."

Clay Stipes grinned, using his tongue to shift a toothpick to the other side of his mouth. He looked to be somewhere in his midforties, at least six feet tall and solidly built with wide shoulders and bulging biceps. *Stout* was the word that came to mind. *Formidable* was another. His hair was dark, his complexion leathery, and his voice had the kind of raspy quality that came from years of smoking. When he turned to observe a passing car, Jon saw the jagged whiteness of an old scar running along his jawline from ear to chin.

He slipped a hand in the pocket of his trousers, letting his fingers close around his phone just in case. "What are you doing here?"

Stipes leaned against the tree trunk and folded his arms as if he didn't have a care in the world. "I heard about Tony. Thought I'd stop by and pay my respects."

"At the morgue?"

"I happened to be in the area."

Sure he had. He'd undoubtedly followed Jon here, which meant Stipes must have been staking out his mother's house. "How did you find out about my brother?"

He bent his left knee and flattened his foot against the tree trunk. "We were supposed to meet up last night. A little honky-tonk Tony knew about out on the highway. Far enough from town so as not to attract unwanted attention but close enough to the action to make things fun. Lolita's." He drew out the middle syllable, giving the name a lascivious pronunciation. "I waited awhile, had a few drinks. When he didn't show, I figured something had happened. I started poking around and found out about the shooting. Tough break." He pushed himself off the tree trunk and took a few steps toward Jon. "All those years he spent behind bars only to get shot dead when he came back home. That must rile you up. I'd be out for blood if he was my brother. How's your mother holding up?" he added without missing a beat.

Jon said with undisguised contempt, "My mother doesn't concern you."

He shrugged. "Just being polite."

"What were you and my brother meeting about?"

"We had unfinished business to discuss." Stipes removed the toothpick from his mouth and pointed it at Jon before flicking it away. "Now you and I have unfinished business."

"I don't think so. Whatever agreement you had with my brother is now null and void."

"That's not the way I see it." Stipes squinted as a thin shaft of sunlight broke through the oak leaves and caught him in the eye. He stepped back into the shade. "Where I come from, honoring your brother's debts is the gentlemanly thing to do."

"I'm no gentleman," Jon said. "And more to the point, I don't have any money."

"Just barely making ends meet on a lowly public servant's salary, is that it? Yep, been there." He removed another toothpick from his shirt pocket and clamped it between his teeth. "I happen to know you can get the cash. I've done some checking. Your family owns property all over the county. What you didn't sell off to pay Tony's legal bills is worth a lot of money these days, what with all the snowbirds moving down here. You've got more than enough to pay your brother's debt and have a nice little nest egg leftover."

"Most of that property belongs to my mother, not me."

"That's what Tony said, but like I told him, I'd rather not involve her in any of our dealings if we can help it. Keep it between us and let the poor woman grieve in peace."

Jon glanced back at the street, automatically checking his surroundings before elevating the confrontation with Stipes. Then he said slowly, "Maybe it hasn't had time to sink in yet or maybe you're just that dense, but whatever leverage you had over my brother is gone. He can't be sent back to prison, so there's nothing you can do to hurt us that hasn't already been done."

Stipes cocked his head. "You sure about that?"

"I'm sure about this. The police know who you are. They've already linked you to my brother. If you're smart, you'll slink back to where you came from before they come looking for you."

The man's grin thickened. "Thanks for the heads-up, but I kind of like it here. Nice town if you don't mind all the murders. I plan on sticking around for a while."

"Suit yourself." Jon turned to walk away. "That'll just make you easier to find."

Stipes said behind him, "Did Tony ever tell you how we met? It's a good story. I think you'll find it interesting."

Jon started to keep walking, but something in Stipes's voice compelled him to turn. "You shared a cell. That's hardly riveting."

"Before that. We crossed paths when he first got off the bus. He was just a green kid back then. Scared spitless like all the other fresh fish. He wouldn't have lasted a month at the farm without someone watching his back."

"And I suppose you were that someone?" Jon asked with no small amount of sarcasm.

"I knew my way around. A cop has to learn pretty fast on the inside who he can trust."

"Don't you mean *former cop*?" Jon eyed him with open derision. "I'm pretty sure they confiscated your badge and gun when you killed your partner."

Stipes didn't seem offended. He said with a shrug, "Son of a bitch had it coming. He agreed to cut me in on the little side business he had going, then he set me up. It was him or me that night. Lucky for me, I had enough information that allowed my attorney to cut a deal. I turned state's evidence against his—let's call them *associates*—and in return, I got a reduced sentence. Twenty years, out in ten for good behavior."

"I don't need your whole life story," Jon said. "Why did my brother come looking for you?"

"He heard I had connections on the outside, heard I had a knack for digging up things. People. Information. He wanted help finding out who killed his girlfriend. You know the drill. Claimed he was innocent. Swore he was framed. Oldest story in the book among convicts. They're all innocent to hear them tell it. But your brother was different."

Jon's attitude subtly shifted. "You believed him."

"Say what you will about how things turned out, but I was once a damn good cop. I knew how to read people. The kid was earnest. But he had a lot of pent-up anger that was going to get him in trouble and maybe me, too, if we didn't find a way to channel his rage. I agreed to help him for a fee to be paid when we both got out."

"I'm sure you found a way to make it worth your while in the meantime."

"Let's just say the partnership was mutually beneficial. I wasn't running a charity, after all. Your brother," he said and pointed with the toothpick again, "he toughened up real quick inside. After a while, nobody dared mess with us. He had my back, and I had his."

"Meaning you used him for muscle."

"He was young, strong. All that anger had to go somewhere. And he wasn't afraid to get his hands dirty. I'll say that for him."

Jon had a sudden image of his brother behind bars, fighting for his life, always looking over his shoulder. He'd downplayed the violence over the years for their mother's sake and maybe for Jon's, too. But his scars told a different story. "And these outside connections of yours?"

Stipes nodded. "They were mainly law enforcement. Buddies I'd worked with in the past. A couple of cousins still on the force. I put out some feelers, and a few days later the information started to trickle in."

"What did you find out?" Jon hated that he'd been so readily hooked. He was starting to see how his brother had gotten mixed up with a guy like Stipes. Despite all the rough edges, he could be persuasive.

"His girlfriend wasn't the angel everyone thought her to be," Stipes said.

Jon frowned. "Lily?"

"Turned out another of my cousins knew her—or at least, knew of her. She used to drive over to Kerrville where she wouldn't be recognized to buy drugs and party. Sometimes, she brought her boyfriend with her. Not Tony. This guy was older, maybe thirty, thirty-five at the time. They both went to great pains to conceal their identities, but a girl like Lily Campion attracts attention. I've seen pictures." He gave a low whistle. "People got curious and started asking questions. Someone who knew someone had a friend who knew someone...that type of thing. Turned out, the guy was married, and his old lady came from money. He had a lot to lose if word got out about his teenaged girlfriend."

"Who is he?" Jon asked. "Does he still live around here?"

The grin flashed again. "So I finally have your attention."

"Did Tony know the man's name?"

"Tony knew everything I knew and then some. He wasn't just my muscle. The kid was smart. Once he had time to think things through, he started putting two and two together."

"If that's true, why wouldn't he have told me? Or his attorneys?"

"Think about it," Stipes said. "Why would he? What could you do about it without hard evidence? Besides, if you started nosing around in the guy's business, you would've tipped him off. That was the last thing Tony wanted. He planned to confront the guy himself."

"How was that going to work with him in prison?"

"He said you'd get him out. The kid was sure of it."

Jon felt a well of emotion at the revelation. He wasn't sure he'd been worthy of his brother's blind faith. How many times had he wanted to give up and walk away?

He swallowed past the lump in his throat and hardened his tone. "Let's talk about the here and now and the opportune way you turned back up in my brother's life. I'm guessing you heard he was out, and you came looking for money. When he had a change of heart, you threatened to go to the police with a made-up story about a murder-for-hire scheme."

"Who says it was made-up? Your brother and me, we had a deal." Something ugly gleamed in Stipes's eyes.

"Even if that's true, it just means you took advantage of a desperate young man who'd been wrongfully sent to prison. When he got out and couldn't or wouldn't come up with the money, you shot him."

"Why would I kill him?" Stipes spat out the toothpick. "He's not worth anything to me dead."

"Except here you are trying to shake me down." At that moment, Jon was only too aware of the kind of person who stood mere feet away from him. An ex-con and a cop-killer who had thought nothing of trying to blackmail his brother.

Stipes feigned surprise. "You think this is a shakedown? This is just business. I'm a private detective, in case you hadn't heard. I get paid to dig up information for my clients."

Yes, but what else do they pay you for? "Whatever you're calling it these days, I'm not interested," Jon said flatly.

"Maybe not yet. Maybe you haven't hit enough brick walls."

"Maybe I just don't like dealing with the person who threatened my brother."

Stipes appeared unthwarted. "Ask yourself this. Why is it you haven't been able to uncover in seventeen years what I was able to dig up in a matter of days from a prison cell?"

"I'm sure you're just dying to enlighten me," Jon said.

"It's simple. Someone like you doesn't have what it takes to do what it takes."

"And how would you know that?" Jon countered. "You don't know anything about me."

Stipes looked him up and down. "I know all I need to know just by looking at you. The way you dress. The way you carry yourself. You think you can find the information on your own? Get back to me when you've been elbow-deep in a ripe dumpster or up to your knees in the sewer. Even then—" he gave Jon another once-over "—the people you need to talk to wouldn't give someone like you the time of day. Like it or not, you need me. I can help you take this creep down. That's what you want, right? Think it over for a day or two and get back to me. You can find my number in Tony's phone."

"The police have his phone."

"The other phone." He gave Jon an enigmatic look. "You've got a lot to learn about your brother. This should be fun."

VEDA SPENT HER first afternoon of unemployment with her mother. They took care of several projects around the house and then worked out in the garden until the heat drove them to the shady back porch. Her mother poured homemade lemonade from a frosty pitcher and served gingersnap cookies on a blue willow plate. The simple treats took Veda back to her childhood when she used to spend so much time with her grandmother. She held the chilled glass to her overheated cheek as she tipped her head to the breeze from the ceiling fan. I could get used to this, she thought. I might even be happy here.

They rocked in companionable silence for the longest time until her mother finally broached the subject of Veda's future plans, and then her pleasant mood vanished.

"I haven't made any decisions yet." She dusted cookie crumbs from her fingers onto a paper napkin. "I've had offers. I'm taking some time to mull over my options."

"It just seems a bit impulsive, and that's not like you." Her mother gave her a worried glance. "You said you took a leave of absence to be with family, then you up and quit your job for good. But instead of staying here with me, you rent a place in town as if you plan to be here for a while. Not that I don't love having you close, but I can't help wondering what brought on this sudden change of heart."

"Nothing," Veda said with a shrug. "I really did come back home to be with family. I knew with Tony Redmond getting out of prison and living here in Milton, you'd be under a lot of stress. I wanted to make things easier for you. I rented my own place because you and I are both too set in our ways. We would have driven each other crazy living under the same roof. You know it's true," she insisted when her mother started to protest. "As far as quitting my job, it wasn't all that sudden. I've been thinking about a change for a while now. Between school and work, I've lived in New Orleans for well over a decade, and as much as I love the city, I'd like to stretch my wings. See what else is out there for me."

Her mother let her say her piece, then asked quietly, "Does this need for a change have anything to do with the doctor you were dating last Christmas?"

"Adam? Of course not."

"I was sorry to hear things didn't work out. You seemed so well-suited."

"Turns out we weren't," Veda said. "We both worked long hours and rarely saw one another. It was easier to go our separate ways."

"Easier for you or for him?"

"It was a mutual decision, Mom."

Her mother frowned as she stared out over the garden. It was an idyllic setting with butterflies dancing through the lantana and honeybees busy in the coneflowers. If Veda let her mind drift, she could almost see Lily out there picking roses.

"I've often wondered why none of you kids has ever married," her mother mused.

Veda turned in surprise. "Really? What's to wonder about? It seems perfectly normal to me. We're all busy building careers and living our lives."

Her mother wouldn't let it go. "You're all in your thirties now. You should be settling down, buying homes. Raising babies of your own."

"That's your dream, not mine." Veda gave her an accusing look. "Are you suddenly pining to be a grandmother? Is that what this is about?"

"I don't know how sudden it is." Her mother tucked back a stray lock of hair. "I won't deny a desire to have children running around this place again, especially now that I'm retired and have time to enjoy them. But this isn't about me. I'd hate for you to miss out on what your dad and I had. We married young, some might say too young, but I never regretted a minute of it. I never felt like I missed out on anything. He was the love of my life."

"I know, Mom. But I'm not you."

Her mother didn't seem to hear her or chose not to. "After the accident, I didn't know how I would find the strength or the will to go on without him. The guilt and grief were almost unbearable."

"Guilt?" Veda found herself enthralled in spite of herself by her parents' tragic love story. "What did you have to feel guilty about? You were devoted to Dad."

"I walked away from the same accident that claimed his life. You don't think I still ask myself why him and not me?" She sounded more pensive than anguished.

"It was an accident. No rhyme or reason."

"It was an accident, yes, but I'm the one who wanted to

drive home in the middle of a rainstorm. You were so young when it happened. I don't know how much you remember, but we'd gotten a call from your grandmother a few days earlier. That was before she moved down here. She'd fallen ill and needed my help. Your dad dropped everything and drove me to Tennessee so that I could take care of her. I'd never spent the night away from you kids and it pained me to leave you for a day, much less a whole week. As soon as your grandmother was on the mend, he came back for me. Instead of waiting until the following morning as we planned, we set out that night. Maybe it was a premonition or maybe I was just being an overprotective mother, but I felt a very strong need to be home."

Veda had heard the story before, but she didn't try to stop her mother's memories. Sometimes a person just needed to get these things out. After the passage of so many years, the accident that claimed her father's life still weighed on her mom.

"I'll never forget that rain," she murmured. "It came down so hard we had to pull over a couple of times, and we saw lightning strike a tree. We were almost home when a truck veered into our lane. Your dad swerved, but the car skidded on the slick pavement. It all happened so fast, and in the silence after the crash, I remember thinking what a close call we'd had. And then I looked over and saw your dad…" She sighed. "The image is still vivid after all these years."

"I'm sorry, Mom."

She was still in her own little world. "I wallowed in that guilt and grief for weeks, barely able to get out of bed, but then I realized how much my misery would have pained him. He would have wanted me to pick up the pieces and get on with my life. Find a way to be happy again. Besides, I had four kids to raise. I had to be strong."

"I don't know how you did it," Veda said. "We were a handful."

"Your grandmother moved down a few months later. She was a godsend, but you kids were what saved me. You gave me a reason to get up in the morning. I thought I'd lived through the worst pain a person could ever go through, and then we lost Lily." She closed her eyes on a shudder. "No mother should ever have to endure that agony."

"I know," Veda said. "But maybe it's not good to dwell on all that sadness."

Her mother nodded. "You're probably right. I didn't mean to get maudlin. But I do have a point to all this. I sometimes wonder if the reason you and your brothers can't commit to a serious relationship is because you've been through so much pain and you're afraid of losing someone else you love."

There might have been some truth in her mother's theory, but Veda wasn't ready to concede. "Did you ever stop to think that maybe the right person hasn't come along yet? Maybe we don't want to settle. Besides, we've still got time. Except for Nate. He's practically an old man now."

Her mother cut her glance. "No. He just acts like one."

The tension lifted as they both chuckled.

Her mother sighed. "Don't mind me. I've been in a mood lately."

"Tony Redmond's release from prison put us all in a mood." Veda flashed back to Owen's fight with Tony. The ferocity of the attack. The verbal threat. And then the loaded glance between Nate and Marcus at the crime scene. She didn't think either of her brothers capable of murder—certainly not the cold-blooded, premeditated act that had claimed Tony Redmond's life—but something had been gnawing at her since Nate's phone call.

"Veda?" Her mother peered at her curiously. "Honey, are you okay? You seemed a million miles away just now."

She snapped back to the conversation. "Sorry. I was just thinking about something. What were you saying?"

"We were talking about Tony. I said it wasn't easy having him come back here. I avoided going places where I thought I might run into him."

"I did the same."

"I'll confess, though," her mother said as she traced a drop of condensation down the side of her glass, "now that he's dead, I'm ashamed of some of the thoughts that went through my head when I heard he was getting out."

"We've all had those thoughts." Veda set her glass aside and curled a leg beneath her. "But under the circumstances, we should allow ourselves a little grace."

"Maybe you're right. I can't help thinking about poor Theresa and what she must be going through."

"She's been on my mind, too."

"Despite everything, my heart goes out to her. I never blamed her for what Tony did, but afterward, I couldn't bring myself to continue our friendship."

"No one can fault you for that." Veda really didn't want to talk about any of the Redmond family, but apparently her mother still had things she needed to get off her chest. Veda vowed to spend more time with her. She obviously had a tendency to brood when left alone with too much time on her hands.

"We had so much in common back in those days," she said with a sigh. "We were both widows raising large families on our own. I remember how pleased we were when Tony and

Lily started going out. We prided ourselves on the fact that we didn't have to worry because we'd each brought up such good kids. And they were so beautiful together. Do you remember? Everyone thought of them as the perfect couple."

"Until they weren't," Veda said bluntly.

"Until they weren't," her mother repeated softly. "Sometimes I wake up in the middle of the night, and I still can't believe it happened. The Tony I knew could be full of himself, but he had a good heart. At least, I thought so. I look back now and think how could I have missed the signs? How could I not have known what that young man was capable of?"

"None of us knew. Something just snapped in him that night. But this is a very depressing conversation," Veda said. "Maybe we should talk about something else. Or better yet, why don't you go inside and cool off in the air-conditioning? I'll pick up the garden tools and put them away."

"I am tired," her mother admitted. "I haven't been sleeping well lately."

"Then, go lie down and take a nap. I'll finish out here."

"Will you be here when I get up?"

"Yes, go on." Veda waved her inside. "I'll just putter around the house until it's time to fix dinner."

She cleaned the shovels and clippers and stored them in the garden shed. Backtracking to the porch, she carried the glasses inside and rinsed them at the kitchen sink. She wiped down the counters and took out the trash, and then she went upstairs and stood in the open doorway of Lily's old room.

Hovering on the threshold, she let her gaze roam over the familiar space. Nothing much had changed in the years since her sister's death. Her mother swore she hadn't kept the room as a shrine or a memorial or anything like that. Raising four kids on her own had simply made her cautious about finances. Why spend good money on new furnishings when the old was still perfectly fine?

The furniture, bedding and linen curtains were all the same, but the band posters had been removed, and the walls had been painted a soft lavender. The subtle color deepened in the afternoon sunlight, giving the room an almost ethereal air that was at once dreamy and a little unsettling. If she closed her eyes, she could see her sister peering in the vanity mirror or sitting on her bed with schoolbooks spread all around her and a phone to her ear. She could hear Lily's favorite song in the background and those heart-tugging whimpers in the middle of the night.

Who were you, Lily? Why do I feel as if I never knew the real you?

Veda wandered around the room, touching trinkets on the dresser, lifting a forgotten candle to her nose. Finally, she went over to the closet and opened the door.

Lily's clothes were all gone. Her mother had tucked away the items she wanted to keep in tissue-lined boxes and donated the rest to a women's shelter. Photo albums and other mementos had been neatly stored in airtight containers on the top shelf. Other than those few plastic bins, the space was empty. Even the hangers had been removed.

Veda was thinking of sorting through a few of the old photographs, but instead she turned off the light and moved to the deepest corner of the closet. Lowering herself to the floor in the dark, she leaned her back against the wall as she drew up her knees.

Memories floated like ghosts through the cramped space. She tried to resist the tug of the past, but exhaustion made her sluggish and vulnerable. With a sigh, she rested her head on her knees and gave in to the lure. She drifted back in time, years before the murder, to the night when she'd first discovered Lily's hiding space. It was storming outside. Veda had been too young to understand the depth of her sister's fear but old enough to want to comfort her. She'd gone looking for Lily after an especially loud clap of thunder. She found her huddled on the floor at the back of the closet with her hands pressed against her ears. Veda had scooted in beside her, offering as much sympathy and comfort as a child knew how to muster.

"Don't worry. It's just a storm," she soothed. "It'll blow over soon. Mom says thunder is always a lot farther away than it sounds."

"But that's not true," Lily whispered back. "She only says that to make me feel better. She doesn't know what the thunder really means."

"What does it mean?"

Her sister raised tear-stained eyes and shuddered. "It means the bad man is coming."

Veda had no idea who or what the bad man *was, but she knew enough to be frightened. She put a trembling hand on her sister's arm. When Lily recoiled, Veda jumped. "What bad man?"*

"He doesn't have a name. All I know is that the thunder summons him. He climbs through my window and sits on the edge of my bed to watch me sleep."

Veda found enough courage to scrabble to the doorway and glance out into the bedroom. "No one's there."

"He'll come. I know he will."

Veda crawled back to her sister's side. "Maybe you just had a bad dream. I have them sometimes, too."

Lily said in a strange voice, "You should go back to your room. If you see him, pretend you don't know."

"Know what?" Veda had a bright idea. "Come back to my room with me. I'll lock the door. I won't let him come inside."

"You're just a little kid. You can't stop him."

"Yes, I can!"

Lily shook her head with a forlorn sigh. "Daddy is the only one who can keep me safe."

"But Daddy's gone. Don't you remember? He had an accident."

Lily hugged her knees tighter. "Of course I remember. I'm the reason he's dead."

The memory drifted away, leaving Veda gloomy and unnerved. She felt a strange combination of emotions. She hugged her legs and rested her chin on her knees. The walls of the closet seemed to close in on her, making it difficult to breathe. She attributed the panicky sensation to claustrophobia, but confined spaces had never really bothered her. The only place she'd ever felt real fear was the attic. One of her brothers had once locked her inside for an entire afternoon, though to this day, neither had ever confessed. They blamed her entrapment on a faulty door latch.

She told herself she'd done enough wallowing in the past. Poking and prodding at all those old memories just made her feel helpless and more than a little unnerved. She needed to get out of that oppressive space and leave the past where it belonged. After all these years, did she really think a memory or a photograph would help her to understand her troubled sister?

But even as she decided to go back downstairs and out into the garden, another memory crept on icy feet from the shadows of her subconscious. She tried to shove the unwelcome creature back into the darkness, back into her mind's lockbox, instinctively realizing that some memories were too painful—and maybe too dangerous—to be unleashed. But already she could hear Lily's whimpers.

It was the night of her sister's eighteenth birthday. The family had had dinner together with Lily's favorite red velvet cake for dessert. Afterward, she and Tony had gone to the movies. They'd graduated from high school a few weeks earlier, and on that fragrant summer night, the two of them seemed to have the whole world at their feet.

Veda had been sound asleep until a clap of thunder awakened her, and she lay for a moment, listening to the storm. She'd left a window open earlier and she could hear tree branches scraping against the side of the house. The sound grated, so she got out of bed and padded over to the window to glance out. She wasn't normally afraid of storms, but every once in a while, her sister's fear rubbed off on her. Tonight was one of those nights. She glanced over her shoulder almost expecting to find the bad man sitting on the edge of her bed.

No one was there, of course. She tried to shrug off her unease. It was just the storm. Nothing to be afraid of.

Lowering the window, she turned and left the room to tiptoe down the hallway to the bathroom she shared with her sister. The door to Lily's room was open, and Veda peeked inside. Her sister's bed was empty. It didn't look as though it had been slept in. Veda's first thought was that her sister hadn't come home yet, and she was going to be in a lot of trouble when their mother found out. Then she heard a strange keening sound coming from the back of the closet.

For the longest moment, Veda hovered on the threshold. She'd been fearless as a little kid, wanting nothing so much as to comfort and protect her big sister. Now she felt the need to protect herself, though she had no idea why.

Swallowing past an inexplicable terror, she'd slipped across the room to the closet door.

"Lily? You in here?"

"Don't turn on the light!"

A spidery sensation crawled up Veda's spine. Something in her sister's voice...

"Are you okay? The storm sounds worse than it is. It'll be over soon."

Nothing but silence came back to her.

She got down on her hands and knees and wove her way through a maze of shoeboxes to the back of the closet. Her sister sat rocking back and forth as she had years ago when they were children.

Veda said in a hushed voice, "What's wrong? Is it the storm?"

Lily drew a tremulous breath. "I saw him again."

"Who?"

"He came through my window and sat on the edge of my bed. I pretended to be asleep. I've always been good at pretending. But I could see him in the flashes of lightning. He wore dark clothes, and he had red eyes."

Veda's heart was thudding by this time. "He isn't real, Lily."

"Then, why could I smell him?"

"You...smelled him?" Somehow the notion of an odor seemed the most horrific of all her sister's revelations.

"It wasn't bad like you would expect. It reminded me of Grandma's old cedar chest." She sounded puzzled. "That can't be right, though, can it? Shouldn't the devil smell like sulfur?"

Veda swallowed back her fear. She didn't know what to say, what to do. She had the strongest urge to scramble out of the closet and run back to her room, pull the covers over her head and pretend she didn't know about her sister's dream. Had never heard the awful keening that had sounded like a frightened kitten in distress.

Awkwardly, she rubbed her sister's arm as she'd done when they were little and whispered a litany of inane platitudes. "You just had a bad dream, that's all it was. The storm brought it on. You've always been afraid of storms. When you were little, you used to have the most awful nightmares. But you don't have to be afraid now. You're all grown up. Nothing can hurt you."

Lily shook her head sadly. "You don't understand. The nightmares went away a long time ago. I thought he'd gone, too, but now he's come back to punish me."

"Punish you for what?"

She sounded numb, distant. "I'm not the person you think I am, Veda. You shouldn't look up to me. If you knew the bad things I've done, you'd hate me."

The hair at the back of Veda's neck prickled. "What things?"

Her head lifted. "Can you keep a secret?"

Veda nodded.

"I shouldn't tell you. I promised I wouldn't say anything. But I can't keep it all inside anymore. Sometimes I feel like I'm going to explode if I don't tell someone."

"What is it, Lily? What did you do?"

She drew a shaky breath. "I've fallen in love with someone else. We're going away together."

Veda drew back in shock. "Who is he?"

"I can't tell you his name. It has to stay a secret for now. Tony doesn't know yet. Neither does Mom or the boys. You're the only one I've told. Promise me you won't say anything."

Her sister's confession rattled Veda. She tried to make sense of it. "You're going away? When?"

"I don't know. Soon, I hope. We haven't worked out the details yet."

"But I thought you loved Tony. You've been together forever."

"I'll always love Tony, but..." *She made a sad little sigh.* "Someday you'll understand. Or maybe you won't. I'm not so sure I understand it myself."

"You have to tell him. He'll be so crushed if he finds out from someone else."

"I will, but the timing has to be right. I don't know how he'll react. A lot of people could get hurt."

Veda wanted to nod in understanding, but at the moment, all she felt was keen disappointment. "Oh, Lily, how could you? He loves you so much."

"I know he does. Maybe too much."

Chapter Six

Veda couldn't take the gloom a moment longer. She scrambled out of the closet into the bedroom. Despite the cool air blowing from the vents, she went over and raised a window, drinking in the fresh air before shutting out the heat. Her mother found her a little while later sitting cross-legged on the floor of Lily's bedroom, surrounded by photo albums and yearbooks.

"I hope you don't mind." She waved her hand over the mementos. "I've been meaning to ask if I could take some of the photos back to my place and scan them."

"That's a good idea. I'd love to have digital copies for safekeeping." Her mother sat down on the bed and plucked at the trim on the coverlet as she glanced around the room. "I've been thinking again that it might be time to change things up in here. Maybe turn it into a sewing room. Isn't that what people do with spare bedrooms? Or a crafting space. Your grandmother's old sewing machine cabinet is still in the attic. Maybe I should have the boys carry it down for me."

"But you don't sew or craft," Veda pointed out. "You said you never had the patience for it."

"True."

She wondered if her mother had known about Lily's nightmares. Not that she was going to bring it up. They'd already spent too much of their visit on depressing topics, and Veda felt worn-out and worn down. "It's getting late," she said. "Should we go down and fix a bite to eat? I need to be getting home soon."

They ate chicken salad on crisp lettuce leaves with fresh strawberries and cantaloupe on the side. Veda stayed to help with the cleanup, then she headed out.

The sun had already dipped beneath the horizon by the time she turned down her street. The light softened as dusk crept closer, and something started to fret around the edges of her mind. She told herself she was just tired. Wandering around in all the old memories had taken a toll. Still, her guard was up. She didn't claim to be clairvoyant, but if there was one thing she'd learned from her time in New Orleans, it was to listen to her instincts.

A car was parked at the curb in front of her house. She thought at first it was the sedan she'd seen across the street from Owen's apartment, but the make and model were different. Nate drove a SUV similar to hers, and Owen owned a truck, so neither of her brothers had come for a visit.

She pulled onto the driveway and parked. Only then did she notice the man seated on her front steps. Jon Redmond waited until she climbed out of the vehicle before he rose to greet her.

Her pulse accelerated as she mentally braced herself and moved onto the brick walkway. She gave him a quick once-over, taking in the dark circles under his eyes and the lines of exhaustion that had deepened around his mouth. She would have sworn he had on the same clothes he'd worn to the crime scene at two o'clock in the morning, only now they were far from crisp, and he didn't seem at all pulled-together. The opposite, in fact. The day had obviously taken a toll.

She said, not unkindly, "You look like death warmed-over, and I would know."

He glanced down at his wrinkled shirt. "Sorry. I was on my way home to shower and change, but I thought I'd stop by here first. Maybe I should have done it the other way around."

"Or maybe you should have called first. How did you get my address, anyway?"

"I asked around. Milton hasn't grown that much." A hint of a smile flashed. "Everyone still knows everyone else's business."

She made no move to join him at the steps but instead kept her distance, slinging her bag over her shoulder and trying to act unmoved despite the tug of sympathy his haggard appearance evoked. "And?"

"And..." he spread his hands in supplication "...I apologize for showing up on your doorstep like this. I didn't think you'd take my call, and you no longer work at the coroner's office, so this seemed the best way to reach you."

"Why go to the trouble? As I understand it, the autopsy was performed earlier today. You've probably already seen a preliminary report."

"I have. But I'm not here about the autopsy. It was never just about the autopsy."

"Right." She gave a curt nod. "You think I know something about my sister's secret boyfriend. And that I withheld information about him on the witness stand. For what purpose, you haven't yet explained. But just to clear things up once and for all—had I known who he was, I would have shouted his name from the top of the courthouse steps."

He ran a hand through his hair, looking indescribably weary. "I don't think you deliberately withheld his name. I think you told the truth as you knew it. But you were just a kid when you were called to testify."

"I was sixteen. Hardly a child."

"That's young to go through the trauma of a murdered sibling." He paused, and she saw him draw a deep breath. "The trial was only a few months later. You must have still been devastated and grieving. We all were. But a lot of time has gone by since then. Sometimes things come back to us when we're no longer stressed. Or when we least expect it."

"Nothing has come back to me." Although, that wasn't exactly true. A lot of memories had surfaced during her time in Lily's closet. She'd always known about her sister's fear of storms, but she'd somehow managed to forget about the bad man in her nightmares. Maybe because even an imaginary demon crawling through windows and sitting on beds terrified her.

"The man she was seeing that summer may have been older, probably in his thirties," Jon said. "He may have been married. Supposedly, his wife's family had money. That could explain the need for secrecy. He had a lot to lose if the affair became public."

Veda looked at him askance. "He may have been this, he may have been that. And just where did these details come from all of a sudden?"

"I have a source who claims to know the man's identity."

"Oh, you have a source." Veda folded her arms. "Why do you need me, then?"

"He's not what I'd call reliable. To tell you the truth, I'm not sure I can believe a word that comes out of his mouth."

"Does he have a name?"

"Clay Stipes. Apparently, your uncle is familiar with him."

Veda said in outrage, "Clay Stipes the cop-killer? *He's* your source?"

"You see the trouble I have putting any faith in him?" His voice remained quietly controlled, but his expression was grim. "I get the impression he'd say or do anything for a payday. But on the slight chance he's telling the truth, I thought the details he provided might help jog your memory."

A rich, older man. *Oh, Lily. What did you get yourself into?*

Something flitted through Veda's head. Not exactly a memory but a faint nudge. There one moment and gone the next. She had no idea what it meant, but questions arose from the prompt. What if Jon was right? What if she knew more than she was willing to remember?

"What is it?" His tone rose slightly. "Do you know who he is?"

She shook her head. "No one fitting that description comes to mind. How did Stipes come by this information?"

"He's also an ex-cop. He claims he still has contacts in law enforcement."

"Then, why don't you just give him what he wants in exchange for a name?"

"It's complicated." He glanced over his shoulder as if worried Stipes might be within hearing distance. "An exchange of cash with a guy like Clay Stipes can result in unintended consequences. He's not someone I want to do business with, much less be indebted to."

"That's probably a wise decision," she agreed. "For the sake of argument, let's say you somehow find Lily's mystery man on your own. What's your plan? Do you go knock on his door and accuse him of killing my sister and your brother without any evidence?"

Another faint smile. "I would hope to be a little more subtle. First, we find out his name, and then we look for the evidence."

"Uh-uh. There is no *we*." She was adamant. "I already told you I don't want any part of this."

"But what if you're the key to uncovering his identity?"

"And what if you're still grasping at straws?" she shot back.

That shut him down but only for a moment. "Think about it. Lily was eighteen and embroiled in a clandestine love affair. Forbidden love at that age can be very romantic, overwhelming even. Put yourself in her place. Would you be able to keep something like that a secret? You'd want to confide in someone close to you, someone you trusted."

Veda sighed. "How many times do I have to say it? She never told me his name."

"Maybe she told a best friend."

"It's been nearly two decades. I wouldn't even know where to find most of her friends. They all scattered years ago. And honestly, if she wouldn't tell me his name, I doubt she told anyone else."

"She may not have deliberately told you anything, but is it possible she let something slip? Maybe a nickname? Maybe his profession or where he lived?"

"If she did, I never caught on. She did say they were planning to go away together, but I already testified to that in court."

"Did she mention where they were going or when?"

"As I said on the stand, they hadn't yet worked out the details."

He paused again. "Do you think he could have been putting her off?"

"While still leading her on? That thought has crossed my mind."

"What about a journal or diary? She would have kept it hidden where no one would have come across it by accident. And what about mementos? Surely, she would have wanted keepsakes from the relationship? Photographs, love letters, *something*. If we could just sit down and talk things through… A few minutes of your time. That's all I'm asking. What have you got to lose?"

Her peace of mind, for one thing. Veda told herself to end it now. Just send him on his way and wash her hands of the whole mess. She was sorry for what he was going through, but nothing he had to say could change the fact that his brother had murdered her sister.

Even as the argument bubbled to her lips, though, an old doubt started to niggle.

He made no move toward her, nor she to him. They seemed to be in something of a standstill, each in their own way trapped in the past as their gazes locked. He looked pale and ghostlike in the fading light. Almost too handsome to be real with his dark, wavy hair falling over his forehead and those blue eyes so electric they could surely pierce her soul. His voice was a deep baritone with only a hint of a drawl. She could well imagine the effect that richness would have on a jury. It was certainly having an effect on her.

The situation was so strange, she thought. She and Jon Redmond standing face-to-face with twilight and honeysuckle weaving a cloak of mystery and nostalgia all around them.

She folded her arms and tried not to shiver. "You should go home." Her moment of weakness made her respond more sharply than she would have liked. "You should be with your family instead of standing here arguing with me."

"They're the reason I'm here," he said quietly. "They need to know the truth. It's all they have left."

"They have you. Go home, Jon. I can't help you."

"Can't or won't?"

"Both." Brushing past him, she climbed the porch steps without looking back. "It's been a long day, and I'm tired."

A car passed by on the street. He waited until the sound of the engine faded before he spoke. "Do you remember the last thing I said to you outside the courtroom that day?"

She slowly turned. "You said, 'My brother isn't a killer, and if it takes the rest of my life I'll find a way to prove it.'"

"Nothing has changed."

The depth of his conviction juxtaposed against the softness of his tone tore at her resolve. "You're conveniently dismissing the fact that your brother was convicted by a jury of his peers."

"A conviction that was overturned."

"For prosecutorial misconduct, not because he was innocent. His release on a legal technicality doesn't negate the fact that he was found with the murder weapon in his truck and my sister's blood all over his hands."

"You're dismissing something pretty damn important yourself. My brother was murdered, too. Less than twenty-four hours ago." He stared up at her from the bottom of the steps. "What if I'm right and Lily's killer is still out there? What if he resurfaced years after her death to murder my brother?"

"Do you even hear yourself?" She came back over to the edge of the porch. "Why would Lily's killer come after Tony? If what you say is true, your brother was the scapegoat. Why cast doubt now on his guilt?"

"Whether you want to admit it or not, the overturned conviction has already cast doubt. Questions are being asked. Old memories are being stirred. I think Tony was murdered because of something he found out while he was still in prison. I think he knew the name of Lily's killer."

"You think, but you don't know. If it were true, why wouldn't he have told you?"

"I can't answer that."

"Can't or won't?" Veda moved back to the door and inserted the key.

"So that's it?" he said from behind her. "I just walk away, and that's the end of it?"

"What did you think was going to happen when you came over here? That I would throw up my hands and say *Go ahead, drag me into your delusion*?"

"It didn't go quite that way in my head."

She said in exasperation, "Why me?"

He answered without hesitation. "You knew Lily better than anyone. You have access to her belongings. You have a vested interest in finding out what really happened that night. And because you're the only Campion who would give me the time of day."

"The truth at last," she muttered as she turned back to the door. "I'm going inside to pour myself a very large glass of wine. It's been that kind of a day. If you're still here when I come back out, I'll give you five more minutes."

He was still at the bottom of the steps. "Thank you."

"Don't thank me yet. If I'm not convinced by the end of our talk, you have to walk away and leave me alone."

"Agreed."

She went inside and uncorked a bottle of wine. Then she went down the hallway to the bathroom to wash her face and straighten her ponytail. She refused to do any primping beyond that. No shower, no makeup, no change of clothing. She didn't need to impress Jon Redmond. The opposite, in fact. She needed to convince him once and for all that he was barking up the wrong Campion.

Returning to the kitchen, she poured a wineglass nearly to the brim, taking a quick sip to make sure none of the merlot spilled over. Then she poured a generous splash of bourbon into another glass and carried both drinks out to the porch.

Jon was seated on her porch swing by this time. He started to get up, but she waved him back down before placing the bourbon on the table in front of the swing. "You look like you could use this."

He picked up the glass. "Thanks, but I'm coasting on fumes as it is. If I drink this, I may fall asleep right here on your porch." He sipped tentatively.

She looked him over. "How long has it been since you slept?"

"I've lost track. Night before last, I think."

She sat down in a chair across from the swing and drank generously. "You look like hell."

"So you've mentioned. Although I believe *death warmed-over* was your previous assessment."

She propped her feet on a wicker ottoman and continued to drink. He did not. The silence that ensued was hardly companionable, yet for some reason, Veda wasn't compelled to hurry him along. Maybe it was those damning circles beneath his eyes or the furrows of grief and worry across his brow. She knew only too well what he was going through. His haunted blue eyes stirred a myriad of emotions. Try as she might to remain hard-hearted or at least wary, she felt her determination slip with each passing moment.

He set the rest of his drink on the table, then leaned back against the swing. "This is a nice place."

"It's a short-term rental. I don't know how long I'll be in town. I never thought I'd be here this long."

"Plans change," he said. "I never thought I'd be a lawyer."

The confession surprised her. She said over the rim of her wineglass, "No? I hear you're pretty good at it."

The swing rocked gently. The motion seemed to hypnotize him. "I wanted to be an architect like my grandfather. Design and build beautiful houses. *Forever homes*, he called them."

Veda idly twirled her ponytail around one finger. "It's never too late."

"Yeah, it is. I made my decision a long time ago. After Tony's conviction, I knew what I had to do. He went to prison, and I went back to school and changed my major to pre-law."

"Never looked back?"

"I wouldn't say never, but not often." He eyed the bourbon but didn't pick up the glass. "What about you? Why pathology?"

She said a little defensively, "Why not pathology? You're not the squeamish type, are you?"

He gave a humorless laugh. "Not anymore. I only asked because I was curious if what happened to Lily had anything to do with your career choice."

Veda shrugged. "Maybe a little. I always knew I wanted a career in medicine. During my junior and senior years, I worked for Dr. Bader after school and on summer break. Mostly clerical work at first, but once I turned eighteen, he allowed me to observe some of the procedures. It took some getting used to."

Jon grimaced. "I'm sure."

She smiled at his tone. "But you do get used to it after a

while. And you learn not to eat certain things before certain procedures. Eventually, I realized that working at the morgue wasn't so different from working in a hospital. A surgeon operates to save a life. A pathologist operates to find out why the person died. And in some cases, we're able to uncover clues along the way as to the who, what, when and where. It's important work."

"Not just important but integral to the criminal justice system," he agreed. "What happens in the autopsy room can free the innocent or send the guilty to jail. Unfortunately, the opposite is sometimes true."

She acknowledged his point with a nod as she studied him in the deepening twilight. She couldn't get over his appearance. Not the disheveled hair or rumpled clothing, but the blue eyes and the chiseled jawline. She supposed he'd always been attractive, but she couldn't remember noticing. Now she'd have a hard time forgetting. Never again would she think of Jon Redmond as anyone's big brother. He was his own man, and somewhere along the way he'd grown exceedingly handsome.

"What's wrong?"

She shrugged and sipped her wine. "I was thinking about our conversation at the cemetery. You made a point of letting me know that Dr. Bader overextends himself and cuts corners, yet I got the impression you were worried about more than his competence. When I mentioned kickbacks, you hesitated before you admitted you didn't have any proof."

He said carefully, "You know why my brother's conviction was overturned, right?"

"Yes, the DA supposedly withheld evidence from the defense."

Jon's eyes flashed in the dusk. "Not supposedly. He did. Two key pieces of exculpatory evidence. Or at the very least, evidence that could have been used by Tony's defense team to create reasonable doubt." He took a breath, seemingly to get his anger under control. "Do you remember the results of Lily's tox screen?"

"Of course. The lab found traces of benzodiazepine in her blood. The DA argued that Tony used Rohypnol to impair her senses so she couldn't fight back."

"Did you know that my brother was also given a blood test?"

She was caught off guard by the question but tried not to show it. "I'm not surprised. It would have been standard operating procedure. Dr. Bader likely collected the sample himself."

"He did. The lab sent back two reports. The preliminary analysis checked for alcohol, prescription and nonprescription medicines, illegal drugs like marijuana, cocaine, heroin, that type of thing. The second, more in-depth analysis turned up the same benzodiazepine found in Lily's blood. That finding was never turned over to the defense, much less presented to the jury."

Veda frowned. "How would that even be possible? Too many people would have known about the second report."

"How many of them followed the trial that closely? The state crime lab is notoriously backlogged. Once they turn over their findings, they move on to the next case unless called to testify."

She came right back at him. "Even if what you're saying is true, the presence of benzodiazepine in Tony's blood test wouldn't have cleared him of murder. He could have dosed himself to numb his senses. Date-rape drugs aren't just used to spike drinks. They're sometimes used recreationally."

"Rarely," Jon argued. "They're considered minor euphoriants at best. But the bigger point is this." He leaned forward. "After the murder, Tony supposedly drove all the way across town to find a railroad crossing. The amount of benzodiazepine in his system would have made that virtually impossible." Then, as if to hammer home his point, he added, "There was also a witness."

She said in shock, "To the murder?"

"Not to the murder, no. A witness saw someone exit Tony's truck and run off into the woods. The witness thought at first the vehicle had stalled on the tracks and the driver had gone for help. He didn't have a working phone so he also went for help. By the time he returned, the truck had been pushed from the tracks and Tony was lying cuffed on the ground surrounded by police."

"Why didn't this person check the vehicle to make sure no one else was inside before he left?"

"He assumed any passengers would have gotten out, too."

"Could he identify the person who ran into the woods?"

"It was too dark, and he was too far away."

Veda shook her head. "Sorry, but his story sounds a little fishy to me. Why did this witness never come forward?"

"He did, but as you can imagine, the scene was chaotic that night. By the time he came back, the police had found the knife in Tony's truck, and they were desperately trying to ascertain where all that blood on his hands and clothing came from. The witness reported what he saw to an officer at the scene, but he was never called in to give a formal statement, much less to testify."

"Then, how did you find out about him?"

"An office assistant who used to work in the DA's office finally came forward. She swore in her deposition that the officer's notes and the second tox screen were originally included in Tony's file. They went missing sometime before his case went to trial."

"Let me guess. Is this assistant a disgruntled former employee?"

"More like someone with a guilty conscience and enough foresight to make duplicates of everything in order to protect herself from a corrupt prosecutor who would have thought nothing of trumping up charges to ruin her life if she tried to go public with the information."

"So why come forward now?" Veda pressed.

"Her former boss has retired from politics. Allegations of corruption, go figure. He doesn't have the power or clout he once hoped to have in this state. But as to the real reason for her timing, only she knows for sure. I would hope that her sense of justice prevailed. What I know is that my brother was denied a fair trial. The DA deliberately withheld those two pieces of evidence because he knew a conviction would help advance his career. It wouldn't be the first time."

"And Dr. Bader? Where does he fit in?"

"The lab would have sent Tony's toxicology report to his office, and he would have made a copy for the police department. At the very least, there was willful negligence on the part of the coroner's office and/or the police department. I have a theory as to why."

"I'm all ears," she said.

He gave her a look she couldn't decipher. "Cops can be notoriously single-minded when they think they have a suspect dead to rights. They found the murder weapon in Tony's truck. Lily's blood was all over his hands and clothing. And he was in what they called an *unresponsive state*. Any piece of evidence that didn't corroborate their case against him could have been easily discounted or ignored."

"You're painting with an awfully broad brush," she accused.

"I don't think so. Not considering the outcome. The tox screen and the eyewitness account along with your testimony about a secret boyfriend could have been used by the defense to create reasonable doubt. Without the other two pieces of evidence, the DA was able to use your testimony to prove motive."

"All I did was tell the truth."

"I know." He turned to glance out over the small front yard, his expression enigmatic. She followed his gaze and wondered if he'd spotted the lone lightning bug she'd seen earlier in the boxwoods. Or maybe he'd drifted back in time before her sister's murder had jaded and changed them all.

And maybe it was time to call it a night and send him on his way. He'd made a good case, but she wasn't yet ready to concede aloud her doubts. His brother had been the bad guy in her head for too many years. She wasn't going to change her mind overnight no matter how persuasive she found his argument.

And yet…

"Tell me about Lily."

She'd been so deep in thought that the request startled her. She shook off her reverie. "What do you want to know?"

"Whatever you want me to know." He watched her from the swing, his eyes blinking drowsily, but the color, even in twilight, was still amazingly vivid. "I didn't know her all that well. Which seems strange, in hindsight. She and Tony were inseparable for years."

"Sometimes I wonder how well I knew her," Veda admitted. "She was smart. Beautiful. Complicated. She could be funny at times but also moody and too often depressed. And secretive. But you already know that. She was also deathly afraid of thunderstorms."

"Why was she afraid of storms?"

"The car wreck that killed our dad happened during a storm. He and Lily were very close. Don't get me wrong. He loved all of us kids. He was a great dad. But even as a child, Lily had this aura about her, this otherworldly beauty that caused people to stop on the street and stare at her. Sometimes they'd even ask my mom if they could take her picture. I think my dad was so protective because he knew her kind of beauty might someday attract the wrong kind of attention."

"In that case, he must have been protective of you, too."

She felt inordinately flattered by the insinuation. Had it been that long since a man had paid her a compliment? Or maybe she was just a little bit tipsy. One very full glass of wine had lowered her defenses.

"I wasn't in Lily's league, and I was okay with that," she said. "This may sound phony and a little too self-aggrandizing, but I never felt jealous of all the attention. Living in her shadow gave me a certain amount of freedom."

"That's a very healthy way of dealing with sibling rivalry. I wasn't that mature. I envied Tony's talent. He didn't just excel at football, he broke records. I was a mediocre baseball player at best." But despite his deprecating tone, he didn't come off as bitter or resentful. He sounded proud. "Did you know he had a full-ride scholarship to Ole Miss? Those aren't easy to come by. He could have ended up in the pros, he was that good. Someone took all that away from him. I want to know why."

Veda's eyes stung unexpectedly. "Someone stole Lily's future, too. Do you really think finding her mystery man is going to give you the answers you need?"

"I think he's a good place to start. One real lead is all we need."

She sighed. "You expect a lot. What makes you think we can undercover something that no one else has been able to do in seventeen years?"

"Because no one else has been looking."

"You have."

"I was more focused on getting my brother out of prison."

"Still..." She gazed down into her empty glass. "I don't think you should get your hopes up."

"I was told the same thing about every stage of the appeal."

"This is different," Veda insisted. "You think Lily left something behind—a photo or a journal or a letter that will give you a clue. She didn't. The police searched her room after the murder. I've been through her things myself. Nothing is there. But—"

"But?" His tone was hopeful.

"I'll take another look just to put your mind at ease."

"Thank you."

Veda decided she must really be feeling no pain to make such an offer. She glanced at his glass on the table. Except for an initial sip or two, he hadn't touched his drink. "It's getting late."

"Yes, you're right. I've worn out my welcome and then some." He stood, and she walked him to the edge of the porch. He caught her arm when she teetered on the top step. "You okay?"

"Just tired."

Dusk had fallen in earnest, and the streetlights were on. The moths had come out to bask in the glow, and the bats had come out to feast.

Jon was still holding onto her arm. "Get some rest. We can talk again if you want. If not...thanks for hearing me out."

Before she could duck or even catch her breath, he bent and kissed her cheek. Far from being repelled, she had the strongest urge to turn her head to meet his lips.

Chapter Seven

Jon was half-dead on his feet as he climbed the outside steps to his apartment. He automatically checked his surroundings as he removed his key from his pocket. The day's events had left him both exhausted and wary. His brother had been murdered less than twenty-four hours ago. He kept waiting for that reality to sink in, but at the moment he mostly felt numb.

He'd grieved for Tony when the verdict had been read aloud in the courtroom and every time thereafter when he'd visited the prison or an appeal had hit a brick wall. He hated to acknowledge that in a very real sense, he'd said goodbye to his brother a long time ago.

His phone pinged with an incoming text message. He checked the screen. Gabby, wanting to know when he was coming back. He thumbed a response: Grabbing a quick shower and change of clothing at the apartment. Be back in a few.

Gabby: You've been gone a long time. Mom's worried.

Jon: Tell her I'm fine. I'll be there soon. Love you both.

His sister's texts momentarily distracted him. The last thing he wanted was to worry his mother, but there were things that required his attention. Still, he needed to be more mindful of his family's needs. To that end, he'd pack a bag while he was at the apartment so that he wouldn't have to come back for a couple of days. He planned to spend the next few nights with his mom and Gabby, not just as a safety precaution but because in his experience, the absence of a loved one was more keenly felt after dark.

His steps slowed as he approached his apartment. The door was ajar. He checked over his shoulder before nudging it open with his foot. The hinges swung silently inward. He'd turned off all the lights when he left early that morning, but enough illumination streamed in through the balcony windows to allow him a view down the narrow foyer and into the living room. No movement. No sound. Everything was silent inside.

Bending to check the doorjamb, he traced his finger across scratches in the wood that could have been made by a jimmy. Then he rose and stepped across the threshold, his gaze darting from one dim corner to the next. Satisfied that he was alone, he closed the door with a soft click. The sound sent a warning chill up his spine, and he paused yet again to listen. The only noise he could detect was the rev of an engine down in the parking lot. Nothing came to him from the depths of the apartment.

Even so, he knew better than to let his guard down. His brother had just been murdered, and now his apartment had been broken into. A connection seemed like a distinct possibility. He wouldn't put it past Clay Stipes to break in looking for money or as a means to coerce and intimidate him.

A vision formed in his head of Tony on his knees, hands

bound behind his back. Jon's heart tripped in trepidation. The safest move was to leave the apartment and call the police from his vehicle. Instead, he held his ground, tuning his senses to the slightest movement or noise.

At first glance, nothing seemed out of place. Maybe the intruder had been caught in the act or gotten cold feet. He was probably long gone by now. As Jon's eyes adjusted to the dark, he noticed one of the drawers in the TV credenza had been left open. A seemingly innocuous detail that on any other day he could have easily blamed on his carelessness. Now he knew with certainty that someone had been in his apartment looking for something.

He moved back to the foyer, extracting a baseball bat from the coat closet. His fingers tightened around the grip as he moved across the living room and down the hallway to his office. He peeked in through the open doorway before stepping inside. The desk drawers were closed, and his laptop and tablet didn't appear to have been touched. Strange, because small electronics would be easy pickings for someone wanting to make a quick buck. But he had a feeling the intruder had been after something else.

Still hovering just inside, he turned to move into the hallway when he caught a slight movement from the corner of his eye. He whirled a split second before the door slammed into him, hitting him in the face and knocking him back into the hallway. His head hit the wall with a thud. Before he could shake off the daze, the door flew back and a shadow sprang from his office.

The intruder body-slammed him against the wall, and Jon went sprawling to the floor even as he swung the bat. He connected with a shin bone. He heard a grunt, and then the attacker lunged. Jon lifted the bat in both hands to deflect the heavy metal flashlight that slashed through the dark toward his head. The casing struck the bat, shattering the lens. Glass shards rained down, piercing him above the left eyebrow.

Blood ran down into his eye, but he didn't have time to wipe it away. He was on his back on the floor, the assailant looming over him. Tossing the flashlight aside, the attacker grabbed the bat with both hands and forced it down against Jon's windpipe. He pushed back hard, but the man was strong and in the position of power, using his body weight for leverage. Jon tried to take in details of his appearance, but it was dark in the hallway and the intruder was dressed all in black. He could have been Stipes; he could have been anyone. They grappled for what seemed an eternity until the man wrested the bat free from Jon's grip. Then he lifted it over his head and swung hard. Jon jerked to the side, dodging a skull-crushing blow, but the bat caught his right temple hard enough to stun him.

He fought his way up through the haze as he braced for a fresh attack. None came. A moment later, he heard the door of his apartment slam shut.

A FULL THIRTY minutes went by before the police arrived. During the interim, Jon called his sister to say that he would be a little longer than expected. Everything was fine, but he had to take care of some business. He'd tell them the real reason for the delay soon enough, but now was not the time to distress his family any more than they already were.

Two uniforms finally showed up at his door. They asked Jon to accompany them through the apartment, checking the contents of drawers and his desk to see what, if anything, was missing. They took pictures with their phones and dusted the flat surfaces and doorknobs for prints.

While they worked, Jon sat on the couch with an ice pack to his right temple and a washcloth pressed to the cut over his left brow to stanch the blood. He felt annoyed, unsettled and mildly embarrassed to have had his own baseball bat used against him. At least he was alive. All things considered he accounted himself respectably if not spectacularly, but this wasn't about ego. This was about turf. Someone had broken into his home and gone through his belongings. If he found out Clay Stipes was behind the intrusion—

The sound of the door buzzer interrupted his misery. He put the ice pack and washcloth aside and got up, glancing down the hallway toward his office as he moved to the door. Marcus Campion stood on the other side. He had his back to Jon as he gazed down at the parking lot.

Jon said in surprise, "Marcus. What are you doing here?"

The police chief turned with a scowl. "I heard you had some trouble here tonight."

"Someone broke in." Jon gestured toward the tool marks on the doorjamb.

Marcus gave the damage a cursory glance, then gazed past Jon into the apartment. "Okay if I come in and have a look around?"

"Sure, but the officers that responded have already taken my statement. They're just down the hall in my office dusting for prints." He stepped aside to allow the chief to enter.

He was out of uniform as he had been at the cemetery, but he'd taken the time to strap on a holster and clip his badge to his belt. His sleeves were rolled up, displaying powerful forearms, and he walked into the apartment with his shoulders thrown back and his head held high, making the most of his six-foot-plus frame. The guy appeared to be in excellent shape for his age, but Jon's admiration ended with his fitness.

He didn't have much use for Marcus Campion as a police chief or as a human being. He remembered only too well the way Marcus had treated his family after Tony's arrest. He hadn't been the police chief back then nor had he been assigned to the case as a detective. However, he'd managed to insinuate himself into the investigation at every turn. Back then, Jon had thought him arrogant, surly and a bully. His opinion had only strengthened since his time as the Webber County DA. They'd managed to hammer out a working relationship, but anytime he was in the police chief's presence, he always sensed a power struggle simmering beneath the surface.

"You seem nervous," Marcus observed.

"Not nervous, just surprised. A B and E seems a few notches below your pay grade."

"The brother of my murder victim has his apartment broken into less than twenty-four hours later, that catches my attention."

Jon was quick to latch onto the observation. "You think there's a connection?"

"You tell me." Marcus stood just inside the doorway, feet slightly apart as his gaze moved slowly around the living room. Then his focus came back to Jon, and his eyes narrowed. "You don't look so good."

"That seems to be the consensus," he muttered.

Marcus gave a nod to the cut above his brow. "Did he do that?"

"Sort of. He tried to clock me with a flashlight. The lens broke, and a piece of glass sliced me."

"Damn. You're still oozing blood there, bud. You should probably get that stitched up."

"I'm fine," he lied. He was starting to feel a little woozy, and the last thing he wanted was to collapse, literally, at Marcus Campion's feet. He moved back into the living room and sat down, giving a laconic wave toward the hallway. "Your officers are down that way."

"I'll just be a minute. Don't go anywhere," Marcus added before he disappeared down the hallway. Jon heard him conversing with the officers, but he couldn't make out what they were saying.

Having Marcus Campion show up at his door was almost as unnerving as the break-in. Garrett Calloway was the lead detective. He should be the one investigating a connection to Tony's murder, but Jon couldn't say he was surprised by the turn of events. He'd suspected all along that Marcus would be running things behind the scene.

He pressed the washcloth to his brow and then lifted the ice pack to his pounding temple. Nausea still roiled a little too close to the surface. He lay his head back against the couch and closed his eyes. Not a good day by any measure. All he'd wanted was a few minutes alone to clean up and maybe have a little time to mourn his brother in peace. Instead, here he sat with blood trickling down his face, an ice pack to his head and an apartment full of cops.

The one bright spot, if he could be so optimistic, was the time he'd spent with Veda. Maybe it was wishful thinking, but she seemed to be coming around to the notion of his brother's innocence. At the very least, he had her thinking. From everything he knew about her professional reputation, she was capable and conscientious and had a keen sense of justice. Whether she'd ultimately decide to help him remained to be seen, but she'd promised to have another look through Lily's things, and at the moment that was really all he could ask for.

Maybe she was right. Maybe it was foolish to think that a clue could still turn up after all this time. The police had searched Lily's room after the murder, and the family had undoubtedly packed away or gotten rid of most of her personal belongings a long time ago. Nothing *should* be there, but Jon's gut told him otherwise. A young woman entangled in a forbidden love affair would want to keep something from her lover close by.

If all else failed, he could still strike a bargain with Clay Stipes, but he had a feeling that would be akin to selling his soul to the devil. Once money exchanged hands, Stipes could claim anything he damn well pleased to try and extract more. A made-up murder-for-hire scheme might be the least of it.

His thoughts continued to ramble until Marcus came back out to the living room and sat down across from him. He didn't take notes or ask questions, just sat staring at Jon for a few seconds, probably trying to intimidate him.

Jon didn't take the bait. He placed the ice pack on the coffee table with careless disregard for the surface. Then he removed the washcloth from his cut and examined the smears of blood. The little tasks were unhurried because he didn't want to leave the impression with Marcus Campion that he could be rattled.

When Marcus finally spoke, his voice was devoid of even the slightest hint of concern, let alone sympathy. "Hasn't been a very good day for you, has it, Jon?"

"Not one of my better ones," he agreed.

"Sounds like you put up a fight, so there's that." He almost sounded impressed.

Jon shrugged. "Not much of a consolation in my book. Were the officers able to lift any prints?"

"A few, but I doubt they belong to the perp. We'll need

a set of yours for comparison." He drummed his fingertips on the arm of the chair as his gaze roamed the space. "Walk me through what happened."

Jon recounted the moments when he'd first arrived home to discover the front door ajar and the tool marks on the doorjamb. Then entering the apartment, he'd noticed the open drawer in the credenza before moving down the hallway to his office.

"Until then, I had no idea he was still in the apartment," Jon said. "He must have been hiding behind the door when I looked inside the office."

"You didn't recognize him?"

"I never got a good look at him. He knocked me back into the hallway with the door. Next thing I knew, I was on the floor fighting for my life."

"You must have noticed something," Marcus pressed.

"I wish I had, but the hallway was dark. I think he closed the blinds in the office to block out the streetlights. Now that I think back, he may have been wearing something over his face."

"Like a mask?"

Jon frowned in concentration. "A ski mask or a hoodie. I can't say for sure."

"What about his height, his build? Tall, short, fat, skinny..."

He shrugged again. "Like I said, it was dark, and it happened fast. I would say he was about my height. Not fat, not thin. Average, I guess. He was strong, though."

"What about distinguishing marks? Tattoos, scars, birthmarks."

"Again, it was dark, and he was dressed in black. I've already gone over this with the responding officers."

"Humor me."

"We were on the floor most of the time. I won't bother giving you a blow-by-blow account, but once he got his hands on the baseball bat, he swung for my skull." Jon pointed to the bump at the side of his head.

"Did you lose consciousness?"

"No, but I was dazed. All I remember afterward was the sound of the front door slamming shut."

"You didn't try to pursue?"

"It took me a minute to get to my feet."

"You've got some blood..." Marcus made an up and down motion with his finger.

Jon grabbed the washcloth and wiped away a fresh trail of blood.

"Are you sure you don't want to go to the ER?"

He was less sure by the moment. "Head injuries always bleed a lot."

"It's your funeral." Marcus leaned in, resting his forearms on his thighs. "Here's my take. The guy was a pro. He had the right tool to get inside the apartment without making too much noise or taking too much time. He went for the drawers and left the electronics." He nodded toward the flat-screen mounted on the wall. "TVs with those kinds of mounts take too long and too much effort, plus he'd then have to carry it down the stairs and out to his vehicle. But your laptop and tablet were in plain sight on your desk. He didn't touch them, either. I'll be honest with you. The prints we found are likely yours. He wouldn't have been that careless."

Jon still had the washcloth pressed to his head. "What about a connection to my brother's murder?"

"Still a possibility. Not much to go on, but I'm not a big believer in coincidences. As of now, though, we'll investigate each crime separately unless and until we can connect them."

Jon gave a vague nod. "Anything new on Tony's case?"

"Since you called Detective Calloway this afternoon? Yeah, that's right. He mentioned he'd already heard from you. Give the man a chance to do his job. It hasn't even been twenty-four hours."

Jon pressed on. "What about ballistics?"

Marcus sighed. "As of yet, no matches. Whoever killed your brother was smart enough to use a clean gun. No fingerprints at the murder scene, no way to distinguish footprints and tire tracks from dozens of others. He knew what he was doing. Just like this guy."

"Dr. Bader said the plastic strap used to restrain Tony's wrists could have been a zip tie." Jon paused, trying not to dwell on the images flashing through his head. His brother on his knees, a gun to his head. "Probably the heavy-duty kind used by law enforcement," he added.

Marcus lifted a brow. "You mean the kind that any DIYer can pick up at a local hardware store?" His eyes flashed a warning. "Remember what I said earlier about throwing around unfounded accusations."

"It was an observation, not an accusation."

"For now, let's just stick to the break-in," Marcus said. "Although, your observations about the assailant haven't been very helpful so far. Assuming the cases are unrelated, is there any reason someone might think you'd have a large amount of cash stashed in here? He could have been watching your place for a couple of days. Have you been to the bank or an ATM recently?"

"Not in the past few days."

"You haven't taken out a cash loan, have you?"

The question caught Jon off guard, though he tried not to

show it. Had Marcus Campion somehow found out about his missed appointment at the bank that morning?

"No loans," he said. "No recent withdrawals. I don't flash money around in public. I don't know why someone would think I'd leave cash lying around the apartment."

"Then, maybe he was looking for information," Marcus suggested. "Maybe the break-in has something to do with one of your cases. I saw a bunch of files back in your office."

"It's possible," Jon conceded. "But anything in those folders is already public knowledge. I don't keep sensitive case-files in my apartment."

Marcus was silent for a moment, but his focus remained on Jon. "Have you heard from Clay Stipes since we talked this morning?"

"I'm hoping he left town."

"That doesn't exactly answer my question. I can't help but wonder about his timing. He showed up in town right after Tony got out of prison. What do you think they were up to?"

Jon was immediately defensive. "What makes you think they were up to something?"

"Both convicted felons. One a cop-killer. Don't tell me they weren't planning something."

Jon took a quick breath and swallowed past the cold anger that had been building since Marcus Campion's phone call early that morning. Now was not the time to antagonize the local police chief, let alone reveal a thirst for revenge.

"My brother wasn't a criminal. He was unjustly charged by a corrupt prosecutor who deliberately withheld evidence from the defense and the jury in order to put another notch in his belt."

Marcus scoffed. "And I suppose the murder weapon just magically appeared in the back of Tony's truck?"

"It was planted, probably by the man who was seen running away from the railroad tracks."

"You mean the man who conveniently came forward when he needed the services of a hotshot law firm to help him beat a third-offense DUI charge? That man?"

"He wasn't compensated for his disposition, if that's what you're trying to imply. He also came forward originally. He told an officer at the scene what he saw, but for some strange reason, he was never called in to give a formal statement. The officer's notes ended up in a file along with a copy of Tony's toxicology screen that showed traces of the same drug found in Lily's blood. Yet both pieces of evidence went missing before the trial."

"What can I tell you? Things happen."

His smirky indifference infuriated Jon despite his best efforts to remain calm. "Did you know about that witness?"

"I didn't much like that question the first time you asked it. But my answer is still the same."

Jon wasn't to be deterred. "Did you know my brother was dosed with benzodiazepine? Tell me you wouldn't let an innocent kid rot in prison because you needed someone to take the blame for Lily's murder."

"Innocent kid." He all but spat the words as he lifted a finger and jabbed it in Jon's direction. "Now, you listen to me, you little—" He broke off as the officers came down the hallway and into the living room. "What is it?"

They kept their distance, either out of reverence, fear or an intense dislike of Marcus Campion. "We're heading back to the station unless you need something else."

Something else? Jon couldn't help but wonder what they'd already done for the man.

"Wait outside," Marcus barked. "I'll be down in a minute."

As soon as the door closed behind them, he jumped to his feet so that he could look down at Jon. "That investigation was conducted by the book. No one needed to withhold anything. The evidence was overwhelming. We had a body, we had a murder weapon, and we had a jilted boyfriend covered in my niece's blood."

"And I have a dead brother." Jon rose slowly. "I'm putting you on notice. If you or anyone in your department try to hide evidence or back-burner this investigation, I'll be coming for you."

Marcus's mouth thinned as his gaze hardened. "You may be the DA—for now—but no one is above the law. If you interfere in an official investigation, I'll have no choice but to have you arrested."

"The district attorney's office has every right to conduct an independent investigation if we deem the local police incapable, unwilling or unfit."

"Do you think that scares me?" Marcus shrugged. "Go ahead. Conduct whatever investigation you like, but you better brace yourself. You might not like what you find."

"I'll take my chances. All I care about is the truth."

Marcus gave him a knowing look. "Sure. Keep telling yourself that."

"What's that supposed to mean?"

"Admit it, Jon. You don't care about the truth. You just want your pound of flesh. You blame me and my family for what happened to your family, but it wasn't a Campion who put a knife in Tony's hand that night. And it wasn't a Campion who shot him in the back of the head."

"You don't know that."

"I know this. You keep harassing my niece, I'll be the one coming for you."

That stopped Jon cold. "*Harassing?* Did she say that?"

"She didn't have to. She feels about you the same way the rest of us do, so I know she didn't seek you out. You accosted her at the cemetery this morning, and your car was spotted at her house earlier this evening. You're not going to deny it, are you?"

Jon's anger flared. "You son of a bitch. Are you having me followed?"

Marcus gave him a tight smile. "I'm keeping an eye on a lot of things. Remember this while you conduct your *independent* investigation. You may be the DA, but this is my town. I take care of my own."

Chapter Eight

The next morning, Veda received a call from her mother inviting her to lunch. Since they'd spent so much time together the day before, not all of it pleasant, she started to beg off. But then she felt guilty and accepted. Between the heart attack and Tony Redmond's release from prison—and now his murder—her mom was having a hard time. She spent too much time alone in that big house with too many painful memories. Wasn't that why Veda had returned to her hometown in the first place? To reconnect with her family and offer moral support when needed? It also didn't hurt that the lunch invitation gave her an opportunity to search through Lily's belongings.

Owen's truck and Nate's SUV were parked in the drive when she got there. She hadn't known beforehand that her brothers were also coming to lunch, and their presence complicated things. They were both observant and nosy and would undoubtedly have questions if she spent too much time in Lily's room. Not that she was doing anything wrong, but she really didn't want to have to explain herself. She could only imagine what they would say if they found out she'd agreed to help Jon Redmond.

She let herself in the front door and called to her mom.

When she didn't get a response, she went through to the kitchen and glanced out the back door. Owen reclined on the patio with a beer while Nate manned the grill, fanning aside thick clouds of smoke that swirled up from the charcoals. When she opened the door to say hello, the scent of mesquite wafted into the kitchen.

Her mother came in carrying an assortment of roses and irises she'd picked from the garden.

"I didn't know the boys would be here," Veda commented.

"Nate offered to grill when he heard you were coming over. He called Owen, and here we all are."

"Don't they both have work today?"

Her mother was busy clipping flower stems at the sink. "Nate has the day off, and Owen is between projects. He's been promising to trim the hedges for weeks, so today seemed as good a time as any." She placed the flowers in a crystal vase, then stood back to admire her handiwork. "What do you think?"

"Absolutely beautiful," Veda said. "And the roses smell divine."

"Don't they? Nothing makes me happier than fresh flowers in the house." Despite her mother's bright tone, she still looked pale and a little careworn as if she hadn't gotten much sleep the night before. Veda couldn't help noticing the dark smudges beneath her eyes and the worry lines across her brow.

"Are you feeling okay, Mom?"

"What?" She seemed momentarily distracted. "Yes, I'm fine. Just a little tired."

"Still not sleeping well?"

"I managed to get a few hours last night. Stop worrying about me, Veda. I'm taking good care of myself, I promise.

I'm eating healthily, I walk every morning, and my blood pressure is normal. Everything is fine."

Except for the fact that she couldn't sleep, but Veda decided to let the matter drop. "What can I do to help?" she asked briskly. "Nate seems to have the grill well in hand."

Her mom passed her a basket. "You can run out to the garden and pick some fresh tomatoes while I rinse the lettuce for the salad."

"I have a better idea. Why don't you sit down and rest while I take care of the salad? I'll make some iced tea, too."

"What did I just say about fussing over me?" Her mom got out the chopping board. "The tea is already made, and I like keeping busy. Now, leave me alone, and go pick my tomatoes."

Veda had always enjoyed working in the garden. She took her time with the tomatoes, promising herself she would come over more often to help with the chores. But she needed to ease up a bit. She could keep an eye on her mom's mental and physical well-being without trying to overcompensate for all the years she'd been away.

A little while later they sat down to an informal lunch at the breakfast table. It was the first time the family had shared an impromptu weekday meal since Veda had returned home. She couldn't help noticing how they all avoided the subject of Tony Redmond. His release from prison had been the topic of conversation for weeks, but now that he was dead, it almost seemed as if his name had become taboo. She wanted to ask Owen if he'd heard from the police, but now was not the time. Besides, if any new developments arose, Nate would surely keep her informed.

She sipped iced tea as her gaze went around the table. Nate, stoic and silent. Owen, careless and confident. Their mom, chatty but with an edge of something that might have been despair below the surface. Tony's release and subsequent murder had stirred a lot of memories, so much so that Lily was almost a presence at the table. Veda wondered again what her family would say if they knew about her conversations with Jon Redmond. They wouldn't like her spending time with him no matter the reason. They might even feel betrayed. Any quarter given to the enemy could drive a wedge through the fragile bond she'd tried to forge with her brothers since her return. But guilt niggled. In trying to uncover Lily's secrets she was now keeping one of her own.

After lunch Nate, not Veda, insisted their mother lie down and rest for a bit. Surprisingly, she didn't argue with her eldest as she had with Veda. Instead, she seemed only too happy to escape to her room for an afternoon respite. Veda loaded the dishwasher and cleaned up the kitchen while Nate went out to cut the grass and Owen tackled the overgrown hedges. As soon as she heard the lawn mower engine, she left the kitchen and went upstairs to Lily's bedroom.

She started with the dresser and methodically searched through the drawers before moving to the plastic bins in the closet. She'd already looked through most of the storage containers the day before, but she made herself go through them again just in case. Satisfied that she hadn't missed anything, she put everything back where she found it and then glanced around the bedroom in contemplation. No obvious hiding place that she could discern. She even checked for loose floorboards and behind the artwork.

The drone of the mower in the backyard drifted up to her. The sound was somnolent in the afternoon heat. She lay down on the bed and stared at the ceiling as memories stirred. She thought about the dream her sister had shared on the night of her eighteenth birthday. The image of someone coming through Lily's window during a storm had been terrifying at the time, but now Veda could easily discern the symbolism. Lily's guilt—not the thunder—had summoned the bad man.

The demonic red eyes, the smell... Veda shivered as she tried to further intuit the meaning. The scent of cedar seemed both incongruous and innocuous, though she vaguely recalled a spiritual significance to the fragrance. But not just cedar. Specifically, the scent of their grandmother's old cedar chest.

Veda hadn't seen that piece in years. Mementos from her grandfather's time in the military had been stored inside, and her grandmother had kept the chest at the foot of her bed. When Veda was a kid, she hadn't given much thought to the placement, only that she'd loved going through all the photos and metals inside. Now she understood. Her grandmother had kept the piece close to her bed because she wanted to be near her beloved husband's keepsakes while she slept.

After her grandmother passed away and her house had been cleared out, Veda's mom had had Nate and Owen haul the chest up to the attic, along with a few other sentimental items she wanted to keep.

Veda bolted upright. Why would Lily's subconscious manifest the distinct scent of their grandmother's cedar chest and associate it with the bad man? Why...unless the cedar chest had been on her mind before she fell asleep that night?

Swinging her legs over the side of the bed, Veda got up and went over to the window to glance down into the backyard. The sound of the mower was more distant now that Nate had moved around to the front. Her brothers would be finishing the yard work soon. She'd have a quick look through the attic and then go back downstairs to wait for them.

She left Lily's room and went to the top of the stairs. The house below was silent. She felt a little foolish going to such lengths to conceal her task, but Tony Redmond had been the literal bad man in her family for so long that she had a hard time justifying her actions even to herself. Nothing would probably come of the search anyway. *Just get it over with and move on.*

Rather than the pull-down ladders found in more modern houses, the attic access was a real staircase hidden behind a latched door. Veda peered up the narrow steps as she recalled the time she'd been locked inside. While she'd waited for someone to come and let her out, her imagination had played cruel tricks. She'd been convinced that the ghosts of previous owners lurked in all the shadowy corners. She'd worked herself into such a state that she'd been willing to risk life and limb by climbing out a window.

More than two decades had passed, and yet she still held a grudge against her brothers for pulling that stunt. She'd never believed the faulty-latch excuse, but she left the door ajar just in case.

The stairwell was unlit, but enough sunlight spilled in through the double windows to guide her up the steps. The space was typical of a hundred-year-old house: creaky floorboards, dusty windows and every inch of space beneath the slanted roofline stacked with boxes, lamps, sporting equipment and the odd piece of furniture.

She had to do some digging and rearranging to get to the cedar chest. Pulling it out into the sunlight, she tried the clasp. It was either locked or stuck. No telling where the key was after all these years. If Lily had used the chest for a hiding place, she may have hidden the key somewhere in the attic, but that could take forever to find. Rummaging through the drawers in her grandmother's old sewing machine, she found a pair of scissors and used one of the blades to pry open the fastener.

The scent of cedar was fainter than she would have expected. After so many years in a musty attic, the wood probably needed to be oiled or treated. She sat down on the rough plank flooring and proceeded to empty the contents one item at a time—her grandfather's uniform, the folded flag that had been presented to her grandmother at his memorial service, a box of metals and photographs. But nothing remotely like a secret stash. Was she relieved or disappointed? Veda wondered. She hadn't expected to find anything, and maybe that was a good thing. Maybe now she could put Jon Redmond and the doubts he'd created out of her head.

She started to return everything to the chest when she noticed a small notch in the bottom. She slipped her finger in the slot and lifted. The wood came up, revealing a space underneath the base large enough to accommodate an old cigar box like the one her grandmother had used to store buttons.

Veda felt a mixture of excitement and trepidation as she removed the box from its hiding space. She shook the contents without opening the lid. Not buttons, she decided. So what was inside? And why was she hesitating to find out?

Assuming the box contained keepsakes from Lily's secret affair, how had she known about the false bottom in the chest unless their grandmother had told her? Veda had never been jealous of Lily's beauty or popularity, but she felt a little sting that in all the times she and her grandmother had gone through her grandfather's things together, she'd never once shared that secret with Veda. In the next instant, she chided herself for being petty. She and her grandmother had always been close. Sharing a secret with Lily had probably been her way of trying to cultivate a relationship with her more aloof granddaughter.

And why did it matter anyway, when she might be holding Lily's secrets in her hand?

Opening the lid, she quickly sorted through the contents—a thin stack of letters tied with a pink ribbon, a dried rose, a gold heart pendant, a small bottle of perfume and a myriad of other items that had no meaning to Veda. At the very bottom of the stash, she found the mystery man's photograph. A snapshot that looked to have caught him unaware.

She peered down at his profile as recognition teased. She couldn't immediately place him or recall his name. Then she had it. He'd been the high-school guidance counselor when Lily was a senior. She'd worked in his office during her free periods and sometimes after school. Veda had only been a sophomore then, but she'd already chosen a career path and had no need of a guidance counselor, or so she'd told herself.

What was his name? Michael Something-or-other. He'd had an odd surname. Legion. No, Legend. Michael Legend. She tried to remember everything she could about the man. He'd been young, good-looking and exceedingly charming. Some of her girlfriends had joked about his name behind his back. *A legend in the sack. A legendary kisser.* The silliness had gone on and on.

Veda had only ever interacted with the man one time that she could remember. She'd stopped by his office after school looking for her sister. He and Lily had been behind his desk standing very close to one another. Veda remembered how they had both looked up startled when she came through the door. And how quickly Lily had stepped away as if she'd been caught in the act. Which, in hindsight, maybe she had been.

Far from the excitement Veda had initially experienced on discovering her sister's hiding place, she now felt unnerved and a little nauseous. She closed the lid and stared at the box for the longest time, debating on whether or not to return it to the cedar chest. She had a bad feeling that she had opened a Pandora's box. If she put it back, no one else would ever have to know. But she'd know. And as she sat there in deep contemplation, Jon's voice whispered through her head: *What if I'm right and Lily's killer is still out there? What if he resurfaced seventeen years later to murder my brother?*

An uncanny silence fell over the attic. Veda lifted her head as something clawed at her senses. She could have sworn she heard footfalls in the stairwell.

She turned slowly, peering through the dust motes floating in sunlight. Someone stood in the shadows watching her. Her heart skipped a beat. Even as the image of Lily's bad man flitted through her head, she realized the watcher was, in fact, her grandmother's old dressmaker form. She tried to laugh at how easily she'd fallen prey to her imagination, but her nerves still bristled with warning. She got up and slipped across the creaky floor to glance down the stairwell. The door at the bottom still gaped open.

Descending a few steps, she called out, "Is someone down there?"

When no one responded, she returned to the attic, placed her grandfather's things back inside the chest and slid it against the wall. Then she gathered up the cigar box and headed downstairs to decide what she wanted to do next.

Owen stood on the other side of the stairwell door. She gasped and visibly started when she saw him.

He gave her a strange look. "What's got into you?"

"After everything that's happened, do you even have to ask?" She took a moment to catch her breath. "Why didn't you answer when I called out?"

"Maybe because I didn't hear you. I just now came upstairs looking for you. I saw the attic door open and figured Mom had forgotten to close it. She's forgetting a lot of things these days, in case you hadn't noticed."

"She's had a lot on her mind. We all have."

His gaze traveled up the narrow staircase behind her. "What were you doing up there, anyway?"

"Nothing," she evaded. "I'm scanning some photographs for Mom. I thought I might find Grandma's old picture box up there."

He nodded to the cigar box. "Is that it?"

"No, just a few things I found while I was up there." She turned and struggled with the door latch for a moment.

He reached around her and fiddled with the mechanism. "Is that thing still broken?"

"There was never anything wrong with it. It's just old." She made sure the door was secure before she turned back to him. "Why were you looking for me?"

"Nate and I are leaving. Mom's still resting. Can you stick around until she wakes up?"

"Yes, of course. I had planned on it, anyway."

He lifted a hand and scratched the back of his neck. "We didn't get a chance to talk at lunch. I didn't want to say anything in front of Mom."

"What is it?"

"You were right. The police came to talk to me."

Her pulse quickened. "What happened?"

"Nothing. They just showed up at the apartment, asked a few questions and left."

"That's it?"

"Yeah. But that's not why I wanted to talk to you. Something has been bothering me about our conversation the other morning when you told me about Tony's murder. What was the real reason you came to see me?"

Veda said in surprise, "That was the real reason."

"But why the urgency? Why didn't you just call like Nate did?"

"I did call."

"And then you felt the need to rush over to Ashley's apartment to see me in person. Why?"

Veda had the unpleasant notion that she was walking into some kind of trap. She chose her words carefully. "I was there when you had that fight with Tony. I heard what you said to him. I knew it would eventually get back to the police, and I wanted you to be prepared if and when they came to question you. Or, worse, to arrest you."

"And I told you, Uncle Marcus would never let it get that far."

"He's not in charge of the investigation, and his powers as chief of police aren't unlimited. He might not have a say in the matter. Just because they left after they questioned you doesn't mean they won't be back."

"You sound as if you think I *should* be arrested."

"Don't be ridiculous."

Her brother fell silent. His gaze was still on her, but he seemed lost in deep contemplation.

She decided to press him. "What else is on your mind, Owen?"

He gave her a quizzical look. "Do you think I did it?"

The point-blank question startled her. "No, of course not. As I said, I want you to be prepared, that's all. Hopefully, they'll catch the real killer soon, and we can get back to normal."

He scoffed at that notion. "We haven't been a normal family since Tony Redmond killed our sister."

His words were truer than she wanted to admit.

He leaned a shoulder against the wall. "You still think *he* did it, don't you?"

She felt on the defensive, all of a sudden. "Why would you even ask that?"

"You never seemed as certain as the rest of us. I always wondered if you had a little crush on Tony."

Veda thought he must be joking at first, but his expression was dead serious. "That's ludicrous."

"Is it, though? Don't you remember how he was back then? Big football star walking through the halls as if he owned the whole school. Girls swooning right and left. What you said at the trial about Lily seeing someone behind his back. I was glad that came out. He needed to be taken down a peg or two."

"Somebody has certainly done that now," she murmured.

"Don't expect me to shed any tears."

Nate had said something similar when he called her with the news. Veda understood their reaction, but their coldness still troubled her.

"Let's get one thing clear," she said. "I didn't have a crush on Tony Redmond. He and Lily were together from the time they were in junior high. Everyone, including me, thought they were the perfect couple."

"And look how that turned out. People are rarely what they seem, Veda."

"That's a cynical outlook."

He shrugged. "Doesn't mean it's not true."

She started to move past him, but he caught her arm. She glanced up. "What is it?"

"Why were you so jumpy when you saw me just now?"

"That's easy." She pulled away from him. "You don't remember the time you locked me in the attic for the better part of an afternoon? I was so freaked out I tried to climb through a window onto the roof. I could have fallen and broken my neck."

His eyes glinted. "I never copped to that."

"I know. But despite what you told Mom, that door couldn't have locked itself."

"Sure, it could. See?" He opened the door and demonstrated how the catch could fall into place with only a slight bump.

"Nice try," she said. "It had to have been you or Nate. No one else was in the house."

"And naturally you assumed it was me." He gave her an enigmatic smile. "I'll let you in on a little secret. Nate wasn't always the good son."

VEDA WAITED UNTIL she was certain her brothers were gone before heading downstairs. The conversation with Owen had left her unsettled. He'd been in such a strange mood. Did he really think she'd had a crush on Tony Redmond, or was he just trying to goad her for some reason? And what did he mean about Nate not always being the good son?

Downstairs, the quiet of the house only deepened her unease. She wanted nothing more than to drive straight home so that she could examine Lily's secrets in private. The letters especially intrigued her, but she reined in her curiosity because she didn't want to take the chance that her mother might see them. Instead, she decided to store the cigar box in her car and put the contents out of her mind for now.

She went out the front door, letting the screen door close softly behind her. Then she stopped cold when she saw her uncle coming up the brick walkway. He was in uniform today, she noticed. Everything pressed and polished with sunlight glinting off his badge as he stepped onto the porch.

"Marcus! I didn't hear you drive up."

He cocked his head in disapproval. "So it's just *Marcus* now, is it? Since when did I stop being your uncle?"

The question caught her by surprise, and she tried to think of an inoffensive answer. "I never even noticed when I dropped it. I suppose after I went to work for the coroner's office, I started thinking of you more as a colleague than a relative. I certainly never meant any disrespect."

He flashed a brief grin. "None taken. I'm just messing with you."

Was it her imagination or was everyone acting odd today? The teasing banter didn't suit Marcus, and the awkwardness made Veda uncomfortable.

"Good one," she offered gamely. "What are you doing here anyway?"

"Guess that means I missed lunch."

"You did. Sorry. Nate and Owen just left."

"Where's Janie?"

"She's resting. Would you like something to drink while you wait?"

"I didn't come to see your mother. Although, I'm glad you and your brothers took my advice to heart. It's nice that you're spending more time with her. It's important to protect her from what's coming."

Veda frowned at his ominous tone. "What *is* coming?"

"Like I told you at the cemetery, there's going to be talk. No way around it. All those rumors about Lily's partying and drug use are bound to resurface. I'll do what I can to head off the worst of it, but you said yourself this is the information age. Everything ends up on the internet sooner or later."

She glanced down at the cigar box, keenly aware of the secrets she held in her hand. "If you didn't come to see Mom, why are you here?"

"I was hoping to have a word with you."

"Is this about Owen?" she asked anxiously.

"Now, why would you think that?"

"He said the police came to his apartment. I assume you knew."

He shrugged. "Routine interview. Nothing to worry about."

"Are you sure?"

His tone turned impatient. "I didn't come here to talk to you about Owen."

"Then, what is it?"

He paused for a moment. "You still consider yourself a Campion, don't you?"

She couldn't help but bristle. "What kind of a question is that?"

"I'm just trying to figure out where your loyalties lie."

"You came all the way out here to ask me that?"

"You've been away for a long time. I need to know you're still one of us."

Veda felt a rush of anger, blunted by the prickle of unease at her nape. Why was he really here? "It's funny you should ask that. Owen said something similar when I went to tell him that Tony Redmond had been murdered."

"I told you and Nate to keep your mouths shut about that murder until I said otherwise."

She took a breath and tempered her response. "I didn't know that included family. You sent Nate to tell Mom, so I figured Owen also had a right to know."

"That was different. I was worried about her health. You should have checked with me before talking to Owen."

Her disquiet deepened. "Why? You said there was nothing to worry about."

"There isn't. I'll take care of your brother like I always have."

Even as a kid, Veda had never felt particularly comfortable in her uncle's presence. A part of her resented the fact that he'd made himself scarce after their dad died when he could have made things easier for their mom. Not that it had been his responsibility, but still. He'd since grown close to her brothers. Nate had even followed in his footsteps, and Owen evidently thought he would keep him out of jail. Sometimes Veda felt like a stranger in her own family, but she supposed that was her fault. For whatever reason, she'd decided to go her own way after college. She was only now realizing what those solitary years had cost her.

Marcus nodded to the cigar box. "You've got a death grip on that thing. Should I be worried about what's inside?"

"I'm scanning some photos for Mom." She was relieved he didn't demand to see the contents. "But that's not the reason you're here. Maybe it's time to tell me why you're suddenly questioning my loyalty."

He glanced toward the screen door as if to make sure they were still alone. "I've been hearing some things that have me worried. I wanted to get your side before I started jumping to any conclusions."

She scowled across the porch at him. "You're hearing things about me?"

"About you and Jon Redmond."

Her heart thudded in spite of herself. That explained the loyalty question. "What are you talking about?"

"Not much goes on in this town that I don't find out about," he said. "Someone sees something curious or troubling, they report back to me. Jon Redmond's car was spotted parked outside your house last evening."

"It's not a crime to have visitors."

"It's not a crime," he agreed. "But I need to know what he's up to."

She stifled her irritation and tried to keep her voice neutral. "He's not up to anything as far as I know. He came to ask me about the autopsy."

"The autopsy?" Marcus looked skeptical. "Why come to you? You made it clear you wouldn't be involved in the postmortem. Why not go straight to Bader?"

"Apparently, he wanted a second opinion. He thinks Dr. Bader's work has been subpar lately. He said he's been taking on a lot of outside contracts. Spreading himself too thin and cutting corners. Is that true?"

"It's no secret the man's getting on in years," Marcus said. "Which is why I'm hoping you'll reconsider a permanent position. We could use someone with your education and experience at the coroner's office."

"I told you I'd think about it." She hesitated. "Is that all you wanted to know?"

"Not quite. Have you talked to Jon since last night?"

"No. Why?"

"Someone broke into his apartment, probably just after

he left your house. The suspect was still inside when he got home. Worked him over pretty good with a baseball bat."

Veda's heart skipped a beat in spite of herself. "Is he okay?"

Her uncle's tone was indifferent. "He's got a few cuts and bruises, but he'll live."

She tried to digest the revelation without appearing to be alarmed. "Do you know who did it?"

"Perp fled the scene, apparently without taking anything. Jon claims he didn't recognize him. Said it was too dark in the apartment and the guy might have been wearing a mask."

"You sound as if you don't believe him."

"I don't think he's been honest about a lot of things," Marcus said. "I'm hoping you'll be able to help shed some light."

"I don't see how. I didn't even know about the break-in until just now. Do you think it's connected to Tony's murder?"

"We're looking into that possibility."

"We?" She gave him a pointed stare. "Isn't Garrett Calloway heading up the investigation? I thought you were going to distance yourself."

"He's lead on the murder case, but I'm still the police chief last time I checked. Every crime in this town falls under my purview. Besides, I wanted to hear Jon's account before he had a chance to change his story."

"Why would he change his story?"

"He's involved in this somehow," Marcus insisted. "I just haven't figured out the details."

"You think he had something to do with his brother's murder?" Veda's tone was almost scolding. "Come on. You don't really believe that. Why would he go to so much trouble to get Tony out of prison only to turn around and shoot him?"

"You tell me."

"He wouldn't," Veda said. "That's your answer."

"I never said he pulled the trigger. But he knows something." Marcus studied her features as if searching for a telltale sign of her complicity. "Before you hear it from someone else, I may as well tell you that he and I got into it while I was at his apartment."

"Physically?"

"We had words. He has a knack for pushing my buttons, but that's neither here nor there at the moment. I want to go back to your meeting with him last evening. Did he happen to mention Clay Stipes?"

Now they were veering into territory that Jon might consider confidential, but Veda wasn't going to lie about their conversation. "He said he didn't trust Stipes, but that's hardly a surprise."

"What was the context?"

"He believes the person Lily was involved with had motive to kill her. That's also not a surprise."

Marcus scoffed. "The so-called mystery man."

"He was real. Lily told me about him." She glanced down at the cigar box, then looked away. "Did the police ever look for him?"

"Of course we did, but there wasn't anything to go on. No name, no description." He shrugged. "We couldn't produce him out of thin air."

"They didn't find anything when they searched through Lily's belongings?"

His gaze sharpened. "Don't you think you would have known if we had?"

"I've just been wondering. It seems like she would have kept a diary or journal. Something."

"You said on the stand she wanted to keep his identity a secret. But we're getting sidetracked," he said with a scowl. "What business did Jon have with Clay Stipes?"

"Stipes claims to know the mystery man's name. He offered to disclose his identity for money."

Her uncle stared at her dumbfounded. "How the hell would Clay Stipes know anything about a man Lily was allegedly involved with seventeen years ago?"

"Apparently, Tony approached him in prison because Stipes had a reputation for being able to dig up information. That's really all I know. Why are you so interested in Stipes, anyway? Do you think he's the one who broke into Jon's apartment?"

"It's possible."

"Do you think he had something to do with Tony's murder?"

"Everyone is a suspect as far as I'm concerned. But I've always had a problem with the timing of that murder. Clay Stipes hits town, and a few days later Tony Redmond turns up dead. My gut tells me they were cooking up something together. Maybe one double-crossed the other. I don't know. But I have a feeling Jon Redmond knows more than he's telling. He may even be in on it, too."

Veda was quick to defend Jon. "You think he'd be involved in something criminal? I don't believe it."

"See how persuasive he can be?" Her uncle made no effort to conceal his scorn. "He's a prosecutor. It's his job to make people believe him."

Veda switched tactics before her uncle jumped to even more conclusions about her and Jon Redmond. "What did the two of you argue about at his apartment?"

"He implied that I conspired with the former DA to conceal evidence in Tony's case."

"Did you?"

His mouth tightened. "You really want to go down that road with me, Veda Louise?"

His use of her middle name annoyed her. Only her brothers were allowed to call her that. "I'm not trying to pick a fight," she said. "But the department must have known about Tony's tox screen and the witness account of someone fleeing his truck. Both pieces of evidence went missing before the trial, and they provided the basis for his appeal."

Marcus didn't bat an eye when he answered. "As far as I know, everything was turned over to the DA's office."

"But no one said anything when he failed to disclose key pieces to the defense."

"That's not our job," Marcus countered. "We interview witnesses and gather the evidence. What the prosecutor does once he brings charges is his business. Besides, why would we say anything? We wanted that bastard behind bars as much as anyone."

Veda asked in a quiet voice, "And if he didn't do it?"

"He did it. Never a doubt in my mind." His eyes glittered dangerously. "I take it you don't feel the same."

"Whether he was guilty or not, he deserved a fair trial."

"You can say that after what he did to your own sister?"

"This isn't about family loyalty," she said. "It's about doing the right thing."

"The right thing." He shook his head in disgust. "You sound just like Jon Redmond. He's making you doubt what you know in your heart to be true. Let me give you a piece of advice. Every time he tries to crawl inside your head, you remind yourself of what his brother did to your sister. He

used a utility knife. The same one he bought to cut carpet. Not quick, not painless—"

Her mother's gasp stopped him midsentence. Veda whirled to find her standing on the other side of the screen gazing out at them. "Mom! How long have you been there?"

She opened the door and stepped out on the porch without answering.

Marcus straightened from the railing. "Janie, I'm sorry. I didn't know you were there—"

"Just stop, Marcus." Her mother's harsh tone surprised Veda.

"I was just trying to explain to Veda why she shouldn't trust Jon Redmond."

"You let me talk to my daughter." Her mother turned. "Why would you ever trust the man who twisted the law to get Lily's killer out of prison?"

"It's not about trust," Veda said. "And he didn't have to twist anything because the former DA gave him plenty of ammunition. Jon's always proclaimed his brother's innocence. That isn't new."

"He got that piece of—" Marcus self-edited in her mother's presence. "He got his brother out of prison. That should have been enough for him, but he just can't let it go."

Her mother's attention was still on Veda. "You don't believe Tony was innocent, do you?"

Veda grew apprehensive. There was a glitter of something she didn't want to define in her mother's eyes. "He's dead. What does it matter what I believe?"

"It matters to me." She moved across the porch and took Veda's arms, her voice dropping to a near whisper. "Don't you understand? I need for that man to be guilty."

Chapter Nine

Veda was still distraught by the time she finally drove home. She couldn't get her mother's anguish out of her mind. The look in her eyes...the desperate plea. *Don't you understand? I need for that man to be guilty.*

The thoughts churning through Veda's head made her physically ill. For a moment, she thought she might have to pull over. The last few weeks had been stressful, and the knots in her stomach had only multiplied after Tony's murder. She told herself to take a deep breath and get a grip. No one in her family had done anything wrong. Their attitude toward Tony Redmond was understandable. Hadn't she felt a momentary relief upon hearing about his death? It was only natural that her mother needed someone to blame, and the evidence against Tony had been overwhelming.

But the other side of the coin had started to nag. He'd spent his whole adult life in prison only to be murdered when he got out. The very notion of his innocence made the reality of those seventeen years almost unbearable.

Yes, Veda thought. We need for that man to be guilty.

Jon was sitting on her porch steps when she got home. She wanted to send him away, but she was the one who had impulsively called him after leaving her mother's house. "I have some news," she'd told him. She should have known he wouldn't be able to wait.

He rose when she came up the walkway, his expression shifting from expectant to worry. "Are you okay? You look—"

She tried to take his concern lightly. "Like death warmed-over?"

"Upset." He stood in front of her but made no move to touch her. At that moment, she wasn't sure how she would have reacted if he had. Something was happening between them. She couldn't deny the flare of attraction in his presence, but that spark was doomed by the insurmountable history that stood between them.

"What's wrong?"

"Nothing." She shook off a sudden melancholy. "This whole business…it's brought back a lot of memories."

His tone noticeably cooled. "By *this whole business*, do you mean my brother's murder?"

She was immediately ashamed. "I'm sorry. I didn't mean to sound so callous."

"I get it. To you, he's still your sister's killer."

She looked him in the eyes. "I can't help how I feel."

He glanced away, searching the street for a moment. "I understand."

But do you? Do you have any idea how hard this is for me? Her loyalty to her family was being questioned even as Jon's unwavering belief in his brother's innocence picked at her doubts. She was being pulled in two different directions, and the tension was taking a toll.

She took in the bruises on his face and the bandage above his eyebrow. Sympathy tugged despite her trepidation, and she softened her tone. "I heard what happened at your apartment. Are *you* okay?"

His gaze came back to her. "Marcus told you?"

She nodded. "He stopped by my mom's house a little while ago. He said the assailant was in your apartment when you got home. He attacked you with a baseball bat."

He smiled, but there was no humor in his eyes. "That's not exactly how it happened, but I'm fine. No permanent damage except to my ego."

"It's nothing to joke about," she said. "You could have been seriously injured or killed." She winced as soon as the words were out of her mouth. Both families had suffered too many tragedies. The thought of Jon meeting an untimely demise triggered an emotion Veda didn't want to explore. "Do you know who did it? Or what they were after? Marcus said the suspect fled without taking anything."

"I didn't get a good look at him, but I have a feeling it has to do with Tony's murder. And with everything you and I talked about last evening. Someone doesn't want us digging up the past."

"But you've been doing that for years," she pointed out.

"Not like this. The appeal was focused on prosecutorial misconduct. Now we're trying to find out the truth about Lily's murder, and it feels as if we may be getting close."

We may be getting close? She suppressed the urge to remind him yet again that just because she'd heard him out didn't mean she accepted his claim. Doubt about Tony's guilt was one thing. Embracing a full exoneration quite another. But maybe that was Marcus talking. Like it or not, her uncle had hit a sore spot when he questioned her loyalty.

She glanced down at the cigar box in her hand. "Let's go inside."

They climbed the porch steps together. Veda couldn't help glancing over her shoulder as she unlocked the front door. She wondered who had reported Jon's car to her uncle. The notion of a neighbor keeping tabs didn't sit well.

He followed her through the small house to the breakfast nook that looked out on the shady backyard. She surreptitiously studied him as she moved aside folders and her laptop on the table. Once she got past the cuts and bruises, she noticed the circles under his eyes were less pronounced, and he didn't look as stricken with shock as he had the day before. His casual attire of collared shirt and trousers made her overly aware of her everyday summer uniform of sandals, jeans and a T-shirt.

She moved around him into the kitchen. "Can I get you something to drink?"

"I'm fine, thanks." He sat down at the table and folded his hands. "I was surprised to get your call."

"Why?" She took a seat across from him and placed the cigar box on the tabletop. "I told you I'd take another look through Lily's things to put your mind at ease."

"And?"

"I found this." She tapped the lid. "Turns out you were right. She did have a secret hiding place."

His expression turned anxious. "What's inside?"

"A photograph of the mystery man, a handful of letters, a few other odds and ends. But no diary."

He glanced up. "Wait a minute. You found a photograph of the secret boyfriend?"

"I think so." Then she added with a note of caution, "You shouldn't get too excited. I haven't read the letters yet, but I doubt any of this will turn out to be a smoking gun."

"I wasn't expecting a smoking gun. Like I said last night, one good lead is all we need."

She opened the box and removed the photograph. "You can only see his profile in this shot. He seems completely unaware of the camera. I have a feeling Lily took it without him knowing. If what we suspect about their relationship is true, he probably discouraged any damning evidence of their affair."

"What about the letters?"

"One thing at a time." She slid the photograph across the table. "Do you recognize him?"

He picked up the image and gave it a careful examination. "I don't think so. Should I?"

"Not necessarily. You would have graduated high school a couple of years before he was hired."

"He was a teacher?"

"Guidance counselor. His name is Michael Legend."

Jon lifted a brow before he dropped his gaze to the photo. "That would be a hard last name to live up to."

"Probably not for him," Veda said. "If memory serves, he thought pretty highly of himself."

"I take it you knew him."

"I knew who he was, of course, but I never had any interaction with him. I didn't think I needed the services of a guidance counselor," she added with a deprecating smile. "I thought I knew everything back then."

"Didn't we all?"

Her heart gave a funny lurch when he smiled back. She glanced down at the box. "A lot of my friends had crushes on him, but I never heard anything untoward about his behavior with students."

Jon placed the photo on the table. "So, this is the mystery man."

"I would assume so. Why else would she have kept his image hidden in the attic underneath a false bottom in our grandmother's old cedar chest?"

He looked both surprised and impressed. "That sounds a little like finding a needle in a haystack. What made you think to look there?"

"Not *what*. *Who*. Lily told me."

He said carefully, "Not literally, I'm guessing."

Her smile was brief. "No, her ghost didn't come to me. It was something I remembered when I was in her room yesterday. She had this recurring nightmare as a kid about someone coming through her window and sitting on her bed to watch her sleep. She called him the bad man, and she said thunder summoned him. She used to hide at the back of her closet and cover her ears to block the sound."

"No wonder she was afraid of storms."

Veda nodded. "Although, I don't know if her fear of storms or the nightmare came first. Anyway, there was a big storm on the night of her eighteenth birthday. She'd been out with Tony and came home late. When I got up to go to the bathroom, I heard a whimper coming from her closet. The way she sounded… I'd never heard anything like it. I was scared to go closer even though I knew my sister was inside."

"Why did it frighten you?" Jon asked, his tone still guarded as if unsure how he was supposed to react to her revelations.

She shivered. "It sounded like a hushed howl, if you can imagine such a thing. Like a trapped or wounded animal."

"That must have been—"

"Hair-raising?" Veda held out her arm. "I still get goose bumps when I think about it."

"What did you do?"

"I was sixteen years old, practically an adult, and yet I had to make myself crawl into that closet. Sounds silly now. Cowardly, even."

He met her gaze across the table. "No, it doesn't."

She took a breath. "You say that, but you don't know how badly I wanted to run back to my room and pretend I never heard that cry."

"But you didn't."

"I couldn't. I had to make sure she was okay."

"Was she?"

"She wasn't physically hurt, but she was distressed. She told me she had the dream again. That the bad man came through the window and sat on her bed while she pretended to sleep. She said he had a *smell*."

"What kind of smell?"

"Like our grandmother's old cedar chest."

"Ah." A light dawned in his eyes.

"You see where I'm going with this. She'd never mentioned a scent before, and she seemed surprised because she said the devil should smell like sulfur."

That took him aback. "The devil?"

"I know." Veda rubbed her hand along the chill bumps. "After she told me about the dream, she confessed to seeing someone behind Tony's back. She said they were planning to go away together." She swallowed past the sudden knot in her throat. How different things might have turned out if she'd been able to convince Lily not to see him again. "Even when we were little, she implied the bad man came because of something she'd done. It seems so obvious now, but it never occurred to me back then. The bad man came to punish her when *she* was bad. He was a manifestation of her guilty conscience."

"That makes sense," Jon said. "It's disturbing, but it makes sense."

"Especially for Lily. Things weighed on her even as a kid. The bad man came back on her birthday because she knew the affair was wrong. I think her subconscious gave him the scent of our grandmother's cedar chest because she hid the evidence of her wrongdoing inside. Maybe she'd been thinking about the chest before she went to sleep that night. She may even have been up in the attic before the storm hit."

"What a heavy burden she must have carried."

Veda felt the sting of unexpected tears at his empathy. That he could be nonjudgmental in the face of everything that had happened was extraordinary. "I never wanted to believe all those terrible rumors that surfaced about my sister during the trial. I thought people were just being gossipy and mean-spirited, and I blamed myself for breaking her confidence on the witness stand. But an affair with a married man…that's serious. That behavior can't be chalked up to youthful indiscretion."

"First of all, you were under oath," he reminded her. "You had to tell the truth. As for the rumors, whether or not they were true, you shouldn't let anyone diminish the memories you have of your sister or how much you loved her. And don't think too harshly of her for being human. She was young and in love. People do foolish things at that age. At any age. God knows I have my share of regrets."

"You didn't have an affair, did you?" She was only half-joking.

He took the question seriously. "No. But I rushed into

marriage when I was in law school. It was an especially stressful time, and I thought our being together would help me get through it. It was selfish and impulsive on my part. Not surprisingly, we only lasted a few months. Technically the split was mutual, but there's no such thing as a clean break. People make mistakes, and people get hurt. You learn to live with regret and move on."

"Lily never had a chance to move on."

"Neither did Tony."

Veda fell silent, both stunned and touched by his confession. Never in a million years could she have imagined a scenario that brought Jon Redmond to her kitchen table, let alone sharing an intimate interlude from his past. She wanted to take it at face value. Just his way of making her see Lily's behavior in a kinder light. Yet a part of her still wondered if he had an ulterior motive. *When he tries to crawl inside your head, you remind yourself of what his brother did to your sister.*

"You mentioned letters," he said.

She removed the stack from the box and handed them to him.

He hesitated before accepting them. "Don't you want to read them first?"

"I don't have it in me right now. I broke my sister's confidence once. Breaching her privacy seems a bridge too far at the moment."

"But you're allowing me to read them. What's the difference?"

She sighed. "Someone has to do it, and I'd rather it be you than me. Just scan the contents, and tell me if there's anything I need to know."

He looked doubtful as he untied the ribbon and sorted

through the envelopes. "No address or postmark. Just her name."

"Yes, I noticed. They probably had a special place for leaving letters and notes to one another. His office, her locker…" Veda shrugged. "They needed to take precautions. If anyone caught on, he would have been fired. Lily may have been past the age of consent in Mississippi, but a married teacher involved with a student would have had serious consequences. Not to mention what his wife would have done if she'd found out."

Jon removed a single page from the first envelope, scanned the text and then glanced up. "It's a love letter." He turned over the paper and examined the back. "No name, no mention of his marital status or profession. Nothing to give away his identity if the letter fell into the wrong hands. He might even have tried to disguise his handwriting. He uses a lot of printed letters rather than cursive. It doesn't flow naturally."

"I imagine he was careful about a lot of things. They both were. I never had a clue until Lily told me." Veda made a rotating motion with her finger, indicating he should move on to the next envelope.

He quickly read through the rest of the letters, lingering on the last one until her curiosity got the better of her.

"What is it?"

"It's more or less a Dear John letter." He folded the paper and handed it back to her. "You should read this one."

She took the page and reluctantly skimmed through the brief lines, then went back to the top and reread everything more carefully. Her voice trembled with emotion when she spoke. "He didn't just break up with her. He threatened her."

"Some might interpret it as more of a warning," Jon said with a note of caution.

She read some of the more egregious lines aloud. *"Stop calling me. Stop writing to me. Stop watching my house. If you ever come near my property again, you'll find out just how angry I can get."* Veda glanced up. "You don't call that a threat? Whose side are you on, anyway?"

"I didn't know we were choosing sides."

"There have always been sides," she said.

"You're right. But the only side we should be concerned about this time is the truth."

Her annoyance faded as she wondered how to broach another subject. "You mean that, don't you?"

"Of course, I do."

"With that in mind... I need to ask you something."

He tied the ribbon around the letters and handed them back to her. "What is it?"

"Did you know the police talked to Owen?"

"I wasn't informed, but I can't say I'm surprised. A lot of people knew about that fight, Veda. A lot of people heard him threaten my brother."

She bit her lip. "Yet you haven't once accused him of Tony's murder."

"I've maintained all along that the same person who killed Lily killed Tony. That wasn't Owen."

She let out a breath. "You don't know how much it means to hear you say that."

"I think I do."

Their gazes held for the longest time until she finally glanced away. "What do we do now?"

"First off, we don't get ahead of ourselves."

"Meaning?"

"If those letters are from Legend, they paint him in a bad light, no question. But as you pointed out earlier, they're not a smoking gun. Nothing in them leads directly to him. That's okay. Neither murder was ever going to be solved overnight, but at least now we have a significant lead. Thanks to you, we have a place to start."

Since when had their roles reversed? Veda wondered. She was supposed to be the cautious, skeptical voice of reason.

"I can't help thinking about the implication," she said. "Lily kept calling and writing. Watching his house. She must have been desperate for his attention."

"She had a broken heart," Jon said.

Veda returned the letter to the stack and placed the envelopes back in the box. "Do you think his wife knew about the affair?"

"I don't know, but he was probably afraid Lily would tell her. The letters may not be evidence of murder, but they are proof of an affair and if we can tie them back to him, that gives him motive."

"But that's not enough to take to the police, is it?"

"We could have a signed confession and it wouldn't be enough for your uncle," Jon said with a bitter edge. "I can't do anything officially, but we're not without resources. The first thing we do is find out everything we can about this guy." He took out his phone.

"You're not calling Clay Stipes, are you?"

He looked up with a scowl. "Why would you think that?"

"You said he was good at digging up information."

"No, *he* said that. Clay Stipes is about the last person I'd ever trust him with sensitive information. We do this on our own, and we start with something safe like an internet search."

Veda slid her laptop toward him. "Use this, then. It'll be easier for both of us to read the results."

While he started the search, she got up and went into the kitchen to pour two glasses of iced tea. When she brought them back to the table, he said, "No bourbon this time?"

"We both need to keep a clear head. Tea is all you get."

"Fair enough." He left the drink untouched as he studied the screen.

Veda came around to look over his shoulder. "What did you find?"

"Quite a lot, actually. He's the vice president of a company that owns hotels and casinos along the Gulf Coast. The owner and CEO is a man named Armand Fontenot. According to this write-up in *Mississippi Business Report*, Legend has been married to Kathryn Fontenot for the past eighteen years. Apparently, Clay Stipes was right about one thing. Our mystery man married into a wealthy, influential family. He had a lot to lose if his wife ever got wind of an affair."

Veda straightened. "You said he and his wife have been married for the past eighteen years?"

"Assuming the information in this article is accurate and up-to-date."

"That means he was practically a newlywed when he started the affair with Lily." She moved back around the table and sat down. "What kind of man does that?"

"A weak man with more ambition than morals." Jon closed the laptop lid. "I'll go back to the office and see what else I can dig up. I doubt he has a criminal record, but you never know."

"And then what?"

"Then, I pay him a visit. If I can catch him off guard, so much the better. It'll be interesting to see how he reacts when he finds out I'm Tony Redmond's brother."

Now it was Veda who offered a note of caution. "What happened to not getting ahead of ourselves?"

He shrugged off her concern. "I'm not going to accuse him of murder. Just rattle his cage a little."

"And what if he is the murderer? What's to keep him from coming after you?"

"Let's hope he does." The glitter in his eyes unnerved her.

"Maybe he already has," she suggested.

"You mean the break-in? The thought crossed my mind. But if that person wanted me dead, he would have come armed with more than a flashlight."

Veda ran her hand across the top of the cigar box. "Then, let me come with you. You want to see how he reacts when he finds out you're Tony Redmond's brother? Well, I want to see his face when I tell him I'm Lily Campion's sister."

He hesitated. "That may not be the best idea."

She was instantly on the defensive. "Why is it a good idea for you and not for me?"

"It may not be a good idea for either of us," he said. "Let's not forget two people have been murdered."

"Which means neither of us should do anything impulsive. Or alone."

"Okay," he conceded. "What do you have in mind?"

She settled back in her chair. "We take the night and think it through. Then we come up with a game plan. We figure out when and where to approach him and what we want to say to him."

The blue eyes gleamed with a different emotion. "So it's *we* now?"

"You're the one who started tossing around that pronoun when you first came to see me. And I'll remind you that you had no problem asking me to dig through Lily's belongings."

"That didn't put you in danger."

"Maybe not, but it wasn't easy." She eyed the box of secrets. "My family would be very upset if they knew I'd found something belonging to Lily and didn't tell them. Let alone that I let you read those letters. Besides, by the sound of that article, Michael Legend is an upstanding citizen. Or at least he pretends to be. He isn't going to try anything in broad daylight in front of two witnesses."

"No, probably not. But your previous point is well-taken. We should take the night and think things through."

She gave him a dubious look. "You sound a little too agreeable. Now that you got what you wanted, you're not going to ghost me, are you?"

His expression sobered. "I would never do that. And I won't try and stop you from coming with me if you still feel the same way in the morning. I owe you that."

Would she still feel the same after a whole night to ponder the consequences? Alone with Jon Redmond in the close confines of a car might be asking for trouble. "Do we even know how to find him?"

"I'll find him." Not a trace of doubt, Veda noticed. He motioned to the cigar box as he stood. "Take care of that. Put it somewhere safe. I'd offer to take it with me, but something tells me you would never go for that."

"No, I wouldn't. This box stays with me."

"Then, take precautions. Whoever broke into my apartment might have been looking for exactly that kind of information."

She rose. "I'll find another hiding place for my sister's secrets. And I'll make sure to lock my doors before I turn in." She didn't feel quite as confident as she sounded. This was getting serious. Tony Redmond had been murdered in cold blood, and less than twenty-four hours later Jon had been attacked in his own apartment. Someone was apparently getting desperate.

"You have my number if you need me. Day or night," he added.

She walked him to the door. He leaned a shoulder against the frame as he stared down at her. His eyes were very blue in the late-afternoon sun shining through the front windows. He looked tired, beat-up and more handsome than any man had a right to be after what he'd been through.

"Thank you," he said. "You didn't have to help me. After everything your family has been through, it couldn't have been easy."

"We've all been through a lot. And you don't need to thank me because it was the right thing to do."

"Still, what you're doing takes courage."

The way he looked at her…the way he lingered at the door…

Veda suddenly felt as if she'd swum a little too far out of her depth. "Jon…"

He smiled. "That's the first time you've used my name."

She swallowed. "Do you ever wish things could be different? Easier? Sometimes I wonder what it would be like to feel normal again."

"I wish for a lot of things." Exhaustion deepened the lines around his eyes. "And what's *normal*, anyway? We all have crosses to bear. The only thing we can do is get on with it the best we can."

"Seventeen years is a long time to get on with it."

He put a hand to her cheek. The touch shocked her. She reached up but not to swat him away. Instead, she closed her fingers over his.

Their gazes connected for the longest time. The brother of the man convicted of killing her sister. It was a loaded moment. Not just because of what had happened to their families in the past, but because of the strange camaraderie that had been born from the tragedy.

When he leaned in this time, Veda turned her head to meet his lips. It was a kiss meant to comfort and reassure, maybe even to solidify their budding relationship, but the passion that simmered beneath the surface made her tremble.

EXCUSES SWIRLED THROUGH Jon's head as he left Veda's house and strode down her walkway. The kiss didn't mean anything. Just two people offering one another a moment of comfort and understanding. A port in the storm. But the truth of the matter was he'd been attracted to Veda Campion long before he'd asked for her help. She'd been on his radar ever since he'd observed her in action in that courtroom in New Orleans. She'd been poised, professional, impressive. And gorgeous.

He hadn't expected to be so taken aback by her appearance when he first read her name on the witness list. She'd lived in the shadow of her sister's stunning good looks for as long as Jon had known her. Apparently, she was one of those people who came into her own in her thirties. She'd had on a simple black suit for court. Her blond hair had been pulled back in a bun, and she'd worn very little makeup. No jewelry. Flat shoes. Nothing in the least sexy or alluring about her attire, and yet Jon found himself leaning forward on the bench, not just to take note of her testimony but to drink in every detail of her appearance. Veda Campion, of all people, had thoroughly captured his attention.

He'd thought about looking her up after court that day, but

it hadn't seemed like a good idea. Instead, he put her out of his head and went home to Atlanta, back to his fifteen-hour days and half-furnished apartment. Back to working on his brother's appeal in addition to the obligations he had with his firm. When he'd approached her at the cemetery after Tony's murder, a relationship had been the last thing on his mind. Yet even then, he couldn't deny his awareness. As much as he might try to convince himself that the kiss had been a culmination of stress, grief and anger, deep down he knew it was more than that. At least for him.

His ringtone sounded. He was still distracted and a little annoyed when he answered.

The voice on the other end said, "Jon Redmond?"

"Speaking. Who is this?"

"Come on, Jon. Don't you recognize my voice?"

The goading tone sent his irritation soaring several notches. "What do you want, Stipes?"

"Look down the street. Black car parked at the curb."

He came to a halt on the sidewalk and turned. A few houses down, Clay Stipes stood leaning against a dark sedan. When he had Jon's attention, he lifted a hand in a brief salute.

"You should thank me," he said in Jon's ear. "I parked down the street because I didn't think you'd want your girlfriend to see us together."

Jon glanced back at the house. "She's not my girlfriend. And I don't want anyone to see us together."

"Maybe not, but you'll want to hear what I have to say."

"Then, say it."

There was a brief silence. "Not over the phone. I'll hang up and wait for you."

The call ended, and Stipes gave another wave as though he were acknowledging an old friend. Jon glanced again at the house as he slipped the phone in his pocket. No sign of Veda at any of the windows. Maybe it was hubris to think she might be staring after him.

He turned back to Stipes. His instincts told him to get in the car and drive away, but instead he started down the street. Apparently, Stipes wasn't going anywhere anytime soon so he may as well have it out with him now.

Stipes straightened as he approached and nodded. "Good to see you again, Jon. I would say you're looking well, but..." He cocked his head. "How does the other guy look?"

Jon had a sudden vision of the intruder standing over him with his own baseball bat. Darkness and possibly a mask had concealed the man's identity, but going by size, history and the viciousness of the attack, he wouldn't rule out Stipes as his assailant.

He studied the man's face. No discernible cuts and bruises. Stipes looked his usual smug self, which only further irritated Jon. "How did you know where to find me?"

"Haven't you heard? It's all over town that you've been spending time with the dead girl's sister. Oh, damn. You didn't know, did you?"

Stipes was obviously trying to get a rise out of him. People could gossip all they wanted as far as Jon was concerned, but talk of that nature could make things difficult for Veda. She'd already gone out on a limb for him.

Leaning back against the car, Stipes folded his arms. "It wasn't hard to find out where she lives. Like I said, I'm good at digging up information. I figured if I waited long enough you'd turn up."

"Congratulations," Jon said. "Did you go to all that trouble for any other reason than to antagonize me? If not, then get in your car and drive back to where you came from."

"I told you before, I'm sticking around. I've still got unfinished business in this town."

"What business?"

"You need a name, and I can get it for you."

Jon allowed himself a tight smile. "It seems you think a little too highly of your skill set. Turns out, you're not the only one who knows how to dig up information. And some of us don't have to crawl through sewers to get it."

Stipes stared back, unimpressed. "So you found him, did you?"

"Found who?"

He grinned. "I guess it helps to have someone do your dirty work for you. What's her name again? Vera? Veda? She's a real looker from the glimpse I had of her on the porch. Not in her sister's league, but I wouldn't kick her out of bed."

A rush of anger burned Jon's face and curled his fingers into fists. He took a step toward Stipes before a cooler head prevailed. The man was obviously needling him on purpose, trying to provoke a physical reaction.

"I gotta hand it to you, Jon. You're more resourceful than I thought. Just one question, though. Did it ever occur to you that she might have known all along who this guy is?"

In fact, that very notion had led to the confrontation outside the courtroom seventeen years ago. Antagonizing a grieving sixteen-year-old had been a low point for Jon. Taking out his anger and frustration—not to mention his fear—on the victim's younger sister wasn't a proud moment by any measure. "Leave her out of this."

"You're quick to jump to her defense, but maybe you should consider this. She testified that Lily never mentioned the boyfriend by name. Technically, she didn't lie if she found out his name from someone else."

Jon reminded himself yet again that Clay Stipes had an agenda. But recognizing the tactic didn't make him immune. The inferences were starting to burrow under his skin as Stipes had no doubt intended. He asked the same question that Veda had asked of him. "Why would she keep his name a secret?"

"Maybe to protect her sister's reputation. Or to make sure Tony got convicted. Her whole family believed he was guilty, didn't they? Would you still feel the same way about her if you found out she could have kept your brother out of prison?"

"Her testimony didn't send Tony to prison."

"But it sure as hell provided motive." Stipes planted his hand on the trunk of his car. With very little effort, Jon could imagine his brother inside. Hands zip-tied behind his back. A gag in his mouth to stifle his pleas for mercy.

He shook off the image. "Why are you really here?"

Stipes smiled. "I came to give you a warning."

"Sure, you did."

"I'm serious. You may have dug up Michael Legend's name, but I doubt you know who he really is."

"Meaning?"

Stipes glanced down the street. "Your brother knew about this guy. We found out his identity years ago, but Tony wanted to keep it quiet. That was his call. He never said a word to anyone, including you, because he wanted to confront Legend mano a mano, if you get my drift."

"And then what?"

The dark eyes gleamed. "What do you think? I told you before, we had a deal. And before you accuse me of taking advantage of a frightened, desperate kid, I didn't have to twist his arm."

"There are many ways of twisting arms in prison," Jon said.

"Yeah, you got that right." Stipes eyed him for a long moment. "Did you know Tony went to see Legend?"

"When?"

"First week he was out. He didn't waste any time. He said he'd know if the guy was guilty just by looking him straight in the eye."

Was that true? Jon wondered. He wanted to believe Tony would have told him about the visit, but his brother had kept a lot of things from him. Maybe he was trying to protect him. Or maybe he didn't want Jon seeing what prison had turned him into.

"Why are you telling me all this now?" he asked.

Stipes shrugged. "Your brother had my back in prison. I figure I owe him one." He squinted into the sun as he waited for Jon's reaction. When none was forthcoming, he said, "I told you the guy married into money, right? His father-in-law is Armand Fontenot. He owns hotels and casinos all up and down the Gulf Coast. His headquarters are in Biloxi."

"I already know all that," Jon said. "It took me about thirty seconds to find the same information on the internet."

Stipes grinned. "What you may not know is how Fontenot got his start. Ever hear of the Dixie Mafia?"

"Anyone who grew up around here has heard of them," Jon said. "But their heyday was over fifty years ago. Their numbers and influence have been dwindling since the eighties."

"They may be low-key, but they're still around, still based in Biloxi last I heard. I did time with a couple of their foot soldiers. Back in the day, they specialized in contract killing. Think about how Tony ended up after he went to see Michael Legend."

Jon didn't have to think about it. His brother's murder was never far from his mind.

"What's your point?"

"If you go nosing around in that man's business, you may end up facedown in the boneyard like your brother."

Chapter Ten

The next morning, Veda was pouring her first coffee when the doorbell rang. She set the cup aside and ran fingers through her tangled hair as she headed through the house, taking a peek out the front window before she answered. Jon's car was parked at the curb directly in front of her house. She glanced up and down the street. If there was a spy in the neighborhood, her uncle would undoubtedly hear about his visit soon enough.

She had no idea why he would show up at her place before eight o'clock in the morning without calling first. Something must have happened or else he'd obtained new information. She braced herself as she drew open the door. "I wasn't expecting you so early. What's wrong?" She searched his face for signs of another attack. "Are you okay?"

"I'm fine." He seemed oblivious to the cotton robe she wore over her summer pajamas. He brushed past her before she had a chance to invite him inside. "We need to talk."

"Come right in," she muttered, but his sense of urgency deepened her anxiety. She automatically skimmed the street before closing the door behind him.

"Before we get into the specifics, I need you to know something."

His blue eyes seemed more penetrating than ever this

morning. Apprehension tickled at the back of her neck. "What is it?"

"You accused me yesterday of trying to ghost you. You implied that I might try to cut you out of the investigation now that I have what I want. That's not what I'm doing. I'm just trying to keep you safe."

"Now you're starting to scare me." She tucked her loose hair behind her ears. "Does this have anything to do with the fact that Clay Stipes was waiting down the street when you left here yesterday afternoon?"

He turned in surprise. "How did you know about that?"

"I have eyes. Your car stayed parked in front of my house for a good fifteen minutes after you left. I went outside to make sure everything was okay, and I saw you talking to someone a few houses down. I didn't recognize the man, but from your body language and the intensity of the discussion, I assumed he was Stipes."

"It was," Jon confirmed.

"Your back was to me, so I knew you didn't see me," she explained. "I didn't want to stand on the sidewalk gawking and I certainly wasn't going to interrupt your conversation. I figured you'd met him down the street for a reason." She motioned for him to follow her back to the kitchen. "I decided if he had anything new to offer, you'd tell me about it. And here you are."

"Here I am." He was dressed for work in a gray suit with a dark blue silk tie that deepened the azure of his eyes. The bruises on his face were starting to fade, but he still wore a butterfly bandage over his left eye.

She said worriedly, "Have you gone back to work already?" Surely it was too soon for that, but was there any real difference in being in the office and conducting an off-the-books investigation? Both were distractions, and maybe that was what he needed at the moment. Everyone grieved in their own way.

"I'm not back full-time, but a few cases needed my attention," he said.

"I assume Tony's murder is one of them."

"Officially, I'm recused from that case. Unofficially, I made some inquiries into Michael Legend's background. That's what I want to talk to you about. Stipes did have new information. I'm not sure how much of it is relevant or even factual, but it concerned me enough to make a few phone calls."

By this time, Veda was in the kitchen getting a second cup from the cabinet. She came back over to the counter. "This sounds serious."

"It could be serious, it could be nothing." He nodded to the empty cup in her hand. "Is that for me?"

"What? Oh, right. How do you take your coffee?"

"Black is fine."

She poured the coffee and handed him a steaming cup. Then she collected her own and came around the counter. "Let's go sit outside before the heat sets in. The backyard is nice this time of morning."

Normally, she would have chosen the front porch, but she kept remembering her uncle's boast that nothing in this town got by him. She also considered excusing herself to throw on some clothes and comb her hair, but his cryptic remarks about Clay Stipes seemed more important than her appearance.

She led him through the back door and across the patio to a pair of oversize chairs strategically placed beneath a canopy of redbud trees. Setting her cup on the table between them, she tucked up her legs and swiveled her body to face him. "What did Stipes say, exactly?"

He took a moment to shed his jacket and tie and roll up his sleeves. A breeze ruffled his thick hair, making Veda wonder what it would be like to run her fingers through those dark strands. When he sat down beside her, she could have sworn she caught a tantalizing whiff of his soap. She closed her eyes on a shiver.

Jon took a tentative sip of coffee, then set his cup aside to cool. "In a nutshell, he implied that Michael Legend has Mafia connections through his father-in-law, Armand Fontenot."

"Mafia connections?" For a moment, she thought he must be joking. The claim struck her as far-fetched to the point of being comical, but she stifled a laugh when she noted his somber expression. "You're serious? You do realize that sounds like something from a bad movie."

"It sounded implausible to me, too, when Stipes first made the claim. Especially dropping it out of the blue the way he did."

"Especially coming from Clay Stipes," she said with a grimace. "Weren't you the one who told me you couldn't believe a word out of his mouth?"

"Yes, but I thought it worth looking into if for no other reason than to disprove his lie. I made a few local inquiries, and then first thing this morning I called a friend of mine who works in the Harrison County DA's Office. He said it was fairly common knowledge around Biloxi that Fontenot got his start with mob money. That got me to thinking about something else Stipes said. He reminded me of the way my brother was murdered. He implied it was a professional hit."

Any bemusement Veda had fled. "Actually, that was Detective Calloway's conclusion, as well. According to him, most of the homicides he's dealt with since moving down here involved drugs or domestic disputes. Tony's murder was different. He said it looked like a professional hit, and you called it an execution."

"Because it was." Jon's voice remained calm, but cold anger flickered in his eyes, reminding Veda that when it came to the murder of a loved one, few were immune to the baser instincts of rage and revenge. Not Jon. Not her brothers. Not even her mother, apparently.

She pulled her robe around her as if she could block her unsettling thoughts. "Let me play devil's advocate for a minute. You've said all along that you think the same person killed both Tony and Lily. My sister's murder was anything but a professional hit. It was—" *Not quick, not painless.*

"I know." He was quiet for a moment. "But think about this. Both Tony and Lily were given knockout drugs. After the murder, Tony's truck was driven across a railroad track to make it look like a murder–suicide attempt. He was found unresponsive inside with the murder weapon in the back of his vehicle. On the surface, it seemed like a crime of passion, but that many steps took planning and coordination."

Veda remained incredulous. "Why would the mob come after an eighteen-year-old girl in Milton, Mississippi, of all places? It sounds ridiculous to even say it out loud."

"Maybe they weren't after Lily. Maybe her murder was meant to send a message to Michael Legend."

She considered the possibility for a moment, then shrugged. "I don't buy it."

"I'm not convinced, either," he admitted.

"Then, why did we just have this conversation?"

"Because I thought you had a right to know about Stipes's

claim. And because you need to be fully aware of the potential risks before we confront Michael Legend."

"Consider me forewarned." She picked up her coffee and sipped.

Jon did the same, though he hardly seemed aware of his action. He had a look on his face as if he were lost in deep thought. "I don't think Lily's death was a revenge killing or a professional hit, but I do think it's possible or even probable that she was murdered to keep her from talking."

"About the affair?"

He nodded. "Michael Legend is the most likely suspect at the moment. And Tony was framed because he was the most likely suspect at the time of the murder. The killer knew if he planted enough evidence, the local police would stop looking." His tone turned almost apologetic. "This whole conversation is guesswork. But I wanted you to know everything I know before I drag you into something we may both end up regretting."

Was he talking about a visit to Michael Legend or something more personal?

"I'm not afraid," she said stubbornly.

"I know. That's why I am."

He was looking at her in that way again, as if he couldn't quite figure out how the two of them had ended up alone in her backyard after all these years. She knew that feeling well. Fate could play some interesting tricks. Here she sat in her pajamas calmly discussing mob hits with the man who had once accused her of lying on the witness stand. But that encounter outside the courtroom was starting to dim. She had an inkling now of what he'd been going through.

His voice dropped as his gaze deepened. "Should we talk about this?"

The question startled her, but she didn't pretend to misunderstand him. "At some point, yes, but not now. You just lost your brother. You haven't even laid him to rest yet. It's only human to want a distraction."

His blue eyes glinted in the morning light. "You think that's all this is? A distraction?"

"I don't know. I do know now is not the time to make any important decisions, let alone commitments. Your emotions and judgment are unreliable. If you still feel the same way six months down the road, then we can talk."

"Six months is a long time." He smiled but there was sadness in his eyes and maybe a hint of resignation that something was over before it had begun.

"The experts would probably say a year, but…" she smiled back "…I'm only human, too."

He took her hand, lightly toying with her fingers. "You said you're only here temporarily. What happens if I still feel the same in six months but you're already gone?"

"Then, come and find me."

LATER THAT MORNING, Jon came by to pick Veda up for the hour and a half drive to Biloxi. She'd been to the resort town many times as a kid. Before her dad died, he would load the family up in his big SUV for a day at the beach. Sometimes they would rent a house and stay for a long weekend. Veda and Lily would usually get the second bedroom and the boys would camp out on the living room floor. Sometimes she and her sister would slip out of their room in the middle of the night and the four siblings would tell ghost stories until all hours. They would spend the next day lazing on the beach, swimming and building sandcastles.

When Veda looked back on the carefree days of her early

childhood, it was like remembering a dream, hazy and idyllic. Then in the blink of an eye, her dad was gone, and all of their lives had changed. Her mother had found a full-time job as a bookkeeper, and she sometimes worked retail on weekends for extra cash. A life insurance policy had provided a cushion, but her mom insisted that money was only to be used for emergencies and education, not for luxuries like family vacations. Her mother's frugality had enabled Veda to graduate medical school with manageable student loans instead of crushing debt, and she would always be thankful for that. She was grateful to her mother for a lot of things. The heart attack six months ago had made her realize just how much she needed her family.

She felt Jon's hand on hers, and she turned in surprise.

"You were deep in thought just now." He removed his hand as if she might take offense at the intimacy. She didn't.

"I was thinking about my dad. He used to take us to the beach a few times every summer. He and my mom would sit under a big umbrella holding hands while we swam and played in the sand. Even after four kids, they were still so much in love." She sighed wistfully. "At the end of the day, we'd head back home, worn-out and sunburned. And just when we were all about to doze off, Dad would stop to buy us ice cream."

Jon smiled. "My experiences in Biloxi were a little different. My buddies and I would drive down for spring break every year. It was a wild time. Tony talked me into letting him come with us once. Two days in, I had to take him back home to be with Lily. They were inseparable back then. It was a little annoying at times."

"It always comes back to them, doesn't it?" Veda leaned her head against the seat. "In some ways, it feels as if we're still living in their shadows." She turned to study his profile. "I didn't mean that the way it must have sounded."

"I know what you mean. Their lives were cut short. It's hard to move on until we know the truth."

"Seventeen years is a long time to put your life on hold," she said.

"I didn't feel I had a choice. I'm sure you didn't, either." He turned and met her gaze. "Let's just get through the next few days and see what happens."

Rather than taking comfort in his measured response, Veda felt a sinking sensation in the pit of her stomach. His words sounded ominous, almost as if he had already dismissed the idea of a personal relationship. What had made him change his mind since their conversation in her backyard earlier that morning? And did it really matter? For all intents and purposes, they barely knew each other. It only seemed as if they had a connection because of a shared tragedy.

She turned her head to the window, trying not to think too hard about the situation. As Jon said, they needed to get through the next few days. Then she would decide about her future, regardless of what happened between her and Jon Redmond.

Once they neared the coast, she lowered the window to enjoy the salt air. The breeze whipping through her hair brought back those nostalgic memories from her childhood. Lily holding her hand as they ran squealing into the surf. Lily floating beside her gazing up at the sky. Lily sunburned and happy and laughing into the wind.

Those were the images Veda wanted to hold onto forever.

MICHAEL LEGEND LIVED on the west side of town in a three-story home shaded by live oaks. Palm trees and hibiscus bushes lined a brick driveway that wound around to the front of the house, where an ornate staircase led up to a second-story entrance. The front landscaping was lush and immaculate, and the back of the house would have sweeping views of the gulf.

No wonder he didn't want to give all this up over an affair with a student, Veda thought as they made their way up the steps to the covered veranda. She could hear the surf, could imagine all too easily her sister's laughter in the sea breeze that rustled the palmettos.

Jon rang the bell, and Veda gave him an anxious look as they waited. A woman wearing a white tennis skirt and sleeveless top answered the door. She was tanned, toned and attractive in the way that middle-aged women of means always seemed to be. Her blond hair was pulled back in a sleek ponytail that set off her high cheekbones and the diamond studs that twinkled in her lobes.

She gazed back at them expectantly. "May I help you?" she asked in a cultured drawl.

"My name is Jon Redmond. I'm with the Webber County District Attorney's Office." He pulled a card from his jacket pocket and handed it to her. "My associate and I would like to speak to Mr. Legend. Is he home?"

She said coolly, "May I inquire as to what business the Webber County DA's Office has with my husband? The last time I checked, we live in Harrison County. And the DA is a personal friend of ours."

Dropping names already, Veda thought.

"We just have a few questions," Jon persisted. "Is he home?"

"Who is it, Kathryn?" a voice called from the foyer. A second later, a man wearing crisp chinos and a knit pull-over appeared behind the woman. He looked to be in his late forties, handsome and fit with crinkles around his eyes and silver threads at his temples. Veda recognized him immediately from the photograph in her sister's secret stash and from his time at Milton High School. She studied him covertly, taking in his expensive yet casual attire, the way he carried himself, the slight lift of one eyebrow as his gaze shifted from Jon to Veda and lingered.

He placed his hands protectively on his wife's shoulders as she turned to gaze up at him. "They're with the Webber County DA's Office." She handed him the card that Jon had presented to her.

"Are you Mr. Legend?" Jon asked. "Michael Legend?"

He glanced up from the card. "I am. What's this about?"

"We're investigating a possible connection between a recent homicide and one that occurred seventeen years ago," Jon explained. "We have a few questions about your time as a guidance counselor at Milton High School. Is now a good time?"

"Homicides?" Kathryn Legend stared back at Jon as if he'd taken leave of his senses. Then her gaze moved to Veda. Something that might have been recognition—or anger—flickered in her eyes. "There must be some mistake."

"No mistake, but the questions are strictly routine," Jon explained. "We'll only take a few minutes of your time."

Kathryn turned and placed her hand on her husband's arm. "Should I call Harry?"

"That won't be necessary. You heard what the man said. The questions are routine." Legend patted her hand. "Everything is fine. You go on without me."

She didn't look convinced. "Are you sure?"

He kissed her forehead. "Yes, absolutely. I'll take care of this matter and meet you at the club for lunch."

She reluctantly turned to disappear back into the house, but not before glancing over her shoulder at Veda.

Legend studied the business card. "You're Jon Redmond?"

"Yes."

"So you're not just *with* the DA's office. You're the district attorney for Webber County."

"Correct."

"Redmond." He repeated the name as if it had struck a chord. "Any relation to Tony Redmond?"

The question must have surprised Jon, but he didn't outwardly react. "He was my brother."

"I thought that might be the case." He gave Jon a sympathetic nod. "My condolences. I read about your brother's death in the paper. The name caught my attention because I remembered a Tony Redmond from my time at Milton High school. He was a football star. Very charismatic, as I recall." His gaze shifted to Veda. "I'm sorry. I didn't catch your name."

"Veda Campion."

He looked startled. "Campion?"

She wanted to be gratified by his reaction, but coming face-to-face with the man who had seduced her sister—possibly even killed her—and keeping her cool was a lot harder than she imagined. "I'm Lily Campion's sister. She was a senior the year you were at Milton High School."

"Yes, I remember her as well. She was an extraordinary young woman." For a moment, he seemed at a loss. "I must say, I would never have expected to find the two of you together at my door. Am I to understand that you're also with the DA's office?"

"I'm a forensic pathologist," Veda told him. "Until a couple of days ago, I was the acting coroner for Webber County."

"Impressive, though hardly surprising," he said with a smile. "I remember you as well. You showed the same promise as your sister."

He was good, Veda thought. Agreeable and charming with only a hint of the arrogance she remembered.

"Perhaps you'd both better come inside." He scanned the scenery behind them as if worried someone walking by might see them on his doorstep.

He led them down a wide hallway to a set of heavy doors which he slid apart and then gestured for them to enter. Closing the doors, he moved around the office and motioned to the chairs across from a large desk. "Please, have a seat." He sat down behind the desk and folded his hands on the surface. "I'm curious. How did you know you would find me at home this morning? I'm usually at work this time of day."

"I called your office," Jon said candidly. "Your assistant said you were taking some time off and wouldn't be available until Friday."

"And you took that as your cue to show up at my house unannounced?"

"As I said, we won't take much of your time."

Legend sat back in his chair, eyeing them across his desk. He didn't look nervous or angry. He seemed more bemused than anything else. "You said you're investigating two homicides that were committed seventeen years apart. I take it you were referring to your brother and Lily Campion?"

"Yes."

"And you think there's a connection that has something to do with my time at Milton High School? I was only there a year."

"You were the guidance counselor, which means you must have spoken to any number of students. Maybe you noticed a pattern of behavior. We're hoping one of our questions may trigger a memory."

He still looked perplexed. "Wasn't your brother convicted of Lily's murder?"

"If you read about his death in the paper, then you probably also know that his conviction was recently overturned."

"Because of prosecutorial misconduct. It wasn't an exoneration."

He seemed well-informed on Tony Redmond's history, Veda noted.

"Let's get back to your time as a guidance counselor," Jon said. "How well did you know Lily Campion?"

He fiddled with a pen on his desk. "As well as I knew any of the students, I suppose. She worked in the office a few hours a week, so perhaps a little better than most."

"What was your impression of her?"

"She was bright, attractive, hardworking. And troubled." He glanced at Veda. "But I'm sure you already know that." He returned his focus to Jon. "I still don't understand why you think any of this is helpful or relevant. And I would imagine asking these kinds of questions brings up a lot of painful memories for her sister."

"Don't worry about me," Veda assured him.

"Just bear with us a little longer," Jon added. "You said Lily was *troubled*. Can you elaborate?"

"She suffered from depression and mood swings. Again, something her family would have noticed as well. She had a hard time opening up to people, but after a while she did tell me a little about her background. Something traumatic happened to her as a child."

"Our father died in a car crash," Veda explained. "He and Lily were very close."

"She mentioned the accident once. Even years later, she had a difficult time talking about it. She seemed completely devastated by the loss. I got the sense that she blamed herself for his death. I don't believe she ever got over it."

Veda leaned in. "Why do you think she blamed herself?"

He gave her a brief, humorless smile. "Surely you would know that better than I."

She'd taken control of the interview without really meaning to, but Jon seemed content to sit quietly and allow her to proceed as she saw fit. "You said Lily had a hard time opening up. She did. Especially to her family. She was very private. Perhaps even secretive. I loved my sister, but in some ways, I feel as if I never really knew her. If there is anything you can tell me about her, about her emotional state during those last few months, I would be grateful."

She had his attention now. Despite his outward reluctance, he seemed intrigued by her request. "She never said why she blamed herself, but my guess is they argued before he died. She was left in an emotional limbo, never able to make things right. She told me once that she had gaps in her memory before and after the accident. The only thing she could remember clearly was her uncle waking her up in the middle of the night to tell her the news about her parents."

"I remember that, too." Veda had rarely shared her memories of that terrible night. She still found it difficult, but something about Legend's expression and body language when he spoke about Lily suggested he was more absorbed in the conversation than he pretended to be. If she could keep him engrossed, perhaps he'd let something important slip about his relationship with her sister.

"That must have been a traumatic time for all of you," he said.

"Yes, but it hit Lily especially hard. After my uncle woke us up, he had us come downstairs to the living room where he told us about the accident together. The first thing he did was assure us that our mother was fine. She had to spend the night in the hospital, but she would be home in a day or two. But Dad...he didn't make it."

"I'm sorry."

She wasn't sure if the murmured condolence had come from Michael Legend or from Jon.

"How old were you when this happened?"

What he really wanted to know was Lily's age, Veda thought.

"I was eight at the time. Lily was ten. My five-year-old brother and I burst into uncontrollable tears. I'm not sure he even comprehended what had happened, but he knew we were all distressed. My older brother came and sat between us. He put his arms around us and told us everything would be all right. He would take care of us. But Lily just sat there alone, stoic and tearless. It was almost as if she didn't hear a word our uncle said until he tried to comfort her. Then she started screaming and didn't stop until he called a local doctor who came and gave her a sedative."

"Pharmaceuticals might account for the gaps in her memory," Legend mused.

Jon still said nothing, but she could feel his gaze on her. She hadn't meant to bare her soul, only to share enough to keep Michael Legend engaged and off guard. But once the words started to flow, she couldn't get them out quickly enough. Maybe Lily wasn't the only one who had carried the burden of that night quietly.

"Veda—" Jon said her name so softly she wondered if she had imagined his voice. Her hand had been gripping the chair arm. She lifted a finger to signal she was okay.

She refocused on Legend. "Did Lily tell you she was planning to run away with someone after graduation?"

He frowned. "Not that I recall. By *someone*, do you mean her boyfriend?"

"I don't mean Tony Redmond. I testified at his trial that she was seeing someone behind his back. She never told me his name, and he never came forward." She paused. "Did she ever mention a name to you, even in passing? Did she ever express interest in anyone other than Tony?"

He took a long moment to answer as if sensing a trap. "We weren't that close."

"Close enough that she told you about our father's death and the guilt she felt afterward."

"That was different."

Jon took over the questioning. "Were you and Lily romantically involved?"

Michael Legend drew a sharp breath, his dark eyes snapping with anger and perhaps a hint of fear, Veda thought. "You have some nerve, coming into my home and making such a monstrous accusation."

"It's not an accusation," Jon said. "Just a simple question."

His expression hardened. "Then, let me make one thing perfectly clear to you. My wife and I were married during the first semester of that school year. We were deeply committed to one another, but even if I'd been single, that is a line I would never have crossed with a student."

"How do you explain these?" Veda set the stack of letters on his desk, followed by the photo.

He examined the image and shrugged. "I've never seen

that photograph in my life. I have no idea when or where it was taken." He picked up the letters and thumbed through the envelopes. "What are these?"

"Love letters to my sister," Veda told him.

He tossed them onto the desk with careless disregard. "They're not from me. That's not even my handwriting."

"Would you be willing to provide a sample for comparison?" Jon asked.

"No, I would not. You're lucky I've been willing to sit here for as long as I have, but my patience is wearing thin."

Veda retrieved the stack from his desk and removed the breakup letter. She took out the single page and read some of the lines aloud. *"Stop calling me. Stop writing to me. Stop watching my house. If you ever come near my property again, you'll find out just how angry I can get."* She glanced up. "You didn't write that?"

He looked momentarily stunned. Then he quickly recovered and nodded to the letter in her hand. "May I?" She handed the page back to him, and he quickly scanned the lines. Then he folded the paper and returned it to Veda. "I didn't write that letter—any of these letters—but I think I know who did."

Veda found herself leaning forward in her chair yet again. "Who?"

"I think Lily wrote them."

Now it was Veda who sat stunned. She felt simultaneously outraged and shattered on her sister's behalf. She told herself he would say anything to keep his secret, but a voice in her head was already starting to whisper. *What if he's right?*

She exchanged a glance with Jon.

He said to Legend, "Why do you think Lily wrote them?"

His anger had evaporated, and he gave Veda a concerned

look. "This may be difficult for you to hear. I didn't write that letter, but I once said those very words to her."

"Why?"

He rubbed a hand over his eyes. "I never suspected she had feelings for me—romantic feelings—until the end of the school year. Then she started leaving anonymous notes in my office. Sometimes little gifts. She even sent letters to my house. She disguised her handwriting so that it took me a while to figure out who they were from. When I confronted her, she readily owned up to it. She said she was in love with me and had been for months."

"And you never had an inkling?" Veda asked.

"I was in love with my wife. The thought never crossed my mind. But Lily insisted that she could tell I felt the same way but couldn't admit it because I didn't want Kathryn to get hurt. I tried to let her down gently, but the more I rebuffed her affection, the more desperate she became. She began leaving explicit voice mail messages. Sometimes, I would see her parked across the street from my house. She even broke in once." He nodded to the letter. "It's true I said those things to her, but I didn't write that letter. I certainly never wrote her any love letters."

"Did you report the break-in to the police?" Jon asked.

"No. I didn't have proof it was her, and I just wanted the situation to go away. I had already decided against renewing my contract for the following school year. I hoped once the semester ended, things would blow over."

"Did you tell anyone else about her behavior?" Jon asked.

"My wife knew."

"Did she and Lily ever have words?"

"Kathryn wanted to confront her, but I told her we were dealing with a very troubled individual. The last thing we needed to do was antagonize her. Eventually the phone calls stopped. Sometime later, I heard she was dead. Murdered." He closed his eyes on a deep sigh. "As much trouble as she caused me, I would never have wished something so tragic on her and her family."

"Why didn't you come forward at the time of her murder?" Jon asked.

He made a helpless gesture with his hand. "Why would I? I had nothing useful to offer the police, and I was about to embark on a new career. Kathryn and I had our whole lives ahead of us. I wanted to put all that unpleasantness behind us. Besides, Lily's family had been through enough. Why inflict more pain?" He shoved back his chair and stood, signaling an end to the meeting. "I've told you everything I remember. If you'll excuse me, I have a lunch date with my wife."

Jon and Veda rose, too. "Just one more question," he said. "Did my brother come to see you after he got out of prison?"

"He most certainly did not. The last time I saw him was seventeen years ago."

"You're sure about that?"

Michael Legend nodded to the door. "You can show yourselves out. Should either of you have further questions, you can contact me through my attorney."

Chapter Eleven

"You're awfully quiet," Jon observed a few minutes later when they were headed back home. He'd remained silent, too, concentrating on his driving until they were well away from Beach Boulevard. Then he turned to search her profile. She was staring straight ahead, hands clasped in her lap. The meeting with Michael Legend had left a sour taste in his mouth. He could only imagine what she must be feeling. "Do you want to talk about it?"

She sighed and let her head drop to the back of the seat. "I think I'm still in shock. I may need a little more time to process what he said about Lily."

"Regarding the letters?"

Her head came up, and he heard a tremor of anger in her voice. "He made her sound like a stalker. Like someone so far removed from reality that she wrote letters to herself and pretended they were from him. Then she broke into his home?" She closed her eyes on a shudder. "I'll be the first to admit that my sister had her emotional ups and downs, but she wasn't deranged."

"Just because he said it doesn't mean it's true," Jon reminded her. "For all we know he was covering his tracks."

She turned to meet his gaze. "But what if he's right? What

if Lily did write those letters? What if the affair was only in her imagination? Where does that leave us?"

"It leaves us exactly where we were before we talked to Michael Legend," he said. "As far as I'm concerned, he's still our lead suspect. Think about it. He knew those letters were out there and that they might eventually surface. He's had seventeen years to come up with a plausible story. Don't take anything he said at face value."

"But why would he write them in the first place? If he was so desperate to keep their relationship a secret, why take the risk?"

"Because the risk of getting caught was part of the thrill." Jon rubbed the back of his neck. "I've dealt with guys like that for most of my career. Their egos almost always trip them up. He loved having the adoration of someone like Lily until she started showing up at his house. He knew if his wife found out about the affair, the lucrative position he had lined up at his father-in-law's company would vanish. He had to do something drastic."

"That's all well and good," Veda said, "but we still don't have any proof. And from where I was sitting, we didn't exactly rattle his cage."

"We'll see." He stopped for a traffic light and scanned their surroundings. Traffic had thinned as they approached the outskirts of town. Businesses dwindled, giving way to litter-strewn ditches and weedy parking lots. He waited for the light to change before he tentatively broached another subject. "That must have been hard for you, recounting the night your dad died to the man who may have murdered your sister. I know what you were trying to do, but you didn't have to open yourself up like that. Not to him."

Veda shrugged. "I wanted to keep him engaged. Despite what he said, I had the impression he enjoyed talking about Lily."

Jon kept his eyes on the road, but he could glimpse her in his periphery. She still sat staring straight ahead, her blond hair loose and wavy about her shoulders, her hazel eyes shadowed and troubled. In some ways, it still seemed strange that they should find themselves working together so closely, yet he couldn't imagine doing this without her. Maybe she was right. Maybe it was too soon to trust his judgment, let alone make any life-altering decisions. But if his brother's death had taught him anything, aside from the unfairness of life, it was that even a moment of happiness was worth fighting for.

He gave her a sidelong glance. "You said Marcus is the one who told you about your parents' accident. You don't have to talk about it if you don't want to," he was quick to add.

"I don't mind talking about it to you. My dad had gone to Tennessee to get my mom. My grandmother had fallen ill, and my mom was taking care of her. She and my dad were supposed to drive back the following day, but my mom said she had the strongest feeling they needed to get home that night. My dad had arranged for a neighbor to come over and stay with us until they got back. Marcus sent her home so that he could tell us the news himself."

"I'm sorry," Jon said. "I know what it's like to lose a parent at a young age. My dad was sick for a long time, so his death didn't come as a shock. But it leaves a void in your life, no matter your age or the circumstances."

"That goes for any loved one," she said. "This must be even harder for you. You've barely taken the time to grieve."

"It helps to have something to focus on. Besides, finding Tony's killer is all that matters to me right now." Sooner or later his brother's death would hit him hard. He knew that. Right now, though, he needed to stay motivated.

He glanced in the rearview and swore.

"What's wrong?"

A police cruiser with flashing blue lights had come out of nowhere to tail them. At first, Jon thought the driver might pass him, but then the siren sounded. "We're being pulled over."

Veda twisted around to stare out the back window. "Were you speeding?"

"Not by much. Not enough to get stopped." He slowed until he found a safe place to pull over. They were still in the area of town where the landscape looked more rural than urban. Little to no traffic. Trees and vines encroaching on deserted buildings. They may as well have been in the middle of nowhere.

Jon had a bad feeling about the stop. "Just stay calm," he told Veda.

She whirled to face him. "Why wouldn't I stay calm? This is just a routine traffic stop, right?"

"I don't know." He lowered his window and killed the engine.

She said in alarm, "What do you mean you don't know? What do you think is going on?"

"We'll soon find out. Whatever happens, just keep a cool head and do what they say." He reached across her legs to retrieve his registration and proof of insurance from the glove box.

The police car pulled up behind them. The siren was shut off, but the blue lights kept flashing. No one got out of the car.

Veda craned back around. "What are they doing?"

"Probably running my plates."

"You don't have any outstanding warrants, do you?" She was only half-joking.

"That would be frowned upon in my line of work." He removed his driver's license from his wallet and waited, his gaze riveted on the rearview mirror.

Veda said uneasily, "I don't like this. Did you happen to notice there's no other traffic on the road?"

"We're a few blocks over from a busy intersection. We'll be fine." He hoped he sounded more encouraging than he actually felt. He told himself it was probably just a speed trap. A couple of patrol cops looking to make their monthly quota.

Another few minutes went by before two officers got out of the cruiser and sauntered toward the car. Jon could hear the sputter of their radios as he tracked their progress in the rearview. A few feet from his car, they split up. One stayed behind the vehicle while the other approached his lowered window.

He kept his hands on the wheel until the officer was beside him, and then he glanced up. "What's the problem, Officer?"

"License, registration and proof of insurance."

Jon handed him the paperwork and returned his hands to the steering wheel.

"Is this still your current address?" He held up the license and squinted at Jon through the window.

"Yes."

"You're from Milton. That's up in Webber County. The DA over there is named Redmond. You wouldn't happen to know him, would you?"

"I'm Jon Redmond."

He nodded. "I figured as much. Just to be clear, this is

Harrison County, so your credentials in Webber County don't mean a lot down here."

Jon kept his voice carefully neutral. "I understand, but you haven't told me why you pulled me over."

"You were weaving across the center line. You haven't been drinking, have you?" He bent to glance in the window at Veda.

"I haven't been drinking." And he knew damn well he hadn't been weaving across the center line.

"Would you mind stepping out of the car?"

Jon's natural inclination was to resist even though he knew better. "Is that really necessary?"

The officer stepped back from the window and placed a hand on his weapon. "Sir, step out of the car now, and keep your hands where I can see them."

The situation had escalated quickly. Too quickly. Jon was getting the impression this was all a setup. It wasn't a coincidence that the officer had recognized his name. He flashed a warning look to Veda as he opened the car door. Her eyes were wide with apprehension, but she didn't appear panicked.

The second officer came around to the passenger side. He opened the door and motioned for her to get out. Jon heard him tell her to stay put. Meanwhile, the first officer instructed him to turn and face the vehicle.

"I don't consent to a search," he said.

"Too bad." The officer grabbed him from behind, twisted his arm back and slammed him against the car. Jon wasn't hurt, but his blood had started to boil. He counted to ten as his legs were kicked apart and the officer proceeded to pat him down. "Just keep your mouth shut, do as we say, and you'll be on your way soon enough. Now." He took a step back. "We're going to need you to open the trunk."

Jon glanced over his shoulder. "Not without a warrant."

"We don't need a warrant when we have probable cause."

"Of what?" he demanded.

"I *said* open the damn trunk." The officer yanked both Jon's arms behind him. Searing pain shot up his biceps and across his shoulder blades. "Don't resist," he warned while he slapped on the cuffs. "Where's the key?"

"Right pocket."

Jon glanced at Veda across the top of the car and mouthed *Are you okay?*

She nodded and gave him a tentative smile to reassure him.

The officer fished out the fob and clicked open the trunk. He moved to the rear of the vehicle to search the space while the second officer rifled through the glove box and console compartment before checking under the floor mats and beneath the seats. Jon kept an eye out as best he could in case they tried to plant something in the car.

When they were finished, he half expected one of them to present a bag of crystal meth and then haul him off to jail. Instead, the officer closed the trunk and came back around to remove the cuffs.

"Sorry for the inconvenience." His tone had completely changed. "We got a tip from a concerned citizen that a car matching this description might be transporting drugs across state lines. Better safe than sorry."

Jon rubbed his wrists. "Who was the concerned citizen?"

The officer gave him back the key fob. "You folks have a good day, now."

They returned to the cruiser, and Jon and Veda climbed back into the car. She gave him a nervous look before turning to glance out the back window. "What was that all about?"

"I think we were just warned," he said.

Her hand flew to her chest. "You think Michael Legend sent them?"

"Let's just say his connection to the Dixie Mafia sounds a little more plausible than it did a few hours ago."

She picked up her purse from the floor and opened the clasp. "I thought certain they were going to plant drugs on us." She rummaged through her belongings.

"The same notion crossed my mind." He pressed the starter button and pulled away from the curb. The cruiser remained parked as if waiting for him to make a wrong move.

"Jon."

"What is it?"

She looked up, stricken. "The letters are gone."

He kept an eye on the rearview. "Are you sure? Could they have fallen out when you climbed out of the car?"

"No. I put them in a zippered compartment in my bag." She kept digging. "The photograph is missing, too."

"I guess we rattled a cage after all."

"It seems as though we did," she agreed. "Good thing I scanned everything to my computer last night before I went to bed."

"Send me a copy as soon as we get home."

She nodded. "You know what this means, don't you? He was lying about the letters. Why else would he go to such lengths to get them back?"

"Assuming he's the one who sent the cops to retrieve them."

Her head came up as her eyes widened. "Who else could it be?"

"Think about it for a minute."

She bit her lip in consternation. "He said his wife knew about the affair."

He nodded.

She dropped her purse to the floor and sat back against the seat. "That makes sense. She's the one with the connections. Maybe it was my imagination, but I could have sworn she recognized me."

Jon interjected a note of caution. "I saw that look, too, but let's not jump to any conclusions. We go slow and think it through, remember? I know how you feel, but promise me you won't do anything rash."

"Like what?"

"Like confront Kathryn Legend." He glanced at her again. "Don't tell me that isn't going through your mind right now."

"It is, but I wouldn't do anything without telling you first. We're in this together. You wouldn't go behind my back, either, would you? We share everything, right?"

"Right." He hoped she hadn't noticed the slight hesitation before he answered.

A DARK SUV was parked at the curb in front of Veda's house when they got home. She recognized the vehicle immediately.

"Were you expecting company?" Jon pulled into the driveway and parked.

"That's Nate. What's he doing here in the middle of the day?" she mused worriedly.

"No jumping to conclusions, remember?"

But Veda was already out of the car. Her brother rose from the porch swing and came down the steps to meet her on the walkway. "Where have you been? I've been waiting here for close to an hour."

She immediately bristled at his accusing tone. Her older brother always had a way of putting her on the defensive. "How is that my fault? Why didn't you call first?"

"I wanted to talk to you in person." His gaze moved past her to Jon, who lingered at his open car door. His mouth thinned as he returned his focus to his sister. "What's he doing here?"

"We'll talk about that later," she said. "Why were you waiting for me?"

His voice lowered. "This is a discussion we need to have in private."

Alarm shot up her spine. "Why? What's going on? Is it Mom?"

"It's not Mom." His gaze moved back to Jon. "I take it he didn't see fit to tell you."

"Tell me what? Nate, what's going on? Just say it, for God's sake."

"Owen has been arrested."

VEDA SPENT THE rest of the day with her family. Nate was allowed to see Owen that afternoon and reported that their brother was handling the situation as well as could be expected, but Veda was worried. The murder weapon had been found in a dumpster near Owen's apartment. That was new information, and coupled with the very public threat—not to mention the vicious fight—it didn't look good. Owen had no alibi for the time in question and a very long history of animosity toward the victim. The evidence against him was circumstantial, but innocent people had been convicted on less.

Nate had already contacted an attorney while Veda and her mother started making arrangements for bail money once Owen was arraigned. Everything that could be done was being done, but the preparations did little to ease Veda's mind. A question kept intruding. Had Jon known that the arrest was forthcoming? Maybe that explained the change in his attitude she'd sensed from the time they'd had coffee in her backyard to their subsequent trip to Biloxi. *Let's just get through the next few days*, he'd said. Had he known what was coming?

By the time Nate dropped her off at her house, she was exhausted and emotionally drained. She wanted nothing so much as a long shower, a glass of wine and hours of sleep.

But a little while later, she was still wide-awake, sitting alone at the breakfast table sipping wine and eating chips when she heard a car pull up outside. She went through the house and glanced out the front window. Jon was just coming up the walkway. She drew open the door and stepped out on the dark porch.

"Jon, it's late. It's been a long day, and I was just going to bed. Can this wait?"

"I won't keep you." He moved across the porch. "I wanted to make sure you're okay."

She wrapped her arms around her middle. "My brother was arrested for murder today, and he's currently sitting in the county jail. I'm not okay."

"Is there anything I can do?"

"Can you get him out?"

"I can't do that," he said. "But I can walk you through what to expect over the next few days. Maybe that will help ease your mind."

"Or make things worse." She couldn't stop shivering all of a sudden. "I need to ask you a question. Did you know Owen was going to be arrested when you came here this morning?"

"I didn't know for certain, but I knew it was a possibility. We talked about that, remember?"

"Would you have told me if you did know?"

He looked her straight in the eyes. "I can't answer that. You're asking me about a hypothetical. All I can say is it would depend on the circumstances."

She leaned back against the doorframe and closed her eyes briefly. "I'm getting a sense of what it must have been like for your family. For you. This feeling of helplessness and anger and disbelief. And loneliness. God, it's so lonely on this side."

"I know."

"It's strange, isn't it? How our roles have suddenly reversed?"

"With one important distinction." His gaze on her even in the dark was intense. "Owen hasn't been convicted of anything yet. There's still time to prove his innocence."

She clung to his words. "He didn't do it," she said fiercely.

"And I'll do everything I can to help you prove that. But you should know my official role is limited. I'm recused from the case."

"You still have contacts, though."

He answered carefully. "Some."

"After I left the crime scene the other night, I went to Owen's apartment. I saw a dark sedan parked across the street. I had the notion that someone may have been watching his apartment. The car even followed me when I left. Do you think the killer planted the gun in the dumpster that night?"

"It's possible. Have you told the police?"

"I told Detective Calloway about it today. But I don't know how much it will help. I didn't get a license plate number. I'm not even sure of the make or model."

"Why didn't you say anything before now?"

"I know this sounds lame, but it slipped my mind." She hesitated. "You believe me, don't you?"

"I believe you."

She drew a deep breath and released it. "I'm sorry."

"For what?"

"For not believing you back then."

"The circumstances are different. You had every reason to believe Tony did it. I don't fault you for that." He paused as their gazes clung in the dark. "Veda." The way he said her name made her heart thud. "I know the other side is lonely, but you're not alone. You have your family, and you have me."

She took his hand and drew him inside. He closed the door and turned. She stood in her tiny foyer, needing his arms around her more than she had ever needed anything in her life. For comfort, yes. But for so much more.

He closed the distance between them and wrapped his arms around her, lifting her up to his kiss. She cupped his face and kissed him back, then threaded her fingers through his hair. Her pajamas were thin cotton, practically nonexistent. She could feel the warmth of his hands on her back, then her breasts. She pulled away and ripped off her top. Then they were kissing again, through the foyer, across the living room and down the short hallway to her bedroom. Somewhere along the way, he lost his shirt and shoes. They stood at the side of the bed and finished undressing. When they finally crawled between the cool sheets, he moved on top of her, propping himself on one arm as he smoothed back her hair.

"This isn't exactly taking our time and thinking things through," he said.

"I don't care."

"Me, either."

The talk died away to sighs and whispers. Their fingers intertwined as their bodies came together. She didn't think about his family or hers. She didn't think about the past or the future. At that very moment, she wanted to feel, not think.

Her breath quickened, and she held on tightly as her body began to shudder.

SOMETIME LATER, Veda walked Jon to the door. He was fully dressed. She was back in her pajamas. Her hair was uncombed, but she didn't care. His kiss was far from gentle, and yet it was. "Try to get some rest. You've a long day ahead of you tomorrow."

"I don't want to think about that right now."

"Then, don't. Get some sleep."

"Jon." She wrapped her arms around him and held on tightly. He hugged her back. Neither of them said anything for the longest moment. They just stood there embracing as the world rushed in on them. Veda had never experienced anything so intimate in her life.

Chapter Twelve

The next morning, Veda was up early, showered, dressed and having her first cup of coffee on the front porch when Nate called. "I don't want to alarm you," he said, which of course immediately alarmed her.

"What's wrong?"

"This time it is Mom. We're at the hospital. She's okay," he quickly added. "I went by her house this morning to check on her. She was having chest pains. I brought her to the ER, and the doctor is in with her now. He says she'll be fine. It wasn't a heart attack. Probably a panic attack, but he wants to keep her in the hospital for a day or two to monitor her blood pressure."

Veda was already on her feet and rushing back inside for her keys. "Why didn't you call me sooner?"

"I'm calling you now. I've arranged to see Owen this morning. Can you come stay with Mom?"

"I'll be there in fifteen minutes. Ten if I don't catch any lights."

She was there in eight. Her mother was still in the ER awaiting a room. She reached for Veda's hand when she walked through the door. "I told Nate not to call you."

"Why?"

"I didn't want to worry you. The doctor says I'll be fine."

"He also wants to keep you here for a couple of days. Just to be on the safe side."

Her grip tightened on Veda's fingers. "I can't stay here. I need to be with Owen."

"Nate is with Owen," Veda reassured her. "You won't be able to see him until after the arraignment, anyway. Mom, just try to rest. That's the best thing you can do for Owen at the moment."

She said on a tremulous sigh, "I feel like I've let you kids down."

"That's not true. You've been both mother and father to us. We couldn't have asked for a better parent."

Tears filled her mother's eyes. "I couldn't protect Lily. Now I can't protect Owen."

"Owen will be fine. He's innocent. We're going to prove that." Veda perched on the edge of the bed, still clinging to her mother's hand. "Jon has a theory. Don't be upset," she was quick to add. "Just hear me out. He thinks the same person who killed Lily also killed Tony. That person wasn't Owen."

"It's true, then." Her mother's voice dropped. "You've been seeing Jon Redmond. I couldn't believe it when Marcus told me."

Veda was quick to his defense. "Jon did nothing that any of us wouldn't do for Owen."

"Owen is innocent," her mother insisted.

"And Jon has always believed Tony was innocent."

"Do you?"

"That's a hard question for me to answer," Veda admitted. "What did Marcus say to you after I left yesterday?"

"He said you've been asking questions about Lily's personal belongings, that you've been looking for her diary."

"Did she have a diary?"

"Why does that matter now?" Her mother looked agitated all of a sudden.

Veda patted her hand. "It doesn't matter. All that matters is that you stay calm and get some rest. Let's talk about something else."

"I can't think about anything but Owen."

"I promise Owen will be fine. He's got Nate looking out for him." He had Jon Redmond, too, but her mom wouldn't want to hear that at the moment.

It was a couple of hours before they came to take her upstairs. Once she was settled, Veda pulled a chair up and sat down at her bedside.

"You don't have to hover, Veda. I'm fine."

"I want to be here, Mom."

"Then, make yourself useful and go pick up a few things from the house. If I have to stay here overnight, I at least want my tablet and reading glasses."

"Make me a list," Veda said. "If it'll make you rest easier, I'll go get them right now."

A little while later, she let herself into the house and went straight to the downstairs bedroom. She collected toiletries from the bathroom and her mother's tablet and reading glasses from the nightstand. Then she went through the house and made sure everything was locked up and all the burners were turned off on the stove. She was just about to leave through the front door when she heard a rustling sound upstairs. Faint but unmistakable. That was strange. No one was home. No other vehicle was parked out front. For a moment, the notion went through Veda's head that Lily's ghost might really be upstairs. Then she chided herself for the fantasy. Maybe a window had been left open.

Even so, she hovered at the foot of the stairs for several moments before she went up. The hair at the back of her neck prickled as she eased down the hallway. She glanced in Lily's room first. Nothing seemed amiss, although she detected the faint scent of...cedarwood?

Her heart started to thud as she backed out of the room and turned down the hallway. The attic door stood ajar.

JANE CAMPION'S HOSPITAL door was open, but Jon knocked and waited in the hallway because he wasn't at all sure he'd be invited inside. She turned her head and visibly started when she saw him. He put up a hand. "I'm sorry. I didn't mean to startle you."

"Did you come to see Veda? She's not here." She sounded more curious than hostile. He was relieved about that. "I sent her home to pick up some of my things. She should be back soon."

"Actually, I came to see you," he said.

"I guess you'd better come in, then." She propped herself up against the pillows and watched with avid eyes as he came into the room and stood at the foot of her bed. "Veda told me about your theory. You think the same person who killed my Lily killed your brother."

"Yes. That's what I think."

"So you don't think Owen is guilty."

"I do not."

Her chin came up. "Do you expect me to say the same about your brother?"

"I don't expect that, no. That'll take some time."

She closed her eyes briefly. "How's your mother holding up? She's been on my mind ever since I heard the news."

"She's doing as well as can be expected. I'll tell her you asked after her."

She gave him a long scrutiny. "But that's not why you're here."

"No." He came around to the side of the bed. "I want you to tell me about the nightmares Lily used to have."

She looked startled. "Why?"

"Because I'm afraid of what they may mean."

SOMETHING TOLD VEDA not to call out or even make a sound. In fact, her every instinct warned her to get out of the house, but instead she found herself climbing the attic stairs slowly. The steps creaked beneath her feet. She paused to listen. The rustling sounded frenzied and determined. She went up quickly, pausing again at the top. Her grandmother's cedar chest was open, the contents strewn about. Her uncle had his back to her frantically rifling through storage boxes, unaware of her presence. Or so it seemed. Then he turned slowly and said her name. "Veda."

If you see him, pretend you don't know.

A shiver went through her as he got to his feet and faced her. He seemed larger than life at that moment. Looming. Menacing. She could imagine him coming through a bedroom window, eyes glowing red, thunder booming behind him.

She tried to act nonchalant, but her heart had started to pound as those terrible images raced through her head. *You did it. It was you.*

"What are you doing up here?" She glanced around at the mess he'd made. "Are you looking for something?"

His pretenses dropped, and he said with a shrug, "I've wondered about what she might have told you. You were very close. If she would have confided in anyone, it would have been you."

Veda swallowed, still thinking she could talk her way out of it. Then something took hold of her, and she said on a near whisper, "You're the bad man she dreamed about. But you didn't just sit on the edge of her bed and watch her sleep. You did something to her."

"I didn't do what you're thinking. God, not that. I just wanted to touch her. Hold her for a moment. She was so beautiful. And mature for her age. You know that's true."

Veda clapped a hand over her mouth to keep from screaming.

He said as if to himself, "I don't know how it happened, what came over me. She promised she wouldn't tell anyone. Not your mom or dad…no one. It was nothing—"

"Nothing!" Veda was trembling so hard she could barely stand. "Don't you dare downplay what you did to her."

"It wasn't like that—"

"Shut up! Don't say another word or I swear—"

"Calm down," he said in a placating tone. "Let me explain."

Bile rose to her throat. She had to choke it back down. "She trusted you. We all trusted you. How could we have been so blind? Those nightmares she had. That was you. She blamed herself for Dad's death because of what you did. She thought she'd done something wrong, but it was *you.*"

He spread his hands in supplication. "You're making it sound so much worse than it was. It only happened once and she forgot about it. I swear she did. I kept my distance, and no one would ever have known. No one would have gotten hurt. We could have gone on with our lives until she met *him*."

"Tony?"

He seemed not to hear her. "She flaunted him in my face. What was I supposed to do? I couldn't let her be with someone like that. He was a married man." His hands clenched in fury. "They thought they were being careful and clever, but I knew. I always knew what she was up to. The drugs. The partying. I went to her and tried to talk sense into her. I said he would end up ruining her life, but she wouldn't listen. She said I'd already done that. *Me*. The person who cared about her more than anything."

Veda's stomach roiled. "You're disgusting."

He went on as if she'd never spoken. "She told me she remembered everything and that if I ever came near her again, she would tell your mother. She would tell everyone. I could kiss my career goodbye. My friends, my family. I'd end up in prison."

Dear God, Veda thought. How could this have happened and no one knew? Guilt washed over her. "You killed her. You killed my sister. Your own flesh and blood." *Not quick, not painless*. "You're a monster."

"No," he said in strange voice. "I'm just a man who had everything to lose."

Veda felt almost numb to his confession. A part of her realized she was in shock. Later, the impact would be profound. "You drugged Tony. You put that knife in his truck. You drove him to the railroad tracks hoping a train would take care of the rest. A murder–suicide made so much sense. But he didn't die. He went to prison instead. And when he got out, he came to find you."

"He said he'd put it all together while he was on the inside.

He said he knew what I'd done, and he was going to make me pay." He shrugged. "Big words. He had no proof, but I knew he wouldn't let it go. I followed him to a place out on the highway that night. He never knew what hit him. That should have been the end of it, but then you and Jon started looking for her diary."

"There isn't a diary. There was never a diary. No one would have ever known."

He looked around at the disarray he'd created. "But now you know. It's over, isn't it?"

"It's over."

She turned and started down the stairs, but she'd misjudged what he meant. It wasn't over for him. It was over for her.

He came down the stairs so quickly he caught her by surprise. He grabbed her around the neck and the waist and hauled her back up the steps. Then he flung her to the floor and straddled her, his hands clamping around her throat. She fought him. Hard. To save her own life, yes, but also for Lily. And Tony. For both their families.

"Shush. It's okay. Everything will be okay." She could smell the undertones of cedarwood in his aftershave as she flailed. "They'll just think the door locked behind you. That latch has always been faulty. You had to climb onto the roof to get out. You fell and broke your neck. I'll make sure Dr. Bader confirms cause of death. Your mother will be devastated, but I'll be there for her and your brothers. We'll all move on eventually. It'll be okay."

Veda tore at his hands, clawed her nails across his face. He squeezed tighter, tighter until her breath grew shallow and her struggles less frantic. She was going to die at the hands of Lily's killer. No one would ever know because he was that good at lying. He was that adept at covering his tracks.

"Veda? Are you up there?"

Jon!

She tried to call for help. Nothing came out but a croak. *I don't want to die. I don't want to die.*

"Let her go."

His voice came from the top of the stairs. Her uncle's grip loosened. He rose and drew his weapon.

Jon! Jon! She tried to scream a warning, but she managed nothing more than a gasp for breath.

"The police are on the way," he told Marcus. "It's over. You've nowhere to go."

Veda was still on the floor, coughing and sputtering. She looked up and saw Marcus put the gun to his mouth. It all happened in the blink of an eye and yet it seemed to unfold in slow motion. Jon lunged across the attic and slammed into her uncle. The momentum sent them crashing into boxes as the report of the weapon temporarily deafened Veda.

Marcus lay on the floor facedown. The gun had fallen from his hand. Veda crawled toward the weapon, but Jon beat her to it. He put the gun to the back of her uncle's head.

"Don't do it," Veda whispered. "That's what he wants."

"Don't worry," Jon said. "He's not getting off that easy."

"How did you know where to find me?" she asked a little while later when the dust had settled and she and Jon had given their statements. Owen would be released as early as that afternoon. Her mother was finally resting. Nate, like Veda, was still processing everything.

She'd driven home from the station to shower and change

clothes. She'd spent a long time scrubbing her skin, but nothing could wash away the awful memories.

Jon put his arm around her and pulled her close. "Your mother told me where you were."

She turned. "You went to the hospital?"

"I saw Nate at the station. He told me what happened. I took the chance that she would talk to me. Something you said about the night your dad died kept bothering me. You said Lily sat stoic and tearless until your uncle tried to comfort her. Then she started screaming."

Veda shivered. "It seems so obvious, doesn't it? I don't know why I never put it together. I should have known. The signs were all there."

"You were a child when it happened. None of this is your fault. It's not your mother's fault, either. She didn't know, although she had a sense something was wrong. That was why she wanted to come back home in the middle of a storm."

"And that's why Marcus disappeared from our lives after Dad died. He was afraid Lily would say something."

"I'm sure he threatened her to keep silent. Probably told her something bad would happen to her parents if she talked. And then something bad did happen."

"That's why she blamed herself." Veda wiped a hand across her eyes. "This is all so messed up. So tragic. Two lives cut short because of him. All our lives changed forever. How do we get past it? I wouldn't blame you if you never wanted to see me again."

"Everything we've been through…the pain, the loss… it's brought us to this moment." His lips brushed her hair. "I could sit here and tell you that I never want to leave your side, which is true. At this moment, it's true. But remember what you told me about making important decisions, let alone commitments. After everything we've been through, our emotions and judgment are unreliable."

She looked up into those piercing blue eyes and managed a smile. "But if we still feel the same way in six months…"

"I'll come and find you," he said. "Wild horses couldn't keep me away."

* * * * *

CONARD COUNTY SECRETS

RACHEL LEE

Chapter One

Audrey Lang was making pretty good time on her drive from Colorado Springs to Conard County, Wyoming. And not only was she making good time, but the day was beautiful and the tall mountains ahead beckoned her like a beacon.

The mountains around her were pretty, too. Gentler slopes, green from recent rains, low enough not to reach the limit of the tree line, unlike the higher, craggier peaks ahead.

She hadn't really wanted to make this move, but her aunt was right: she needed to escape Paul Lang. The ex-husband who wasn't ex enough. A constant threat who had been riding her spine like ice.

Just as she leaned forward to punch the CD button and listen to some Willie Nelson, Aunt Gladys's voice came loudly from the cargo area of the Suburban. *Oh, God*, Audrey thought. *Not again.*

"When are we gonna get there?"

"When we do," Audrey answered sharply.

"I'm sick of being locked up!"

"Too bad."

"You have no right to kidnap me! Help! I'm being kidnapped!"

Periodically, throughout this trip, Aunt Gladys's African

gray parrot kicked up a fuss. Audrey found that bird unnerving. He talked just like a human being, almost always made sense and could imitate just about anyone's voice. Including Aunt Gladys's, which was making Audrey a bit jumpy.

It felt as if Aunt Gladys was sitting in the back complaining about the trip by the mile.

"You're not being kidnapped. Unfortunately for me, Aunt Gladys asked me to take care of you, Clyde. You're stuck with me."

"Being in a cage is insulting and dangerous," Clyde announced. "I could break a wing in here!"

"As if," Audrey answered, long past the point of feeling foolish for responding to a bird as if he were human. "You're too smart to do that, Clyde."

The compliment seemed to settle the bird for the next few miles. Audrey's ears were grateful. Dang bird had quite some volume when he wanted.

But Clyde couldn't remain silent forever. "Why the hell are we doing this?"

A bit of a salty mouth, too. "You heard Gladys. She wants me to supervise the remodeling of her house."

"Yeah, yeah," Clyde answered grumpily. "But why do *I* have to go?"

Audrey had reached her limit with noisy, nasty birds. "Because you're barely twenty, Clyde. Because you'll probably still be squawking at me when I'm in a nursing home like Gladys. You're lucky I'll take you."

That silenced Clyde, but only briefly. "She should have let *me* choose."

Audrey agreed with him. Except Gladys was right. The bird couldn't go with her into assisted living. Someone was going to have to take on the task of caring for this loud-mouthed bundle of feathers. That someone had turned out to be Audrey, and how was she going to deny her aunt anything?

But there was another truth, one she didn't want to share with Clyde. Aunt Gladys had feared that if she died in that home, the bird would have no protection. He might be put up for adoption if he was lucky. Or someone might kill him just to shut him up, not far from Audrey's thought on that subject. There were darker things, too, which Gladys hated to even think. Sideshow?

Nope, Clyde was stuck with her and she with him.

Then Clyde resumed his endless criticism of the journey and even indulged in some back-seat driving.

Finally she snapped. "Oh, just shut up, Clyde. Give me some peace."

Amazingly he did. For a while.

Then the bird said, sounding eerily like her ex-husband, "You'll pay for that, sweetie."

That did it. Audrey pulled to a sharp stop on the shoulder, spinning out a spray of gravel. She jammed the car into Park then climbed out to open the side door.

Clyde gave her a side-eye from the cargo space from where he roosted in a cage fit for a maharaja.

"You listen to me," Audrey said, between her teeth, "you ever use that man's voice in my presence again, I'll give you to the first four-year-old with sticky hands that I can find. Got it?"

For a moment Clyde didn't respond. Then he nonchalantly spread a gray wing and pecked at it. "Have it your way."

"As if. I'm not kidding, Clyde."

Then, when she was back behind the wheel, Clyde finally silent behind her, she resumed her trip.

She thought again about playing Willie Nelson on the car stereo. She loved driving to the upbeat song "On the Road Again."

Then she remembered Clyde. He hadn't quite mastered Willie's voice. Which meant, given that Clyde loved to sing, Audrey would be listening to Willie in stereo, one version slightly out of tune. Or worse.

Nah. Smarter not to stir up Clyde. Right now, in the rearview mirror, he appeared to be sleeping. Let sleeping birds lie and all that.

She suppressed a snicker, realizing that whether or not she enjoyed this task her aunt had given her, it promised to distract from her other troubles.

Her only serious concern right now was meeting Cameron McKay, the contractor Gladys had hired for the renovations to her house.

Men. As far as Audrey was concerned, they could all fall off the planet as fast as possible. She sure as hell didn't want anything to do with one again.

But she was going to have to deal with this contractor. Gladys had already hired him.

"Crap," she said under her breath.

"Don't use that language," Clyde scolded from his confinement, sounding exactly like Aunt Gladys.

"As if you don't," Audrey snapped. But the bird was right. She shouldn't use that language, much as she wanted to. Gladys had been quite stern about that.

So, okay. The bird could use those words, but Audrey couldn't. There was something very unequal in this relationship.

And no reason to think that inequality would change.

CAMERON MCKAY WAITED for Audrey Lang's arrival like the sentence of a jury. Except that he already had his sentence from Gladys. If she hadn't done so much for him over the years, Cam would have gladly told her where to take her remodeling project.

But Gladys had helped Cam get his own business started, had helped it grow, and he owed her big-time. Not that Gladys had ever intimated that. She wasn't the type. Probably never even once thought it.

But Cam did. Often. He loved Gladys, too, which made it impossible to refuse her anything.

But Gladys had moved away a decade ago to follow warmer opportunities in Colorado Springs, had closed up her house…

Cam stood in that house. He'd been through it twice already and could only sigh and shake his head. Why the hell hadn't Gladys asked him to keep an eye on it over these years? The repairs and remodeling the house now needed had gone out of sight.

Hell, when he'd first peeked in, he'd been aghast to find frozen water had cracked a toilet bowl and risen like a glacier from what was left of the ceramic. Winterizing? Gladys hadn't even thought of that? He didn't want to begin to imagine the state of the rest of the plumbing.

Might as well get a bulldozer, clear the land and build again from the basement up.

He stepped out on the front porch, feeling the icy knife of the wind, but didn't bother to button his shearling jacket. Winter had only begun to ease into the usually cold spring, and since it appeared Gladys's niece was going to be living here, he had been moving swiftly to batter at least part of this wreck into a livable space. No renovation there. No time. Just make sure Audrey wouldn't freeze to death.

"You know, Gladys," he said to the empty wind, "it would have been nice if you'd told me Audrey was going to live here. Instead of just telling me a month ago you wanted the place fixed up. Which left me dallying around thinking I had time…"

He silenced himself. No point in spewing irritable thoughts to the icy wind. He should have gone down to the Springs and spewed them there.

Much as he loved Gladys, sometimes she could drive a man mad. He was getting there with this round. Hadn't it ever occurred to her, at the very least, that he had other work on his plate? That he couldn't just drop everything to race in and recover this place?

Because that's where he was right now: recovery. Renovation had moved squarely to the back burner.

"Nice project," he muttered to himself. Yeah, that's what he'd anticipated when Gladys called him. Remodeling and renovation to fill the cold days of late winter when most of his construction work dried up. Now he faced an emergency.

Then he felt bad. Gladys had moved away to pursue a great job as the director of a large art gallery. A choice plum. And she couldn't help that she'd been stricken with cancer. No one volunteered for that.

So okay, maybe she wasn't thinking too clearly about some things right now. Who would?

Then Paul had been released from prison. But Gladys had been clear about one thing: keep that son of a gun ex-husband, ex-con, away from Audrey. The entire point of sending Audrey to the back of beyond.

Which, when Cam thought about it, likely meant that Audrey wasn't any happier about this than he was. And that she was running scared.

"Hell," he said to the wind. The wind slapped him back. He nearly laughed aloud because the response of the wind felt so much like an irritated Gladys.

WHEN GLADYS'S HOUSE on the edge of Conard City lay only ten miles ahead, Audrey had to pull over to the side of the road and search for some inner calm. Inner Zen, a friend had called it.

She needed it now.

Clyde spoke from the back, this time in his own voice. "What's wrong, Audrey?" Then he fell silent, making not another peep.

So the bird sensed it. Audrey didn't care. Until just this moment she'd been trying to dance away from fear. A fear she'd never been able to name.

As a child she'd often visited Aunt Gladys, spent a few nights with her. Fun times. After Uncle Herb had died, she'd shared Aunt Gladys's bed at night. A time when Gladys had recited riddles for her, riddles that Audrey had always recognized but still couldn't recall the answers. The candy corn in the drawer of the big chest in the dining room. The Regulator clock on the wall, ticking steadily, a familiar sound throughout the days and nights.

All good memories. She should be happily driving toward them.

Except there weren't just the memories. There were the dreams bordering on nightmares.

Audrey could never explain them to herself. Why should she have nightmares about a house that had offered her some of the best times in her childhood? Why should short hallways suddenly become endless, two rows of closed doors she feared to open?

The basement she could have understood, although it had never been very scary to her. Plenty of light, a cistern in one corner, a wringer washing machine in another with a laundry tub, and the shelves of neat rows of canned vegetables and homemade jams and jellies. Nope, not real scary even in her dreams.

But the rest of the house? Especially the upstairs?

What in the hell was wrong with her?

But she didn't want to drive forward. Not toward the house of smiles and dreams. Not toward the fears and joys that place had somehow birthed in her.

And most especially not toward the man Gladys had set on her. Cam McKay. Contractor. Since Gladys had known him for years, he was probably okay. No one to fear.

Except some fears had become engraved on her very cells, rational or not, and fear of her ex, Paul, was entirely rational. Those fears had extended to other men, but not since Paul had she been entirely alone with one.

But now there was Cameron McKay. Now she was going to have to deal with a huge set of her fears.

Eventually Clyde added his two cents. "Will you *please* move this car and get me somewhere so I can escape this cage? This is animal cruelty!"

"You're not an animal."

"Ha!"

But another silence fell as Audrey released the brake and started once again toward Gladys's house. Not much farther. Not at all.

Every fiber of her being tightened.

CAM SAW THE dark green Suburban while it was still a couple of miles away. On the state highway, barreling along toward the edge of town. The wealthier end of town, graced by Edwardian and Victorian architecture. Large houses, like Gladys's, too big now without a huge family or a great deal of entertaining. Remnants of an older, more gracious age. Well, older at least, Cam thought. He wasn't sure about the more gracious part.

Regardless, in this direction he looked out over waving fields of deep grasses and brush. Turn a little and he'd be looking up at the high mountains. Another turn and he was looking down a busy street. Contrasts. To his way of thinking that was one of the things that made this house such a prize.

No shoulder-to-shoulder construction with tiny backyards and only slightly larger front yards. This house still had spacious acreage, once probably farmed or grazed before the house had been nearly consumed by the town. And now it desperately needed loving attention. Kind of surprising that Gladys had allowed it to be neglected so long.

Or maybe not. Maybe she'd grown sicker earlier than anyone knew. Tired. Overwhelmed. Or unable to afford the constant upkeep? He'd never know now.

The green Suburban turned into the driveway, no longer an approaching destiny but here and now. He waved, as welcomingly as he could, wondering what Audrey Lang would be like. Surprised that she didn't jump immediately from the car as soon as it rolled to a stop.

Oh, yeah. Her ex. It probably extended to all men. Great. That ought to help matters. Right.

So he waited, giving her time and space. If Gladys was worried about the ex, then he should be, too, as worried as this young woman might need him to be.

So he waited, the icy wind crawling up under his jacket.

AUDREY SAT, ENGINE RUNNING, taking in the tall man in his shearling jacket, denim jeans and chambray shirt, with a battered cowboy hat that looked as if it might want to take sail in the freshening wind.

"Can we *please* get out?" Clyde demanded. "We're here, aren't we?"

"Oh, yeah." In correct English as well. The bird had evidently learned or been taught by Gladys. "But it's cold out there, Clyde. I gotta figure out how to keep you warm enough."

Clyde's answer was surprisingly dry. "I won't freeze in a few minutes."

"Probably not, but I don't know how warm the house is inside."

Clyde had had enough. He squawked, a very unpleasant bird sound. "Then find out!"

Well, that was the entire problem, Audrey thought. A man. She'd have to get out and talk to a stranger. But still, Clyde was right in one way. She had to find a warm place to stash him and his palace.

Gritting her teeth, she reached for the red parka on the seat beside her and shoved her arms into it. Now or never.

"It's about time," Clyde groused.

Maybe it was. One man. One who Gladys trusted enough to hire to work on her house while Audrey was there. She wondered if Gladys ever would have trusted Paul. Maybe, maybe not. Audrey had never asked anyone's opinion of the man, probably her first, and possibly biggest, mistake.

She opened the car door and climbed out, closing it quickly behind her. She'd have preferred to leave it open for quick escape, but she couldn't freeze Clyde.

"Hi," she said, trying to make her voice strong. Damn, that man looked big.

"Hi," he answered, smiling. "You must be Audrey. I've been looking forward to meeting you."

Audrey doubted that, and somewhere during the last few years she seemed to have lost the skills of common courtesy. Couldn't even say something pleasant.

"Is there a warm enough place for Clyde?"

He stilled. "Gladys's bird?"

"The same. I'm the new lifelong babysitter." Clyde squawked an objection from inside the car. Too bad. "Anyway, he has to stay warm, at least seventy-five degrees."

Cam descended the three steps to the front walk. "I've got a room at seventy-two for you. Won't take long to bring it up. Gladys never said much about him, but I can keep him warm."

"Good. I wouldn't want him to freeze. Trust me, he wouldn't do it quietly."

That was apparently too much. Cam guffawed. "Like that?"

"Wait until you hear his mouth." She turned, now convinced that Gladys had never told Cam much of the ugly truth about Clyde. "Anyway, I have to cover his cage with a blanket and get him inside."

"Can I help?"

Clyde's resounding *no*, muffled from inside the vehicle, answered that question for Audrey. She smiled. "That would be great!"

"Wow, that's some bird," Cam said as Audrey lifted the tailgate. "What? Thirty inches long?"

"Something like that. Most of it is mouth."

Clyde snorted but refrained from showing off his vocabulary. Audrey pulled a fleece blanket from the floor and started spreading it over the cage. Cam was quick to help.

Then came the fun part: lifting the Taj Mahal out of the cargo space and carrying it inside. Audrey had needed help when she'd done this at the nursing home, and much as she hated it, she was glad for Cam's help now. It wasn't that Clyde was so heavy, but that the cage was, all that black steel woven into fantastic shapes. And the toys. And the perches, and...

Well, if there was anything an African gray needed, Clyde probably had it and some extra, too.

"Gladys spoiled this bird," Audrey remarked, risking Clyde's wrath. Not a peep from under the blanket, though.

"Well, I'm sure he's cute," Cam said.

Audrey rolled her eyes. "Man, are you in for a shock."

A rumble of disgust emerged from beneath the blanket but subsided quickly. Audrey would have bet that dang bird was saving his best show for later. Once he was safely inside. Once a human couldn't drop his cage in sudden shock.

"I wasn't expecting a cage this big," Cam remarked as he and Audrey eased their way along a hallway past a large kitchen. "I guess he needs it, since he's so big."

Around a corner into a bedroom beside the kitchen that felt palpably warmer. There was even a large table along one wall. Big enough. "I guess Gladys didn't tell you much about Clyde."

"That she loves him, of course. That sometimes he talks. I didn't imagine him quite *this* big, though."

"Few people do." Yeah, birdies. Little things, for the most part, unless an egret or a heron wandered by. The mind didn't want to accept something as big as a pterodactyl. Or as noisy.

Well, okay, not that big or noisy, but sometimes Clyde felt close to it.

Once the cage was safely settled on the table, Audrey reached for the blanket, bracing for the angry spew that was about to come.

But Clyde had different ideas. At least for now. He lifted a claw and pecked gently at it. Then he looked up, his head turned to one side, regarding Cam with one golden eye. "You must be Cam. Gladys said so much about you."

Audrey's head snapped around to see Cam's reaction. He *did* look a bit startled.

"No parakeet, this one," Audrey said dryly. "Plenty to say, he's a griper, and wait until he imitates your voice."

Clyde gave her the side-eye. "Thanks for the intro, Audrey." Now he sounded like Gladys, which made Cam appear even more startled.

"Get used to it," Audrey said to Cam. "Clyde comes with a whole box of voices, half the dictionary at his command and plenty to complain about."

Cam cleared his throat. "Coffee or something else warm?" he said after a half minute, gesturing toward the kitchen. "And I got some bagels at the bakery."

Audrey summoned a smile, even though he was suggesting she go to another room with him. "Sounds good. Thanks."

"Don't forget *my* bagel," Clyde said from behind them as they left the room. Once again he became Gladys.

Cam shook his head. "He does that all the time? Gladys never mentioned."

"Gladys loves it. Maybe he'll settle down. Right now he's beginning to sound tired. Considering the way he complained and ranted all the way up here, he must be exhausted."

In the kitchen, which Cam had warmed up, too, he poured coffee, since Audrey hadn't asked for anything else, and set out a plate of bagels and cream cheese. "Help yourself. That was a long drive."

Now that Clyde was settled, Audrey began to feel the creeping unease that never quite left her. Not since Paul had she felt any other way. He'd ripped security from her.

Turning her head to look out the kitchen window at the fading day, she wondered if she would ever feel secure again. Ever feel like that bright and shiny innocent she'd once been.

Probably not, she thought glumly. Too much had happened and couldn't be erased. But maybe she could stop feeling like a cat on a hot tin roof every time she was near a male.

Not *all* men were bad, right?

Except these days she didn't believe it. Paul had seemed loving and sweet when they'd met. When they'd married. The ugliness had come on slowly at first. Like having herself nibbled away and not even realizing it.

With effort, she reached for a bagel and smeared it with a bit of cream cheese. Evidently relaxing once Audrey took some food, Cam poured coffee then sat at the far end of the kitchen table.

He evidently sought a safe area of conversation. "Did you know what you might be getting into with that bird?"

In spite of herself, Audrey grinned. "Pretty much, but you haven't heard a bit of it yet. Wait until he decides to impress you with something besides his gentlemanly manners."

Cam appeared dubious, and Audrey couldn't blame him. He'd learn, the way everyone learned soon enough about Clyde. Damn bird wouldn't be able to restrain himself forever. Then the real shocks would begin to shiver down human spines.

"So what temperature does he need?" Cam asked.

Audrey swallowed some bagel before answering. "Ideally between seventy-six and eighty-four. But that's ideal. I'd worry more about the lower number."

"Easily frozen?"

"Too easily. He's a subtropical bird, and don't ask me what Gladys was thinking. Clyde probably charmed her to death. He's good at that when he wants to be."

Again Cam looked dubious. When had Gladys bought this bird and why? Sometime after she'd moved away for certain. Oh, boy, did he have a lot to learn. It was to his advantage, though, that he could escape whenever he wanted. Well, he supposed Audrey could, too, for short spells, but where would she go? Certainly Gladys thought she was better off here.

She spoke. "Has much changed around here over the years? The last time I visited was for two weeks when I was ten. Twenty years ago." The passage of the years startled Audrey. So much had happened that those years had felt endless, but now they were gone.

"Not much, I don't think," Cam answered. "Maude's still running her diner like a dragon with the help of her daughter, Mavis. Peas in a pod. Linda opened her bakery, which is busy from the morning hours until just afternoon. We've got an organic foods store."

Audrey lifted her head. "Seriously? *Here?*"

Cam smiled. "Yup. I don't think anyone thought it would survive, but it prospered. Mostly veggies from home gardens. The bookstore is shrinking because even here people find ebooks easier, especially out on the ranches. The library thrives, but Miss Emma has to work hard at it these days. Computer stations, meeting rooms for local organizations…" He trailed off. "I'm boring you. You can find out most of this yourself."

If she ever dared to walk these streets again. She couldn't for the life of her remember if she'd ever mentioned Conard City or Conard County to Paul.

Probably, she thought glumly. In the early days, when sharing good memories had been fun. Before the man had started limiting her social circle, even including Aunt Gladys.

Sometimes she could only stare into space and wonder how she had let that happen. In fact, a lot about herself over the past years left her wondering who she really was. How had she succumbed?

Clyde, who'd been behaving himself as long as he could manage, or sneaking a nap, suddenly called out from the next bedroom in Aunt Gladys's voice. "Audrey! Where's my bagel?"

Now Cam looked truly astonished. "Clyde?"

"Oh, definitely." Audrey reached for a plain bagel and broke off a few small pieces.

"I knew parrots could talk, but this?"

She gave him a crooked smile. "The best is yet to come."

Cam simply shook his head and followed Audrey into the bedroom. She flipped on the overhead light and approached Clyde's cage.

"I want out of here," Clyde demanded, now sounding like Humphrey Bogart. "This is no place to keep a lady."

"Oh, for Pete's sake," Audrey said a bit sharply. "You ain't no lady."

"Am not," Clyde agreed firmly, once again Aunt Gladys. "Your English grammar is appalling." He moved to the side of his perch and watched as Audrey pulled out his food tray and put the crumbs of bagel in it. "Fresh?" he asked.

"As good as mine. Cam bought them specially."

At that, Clyde ignored the bagel crumbs and eyed the man, turning his head from one side to the other, giving each golden eye a view. "So this is the man."

Audrey blew a breath, feathering her light bangs. "Yes, this is the man. Mr. Cameron McKay."

"Well, he can leave. We don't like men, do we?" Clyde said.

Audrey wondered if it was legal to give a bird a tap on the cheek. A warning tap. Just a light one. "You're a man," Audrey pointed out. "What's more, you'll freeze to death without the help of Cam, so I suggest you remember some of your manners."

Clyde grumbled, then helped himself to bits of bagel.

Cam spoke. "I wouldn't believe this if I hadn't seen it myself."

"African grays are not only intelligent, but they're mouthy," Audrey replied.

"When do I get out of prison?" Clyde asked, pausing over his bagel crumbs.

"When I'm sure you understand the ground rules."

For once the *bird* managed to look surprised.

"I'm going back to my coffee," Audrey announced. Then she turned her back on Clyde, who'd been taking entirely too much of her attention, and returned to the kitchen, where she poured herself a fresh cup of coffee and began to pace, hardly touching her mug.

"Sorry," she said. "Too many hours in the car."

"I get it. If the wind would cut out, we could go for a walk, stretch your legs. Too bad it's only the beginning of March."

A walk. Audrey had been doing little enough of that since Paul had tried to kill her. Even though she was now hundreds of miles away, she didn't feel safe. Then it struck her that Cam had said *we* could go for a walk. Both of them. Why?

Arms folded, she turned slowly to look at him. "Has Gladys been talking about my situation?"

Both of his eyebrows lifted. "What are you concerned about? Gladys, as far as I can tell, hasn't been one to gossip."

"Not usually." Audrey leaned back against the counter, arms still wrapped around herself in a protective embrace. "But she said something about *me*, didn't she? Something about my divorce. About my ex."

"Well, yes. But only that there was a restraining order against him, that she considered him dangerous, and she asked that I keep an eye out for strangers near the house. Nothing major."

"Nothing *major*?" The stress of the past few months seeped out of her, sounding angry. Sounding furious. It was all major enough to her.

Cam rose from the table, the chair scratching on the floor as he pushed it back. "That isn't what I meant. Damn it, Audrey, let's start on a better foot than this."

Another man criticizing her. Another man blaming her for something. It didn't matter what. Everything was *her* fault.

Summoning every bit of courage she had managed to regather in the time since she had escaped Paul, she unfolded her arms and clenched her hands into fist. "Leave," she said hoarsely. "Leave now."

Cam didn't move, and she felt an icy hand grip the

back of her neck. But he didn't stay still for long, relieving her almost as soon as the fear began to slide through her.

"I'm leaving," he said, pulling his jacket off the back of the chair and slipping it on. "The temperature in the bird's room should stay between seventy-four and seventy-six. The cot in there is for you. If you can't sleep with Gladys's bird, let me know tomorrow and I'll heat up another room for you."

Then he left, striding from the kitchen, his footsteps loud in the wood-floored hallway, then she heard the sound of the front door closing.

Clyde had found his voice again, calling loudly from the next room, "Really, Audrey. That was foolish. Did you ever think that Gladys chose him to be your protector?"

"Just zip it, Clyde," she snapped. "God, you're driving me crazy!"

"You were already crazy," the voice of Dolly Parton answered. "I can't make it any worse."

"Damn it!" Uncharacteristically, Audrey threw her cup into the sink. It was plastic, so it didn't shatter, but it sure made a mess with the coffee. Everywhere. A mess to clean up, like her entire life.

"Tsk," said Clyde/Parton. "That man taught you some bad habits."

That was enough. "It's your bedtime." Around the corner in the bedroom, she found the travel blanket and threw it over the cage Mahal.

"But…"

"The clock says it's your bedtime. So it is. You can argue with a lot, Clyde, but not with the clock."

She heard some irritable sounds from within the cage, a bit of fluttering as Clyde settled his wings, then silence.

At least African grays slept all night. Audrey could be grateful for that.

Chapter Two

Outside, in a wind that had grown even chillier, promising winter on every gust, Cam unlocked the tonneau of his crew-cab pickup truck. He'd emptied it of all his tools earlier, before Audrey arrived, stacking them in the detached garage that had once been a stable.

He'd known he was going to have to sleep here most nights, at least until he made the house fully secure, but he'd planned on sleeping in the cold living room when he couldn't go home. But how could he just drive away after Gladys's plea and warning? And now he'd managed to get himself thrown out.

The one thing he hadn't counted on was how easily Audrey could become offended or upset. Given what Gladys had told him about Paul, maybe he should have expected this. Except Gladys hadn't told him *this* much.

God. He unrolled his sleeping bag, ditched his shoes and jacket, and slid in. A few minutes until his body started to warm the thing. Pulling down the tonneau cover added to the warmth the truck bed started to capture.

He'd spent a lot of nights like this on the job. He could spend quite a few more if necessary. He grinned into the darkness, grateful that his body hadn't reached the point of stiffening overnight in the cold.

He wished Gladys had told him more about that bird, though. *Mouthy* was Audrey's description, and from just the little he'd heard, Cam was inclined to agree.

His sister had been fond of parakeets, and the little things never stopped singing. Round the clock, night and day. But it was a pretty sound. Clyde's was far less pretty and a whole lot more than singing.

Beautiful bird, though. All those gray feathers, darker around his head, and then a surprisingly red tail. Unexpected.

Quite a repertoire of voices, too. He'd heard, of course, that some parrots could speak a few words. Most people delighted in that. But Clyde was a creature unto himself. Surprisingly intelligent, from what Cam could tell. Of course, it might have been accidental, but Cam was already waving away such doubts. He'd heard some of Clyde but more than enough of Audrey's reaction to warn him that the bird wasn't a simple collection of cute statements or even cusswords.

Well, time would judge that one, and from the look of it, he was going to have plenty of time.

Gladys had asked him to keep an eye on Audrey. Sounded simple enough: drop by every few days, do some more renovation, talk about anything that came to her mind.

Except he'd seen enough of Audrey to know this was going to be no simple task.

She was worried about what her aunt might have told him, but Audrey had told him more than anything anyone could have said. Just by her reactions. Just by the way terror appeared on her face. The way she was unnerved by the idea that Gladys might have given him any details.

So no simple task indeed. Scared as she appeared to be of men, at least of him, he'd better hang around. Especially since Gladys had said the creep was out of the slammer. No running back for a few days to take care of his own business, unless he could persuade Audrey to go with him. Right now, that didn't look too likely. So he could rely on his partner Dan.

Sighing, he rolled onto his side. Tomorrow he had to get another room ready for Audrey. She might seem to be all right sleeping with Clyde, but he wouldn't bet on it. The bird apparently had too much to say. At least Cam had gotten ahead of the game, thawing and repairing all the pipes in the house before Audrey arrived. Of course, that had been his first priority but it was still one step forward.

AUDREY COULDN'T SLEEP, and it had nothing to do with Clyde. He'd gone into his nightly coma, only making occasional soft sounds that might indicate he was dreaming. She wondered if he could dream and then wondered if she could ask him. Well, of course she could *ask*. The question was whether he would understand her meaning. Or even deign to answer.

She almost sat up. Was she really lying here wondering if a bird could understand the concept of dreaming? Yeah, she was, and with Clyde everything seemed possible.

Man! Rolling over, she wrapped her arms around her pillow, then tried to remember all the joyous times she'd had here. Remembering Gladys before the years had begun to steal her vigor. The games of dominoes on the card table in the living room. Remembering them, Audrey also remembered how she couldn't get the point of the game. Her aunt and uncle had been endlessly patient with her and had very much seemed to enjoy the game, poorly as she played.

But then they, more than anyone else in her life, including her parents, had made her feel loved. Loved just as she was, without expectations.

Their love had stayed with her throughout her life, buoying her through some tough times. Giving her the confidence to carry on. Or to step into adventures.

Until Paul. Almost everything was "until Paul." Closing her eyes tightly, she tried to reach back across those appalling years to the young woman, hardly more than a child, she had once been. It was sad to realize that all that confidence had been shredded, but even sadder to realize that she felt like a total stranger to the girl she'd been. That she could lie there wondering what the hell had happened to her. How she had let it happen.

All the things the psychologist had told her about how it wasn't her fault, that abusers tended to be people who were amazingly good at manipulation. Consciously or unconsciously, they knew how to slowly but steadily take total control of another person.

She'd been victimized and hadn't even realized it while it was happening.

Hard to swallow. Hard indeed. Hard to remember who she'd been in her distant past, but sickening to think about who she'd become.

Apparently she'd grown restless, because Clyde's voice emerged from beneath the blanket. "For heaven's sake," he said irritably. "Get yourself some warm milk. A bird needs to sleep."

She was absolutely in no mood to be scolded by him. "Shove it, Clyde. I've got things on my mind."

"Next you'll be saying I don't have enough of a mind to have anything on it," Clyde grumbled.

"The thought had occurred to me." But Audrey sighed and rolled onto her back. Verbally jousting with that bird was childish. Maybe it was unkind. Clyde seemed to like it, but how could she know it wasn't some kind of pretense on his part?

Just like that, she snapped upright. Clyde? Pretense? Seriously? Could he even...?

Laughter burst out of her, the most genuine that had escaped her in months if not years. It rolled up inside her, making her sides ache.

Clyde tsked loudly, but he didn't sound irritated at all. Maybe amused.

At last, having left Audrey breathless, laughter slipped away, bringing a deep sense of peace in its wake.

There was a small lamp beside the bed and Audrey reached out, turning it on. The yellowish glow dispelled the gloom. "You need anything, Clyde?" Might as well be pleasant since she'd wrecked his sleep.

"Water," he answered. "And some millet would make a nice snack."

Shoving her feet into fuzzy gray slippers that had seen better years and pulling on the thick yellow sherpa robe that Gladys had given her, she rose. "Millet and water? Is that all?"

"It's all you can carry."

She paused, looking into the golden eye of that parrot, and wondered if he was engaging in some manipulation himself. Nah, it was just a broad hint. Clyde was good at those hints when he chose not to be blunt.

Maybe she was anthropomorphizing too much anyway. However human Clyde *seemed*, he wasn't. Just a very smart bird.

Although using the word *just* with Clyde never felt right, either.

Reminding herself that she was standing there with a plan that included some hot chocolate, if there was any in the house, she stepped over and released the top and bottom latches on Clyde's cage.

"Well, it's about time," he said sharply, shaking his wings out and hopping forward onto Audrey's shoulder. Through the thick fabric of her robe, his talons didn't feel especially sharp. Although he was usually careful not to hurt her.

"Am I allowed to fly, Madam?"

"If you want. If you can find room. If it's not too dark. And if you promise to stay in these two warm rooms. I don't want to be looking for a hot water bottle."

"Sheesh. Any more rules?"

She walked around the corner to the kitchen, flipping on the overhead lights. Clyde flapped his wings, and after a brush against her ear he flew the short circumference of the room then settled on the edge of a counter.

"Do you want the millet in here or in your cage?"

"Here."

Okay. Not a problem either way, except she'd have to do some sweeping up after.

She dug around in one of the plastic bags she'd dropped on the table and found her Clyde supplies. Millet. Man, he loved those twigs with all the seeds on them. Probably made him more content than almost anything. A small bowl of water nearby completed her duties.

Then she headed for the pantry, wondering how much might be in there, and how much shopping she'd have to do in the morning. She wasn't looking forward to going to the grocery because it was a strange place and would be full of strange men. At home she had almost everything delivered to her door. She wouldn't be as fortunate here. But Gladys had said Cam would put a few things in the fridge, hadn't she?

She honestly didn't expect to find anything in the pantry except some old cans and some mouse-gnawed dried goods. No one had lived here in a while, and she was sure Gladys hadn't even come up to check on things, not for the last couple of years since she started to grow ill.

The pantry lights turned on, much to her relief. Then she looked around in amazement. Gladys apparently hadn't wanted to leave a bare cupboard, probably because she expected to visit again soon.

Regardless, Audrey looked around at rows of sealed plastic containers, all neatly labeled in Gladys's perfect hand. Food, plenty of it. Dried milk. Powdered eggs.

"Heavens, Gladys, were you getting ready for the apocalypse?"

Clyde made an unidentifiable sound, probably a comment he didn't want to bother translating.

"Did you see all this in here, Clyde?"

"Can now. At least you won't starve before you can get me more millet."

"Selfish bird."

"Always." Then he went back to cracking millet seeds.

Much to Audrey's delight, she found some instant hot chocolate mix that didn't require milk. For whatever reason, Gladys had prepared for just about everything. Maybe getting stuck up here in a winter storm?

Cam had bought some of the necessities, too. The refrigerator was pleasantly full. The gas stove turned on with a flick of the knob, so he'd gotten that working again. Soon water was steaming in a small saucepan, instant powder at the bottom of a cup waiting for it. In no time at all, Audrey sat at the kitchen table, listening to Clyde and his millet. He seemed to be taking his time with it.

Stirring her cocoa, resting her chin in her hand, she noticed. "Clyde? Are you okay? You're eating slow."

"I'm fine," he said irritably. "I'm making it last longer because the glaciers will cover this country before I get another."

A giggle escaped Audrey. "You're too much."

Clyde imitated Gladys again. "No, Clyde. Millet is fattening." He shook his feathers, settling them again. "I need a diet?"

"She might have a point. Anyway, I'll give you another one, just tonight. Don't expect it every time."

Clyde muttered something about not being able to expect anything, but Audrey had drifted away on her own thoughts. Clyde was a great distraction, but that's all he was. He couldn't help her over the rocky patches she still faced. The fears that wouldn't leave her.

Six years in jail. That's all Paul had gotten. Six years was all Audrey's life was worth. Sometimes that made her angry, and at others it filled her with despair. He had tried to kill her. What if he had succeeded? Would her life have been worth much more with her dead?

The night beyond the kitchen windows was black, lacking any moonlight out there. They reflected the interior of the kitchen, creating an odd double-image effect. A faded world compared to the one inside.

Faded like her own soul, she figured. A long road of recovery lay ahead of her. Without being asked, she rose and gave Clyde a second millet stick. He even thanked her.

But she was miles away. She turned on water for more cocoa, but the action was hardly conscious. Instead she stood looking out at the inky night, telling herself there was nothing out there to fear. He could never find her here, thanks to Gladys. But an icy chill ran down her spine anyway, and she had to shake herself.

Telling herself that tomorrow, whatever it took, she was getting curtains to cover these windows. God, she felt like she was on TV.

The icy chill ran down her back once again. Someday that would stop. Or at least happen a lot less. That's what the therapist had said. It was hard to believe. The feeling was a nearly constant companion.

The water nearby began to bubble as it boiled, but she gripped the edge of the counter, staring into night and hopelessness.

OUT IN HIS TRUCK, Cam was having a restless night, too. He hadn't been prepared for most of this, and he wondered if Gladys had purposely kept him in the dark. Telling him to keep an eye on her niece who'd just escaped an abusive marriage didn't sound like such a huge thing. He wasn't a counselor, merely the guy who was supposed to fix this damn house.

Besides, a friend of his had once been abused, and he'd spent plenty of time with her when she got away. Mostly she'd seemed to need a shoulder until the worst of the shock passed.

Was this different? He had a feeling it was. Here Audrey was, hundreds of miles from her abuser, yet terror still ran across her face. With no obvious cause that he could determine.

Then there was Clyde. Hell. That was no *just a parrot*, as Gladys had told him. He hadn't seen much of that bird yet, but he'd seen enough to think Audrey had brought a pain-in-the-butt two-year-old with her, except this one had feathers. And the disturbing ability to mimic other people.

Hard to believe it was a bird.

"Just a parrot, my foot," he muttered. Then he rolled over, and through a small opening in the tonneau he saw the kitchen lights were on. Strange place. A bucket full of worries. Maybe even a noisy bird. Yeah, it would be hard to sleep.

Well, hell. He was getting cold out here, there was coffee inside, and maybe he wouldn't scare the life out of her if he let her know he was approaching.

He weighed that fear thing for a few minutes, then pulled on his boots and jacket. He was going to be hanging around her a whole lot, and somehow he was going to have to help her over her fear of him or nothing was going to get done on Gladys's house.

He crunched his way over to the side door that opened to a mudroom and knocked. Silence from within. He hesitated. He sure didn't want to show his face at the kitchen window. *That* would probably shave twenty years off her life.

So he knocked again more loudly and called, "Audrey, it's Cam." Again, silence. He wondered if she'd heard him.

Then he thought he heard Clyde—boy, that bird was loud—and the door between the mudroom and kitchen opened hesitantly.

"Cam?" Audrey asked.

Before he could answer, Clyde said, "I *told* you it was Cam."

Audrey just shook her head. "Do you need something?"

"A hot drink, if that's okay. I'm sleeping in the bed of my truck. I should have thought of bringing better camping supplies." But then, he hadn't initially imagined she would throw him out and that he couldn't sleep in the somewhat warmer living room. Nor had he anticipated just how cold it was going to get out there.

He should have been better prepared instead of acting like a greenhorn.

Audrey opened the door wider. "Of course. Come in."

He felt the warmth of the room almost like a slap in the face. After the below-freezing temp out there, seventy-five felt like a sauna. He pulled off his jacket, hanging it over the back of the chair. "Warm enough for the bird?"

Clyde regarded him with one eye. "Rude."

"Don't mind him," Audrey said. "He'll let us know everything he thinks. What can I make for you?"

"You just take a seat. I'm pretty familiar with this kitchen, Audrey."

When he thought about it, he knew he'd spent more time in this very room during the last fifteen years than Audrey had. He also remembered Gladys's growing concerns as Audrey drew away from her. "This isn't like her," Gladys had said more than once. "And when I ask her what's wrong, she denies that anything is." Every single time Gladys had shaken her head and wondered what, if anything, she could do about it.

"She's an adult, Cam. She has a right to run her life the way she sees fit."

He couldn't rightly argue that. But now, with Audrey right in front of him, he wished there'd been an answer back then.

He made the coffee with the skill of long years of practice. He noticed Audrey had been drinking instant hot chocolate and asked if she wanted more.

"No, thanks." She sighed and closed her eyes.

"Couldn't sleep?"

"Not really. I was bothering Clyde, though, and he let it be known. Then he wanted a midnight snack."

Clyde grumbled.

Cam faced the bird, feeling foolish as he said, "Don't you think it would be nice to let Audrey sleep?"

Clyde grumbled again and stuck his beak beneath a wing, where it stayed.

"Score one," Audrey said wearily. "It won't last."

"Why'd you agree to take him?"

"Because Aunt Gladys was worried about him. She couldn't take him into the facility with her, and she didn't want him to wind up with a stranger. Or worse. So…" Then she gave a half smile. "I kinda like him, sassy as he is."

Clyde pulled his head from beneath his wing to say, "I'm also a good alarm." And with that he tucked his beak away again.

Audrey shrugged. "I guess he's taking care of me, too."

Cam studied the bird, already curious but growing even more so with longer interaction. "Are all parrots this…talkative?"

Clyde's head snapped up. "Talk about me like I'm not here?" He huffed and took wing, saying in Gladys's voice, "Good night!"

He disappeared around the corner, and Audrey heard his cage door clang shut. She sighed. "Annoyed again."

"What was that clang?"

"He closed his cage door without locking it, making it

known he doesn't want to be disturbed. Which is fine, because he's supposed to sleep all night the way we do."

"Or try to," he said dryly. "Look at us. But to get back to Clyde, whether he likes it or not, are all parrots as talkative?"

"No way. African grays, like Clyde, seem to take to it more readily, but Clyde is unique. Absolutely unique. And one of the things I didn't say earlier was that Aunt Gladys always worried that someone would steal him, then sell him to some lab for study. Or turn him into some sort of moneymaking act. That kind of treatment would probably depress Clyde to death."

Thinking over how lovingly raised Clyde had clearly been, Cam believed it. But then, wouldn't almost any animal torn from its home and thrown into unnatural circumstances be depressed? Maybe that part wouldn't be unique to Clyde.

"Well, he's something else. I wonder if I could ever get used to him. It's like having another person around."

Audrey put her chin in her hand. "I do think of him as another person. As a precocious toddler. Because he might as well be one."

Clyde's Willie Nelson voice drifted from the other room, sounding sleepy. "I heard that."

But then Cam could have sworn he heard a quiet snore.

"All righty, then," Cam said and couldn't help grinning. "I'll get used to this."

"You won't have much choice." Audrey yawned, covering her mouth.

So pretty, Cam thought. So very pretty. And so very exhausted from the look of her. "You need to get back to bed. I'll be right outside in my truck."

She hesitated visibly, clearly uneasy, then took a risk that very nearly snatched his breath. "Couldn't you find a more comfortable place in the house?"

That was quite an offer, considering what she'd been through. Why she was here. That Gladys feared, probably rightly, that the ex would want to settle a score with Audrey.

He should say no, should give her the space from men that she probably desperately needed.

But instead he said, "If you don't mind, I can put my bedroll on the living room couch."

She looked down. "I guess it'll be slightly warmer, and it's got to be more comfortable."

Then, abruptly, she rose, leaving her mug where it was. "Good night."

With a sharp turn, she walked away to the bedroom. The door closed quietly behind her.

Cam leaned back in the chair, coffee mug at hand, and tried to work through this situation.

It was nothing at all like his expectations. He'd been told about a bird, but no bird like this one. He wondered for how long Clyde was going to startle him.

But mostly he thought about Audrey. Gladys feared for her. Wanted her well away from Colorado Springs. He understood all that and couldn't disagree. He was more than willing to play security guard but at the time he hadn't considered it might be an all-day, every-day job. "Keep an eye on her," Gladys had said. A far cry from thinking the threat was unlikely.

But he hadn't expected a woman hurting to this degree. When she talked about that damn bird, she brightened, but then the fear crept back onto her face, into her posture.

Some part of her was seriously convinced that her ex was going to come after her.

It happened all too often. Cam didn't have much direct experience, but he'd read enough to know that a restraining order wasn't worth the paper it was written on. Abusers frequently violated them, and the cops seemed reluctant to throw a guy in jail for getting too close. It was a situation, in their minds, that only called for a warning.

But violating that order even once could be quite enough. Women who got their abusers arrested entered the most dangerous time of all. Cam could imagine how much worse that got when a guy went to jail and developed a serious grudge. And this one had just gotten out, according to Gladys.

Rising, he washed his cup and the coffeepot, deciding to bring a few things inside and take advantage of the living room floor.

But also thinking in a way that awoke old lessons from his stint in the military. A way of thinking he hadn't needed in over a decade. Ideas for protection. Places of vulnerability.

And curtains for these damn kitchen windows.

Cussing under his breath, he stepped out into the cold, moonless night and got ready to move into the house.

He wasn't at all as sure as Gladys had seemed that Paul wouldn't find his way here. Gladys had asked for his help in a way that made him think she was only slightly worried about her niece. And she might have been right.

But Cam wasn't going to bet the farm on it.

Seeing his familiar world anew, with vision he thought he'd left behind with the army, he knew he'd have to do more than just hang around. At least for a while.

Gladys's house was past the end of the once-wealthiest

street in town, big old houses, many of which the economy had turned into duplexes or apartments. But Gladys's house, while not huge by today's standards of McMansions, owned more privacy than the rest.

This property had once been part of a larger ranch, and subdivision of the land had left two acres between this house and the next one on the street. Not much space, but when she'd lived there, Gladys had kept some goats to keep it all trimmed. Now it had become scraggly. There were several copses of trees providing privacy. Maybe too much privacy.

Okay, tomorrow he was going to have to make a serious survey of the immediate area.

Because if Paul decided to chase down his ex-wife and succeeded finding her, he might not just burst onto the scene. He might be wilier. Much wilier. And likely dangerous as so many men of his ilk were.

Chapter Three

Morning arrived with bright light slipping in small stripes beneath the bedroom curtains. It also arrived with Clyde sitting on the headboard staring down at her. If those golden eyes could bore holes, his were.

"Oh, hell, Clyde." She squeezed her eyes shut. She needed time to ease out of sleep, get her brain rolling, stretch her body, which, frankly, felt too good to move.

But Clyde didn't answer. He merely continued to perch and preen.

What the dickens? He should at least have made a comment about breakfast, how he was starving to death, how she was lying about uselessly.

But he said nothing. Instead he was acting like an ordinary bird.

That brought her wide-awake. Was something wrong with him?

She twisted to look fully at him. "Clyde? What's wrong? Aren't you hungry?"

He looked up from his preening, giving her the side-eye. "Cam" was all he said, then returned to smoothing out his feathers.

Cam had fed him? Wow. She wasn't used to not being

responsible for every minute of Clyde's life. Certainly not now, not since Gladys had turned him into Audrey's eternal endowment.

Awake now, she hopped out of bed and grabbed jeans and a warm blue fleece shirt before heading to the kitchen. There sat Cam at the table with a big sheet of paper in front of him that almost looked like a blueprint of the house. Except it was no blueprint.

The aroma of coffee filled the room, and Cam had a mug right beside him. Audrey headed immediately for the pot. "Thanks for making the coffee." What a luxury to have that done for her.

"Can't function without it." He kept studying the drawing in front of him.

"Clyde said you fed him."

"Squealer. He said he was starving to death. That bird is hard to shut up." Cam looked up, giving her a cockeyed smile. "Wouldn't have believed it."

"Who would?" She sat across the table from him. "What are you doing?"

"I went through this entire house, making my own layout of where everything is. Like a blueprint. Except something is nagging me and I'm running over it again."

"Gotta be nitpicky, huh?"

"Believe it. A few centimeters this way or that could cause a lot of trouble and cost a lot of repairs. I'm on the triple check for this."

Clyde flew into the room, perched briefly on Cam's shoulder, looking down at the paper, then shook his feathers in disapproval and flew once around the room before settling on the edge of the table beside Audrey. Cam seemed undisturbed.

"Well, you're quiet this morning," Audrey said to Clyde.

"Boring." Then he tucked his head beneath his wing, telling the world what he thought of it.

Audrey almost giggled. Such disapproval from a bird. She might have shared it briefly, except she still needed to drink her coffee. And then she had to think about what kind of life she was going to make for herself—if Paul didn't show up like a wrecking ball.

No reason he should. He'd already been in prison once. Maybe he'd actually have smarts enough to just drop it. Maybe Aunt Gladys was being overly cautious.

Except it was hard for Audrey to dismiss her fears when she'd had to travel hundreds of miles to escape the terror. She should be able to, right? Now?

Oh, hell, she couldn't dismiss it at all. She wished she could just shake herself hard and get rid of everything that clung to her. Instead every time she looked at Cam she felt a bit of uneasiness. *A man*.

Cam began to roll up the huge piece of paper.

"Did you find a problem?" Audrey asked.

He shook his head. "Just a few places I want to check my measurements one more time so I can start the necessary work to bring heat to the living room and one more bedroom. Oh, and more of it to the bath. I doubt you want to shower in tepid water."

She smiled. "Absolutely not."

"There's hot water in here now obviously, but at the time I couldn't see a reason to run it everywhere. As long as the water, even cold water, trickles, the pipes won't freeze again. But I diverted things to save on energy while I was working. No point in heating the entire state or wearing out the water heater when I didn't need much."

Audrey looked at the windows. Ice did indeed lace the edges of them. "I guess it got colder."

"That time of year." He got himself some more coffee. "Now, to get to town. I want some curtains for the kitchen window. Bet you do, too."

She nodded slowly. "It'd be nice."

"Basic café curtains with tension rods," he decided. "Practically an instant fix. Then—" he studied her "—after I get these problems taken care of, would you like to go out tomorrow and meet some of your neighbors?"

Audrey started and simply didn't answer. She'd become so withdrawn, so agoraphobic, so afraid of conversing with people… After a minute she said, "I'll think about it." Actually, she'd be more likely to try to figure out how to hang a blanket over those windows.

Clyde stirred, and Audrey could tell he wanted to say something but didn't. What was going on with that bird, anyway?

Cam spoke again. "I hope I didn't do anything wrong. Clyde wanted sunflower seeds this morning. At least, that was the bag he pecked at."

"That's okay." Audrey summoned a smile. "So he didn't tell you, he just pointed?"

"Yup."

"How strange." She twisted her neck, trying to look at Clyde, but couldn't quite make it. "Are you sick, Clyde?"

He replied irritably in his own scratchy voice, "I told you I'm fine."

"Okay." Sighing, she looked at Cam. "It's going to be one of those days. He gets cranky and stubborn sometimes."

"And you don't?" Clyde snapped, then went back to preening.

"Bath?" Audrey asked.

Clyde stopped preening. After a couple of seconds, he fluttered and landed beside the sink.

"Guess so," Audrey remarked. She took a long drink of her coffee, then went to the sink, adjusting the taps until there was hope that tepid water would emerge. The hot water arrived as Cam had promised. "You're gonna get splashed," she warned Cam. "This is not a neat process."

"I've been wet before. I should go to work on the heating, though, make the rest of the house warmer. I'll leave the rest of the water until you're done there."

"Thank you."

She pulled out a fuzzy dish towel and spread it by the sink on the chipped plastic countertop. Then she tested the water with the inside of her wrist. "Okay, my friend. Have at it."

He stood a moment longer on the edge of the counter. "You know, we *can* bathe outside when the conditions aren't perfect."

"Tell me you don't like being babied. Anyway, this is it, and you sure as hell can't bathe outside right now."

She'd filled the sink to about half an inch, more than enough, then got fresh coffee while Clyde got busy. Birds loved water, she'd learned. Sometimes she misted Clyde and he enjoyed it. Almost as much as getting into the puddle she'd made for him.

Thank God she'd had time to learn from Aunt Gladys before setting out with Clyde. That poor bird would probably have gone nuts from her lack of knowledge.

Sighing, listening to Clyde's splashing, she closed her eyes and tried to dream of a better future. Once she had believed that dreams were the building blocks of days, weeks and years to come. Paul had crushed that out of her. He'd never been her dream, except at the beginning.

But now, now maybe she could try a little dreaming of good things again. Small things to start with. Maybe now would be a good time to take out her pencils and pens and ink. Then later she could order the proper paper and water colors. But no, first the sketching. It had been so long, she doubted many of her skills were in decent condition.

But it would take her out of herself, something she desperately needed to do. To drive away the shadows and fill them with creation, however poor it might be.

The flutter from the sink was loud and pointed. Opening her eyes, she saw that Clyde had hopped out of the sink and was sitting on the towel, once again organizing his feathers.

"Feel good?" she asked him, reluctant to rise and go clean up the water that he had splashed everywhere.

He simply looked at her.

"Sheesh, bird, what made you so quiet?"

Like pointing out the sunflower seeds to Cam rather than just stating his desire. Saying enough to let Cam know he was hungry then silencing himself.

Then it struck her. Cam was still a stranger, and Clyde hadn't decided what to make of him. Come to that, Audrey hadn't decided, either.

As she started wiping up the water that had splashed all over the windows and the floor and what counter it could reach, she paused and gave Clyde the eyeball. He returned the same.

She could hear Cam down in the basement banging around. "Do you have a reason not to like him?"

Clyde shifted his weight on his feet. "Not sure."

"He's Aunt Gladys's friend."

Clyde made a sound very much like a human sniff. "Gladys made mistakes."

"Ooooh. Burn."

A Gladys giggle escaped him. "True. I'll watch him. You, too."

Now she was conspiring with a bird. Yup, she'd lost her mind.

But he was right. Gladys had picked Cam to be her contractor. He said she'd given him a leg up to get started in business. But that didn't mean he was always a good guy. How well did Gladys know him after all this time when they hadn't see one another often?

Audrey felt her barriers start to rise, barriers that had only just begun to lower.

No reason, she told herself. No reason at all to think the worst.

But it was easy to think the worst of men now. After all the times the cops had come then walked away, even though she'd been bloodied and bruised because Paul gave them an explanation they chose to believe. Because she didn't dare say anything with Paul standing right there. Leaving her to face even greater wrath until she gave up calling for help. Even in this century most people were quicker to believe a man. A woman could do most of those things to herself, right?

Other men, neighbors who must have known. Doctors at hospitals who didn't seem to think it at all odd how often she was there in the ER. But Paul had always been standing there, looming, a silent threat. Keeping her mute.

But then, that was the problem all the time, wasn't it? She had become too scared to speak for herself until the end. Too frightened and ashamed. And it wasn't *men* who were the problem. Not all of them. But deep within, she believed it was.

Because when she'd met him, Paul had been a man just like any other man. How could you tell what was behind the facade?

CAM OPENED HEATING DUCTS, allowing warm air to pass into other parts of the house. Considering the shape he'd found the plumbing in when he came to estimate repairs, he was just grateful that all the neglect hadn't out-and-out killed the house. The second floor...well, maybe he should start heating that, too. Except right now he had plenty to do on the first floor and didn't need problems growing overhead until he was ready for them.

Anyway, the heat downstairs would suck some of the cold out of the upper level. A slow thaw, maybe. At least he'd dealt with that frozen fountain that had once been a toilet.

When he finished shunting hot air to the first floor, he headed upstairs, plumbing and construction materials in mind, then saw the window as he entered the kitchen.

"Colors," he said suddenly.

Turning from the counter where she'd been wiping up water, Audrey said, "Colors?"

"For the café curtains. You'll be the one looking at them every day, at least until you find something better you want. What colors do you like? Or would you like to come along? Clyde can be on his own, right?"

Clyde let out a squawk and winged from the room.

"Oops," Cam said.

"I can't come, Cam. Not yet."

He nodded, appearing to read her deeper meaning. "So, colors?"

No hassle, no argument, no shouting that she was a miserable, incompetent woman. No, Cam was just asking her pleasantly what color of curtains she would like.

A hard decision after so many years of not being allowed to make one, not even about the brand of laundry soap. She stood there hesitating, feeling like a fool for being unable to answer such a simple question.

And Cam just waited as if he had all the time in the world.

Clyde, evidently satisfied that he'd preened himself nearly dry, lifted from the counter and landed on her shoulder.

"Red," he said.

Jerkily, feeling as if her neck had been frozen, she turned her head to get a view of him. "Why?"

He twisted his head, pecking at a feather. "Yellow."

"Oh, for Pete's sake." Audrey emerged from her temporary paralysis. She looked at Cam. "He's acting like a preschooler again."

Cam smiled. "Well, do *you* have a preference, or is Clyde the final word?"

Audrey pulled the words out of the cave her spirit had been thrust into. "Something bright and cheerful," she managed. "Yellow? Green? Just no pattern."

Why no pattern, she wondered when Cam left a few minutes later. Why no pattern? Something buried inside her tried to stir, but she shoved it back into the iron cage where she kept bad things.

She shook herself, trying to gather her scattered thoughts. "Breakfast," she said, homing in on one thing she could take control of.

"Me, too," said Clyde, flapping from her shoulder to the table.

"You already had sunflower seeds, Cam said."

Clyde clacked his beak. "Stingy. I need more."

Well, maybe he did. A little extra feed once in a while was unlikely to make him heavy. At least she had a bag of nutritious pellets for him, but she was going to need some fresh veggies. As if she didn't need some for herself.

A sense of being overwhelmed struck her, as it had too often since her break with Paul. He had emptied her so thoroughly that she had trouble thinking for herself. But she could take care of Clyde. First. Then she'd try to figure out something for herself.

Oh, yeah, she needed to clean Clyde's cage, too. How could she have forgotten to do that last night?

It had become part of her life, like brushing her teeth.

Clyde wanted to eat in his cage, as he usually did. She left him pecking away at his pellets and took herself to the kitchen, where she faced the pantry that was surprisingly full of items that required cooking or baking. Then the refrigerator. Bless Cam, only he could be responsible for the quart of milk, the stick of butter, and the half dozen eggs and more. A small package of sliced cheese, another of sliced ham and turkey. Seeing that, she started to smile and dared to open the bread box. A nice loaf of bakery bread greeted her. Wow, he'd done more than just get a few things. She hadn't really looked yesterday.

Everything she needed to make herself a breakfast or lunch, right down to mayonnaise and mustard.

She decided on the sandwich, although it took her a few minutes to make up her mind, such a simple thing! Shaking her head at herself, she set about making a thin ham sandwich. With Paul, everything, even simple things like this, could become a trial by fire.

It was a fact, one she needed to face, that she wouldn't be able to live on this largesse for long. Sooner or later she was going to have to gather up every bit of courage and go to the grocery. And make her own decisions about food.

She doubted many people would be able to believe that she'd walked alongside Paul at the grocery but hadn't been able to say a word about what went into that basket. *He* had decided, the way he had decided everything else, including what she wore. Even after six years, some of that remained. Branded for life.

Forcing that man to the bottom of her thoughts, into that iron cage, she focused her attention on the sandwich. It tasted good, far better than the food she had eaten for years. For so long everything had tasted like ashes, but not now. Now she could savor every flavor that burst from the bread, the ham and the mustard.

Closing her eyes, she allowed herself to enjoy every single mouthful.

Life could be good, she told herself. Life was getting better. Two mantras near at hand all the time.

Life can be good.

CAM FELT BAD about leaving Audrey alone, but it was ridiculous to think he could be with her every minute. Whatever had happened to her, he couldn't fix it. In the meantime, he had other matters to take care of, like his construction company. Like getting parts for repairing Gladys's house.

And Audrey was just going to have to find some way to poke a hole in her shell and meet some other people. It was awful, of course, what she'd been through.

Dealing with his business was easy enough that day. He had a good second-in-command, Dan Shaw, who could be trusted to take care of most things without a problem. Not that Cam could let him run it indefinitely on his own. Having a business did not mean you could just walk away from it for extended periods.

But today a quick updating was all he needed. Then he set off for the building supplies business and filled the back of his truck with items he needed for Gladys's house. In one corner at the very back, the business had provided for the more modern buyer, so he was able to find some café curtains and rods. Yellow curtains, no pattern. Which was an odd request, but he shrugged it aside. Maybe it had to do with her marriage. Avoiding anything that might remind her.

On his way back to Gladys's place, however, he started thinking seriously about Audrey. A beautiful young woman, so scarred by life that she might spend the rest of her days in virtual hiding. God, that would be awful.

His hands tightened around the steering wheel, then loosened. Truth was, all he could do was work on Gladys's house and be around if Audrey needed him. That was the extent.

Still, damn it, he was a man who wanted to solve problems, not just let them be.

As he was approaching the town, rangeland surrounding him, he thought of groceries. He'd put a few necessities in the house, but not nearly enough. Picking up his phone, he dialed the number Gladys had given him.

All of a sudden, he wondered if Audrey would even answer a phone these days. With all her fears and scars, it might look like a threat, especially from an anonymous number.

As he listened to her phone ring, he became convinced she'd never answer and hoped that she was okay. As for the groceries, that could wait until he got back to house and asked her.

But just as he was about to hang up, she answered. Her

voice was just a little uncertain, but not as much as he might have forgiven her for.

"Hello?"

"Hi, Audrey, it's Cam. I'm just coming up on the grocery store and wondered if you wanted me to pick up anything."

Pause. Then, "I'm okay."

Okay? With a pantry full of dry goods and bird food, with one loaf of bread, coffee, milk... He hadn't stocked that refrigerator with enough food to get her through most of a week.

His thoughts trailed off. Like hell she was okay. Couldn't even decide on something from the market? Not even a color for the curtains. That was bad.

From what little he'd seen, she had courage to take care of Clyde, to talk about him, even to make a little fun of him, but that was Clyde. A bird. Not a human male.

He cussed several choice words in a row and wondered how the hell he could deal with this. Ask Clyde to make a shopping list? For the first time he considered how deep Audrey's problems might run if a bird was her only safe point of contact.

He swore a few more times, a totally useless occupation, but otherwise a good way to fill the truck cab with some of his useless feelings about this.

Damn, Gladys, he thought, *the woman needs a therapist, not me.*

Then he recalled Gladys's overriding concern: that Paul would come after Audrey. While Gladys hadn't said much about what had happened, Cam had understood she was scared to death for Audrey.

And that, he reminded himself, was why he was here. To keep some beast from reaching Audrey. To hell with groceries. She'd either have to screw up some courage to make choices or he would have to make them for her. He cursed again. No hint, even for the curtains, and no request for anything from the grocery.

Leaving her on her own where making choices was necessary, forcing her to decide how to take care of herself, was probably entirely the wrong way to go about this problem, but Cam was Cam, and he didn't have an education for this. Guess he'd have to bull his way into the middle of this.

Chapter Four

Clyde seemed to be having a great time in the two new rooms. At least he was swooping around everywhere there was space, perching on every possible surface and checking things out if they caught his eye.

Audrey watched him, smiling faintly. Such a joy, a blanket of light in a world that for her had become lackluster. Clyde, she decided, lived very much in the minute. He sure as hell wasn't worrying about much that she could tell.

But why was *she* worrying? She'd escaped Paul. She was fairly certain he'd never find her here. No need to worry about him, not really.

No, a greater need was getting those extra drawing supplies Audrey had ordered. They'd be here in a couple of days, and that brought another smile to her face. After years of scribbling on the backs of receipts because Paul thought she was wasting both money and time with her art, she felt like a five-year-old waiting for Christmas morning. Such a good feeling that she hugged it to herself.

A crunch from the driveway made Audrey jump up and look out the kitchen window. It was Cam.

For just a second, she felt her heart lift with relief, then it crashed again. What would he think of her ordering art supplies? He'd probably be mad. She had no money to waste on such things. None. And he'd have every right to tell her so. Maybe he'd even rip up her sketchbook. Or throw it in the trash to get messed up with coffee grounds. She could think of so many ways he could express his displeasure. Was it so wrong to want a different kind of paper because the paper could have a huge effect?

She almost reached for her phone to cancel the order—the brand-new cell phone that Gladys had given her—but Cam came walking through the door with a plastic package and two long brass rods. He was smiling. She wondered how long that would last. How long before he erupted in fury.

"The curtains you wanted. At least I hope they are."

Two things struck her: she'd dared to state her preference for plain, not patterned curtains, and Cam had granted her wish. She'd have seen neither with Paul.

A little bit of her perennial tension eased.

"Well, let's unwrap them and see what you think." He handed her the package. Easy enough to open with its zip closure.

Then she pulled out the first curtain and drew a breath. It was so pretty and glimmered almost like yellow satin. "These are too good…"

He chuckled. "Hardly. But since you'll have to look at them so often, you ought to like them."

She watched him feed the curtains onto the rod and raise it, expanding it to fit the opening. "What a change that makes," she breathed.

"It does, doesn't it?" he agreed, stepping back. "I've got that ruffle thingy if you want it across the top." He indicated the second rod.

After a minute, she realized he was waiting for her to decide whether to use the ruffle. She glanced at him. He was still smiling. Well, she'd summoned the courage to ask for curtains without a pattern, so why not express her opinion about this?

But her throat seemed to clutch, and the words didn't want to emerge. God, was she ever going to get past this? What words? She couldn't seem to make a decision about the ruffle anyway. She stared at the window, silent.

"How about this," Cam said after a bit. "I'll feed the ruffle onto the rod and hold it up. That oughta make it easier to decide."

Now she was embarrassed. Every time she thought she might have been crawling out of the pit Paul had left her in, something would rear up to remind her. To cast her down again.

But Cam put up the curtain on its own tension rod and adjusted the ruffle before stepping down from the stool. "Whaddya think?"

Clyde chose that moment to fly in. "Awk! You covered my window!"

"*Your* window?" Cam asked. "You want any more early-morning sunflower seeds from me, you'd better change your attitude."

Clyde settled on Audrey's shoulder, grumbling quietly. That grumble always got to her, always amused her. How could he do that?

Clyde seemed to think about that, then with a push of his legs and a flap of his wings, he lifted into the air and landed on the sill over the sink, now behind the curtains. He stood there eyeing the curtains from every angle, then stuck his head through the slit between two of them.

"Will do," he announced and winged away.

"I didn't buy them for him," Cam said. "They're for you. The bird is selfish. I wouldn't have thought…" Then he shook his head. "I would never have imagined this bird at all."

"Many wouldn't." Audrey looked at the yellow curtains with their slight shimmer and felt her throat tighten. Other than Gladys, it had been ages since anyone had done something so nice for her.

"Thank you," she murmured to Cam. "This is so nice of you."

"It's been rumored that I'm not all that bad. But now we have to discuss groceries. You need more food in here or you're going to starve to death. So let's sit down and make a list."

A list? Going for groceries had always meant walking down an aisle, pushing a cart while Paul threw into it whatever he wanted. Not exactly abuse, but far from caring.

She sat down facing Cam, realizing that his closeness was no longer setting her on edge. Realizing that if she didn't get some kind of grip on herself, Paul was going to be a permanent part of her life. She couldn't stand that. Five years of marriage had been more than enough. And since her ex had gone to prison, she'd ordered everything by delivery, even her food.

Cam had twisted to grab a magnet pad off the fridge and pulled a pen from his breast pocket. "Okay," he said. "Doesn't have to be complicated, but I want to know what you like to eat. Or what you might want to cook."

He paused, a pause that felt significant. Audrey raised her head and met his gaze. She even managed to hold it.

"This would all go a whole lot better if you'd come to the store with me and choose what you want."

Audrey drew a sharp breath. She had only one memory of going to the store, and it was with Paul.

Apparently Cam read something on her face. "I'm not Paul," he said quietly. "Whatever you remember, I promise it'll be different with me. And you've got to get out of here, Audrey. Get a breath of fresh air. See the world again."

He was right, so right. That didn't make it any easier for her.

Damn, she'd managed to visit Gladys almost daily in the home. She'd gotten all the way up here on her own. She'd climbed into a car with a parrot and started driving. She'd stopped for gas, but that wasn't a personal experience, not anymore. So what had happened to her once she arrived here? What had made her so much worse?

She was backsliding, and she wondered if it had to do with a man being so close. Maybe. Or maybe being within the protected shelter of a house, a familiar one.

But in that moment she knew exactly what she needed to do. There was only one way to start getting past this, a bit at a time.

"I'll come with you."

"Good. That'll be a great help."

She was dressed well enough in her jeans and a fleece shirt, so she just jammed her feet into boots and pulled on a jacket. An old one. Paul hadn't let her buy a newer one. Well, she decided boldly, she was going to fix that, too.

Another moment of fright hit her as she was about to climb into Cam's truck, but she tightened her jaw and did it. Inside the cab the fear didn't entirely dissipate. Paul had often gotten violent in the relative privacy of *his* truck.

But this was a different truck and a different man. In fact, unlike Paul's, which was spit-shined every week at a shop by their home, this truck was dusty and looked like it knew how to drive in rough, dirty places. She liked that.

Cam had put some quiet country music on the radio, just enough to ease any need for conversation. She was grateful for that.

But finally, after driving through quiet residential streets, they reached the northern outskirts of town and the grocery rose ahead of her. The tightening once again began.

"Not too busy this afternoon," Cam remarked as he turned off the ignition. Audrey retained a faint memory of this store. Gladys had brought her here a few times when she visited.

Okay, she knew where she was going, not that it had made much difference with Paul.

In a surprisingly gentlemanly way, Cam came around the truck and opened the door for her. Maybe he was afraid she'd refuse to get out. She didn't. She *was* glad, however, that he didn't offer her a hand. Didn't try to touch her, even with a gesture of courtesy.

Audrey gave herself an internal shake of her head, nearly ashamed of herself for all this fear. Paul's gift to her, all that fear and shame.

She climbed down and headed for the store's doors with Cam beside her. They passed a few women trundling carts filled with full sacks. The women smiled and said hi as they continued past. Cam answered, and Audrey dragged a smile out to offer.

She could still smile, couldn't she? She sure smiled at Clyde when she didn't get annoyed with him.

Stepping inside the store helped a lot. She remembered the floors being wood, but now they were a white linoleum. Everything else remained pretty much the same. Even the butcher behind his showcase. Harvey? She wasn't sure of his name, maybe because as a child she hadn't needed to use it. Or maybe she didn't remember as much of those good times as she'd like to believe.

CAM THOUGHT HE detected a relaxation in Audrey, as if the familiarity of the store was helping her. He noted, though, on their first trip around the store, she didn't want to make any choices, so he started walking her around again. If they had to make this circuit a dozen times, he'd willingly do it until she put something *she* chose in the damn basket.

God, that guy had messed her up good. She ought to be feeling a whole lot better with her freedom, at least a bit, but he couldn't see it at all. This trip to the store was evidently a major triumph for her.

But at last she did it. She picked up a package of ham steaks. "Will you eat with me?"

Hallelujah! "Only if you want me to."

She nodded and picked up a second package. Pork chops. Rye bread unlike the white bread he'd bought for her before she arrived. Little by little, the basket filled up halfway.

Well, thought Cam, they could do this again in a few days. More trips, more relaxation. He *did* notice, however, that on the return trip to his truck, she walked straighter. A little taller. Man, did *that* make him feel good. It also gave him a measure of her wounding, that such a little thing could make such a big difference.

Cam put the groceries in the back of his crew cab, then drove them back toward the house. As they were pulling into her driveway, he asked, "Any idea where we can get food for Clyde?"

"I brought a lot with me. A feed store should do it, though."

"Just regular parrot food?"

At last she looked at him, and he caught a faint smile on her face. "Clyde would settle for nothing so ordinary. He pigs out on millet. He likes berries. Regular nuts."

"A gourmet, huh?"

"I think Gladys spoiled him a bit, but that's okay. He's obviously healthy."

"And, like you said, mouthy."

"Well, he tested the café curtains and approved."

"I could hardly believe that." He was still having trouble with it. He could only imagine trying to share that with the guys he employed. But Audrey was talking. Maybe about that damn bird, but at least she was talking. And inviting him to dinner.

Baby steps. He just wished Gladys had warned him how bad this was. But then, maybe Gladys didn't know. Audrey was clearly capable of appearing okay when the moment was right. Maybe Gladys had been a haven for her.

As they pulled up near the house, Cam noted for the first time the amount of brush that surrounded the house. He'd paid scant thought to it, or the islands of trees that were scattered around.

Something needed to be done about that. Because Cam simply didn't believe that man couldn't find Audrey if he wanted to get to her. Domestic abusers too often did.

There wasn't a whole lot of food in the tail of the truck, but enough to assure him that Audrey would be okay for a few days at least.

For a few days? Was he losing his mind? Like he was going to leave her alone that long? No, a piece of paper from a court didn't stop one of those guys. Nor did distance or much else.

Before he could sink further into angry thoughts, a large gray bird flew out through the front door and landed on his shoulder. "Got a problem, big guy?"

What the hell? He turned his head to the left, met a golden eye peering at him and remembered the porch steps just in time. No accident, no thanks to that damn bird. "Where did you come from?" he demanded.

Clyde chose that moment to shut his mouth. Then, before he could get through the screen door, Audrey appeared. Her look of anger was one Cam hoped never came his way.

"Damn it, Clyde," she fumed. "How many times do you have to be told that it's dangerous out there? More dangerous than Colorado Springs."

Clyde chose that moment to hop from Cam to Audrey's shoulder, where he started nuzzling her with the side of his head.

"Cut it out, Clyde," she snapped. She stepped back, giving Cam space to enter the house. "Sorry," she said to him. Then she reached up and pushed gently on the bird. Clyde jumped to the side of her hand.

"I'm telling you, bird," she continued as she closed the front door with a bit of a bang, "there are things out there that would take one look at you and think you'd make a wonderful lunch. Eagles, hawks. You're not as big as you think!"

Clyde spread his wings, flapping them irritably.

"Oh, don't give me a hard time. I don't have to give you millet, you know."

Clyde stopped flapping. Cam, still holding two plastic bags of groceries as he watched all this with amusement, said after the conflict seemed to have settled, "When did Clyde learn to talk like Peter Falk?"

Audrey gave a little movement of her hand and Clyde

jumped back to her shoulder. "How should I know?" she answered Cam. She paused, then said, "I'm sorry, Cam. My mood sucks."

"You don't have to apologize for your mood."

That seemed to surprise her, and he felt an ache as he wondered what this woman had lived with for so long.

"Yes, I do," she said and turned toward the kitchen. "Common courtesy."

He followed Audrey and the bird into the kitchen and began unpacking the two plastic bags.

"Please, take a seat," Audrey said. "Maybe make yourself some coffee. I can put all of this away."

Cam saw the instant where she caught herself, when she realized she had just suggested he do something. Such a small thing, such a big reaction. He moved in swiftly.

"That's nice of you, Audrey. A cup of coffee sounds good."

"I can make it for you."

He laughed. "I'm not a baby. I can do it myself. But it's kind of you to offer."

God, the longer he was with her, the clearer his picture of how she had been treated became. He pushed down a desire to kill the SOB who had done this to her. Wouldn't do a damn bit of good now.

But if the monster tried to get within five feet of Audrey, Cam would tear him to pieces. And while it had been years since Cam had been in special ops—he'd been just a kid, really—there was plenty he remembered. Enough to take out a creep like this Paul Lang.

By the time Audrey finished putting away the groceries, the coffee had brewed. "Want some?" he asked her.

"That sounds good." A faint smile. And that damn parrot sitting on her shoulder like a pirate's familiar.

He brought coffee for both of them, Audrey once again taking her place on the far side of the table. As much distance as she could get from him.

He decided to talk to the bird. Maybe that would help Audrey relax even more. "Hey, Clyde."

The bird cocked his head, looking at him from one golden eye. Red tail feathers fluttered just a bit before settling. Regardless, while Clyde must have heard him, he wasn't talking.

Now, that was interesting. What next? "I asked before, but you didn't answer. How did you learn to talk like Peter Falk?"

No answer. Well, hell, the bird had decided to go silent, at least around him. Which made it impossible to use it as a way to get Audrey to converse. "Audrey?"

"Hmm?" She looked at him, her face completely relaxed for the first time that day.

"Where are Clyde's millet sticks?"

Now, that got the bird's full attention. Hard to believe it, but all of a sudden it was clear that Clyde had stopped giving him the side-eye.

"Just inside the pantry door," Audrey answered. "Second shelf. But only one. They're fattening."

Cam saw enough to realize that Clyde, silent or not, did not like that stricture. He smothered a smile, aware of a bird watching every step he took.

He found the package and was surprised to find the millet on narrow little sticks, not too long, but packed with seeds. "Just one?" he asked and waited to hear Clyde's response.

He heard the bird grumble. Not speak, but grumble. He had to admit that amused him, that sound. "Hey, Clyde, you heard Audrey." Then he emerged from the pantry with two millet sticks. Audrey eyed them about the same way Clyde did, except Clyde looked happy and Audrey quite the opposite.

Cam looked at her. "I spoil dogs, too."

A laugh escaped her, blowing out through her lips to release a happy sound.

Clyde spoke. "I am *not* a dog."

"No," Cam replied, "a dog is more loving and useful. What's your excuse, Captain Kidd?"

The squawk that escaped Clyde right then was enough to make Audrey wince and lean away. Clyde hopped down from her shoulder onto the table and regarded the man, his golden eyes able to stare holes.

"That is not my name," Clyde said angrily.

"Really? Then tell me what it is."

Clyde simply stared at him, so Cam held up one of the millet sticks. "Try talking politely to me if you want one of these." God, he thought, he was giving a bird a hard time. Time to visit a shrink.

Clyde huffed. Then he said, "What's wrong with you?"

"You didn't answer my question. How'd you learn to talk like Peter Falk?"

If Clyde could have looked stubborn, he would have, Cam was convinced. Instead the bird looked away.

"Okay then," Cam said, rising, millet sticks in hand. "Do you have to argue with this bird every day, Audrey?"

"Almost constantly," she answered, but a faint smile showed in her blue eyes. "He's being good for you."

Clyde made his inimitable huffing sound.

"Well, if he doesn't want to answer a simple question, he can't want this millet that much. All I want to know is where he learned that voice. You don't hear it often anymore, if at all."

He hadn't taken his first step away from the table when the millet won the day. "From the movies," Clyde said.

"What movies?" Cam asked.

"Gladys likes them." But now he was staring at the millet in a predatory way. Cam decided it might be wise to give him one of the twigs. Apparently so, because Clyde wasted no time pulling the seeds off and cracking them open.

Cam looked at Audrey, who was watching the bird with evident enjoyment. "I never would have thought of eagles and hawks," he remarked. "They're around so much I don't even see them."

She raised her eyes to look at him. "It occurred to me as we were driving up here. Lots in the sky riding the thermals. Such a beautiful sight. Plenty of buzzards, too, from what I could tell."

"Nature's cleanup crew," he answered. "But that's a good warning about Clyde."

"I hope he listens."

Clyde raised his head from cracking seeds. "I *always* listen."

"Always," Audrey agreed. "Whether you'll pay any attention is another matter."

The bird chose to ignore the provocation and returned his attention to millet.

"It's about time to make dinner," Audrey said. She looked at the clock as she did so, and her entire body tightened visibly. "I'm late."

Late? What made her so tense? "Do you have a time schedule?"

Her head snapped around, and he could hear that she

was dissembling. "Not...really. I just don't want to have to clean up later."

He nodded, though he didn't accept that as her reason. He didn't consider her a liar, though. No, this was something else. Like maybe years of hell with a tyrant? "Well, if you want to start now, I'll help. Then I'll do the cleanup."

Her brows lifted, her mouth opened slightly. Surprise? That would be his guess.

"After dinner I want to take a walk around outside," he added. "I'd like it if you'd come with me."

She looked toward the window. Outside the twilight was deepening. "I...don't think so. But thank you."

Damn, he wished Gladys had given him some kind of road map to Audrey's problems. There sure seemed to be a mess of them.

Maybe he should phone Gladys tomorrow and outright ask her. Telling him her niece had been the victim of domestic violence might be all that was on a police blotter. Not enough. He needed to know so much more.

The night had fully fallen by the time Cam had finished helping to wash up after dinner. "Sure you don't want to come?" he asked Audrey as he pulled on his jacket.

She shook her head. "No, thank you." He watched her straighten her shoulders as she spoke. Apparently that refusal meant a great deal to her. A choice.

Well, good. The night had not only darkened but had decided that adding another touch of winter would be good. He buttoned his jacket and retrieved a flashlight from his truck.

He honestly didn't think Paul Lang, who had only recently been released from a disgustingly short prison sentence, could have found where Audrey had gone. Gladys had been certain neither she nor Audrey had mentioned this house, or locale.

Memory, however, was a shaky thing, often untrustworthy. Gladys and Audrey, either one of them, could have forgotten a passing, absent mention over the years. And Paul was just the kind of man to remember such an important piece of information.

But to get up here so quickly? He'd need money and transportation, neither of which the prison would have given him. No, they gave just enough to eat for a day or two and a bus ticket to his last place of residence and a bus ticket that he couldn't crash in. The guy was seriously hampered. For now. Cam hoped.

Except for the freshening breeze that stirred some early leaves on the cottonwoods, the area around the house was silent. Those cottonwoods, he thought with humor, must be wishing they hadn't grown *any* leaves so early. Their rustling in the breeze sounded more like shivering. He heard an owl's lonely call. He loved owls but didn't think Clyde would agree.

Which brought him around to thinking about Clyde. That damn bird was amazing. He'd heard over the years of African grays becoming able to say simple words and sentences, but Clyde went ever so far beyond that. So much so he didn't seem real.

But given what Clyde could do, Cam had no trouble understanding why Gladys had insisted that Audrey take him away. He'd be a boon to any scientist or huckster. Plenty of reasons to snatch that bird.

Too many. If word of Clyde's talent had gotten out anyhow, then Cam couldn't imagine how many people might be hunting *him*.

God, Gladys, what have you dumped on me? Without any warning or suggestions. Just a mouthy bird, as Audrey said, and a possibly hunted woman.

And he was somehow supposed to protect all this?

THE HEAT WAS turning on frequently now. Clyde had taken himself to his palace to sleep for the night. Which left Audrey standing at the kitchen window staring out into the dark. She should have closed the café curtains but for some reason didn't. Or couldn't.

Maybe because Cam was out there? A shiver passed through her at the idea she could be waiting for a man, any man, for any reason.

Yet there she stood, feeling torn between a past that didn't bear remembering and a future that was a big black hole, offering no plans and no promises.

God, she hoped her new art materials arrived tomorrow. She had enough right now, but the new ones already felt like Christmas gifts. Joy and excitement in cardboard boxes.

At last she closed the café curtains and decided the house, despite the best efforts of the blowing heat, felt as if a chill snaked through it. Going into her bedroom, she paused to look at Clyde, who slept on his perch. That perch part always amazed her. However did he manage to balance that way all night? Well, except for the occasional stirring as he shifted a little bit on the thick sideways pole that was his bed.

She grabbed a cardigan from the foot of her bed, reminding herself to unpack tomorrow. Reminding herself that she needed to assemble Clyde's five-level play toy, kind of like a cat tree, only built for big birds.

Never let it be said that bird lacks for anything, she thought wryly as she left the room.

She stepped into the kitchen just as Cam came from the mudroom, bringing the night's cold with him.

"I'm no weather expert," he said, "but I'd bet on snow by morning."

"Sheesh." Not that it mattered. She wasn't planning on going anywhere.

"Mind if I make coffee? I need a hot drink."

"Help yourself. Or there's that instant hot chocolate in the pantry."

Sitting at the table, she wondered why she hadn't just gone to bed. Sure it was still early, but so? She could have turned on her ebook for the first time in ages. She could have even used the tablet Aunt Gladys had given her recently, one she could draw on with her finger. She didn't have any of the fancy software for art, but her finger would be good for doodling. Then there was the shiny new laptop that Gladys had pressed on her. Barely out of rags, working her way back to a normal world, she was already carrying three electronic items. Amusing.

Cam put a cup of coffee in front of her. "Cream?"

"No, thanks."

She stared down into the dark liquid, watching the steam rise. And, she realized, she had done something important this evening. She had declined an invitation to take a walk. Paul would never have let her do that, but she'd done it anyway. A touch of courage? For the first time in how long?

And nothing bad had happened.

Relaxation eased through her, making the world look a bit brighter. Then she looked at the window and the café curtains. "Cam?"

"Hmm?"

"Why were you worried those windows weren't covered?" Her stomach tightened in expectation, the brief moments of relaxation starting to slip away. He'd practically insisted on getting the curtains today. Immediately.

"Warmth," he answered. "Should have been done a long time ago. Everywhere else this house has insulated curtains, and it struck me they'd be useful here, too. Especially because of Mr. Toasty Toes."

She felt her eyes widen. "Toasty Toes?" Then she got it and started laughing.

"Well, he's so temperature delicate, from what you said about his safe comfort range. You'd think he'd have the sense to fly to a warmer area in the house if he started to get cold, but who needs to risk it?"

Audrey wanted to take umbrage at his description of Clyde but couldn't. Smart bird, yes. Maybe too smart for his own good. But she'd also known a lot of smart people who could be oblivious to the obvious. What's more, ever since he'd come to Gladys, Clyde had been pampered in every way. He might not *know* how dangerous a chill could be.

She studied Cam for a minute. He had his head turned slightly to one side, his gaze distant as if he were thinking. Leaving her free to take him in for the first time. Until that moment, she'd mostly avoided looking at him.

In another time, pre-Paul, she'd have a very different reaction. She could distantly remember when a ruggedly handsome face like Cam's could have made her heart skip beats. He rose to get himself more coffee, and there was time, too, to notice his narrow hips and flat butt. A man who worked hard.

Then, just as he started to turn back to the table, she snatched her gaze away from him and looked down. "I think I'll turn in. Good night."

"Sleep well," he answered.

She scooted around the corner into the bedroom, separated by only one wall from the kitchen. Then she leaned back against the wall with an urgent need to catch her breath. What had just happened? Better yet, what was happening to *her*?

Cam's face floated up before her mind's eye, so good-looking. So friendly.

Then Paul's erased it. His ugly, angry face wiped out everything. Oh, God, how was she ever going to escape?

Chapter Five

There was an old sofa in the living room that Gladys had left behind. Considering it had spent its life in solitude, covered by a sheet, it must have been padded with something durable, because it was still damn comfortable. Cam made his bed there, using an old throw pillow and his sleeping bag.

Comfortable, when all was said and done. But his mind didn't want to let go. Sleep eluded him like a buzzing mosquito. Every time he thought he would slip away from it, it started buzzing in his head again. No point trying to slap it, either.

He rolled onto his side and stared into the darkened room, tempted to open those front curtains over the bay window and let in the moonlight.

He enjoyed moonlight in general, especially those rare nights when it would be at just the right position and height to strike his sleeping eyes and bring him fully awake to its glorious light.

And there was a fingernail moon out there. It couldn't have finished traversing the sky for the night yet.

He threw back the flap of his sleeping bag and padded over to the window, pulling back one of the heavy curtains. The faintest moonlight still silvered the world, a special kind of magic. The kind of night when he often liked to take a lazy ride on his horse.

Then he got to thinking about this Paul guy. Audrey's face revealed nearly every feeling she had, which couldn't have made her life one bit easier with an abuser.

Would the guy really come after her? Like Gladys, he couldn't trust that Paul wouldn't. And Gladys probably had a better measure of the man than he did.

Sticking his fingers in his back jeans pockets, he wondered just how long he'd need to worry about Audrey. Not that he resented having to do it, because he didn't. But when would that day of freedom come for her? When she truly knew that she was safe and able to live again. Could there ever be any guarantee?

Not likely, and that concerned him. A problem like this needed some kind of ending. Would time be able to do that, thinking that if he hadn't come for her after six months or a year, he never would?

That would depend entirely on how deeply fear had scarred her. Those scars might even be deep gouges in her psyche.

Smashing faces wasn't a common urge for him, not by any means, but he'd have liked to smash Paul Lang's. Put the fear of God into him. Power and sadism were the only things a man like Lang acknowledged, and a good taste of his own medicine might change his mind about some things.

But Cam knew better. He'd met a few men like that in his life, totally devoid of even minor empathy or caring. Psychotic in the truest sense. Nothing shocked them out of their natures.

Which meant there was no point in going after Paul that way, satisfying though it might be.

"Hell," he swore under his breath. Keeping an eye on Audrey was turning out to be a little different from his expectation when Gladys had first asked him. Or so it felt now, maybe because he hadn't really thought about it when he agreed.

Other things on his mind. Look after Gladys's niece? Sure. Poor woman must be a wreck and probably needed a little company. Maybe the feeling of being protected.

But he hadn't really registered Gladys's true worry about Paul, maybe because it was too horrible for him to think about. Even though he knew it happened.

But Gladys was sending Audrey hundreds of miles away and...

Yeah. Okay. He'd been looking at the bright side. But since Audrey had arrived here with that dang bird, he'd realized that he hadn't truly been prepared for what Audrey might be facing. What she had every reason to be terrified of. Now that he knew her a little, having put together the pieces Gladys had given him and Audrey's endless fear he faced the truth of her ugly, sordid past. Of how much terror she held in her slender body. More than he ever wanted to see in another human being.

And that was his own damn fault for not having paid closer attention to Gladys. She'd told him. She hadn't force-fed it to him, but she'd told him. And he hadn't really listened.

Gladys had sent Audrey here for her *safety*, not because she needed a change of scenery. Hell, Gladys had made no secret of it. Had thought he'd *get* it.

There was nothing quite like feeling like a total ass. All the pieces had been there, and he'd believed he understood them.

Then, over the last twenty-four hours, it had begun to sink home. Reality had finally switched on.

Audrey was in fear for her life, and Gladys believed she had every right to be.

Duh.

And he had been thinking that it would take Paul a long time to get here and maybe wasn't even thinking about it after six years in prison.

Gladys clearly wouldn't share that Pollyanna attitude and would probably be disappointed in him that he hadn't acknowledged the real depth of concern.

Paul Lang couldn't make it here easily. Paul Lang would probably have other irons to concern him, Audrey long in his past.

Although Paul had had a good long time to nurse a grudge about the woman who had put him in prison. Not a grudge-holding man himself, Cam couldn't imagine carrying an anger or hatred that long. Nursing it. Making it grow. But what else did you have to do in prison? Little enough to erase bad memories and replace them with better ones.

Prison was punishment, pure and simple, not the rehabilitation people had once claimed. In that environment, who could ever change? So, yeah, sitting there for years, a grudge could be honed as if sharpening a knife or making a shiv.

Gladys had been right to send Audrey up here. And he needed to get his head out of his butt. He hadn't been treating this seriously enough. Walking around outside checking for hiding places? Well, he hadn't done a very good check, had he? Walking around the edge of the growth near the house. He needed to check a wider perimeter. He needed to examine all the locks on the doors and windows to make sure they were sturdy.

This might require a whole hell of a lot more than just keeping a general eye on the situation.

Audrey deserved that. So did Gladys, come to that.

He could only be glad that he'd finally awakened to the truth of all this. That he was no longer distracted by a talkative bird and a pretty young woman with a sad face.

Some threats could be real. He hadn't faced one in a long time, but he was facing one now.

Time to saddle up and reach back in time for his military training, something he'd believed he'd never need again. He was going to be depending on a lot of muscle memory in order to keep Audrey safe.

WHEN HE SLEPT, Clyde did so soundly, although like humans he moved during the night, easing his way along the perch an inch or two. Sometimes making quiet sounds as if he were dreaming.

Did birds dream?

Audrey found herself incapable of sleep. Too many changes, she thought. Fighting for freedom from the past the entire time Paul had been in prison. A therapist helping her.

And with one letter, the one telling her that Paul was being released, all her hard work had blown up in her face. All the strength she'd been building and there she was, quivering gelatin again. Small. Defenseless.

Continuing with her counselor hadn't helped. Not at all, not now. Paul was out there.

Then Gladys had stepped in, telling her that she needed to protect Clyde by sending him to her old home. Right. It hadn't just been Clyde that Gladys had been protecting. Audrey knew it, but she'd grabbed the lifeline anyway. Taken the chance to get as far away as she could.

And through her entire journey up here, with every mile she'd traveled, she'd believed she was growing stronger, that she really *was* free at last. Why? Why not before? She didn't want to face the reality that she was just getting farther from Paul. Just because of that.

Then...what? What had happened? Cam, a stranger. Or maybe she just hadn't recovered as much as she'd thought. Because she was feeling small again.

Clyde's scratchy voice, imitating no one but himself, emerged into the darkness. "Are you ever going to sleep, woman?"

"You might try treating me with some respect."

"And you might try letting me sleep. All that sighing and tossing."

"You're selfish."

"Never claimed anything else."

Which was true, Audrey thought. She flipped on the bedside lamp, jammed her feet into some mules and grabbed her dark green sherpa robe to wrap around herself. No place to go except the kitchen. Maybe some cocoa would help.

Despite the heat, the house still felt chilly. That chill made some of her old injuries ache. The ones Paul had given her. The ones that would remind her forever every time she got cold.

She shook that off. Lots of people hurt. Lots had memories of accidents, or whatever, and carried the physical scars. She was unique in no way and needed to remember that.

Then, cocoa made, she sat with her steaming mug and tried to concentrate on the drawing supplies that might come later. Tomorrow at the latest. She hadn't the least idea what she might sketch, given that she wasn't ready to step out of the confines of this house yet.

She'd have to get over that soon. Maybe meet her neighbors. That would be a good thing, making her feel more secure, surrounded by people she knew. But she had only been here three days, not long enough to feel any desire for the company of others. She needed to get herself grounded before she took a chance on other people.

Once, before Paul, she'd been outgoing, with good friends and an enviable social calendar. Where had that young woman gone? Audrey closed her eyes, reaching for those feelings that had once guided her days.

Suddenly, Clyde startled her. He landed on her shoulder and squawked, quite loudly, "Noise outside."

Just as quickly, Cam appeared in the kitchen, looking as if he hadn't slept at all. He didn't bother talking to Audrey but looked straight at Clyde. "Where?"

Clyde flapped his wings, dropping from Audrey's shoulder to grab the back of a chair. "Outside."

"Damn, Clyde. More detail would help." Then Cam gave his attention to Audrey. "I'm going to check on this noise, whatever it is. I'll be right back."

"You hope," Clyde said darkly in a Vincent Price voice.

"Shut up," Cam snapped. "There's a breeze out there. It might just be some tumbleweed."

Audrey didn't want Cam to go. She wanted him inside where she could see him, not out there where he might get hurt and she'd never know it.

As Cam departed through the mudroom, Clyde flew over to land once again on Audrey's shoulder. Then he astonished her nearly out of her fear.

"I'll protect you," he said.

She just shook her head, seeking an internal balance. The snappy part that had once been Audrey. "Getting too big for your talons, huh?"

"Actually," Clyde said stiffly, sounding once again like Gladys, "you're discounting my claws and beak. And my speed."

Maybe she *was* underestimating him, Audrey thought as she tightened with renewed terror. It couldn't be Paul. No way could it be Paul.

And yet she feared that it was.

Cam returned twenty minutes later. "Tumbleweed," he said. "The wind has gotten pretty strong. Clyde has good hearing. I don't think either of us would have heard that."

Good news, Audrey thought. Right? "Thanks so much for checking it out."

"This is one time I wouldn't have minded punching someone, but a bunch of brush just wouldn't have been satisfying." He plopped on the chair facing her. "Can't sleep?"

"I guess not. Clyde complained about me tossing and turning."

Cam reared back a bit and eyed the bird sitting on Audrey's shoulder. "That's not polite."

Clyde chose silence.

"You've convinced me you're not stupid, bird, so I'd be willing to bet you learned some manners along the way. Take care of the woman who takes care of you. Or there could be an accident with your millet."

Clyde couldn't ignore that. "You wouldn't!"

"Last time I looked, depriving you of a snack doesn't constitute bird abuse."

Muttering, Clyde settled.

Cam looked at Audrey. "Someday, when all this settles down, I want you to deny that I ever talked to that bird."

A weary laugh escaped Audrey. "Worried about your sanity?"

"My sanity is just fine. But other people might not think so."

Somehow feeling a whole lot better, Audrey went to bed, and this time Clyde didn't complain about anything at all.

And it *wasn't* Paul out there making noise. It *wasn't* Paul.

Chapter Six

Soon it *would* be Paul. He'd had plenty of time in prison to build up a whole lot of sad feelings for the woman who'd put him there. Where did she get off, lying about him? It was a wife's duty to take care of her man, and she'd provoked him every single time he'd blown up at her. He hadn't wanted to explode like that, hated his memories of the betrayed look in her eyes every time he did.

He hadn't wanted much from her. Just basic care, the kind of care one could reasonably expect from a loving wife. Was it too much to ask for a properly cooked meal? That his clothes were all carefully folded or pressed if they needed it? God, it wasn't like he didn't have to go to work looking neat. Even in his job as a delivery driver. And the hours he had worked out of love for her, often eighteen a day for the overtime. So he could keep her in the best comfort he could provide.

Then she'd proved she didn't love him after all. She went to the police just because he got a little mad. She sure should have understood that. He'd apologized and apologized, but apparently that had meant nothing to her. He had to find her. Nothing was going to stop him. Nothing.

Because he loved Audrey. Loved her with all his heart

and soul. He had to persuade her to return. Love couldn't be kicked to the curb, could it?

But Gladys hadn't seemed to recognize him and was no help at all. She didn't know where Audrey was. That she'd seemed frail and out of it on drugs, she should have been more willing to answer his questions, but she hadn't. Had acted senile. Maybe she was. He nearly begged her, telling her how much he loved her niece, how he only wanted to make her happy.

Gladys had just looked more confused.

The bus from the prison in Cañon City had dropped him right in Colorado Springs. Helpful. But not helpful enough. No, he'd have to do more legwork than he'd thought. He'd been sure that aunt of hers would tell him everything he needed to know. Strikeout. There had to be other people he could ask about Audrey. Before she'd married him, she'd had a lot of friends. People who would want to help her out by bringing Audrey back to him.

He still needed both a car and some cash. Neither would be extraordinarily difficult to get. He hadn't forgotten everything he knew about stealing while he was locked up.

The first step, the one he'd believed would be so easy, hadn't been easy at all. But there were other people who'd been in Audrey's life after she'd put him in prison. After his arrest, he'd learned who they were.

Yeah, he'd get the information he needed, while dealing with the car and cash problem.

ALMOST AS SOON as the door closed behind him, Gladys picked up her phone.

AUDREY DRAGGED HERSELF into the kitchen, following the aroma of coffee. Cam was there, papers again spread out in front of him. "I'll get you your coffee," he offered.

"I need to keep moving."

"That might keep you awake."

She snorted. "I don't think anything is going to *let* me sleep." Coffee in hand, she returned to the table. "Plans for another job?"

"Getting ready to write a proposal for one."

She'd never thought about that. "So you have to propose a job?"

One corner of his mouth lifted. "Jobs don't walk through the door, unfortunately. Think of this as just a complicated estimate. Although it's a lot more."

She eyed the papers. "Looks like it. Are you doing this from an architect's design?"

"Not this time. This time it's a remodel."

Clyde wafted into the room and settled on the back of a chair. "Hungry," he announced.

"Bet you are. Never mind that you always have a full tray of food in your palace."

Clyde eyed her but said nothing.

Cam raised his gaze from his papers. "Maybe he just wants to eat with us."

Audrey hadn't thought of that. Maybe he did, she decided as she went to fill a small custard bowl with some of his mixed food. Why should that surprise her? Because *everything* about Clyde still surprised her. But then, she hadn't been caring for him all that long.

She put the bowl in front of the bird and sat to drink her coffee. "You're going to get cracked seed shells all over those papers," she warned Cam. "He's a messy eater."

Cam shrugged and turned his attention to work.

Clyde dipped his head, bringing up some seeds to crack. Halfway through her cup of coffee, it occurred to her that

Clyde was being too quiet. It seemed to her like he was always talking. He sure should have objected to her description of him as a messy eater.

But before she could look into it, her cell phone rang. "Gladys," she said with delight. "Clyde, you can talk to her after I'm done. Just keep eating."

She swore softly when Clyde hopped over anyway and put his head near the phone, near as her own.

"That must be Clyde you're cussing," Gladys said dryly. "Clyde, you'd better behave for Audrey. She doesn't have to take care of you."

But Audrey immediately picked up on the fact that her aunt didn't sound right. "Aunt Gladys? What's wrong?"

"Some man was here just a short while ago. Said he loved you desperately, that he needed to talk to you because you were his soulmate."

Audrey sucked a deep breath. "Gladys…"

"I know, I know. I didn't tell him one word about you. Acted senile. He was an oily jerk, by the way. Anyway, I wasn't quite awake when he got here, but I was totally awake when he left. So I'm letting you know someone's looking for you."

"But it wasn't Paul?"

"Honey, I wouldn't recognize Paul if he introduced himself. I didn't make your wedding and you told me you didn't want me at the courthouse for his trial, remember? I can only speculate."

Audrey's stomach was sinking like a stone. Of course Gladys wouldn't recognize Paul. He'd made sure they'd never met and had even managed to get Audrey to avoid her aunt. God, what that man had done to her.

"Thanks for letting me know, Aunt Gladys."

"I'm not sure what I just let you know and how helpful it might be. Right now I'm furious with myself. Damn sleeping pill the doctor put me on. If I'd been more awake, I could have found out something about him. Maybe give him a misdirection."

"You did everything you could," Audrey assured her, trying to sound as firm as she could. It was hard. Not only was her stomach sinking, but that crawling, icy fear was climbing its way up her spine again. Maybe she should just take Clyde and vanish somewhere?

But Gladys had sent her here to be safe, and she probably was. As safe as she could be.

What now? she wondered.

Cam spoke. "That wasn't good news."

She lifted her head to look at him. "I don't know what kind of news it is, not for sure. Somebody's looking for me, claiming to be my soulmate. Gladys didn't tell him a thing about where I am."

Cam nodded slowly. "Who was he?"

"She doesn't know. Gladys never met him. If it was Paul, she wouldn't have known because she never met him."

Cam had begun to frown and closed his eyes briefly. "Okay. Six years in prison, right?"

"Right."

She didn't want to think about that. Still couldn't bear to think about it. But she dredged up one thing. "He was there at the hospital, begging me to forgive him. But the nurses and the police wouldn't listen, but they reported my condition. It seems the prosecutor can file charges for domestic violence even if the cops don't. When I asked about it, that's what they told me. Someone had put my file on his desk. I don't know who. A clerk I guess." She trailed away. No. She wasn't going to think about that.

"Even if you don't want to." Cam picked up his pencil and rapped it on the tabletop, a familiar rhythm. After five minutes or so, he looked at Audrey.

"Security cameras," he said. Then picked up his own phone. "Dan? I'm going to need some security cameras out here at Gladys McMahon's house and some help to put them up."

Audrey mentally cut off the last of the conversation, not wanting to hear this, either. She had turned into a coward and hated it.

Then she felt a softness on her cheek and realized Clyde had come over to lay his head against hers. A particular sign of affection.

"I'll keep watch," the bird said. "I'm better than any camera."

Audrey didn't doubt it, but she also wondered when she was going to get enough backbone to start protecting herself. She couldn't spend the rest of her life cowering while others protected her.

She also knew that if she ever got into a dangerous situation with Paul and she had a gun, she was going to shoot him without remorse.

That man wasn't fit to live.

THE GUY BELIEVED he was Audrey's *soulmate*? The mere idea sickened Cam. Talk about obsessed. And how did his treatment of Audrey fit into his insistence of love?

Cam was the first to admit he didn't know human nature that well. Maybe it was possible in some distorted kind of love to harm the object of that love. Maybe obsession was all the cause that was needed.

From what he had seen, men who abused their wives got relatively short sentences, a crime itself to Cam's way of thinking. But Paul had gotten six years. Cam's stomach churned to think how badly Paul must have hurt her. And for a prosecutor to step in without a formal complaint from the victim? Yeah, that was unusual. Evidently the claims that had been ignored for so long had been recorded somewhere and were substantial.

So this had to have been magnitudes beyond that. It was hard to even imagine, and frankly he didn't want to.

Dan showed up an hour later with all the security gear in the back of his truck. The stuff could run on lithium batteries or house current, but given the state of parts of Gladys's house, Cam didn't want to rely on the house power only.

"I figured," Dan said, "that you'd want a camera on every corner of the house, on both floors. Long and close range."

"Good thinking."

Dan gave him a lopsided smile. "Have I ever given you reason to think otherwise? I brought some infrared motion detectors, too, but I didn't know if you'd think they'd be helpful."

Cam gave it a moment's thought. "I'm not really sure. It's not like we have a dog or something large running around in there, but we do have a kinda big parrot."

Dan lifted a brow. "How big is kinda big?"

Cam decided to introduce Dan and Clyde. "Come on. You can tell me if I'm still sane."

Now Dan looked quizzical. "Cam…"

"Trust me."

Inside, Cam found Audrey with a laptop at the kitchen table. She looked up and smiled uncertainly. "Hi."

"This is Dan, my partner. I'd like his help to put up the security cameras. It'll go faster. But I'd like him to meet Clyde. Where is he?"

Audrey bit her lower lip, then shook her head. "I don't want to advertise him, Cam. That could identify my whereabouts. Plus, it might put him at risk."

Cam put his hands on his hips and regarded her. In a way she was right. In another, he didn't agree.

"Audrey, Dan is my partner. We've been partners for nearly fifteen years. I'd trust him with my life. Or with yours."

She met his gaze forthrightly. "Why do you want Dan to meet him?"

"Because I seriously need someone to confirm my sanity. I've spent three days trying to feel as if I haven't fallen down the rabbit hole."

Audrey continued to look at him for another few seconds. Was her mouth twitching? He didn't have to wonder for long, because she burst into laughter, a very nice sound. "The rabbit hole?" Then she laughed some more. Cam had to join her. Even Dan started grinning.

Audrey spoke again when she caught her breath. "I think you've fallen into a Clyde hole."

Which unleashed another laugh from Cam. "It's weird, all right."

Leaning back, still half smiling, Cam watched Audrey reach her decision. Like almost everything else, it was written clearly on her face.

"Clyde?" she called. "Wanna meet the company?"

"You told me to hide." Gladys's voice again.

Clyde came in from the bedroom with a quiet flap of wings to land on Audrey's shoulder.

"It's about time," he said, still sounding like Aunt Gladys. "Not nice to keep me away from the guests."

Dan's jaw dropped.

Cam looked at him. "So I'm not crazy?"

Clyde clucked his tongue several times. "Knowing me doesn't make anyone crazy."

"That's debatable," Audrey said sarcastically. "No one believes you exist."

"Then why am I a secret?"

"Paul," she said, one distinct word. Then she added, "Science labs and sideshows."

Clyde fell silent, then said, "Okay."

Dan still looked gobsmacked.

"Better sit down," Cam said, pulling out a chair for him. "Coffee?"

Dan cleared his throat. "Two fingers of whiskey would be better."

Clyde issued a crackly, squawky laugh. "I *do* have that effect sometimes."

"And I'm clearly not crazy," Cam said.

"I could have told you that," said the irrepressible Clyde.

"That," Cam remarked, "wouldn't be any help at all."

Clyde didn't move for a couple of seconds, then lifted off Audrey's shoulder with a flutter of wings. "Sayonara."

For several interminable minutes, the kitchen remained nearly as silent as a grave except for a click as the coffeepot turned on its heating element.

Then Dan cleared his throat. "I *did* see and hear that, right?"

Cam answered. "Why do you think I wanted you to verify this whole thing? Really, that bird is overwhelming."

Dan nodded. "I knew they could speak, but nothing like that."

"Apparently Clyde is unique." Both men looked at Audrey.

She shrugged. "He's unique, all right, but don't ask me to explain it. African grays are notoriously smart and evidently can talk more than most parrots. But I don't think 'more than most' covers Clyde."

"Nothing could," Cam said, shrugging his shoulders. "Okay, I'm officially down the rabbit hole. Wanna get going on that security stuff, Dan? After your coffee?"

Dan looked as if he'd be thrilled to get outside to the normal world again. Cam definitely understood, although he realized he was already adapting to that damn bird.

Dan stood immediately. "No coffee, thanks." Four steps and he was out the mudroom door.

THE CAMERA INSTALLATION went on throughout the afternoon. Audrey was surprised by how many Cam and Dan were putting up: upstairs, every corner. Downstairs, every corner plus extras near outside doorways.

Then Dan took off with his truck, and Cam joined her in the kitchen. She still sat at her laptop.

"Whatcha doing?" he asked.

She snorted. "Tracking a delivery as if I were a bloodhound on the scent."

"Eager for something?"

"Art supplies," she admitted. "I need some additional stuff. They're supposed to be here today."

"Gladys never mentioned you're an artist."

"I sell some."

"Doing art, especially under these circumstances, sounds like a great idea."

"Feels like one." Anything to distract her from thoughts

of Paul. Anything to resist fearing he might actually find her. Trying not to remember that he *was* looking for her.

"What about the security cameras? You put up a lot of them."

"Enough to keep the entire area covered. I'm going to get you a monitor so you can watch if you ever feel uneasy. And then tomorrow I've got another job, one I can do myself."

"What's that?"

"Protection against broken windows."

Audrey drew a sharp breath. "That's a whole lot." Thinking about all of it gave her a faint sense of claustrophobia. Surrounded by cameras and God knew what? Like being trapped.

"You can turn the whole thing off," he said, as if he sensed her reaction. "You're not stuck inside by the alarms. Or you can turn it off and set it to turn on once you're outside—the safest option, in my opinion. Regardless, those cameras will always be recording."

"My God, this must be the same kind of security they have at the White House!" And it must have cost a fortune. But she didn't know how to ask.

"One thing you'll have to get used to?"

She arched a brow at him.

"You'll hear a chime every time an exterior door opens."

This whole security thing seemed to be growing fast. She thought Gladys had asked him to keep an eye on her, not to build her a fortress. "How long is this going to go on?" Being shut in. Being surrounded by observation.

"I wish I could answer that."

She drew another sharp breath and saw absolute, hard-edged determination in his eyes. "That might be a long time."

"Maybe not as long as you think."

Then he rose. "I'm going to get that monitor in here and check the alignment of all those cameras."

Alone in the kitchen once more, Audrey felt a hunger pang for the first time in what felt like forever. Thank goodness she'd thrown all those frozen meals into the cart yesterday.

She lifted her hands from the keyboard and looked at them. They were trembling like leaves. The way she felt inside. Anxiety ruled.

Then she made herself stand up and go to the freezer. Distraction. The world right now didn't hold enough of it for her.

Then she felt a flutter, a movement of air, and her favorite—well, sometimes favorite—bird landed on her shoulder. "What's for dinner?" Clyde wanted to know, using his own voice instead of borrowing someone else's.

"You're getting the usual. I don't want to make you sick."

Clyde edged closer. "I see frozen blueberries…"

Damn, he was reading bags now? She looked at the bottom of the freezer and saw the picture sticking out. Relief. "Okay, a few berries for you tonight."

"Millet?" Clyde purred. Literally purred. Evidently *cat* had come into his list of voices. At least it wasn't a yapping dog.

"One or the other. Don't argue, damn it. You don't want to get too fat to fly."

"That's an offensive term."

"Okay, I agree. I hate the word myself. But you don't want to get too *heavy* to fly."

Clyde muttered, then stuck his head beneath his wing.

The frozen lasagna looked big enough for two, even with a large guy like Cam joining them. She popped it in the oven, wishing she had thought to get some garlic bread. She had the stuff to make a nice side salad, though.

But she had over an hour before the lasagna would be done, so she sat at her end of the table and looked at the laptop again. At least she was able to get internet out here. She'd been half afraid she wouldn't. Not that she used social media. Paul had cut that out of her life, too. Still, it gave her access to the outside world.

After a while, she looked up and realized Clyde was still with her. On a whim, she asked a question that had been bugging her. "You're too smart. How'd you get this way?"

Clyde preened a feather. "Most people think parrots are merely mimics."

Audrey caught her breath. "There are more like *you*?"

"Must be. Except most of them have the sense to stay quiet. I should have paid attention to that, but I had so much fun talking to Gladys. I would be safer."

He might have a point. She knew what Gladys feared, and understood it, but now Cam and Dan both knew as well.

Then there was Paul. He wasn't supposed to know she was here. She was positive that she'd never mentioned where her aunt had lived. But a doubt niggled anyway.

She could hear Cam doing something upstairs and felt the chill creep along her spine again. Yeah, he was renovating and Gladys had asked him to keep an eye on her. But it appeared a lot of work had taken a back seat.

Then she looked at Clyde. She hadn't really thought about it, but now she needed to protect Clyde as well as herself. She knew all the worries Gladys had for the bird's safety, but neither of them had counted Paul.

She hated to think what Paul might do to Clyde. A man so jealous...

She shuddered. Jealousy. A dangerous emotion.

CAM WAS WORKING on the outside lights when a sheriff's Suburban pulled up. He climbed down from his ladder in time to greet Gage Dalton, the sheriff himself, a man with such a complicated history it was a wonder he'd survived. The shiny burn scar covering one side of his face must make every look in the mirror a reminder of the family he'd lost years ago to a car bomb. A bomb that had left him nearly disabled himself. Since then, he'd put together a new life with the librarian, known as Miss Emma, and their adopted son, Justin.

He shook Cam's hand, giving him that patented half smile that still tugged a lot of hearts in a county that had once called him "hell's own archangel."

Gage's visit wasn't unexpected, since Cam had called him yesterday with questions about Audrey's situation. It was clear Audrey wasn't going to tell him a damn thing, and if he was to look after her, he had to know something.

"Been a while," he said to Cam. "Guess you're staying out of trouble." The two of them had had a couple of run-ins when Cam had been in his midteens.

Cam chuckled. "You could say that. How's Emma?"

"A whirling dervish trying to bring the library into the twenty-first century. There's a pretty even tug-of-war, I guess, between people who still want regular books, people who want electronic books and kids who think everything should be plugged in."

"Now, that I can imagine. Sounds like a heckuva balancing act."

"It is." Gage leaned back against the side of his Suburban. "So, what's this about wanting records of this old case in Colorado Springs?"

Cam had made a brief call about that, leaving a message just yesterday. "Gladys McMahon asked me to keep an eye on her niece while I'm remodeling. The thing is, Audrey—Audrey Lang—was married to a guy who abused her so badly the prosecutor filed the charges himself and the guy got sent up for six years. He's out now."

Gage gave a low whistle. "Not good."

"I wanna know one thing," Cam said. "Why this deal in the record about the prosecutor filing the charges himself. Isn't that unusual?"

"Sure. But in domestics, no matter how bad the damage, if the victim denies the assailant had anything to do with it, withdraws her charge, whatever, sometimes the prosecutor will go ahead anyway. If it's egregious enough, if history builds the case for him."

"God!" Cam put his hands on his hips, tipped them to one side, and stared off into the wide blue sky and the snow-capped purple mountain range.

Still trying to absorb what Gage had just hinted at, he said, "I know how much value a restraining order has. Might as well be toilet tissue. But I need to know what I might be facing here if he locates Audrey."

Gage nodded slowly, looking up at the cameras. "I see you're doing the security thing to the nines."

"Which is all well and good, but Audrey can't stay locked up in that house indefinitely. She needs to be able to do some shopping, be self-reliant. Get out and meet some people so she doesn't feel alone and isolated. This is just exchanging one prison for another."

Gage nodded again. "I take your point. And you need to know what the two of you might be up against." With a wince from a back that never stopped paining him, Gage moved and opened the door of the Suburban. He handed Cam a thick manila envelope. "Here it is. Charges filed, her hospital records, court testimony…" He paused then continued. "There's also some photos you might not want to look at. In a separate envelope."

Cam took the file gingerly, wondering how Audrey would feel if she knew he'd invaded her privacy this way. Sure, it was all public record, but that wasn't proof against a sense of invasion.

Hell.

He and Gage chatted for a few more minutes. Before leaving, Gage told Cam, "You need anything, holler. I'm serious."

Holding the file, Cam watched Gage drive away, a cloud of dust lifting behind him.

He couldn't say why he was getting so worried. Why he was elevating this beyond keeping an eye on Audrey.

Well, yeah, there was a big red flag. Gladys had called to warn Audrey that Paul might be looking for her.

How many red flags did he need?

LIFE SETTLED INTO a routine. Cam left for a few hours every day to keep up with his business. When he did so, he warned Audrey to keep an eye on the monitors and not to shut down the security system while he was gone. Then when he came back, he spent a lot of hours working on Gladys's house.

She was agreeable to that. Even if the thought of Paul getting within a dozen miles of her was enough to make her go cold.

But what had totally changed was her reaction to Cam. He no longer seemed to carry that male threat that she'd learned years ago from Paul.

He'd escaped her personal ring of fire. She didn't know how or why. She certainly heard him cuss and bang things from time to time, but with Cam that didn't seem at all threatening. It sounded like a guy at work having occasional bursts of frustration.

She never dreamed that some of the frustration he was expending had a lot to do with that, a lot to do with a need to wrap his hands around Paul's throat.

How could she even guess when he was always so pleasant to her?

Clyde seemed to have settled into his new space. Not a whole lot of complaints anymore, which was a relief. She'd begun to wonder if anything would please that bird.

In fact, though, Clyde seemed to have reverted to ordinary bird state. He sang sometimes, a beautiful sound escaping him, making her smile with pleasure. He clacked his beak, though she couldn't always tell why.

Unfortunately, he often stood at the kitchen window when the curtain was open. She couldn't miss his wistfulness, guessing that he wanted to be out there soaring through those blue skies. She could understand that. Her own soul felt that way.

Chapter Seven

Three days later, a large flat monitor hung from one wall in the kitchen. With a touch of a button, Audrey could flip the view from upstairs to downstairs cameras. She also had a smaller monitor in her bedroom, which Clyde complained about until she asked if he wanted his palace covered at night. The bird shut up.

Cam had managed to read Audrey's file in the late hours when she slept, and his stomach actually heaved at the amount of damage he saw had been done to that woman's body. He had no doubt why the prosecutor had decided to file the charges himself without a complaint.

Domestic or not, this was the worst kind of battery you might see in a late-night street robbery or attempted murder. The kind of thing for which charges were filed simply on the evidence.

But in Audrey's case, medical professional after professional had recorded her explanations of her injuries, and she'd told them none of them had to do with Paul.

The last one, though, the one that had put him in prison, couldn't be explained as some kind of accident. Too much, too horrific. He'd claimed someone else had attacked her, but fingerprints and DNA proved his lie. That and all the times she'd been in the hospital before created a picture of escalating violence.

And six years was all he got, Cam thought, a wave of fury ripping through him. Six years. He had to believe they'd have given him more if they could have. To Cam's way of thinking, Paul should have been charged for every single hospitalization.

But he hadn't been, and now that he was out, Gladys was worried that he was looking for Audrey, and Cam's thinking that this might be a relatively easy assignment when he'd agreed to it now tasted like ashes in his mouth.

Man, didn't he know enough about things like this? About men coming after their ex-wives years later? And this guy probably had a real burr under his saddle, feeling that Audrey was the cause of his jail time.

He should never have underestimated the possibilities here and wondered now how he could have been such a fool. And now he had to worry about that damn parrot as well. Although that bird was growing on him. Seemed to have settled down into a more reasonable quiet.

Audrey had received her sketching supplies and was enjoying them more every hour. Clyde, of course, had more than one opinion about the sketch she did of him, but overall, when he could have been truly nasty, his comments were few and not entirely critical.

"I look good in black and white," he said at one point.

"You *are* black and white except for those red tail feathers."

"I'm gray," Clyde remarked, then dropped it.

Which was a good thing, Cam thought, because it must be hard for an artist to have someone right on her shoulder watching and criticizing the whole time she was trying to draw.

Now he was wondering if he could persuade Audrey to come out of the house with him. God, she must need a change of scenery, if only to shop. Or maybe she'd let him invite the neighbors over. The Redwings were a nice couple, only one house up the street. Only problem was that Valerie was still working out of Gunnison and the two were meeting somewhere in the middle distance.

Cam snorted, wondering how those two made a go of such a mixed-up schedule.

Or maybe Jenna and Kell. They both had nice dogs, including Kell's K-9, and maybe Audrey would like that.

"How are you with dogs?" he asked Audrey.

"The question is, how is *Clyde* with dogs?"

Cam hadn't been thinking of that, but now he did. "Well, the dogs are both very well-trained. Kell's dog was a military K-9."

Audrey lifted her head from her sketch to look at him. "Why are you asking? Or are you plotting something?"

He almost grinned at the suggestion. "I thought maybe you'd like a break from this isolation. Meet some people. Up to you."

He *had* been plotting, he realized. Trying to do something nice and instead may have put his foot in it big-time. She might be annoyed that he'd been coming up with all this without consulting her. And she'd have every right.

"Just kinda thinking out loud," he hastened to say, which was also true. "Of course, you make any decisions. I was just wondering about people nearby."

"I'll think about it."

Which left him wondering if she'd gone through the last

six years of her life while Paul was in prison without any friends at all. Was she that introverted? If so, was it natural or learned?

He had an awful lot to learn about this woman, then wondered why he should bother. Somehow this mess would be taken care of and he'd go back to his business and his own life. To working hard every day and finishing off with a couple of beers with a few friends at the Watering Hole.

Yeah, it was a good life. And now he might have a great big gaping hole in it. Audrey. When she left, because she probably would. Maybe the amazing part was that he didn't mind it.

"Hell," he muttered under his breath, then said, "I'm going outside to take some measurements. Still trying to decide if it'd be wiser to put up aluminum clapboard or wood. I know which would be cheaper."

"Which means you've already made up your mind." The smile she gave him was almost saucy.

"I guess I have," he admitted.

"So how do you get all that clapboard?"

"I order it and have it delivered here. Me and a couple of other guys can get it up pretty fast. But I warn you, there's going to be a lot of noise. Trucks. Heavy equipment, hammering."

"I can live."

"Good. After that, I'll move inside and start making repairs in here. Gladys wants it all up to snuff."

He was just about to rise when he saw Clyde perched on the kitchen windowsill, staring out into a sky that was so blue it was nearly blinding.

"What's with him?" he asked, nodding toward the bird.

"He wants to be out there flying. I don't blame him.

But the hawks, the eagles and the owls... Frankly, Cam, I couldn't stand it if all I saw fall from the sky was a mouthful of feathers."

"I get it," Clyde answered querulously. "I get it. And in case you haven't noticed, I'm smart. But I can still dream."

"Ouch," Cam said. Audrey closed her eyes tightly and looked as if she might cry.

Clyde suddenly lifted from the sill and with a strong wave of his wings crossed the distance to land on Audrey's shoulder.

He pressed his feathery head to her cheek. "Hard on everyone. I get that, too."

Then he turned his golden gaze on Cam. "Except for you."

Audrey spoke. "Clyde, be polite."

"He's not running for his life," Clyde snapped, then rose and disappeared into the bedroom.

Audrey looked at Cam. His weather-hardened face revealed nothing. "I'm so sorry."

He waved a hand, dismissing it. "Clyde's right. Besides, you couldn't possibly be responsible for anything that damn bird says. Never has the phrase *mind of his own* been more true. I just wonder about him."

"How so?"

Cam tipped his head a little, looking thoughtful. "I read up on the talking parrots. Pretty smart, all right. Like the one who taught his companion how to spell *color* when the younger bird kept messing up, no prompting, just impatience from the older bird." He shook his head.

"I've read about that, too. Any questions, well, Clyde kind of deals with them."

"Clyde is still extraordinary. No explaining him, no believing in him unless he squawks something in your face." Cam snorted. "I can see why Gladys was afraid he might be stolen. Somebody might give him right back, though. Pain in the neck with his commentary."

Clyde's voice came from the bedroom. "I heard that."

A guffaw escaped Cam, and his eyes danced. "That kind of thing. And what about your drawing? What's wrong with that, for Pete's sake? Looks like Clyde to me."

"I've been thinking about that." Audrey turned her sketchbook around so Cam could see it easily. "Clyde thinks he's all gray except for his tail feathers."

"He is, isn't he?"

"Sure. But he also has shadows, and what gives his feathers and head their definition? Shadows. Without them he wouldn't look like Clyde. Heck, he wouldn't look like anything at all except a gray outline."

As she spoke, Cam's perception of Audrey's sketch shifted, and he saw what she meant. "I'll be damned."

"If you look even closer, you'll see there's not a line in here. Just shadows."

Cam stared, growing increasingly impressed. "You've got a lot of talent."

"Talent is really nothing but a lot of hard work."

"Then why aren't I a great artist, too?"

She giggled, the sweetest sound he'd ever heard.

JUST OVER THREE hundred miles away, Paul Lang found himself a suitable vehicle for his trip. A battered old pickup, rust-ridden and well splotched from rust paint. Nothing to stand out.

But it must have been preserved for its engine, sitting there on the back of a junk lot. That engine purred, man.

Probably five thousand bucks to install it in another vehicle, but worth every penny. Tires stolen from totaled cars of newer vintage. *"Go, baby, go."*

He had his wheels. Now he needed some money and a five-gallon gas can. The money was easy. A lot of stores were open at night and didn't make a deposit till morning. Trusting jerks. Made it easy for Paul to pick up a few hundred. Then the gas can at the nearest overnight. Ha!

He was feeling pretty damn good when he at last drove that heap of junk away from the lot. Yeah. It was all good.

One of her so-called friends had told him she was in a place in Wyoming. Except that he still didn't have Audrey's exact address and was aching for her like a lovesick cow. He wanted her back. He'd beg her to come back.

But Wyoming was a pretty big place. Not that many people there but a lot of square miles of land. Still, considering how far he'd managed to come since he'd left Cañon City behind, he had every confidence that he was smart enough to find his wife.

Often enough he closed his eyes, recalling Audrey's beauty, the silkiness of her skin beneath his hands, her wonderful scent. He yearned for her, loved her and couldn't understand why she'd left, why she'd hadn't visited him in prison.

Paul needed a lot of answers to a lot of questions. But first he'd put that smile back on her face, the one he'd seen often when they first married.

He'd never understand why it went away.

Chapter Eight

"If you come outside with me," Audrey warned Clyde, "you stay under the porch roof and go no farther than your perch. Got it?"

"Yeah, yeah." The bird was eager to get out there.

Audrey was scared half to death.

Cam had insisted on screening the entire porch. "We're about to go into mosquito season, and you ought to be able to enjoy your time out here."

Because of that, she felt obligated to sit on that damn porch even if she was afraid to. Despite the fact that with Paul out there somewhere, she'd have gladly stayed inside forever. He'd break her. He'd broken her once before. But she wasn't the only one involved.

There was Clyde.

Cam spoke to the bird. "There's netting out there to protect you, but you'd better not tear at it with your claws."

Then he exited the house.

"Does he think I'm stupid?" Clyde asked.

"You can be at times."

Which put Clyde on a slow burn, but he didn't make any additional comments.

But feeling emotionally naked or not, Audrey gritted her

teeth and went out to the big front porch with Clyde on her shoulder. It was still chilly, so she wore her jacket but didn't expect to be outside for long.

Clyde's claws dug gently into her shoulder as he danced back and forth impatiently while she carefully lowered herself to an Adirondack chair. Instantly she felt uneasy, as if she couldn't get out of chair fast if she needed to. She wanted to be sitting upright, for ease of escaping.

Ridiculous, she told herself. More than once. As well cleared as the land was right around the house, she could see anyone approaching.

And Cam was out there hammering away with his partner, Dan, putting the last of the siding in place. Vinyl, Cam had decided. Less maintenance, longer durability.

None of which mattered to Audrey. She'd been sent here to keep an eye on things. In reality, though, she'd been sent to hide.

She honestly wondered if there *was* any place to hide.

Clyde took the opportunity to fly around the spacious porch several times before settling on his freestanding wood perch. A perch that needed frequent cleaning, but it made the bird happy. One of his favorite places and not as much of a pain to clean as his palace.

As her thoughts returned to Gladys and Clyde preened his feathers, Audrey remembered the conversation with her aunt when word came that Paul was out of prison.

Audrey had been shaking with the news. Couldn't stop shaking. Gladys's brown eyes sparked with anger.

For a long time, few words passed between them, most of them from Gladys, who kept saying, "We'll find a way to deal with this."

Audrey had felt trapped. She couldn't even go around to sell her paintings and sketches. No money coming in.

And what about her friends? She didn't want to lose them either, not after all these years of emerging from her shell long enough to build those friendships. They were priceless.

But terror was taking charge. She knew exactly what she'd face if Paul got hold of her again.

Then Gladys had said, "I have a plan."

Now here, Audrey sat nervously on a porch slightly shaded from a brilliant afternoon sun that ought to make her feel good. It had before, once upon a time. A glance at Clyde told her all was well in that department.

For the first time in a long time, she wished she could be less of an introvert. But would that change her at heart? She'd always found it a bit exhausting to be with other people for very long. Even her new friends. Nothing about them, all about her. Reaching out was exhausting. Like an emotional marathon, although she didn't try to completely avoid it.

Sighing, she tipped her head back, closed her eyes and let the chilly breeze wash over her. At some level it seemed to freshen her. Thank God.

Then Clyde spoke. "I'm watching out for you."

The words snapped her eyes open, and she sat up as best she could in that chair. "What are you talking about?"

"Gladys." The bird seemed content with that and began to whistle a surprisingly beautiful song, given the scratchiness of his voice by comparison.

Gladys? Then she remembered that Clyde had been in the room the entire time she and Gladys had discussed the situation. At Gladys's place. That Gladys had a friend she was going to ask to keep an eye on Audrey.

So the bird had heard. And decided to join the security crowd. But then she remembered when Clyde had listed all the ways he had of inflicting damage on an opponent.

Sheesh, had she missed that, too? That Clyde could be dangerous? Was she skipping over everything? Remembering only what she wanted to?

That was a chilling thought.

"Audrey?"

She turned and saw Cam approaching, tool belt still hanging from his waist.

"Dan is going to run into town and get dinner. Maude's. Can you give us your order?"

"Will Dan join us?" She had to be polite. She knew Dan was nice enough, but he was a relative stranger. Still, he'd been working hard on Aunt Gladys's house and seemed always ready to accept a cup of coffee. Only a dinner invitation would do.

Cam halted at the foot of the porch steps. "He can't. He wants to get home to his family, and I can finish the work here."

"And he probably doesn't want to sleep in his truck anymore."

Cam flashed a grin. "That cab-over camper of his has heat. And a minuscule kitchen. He's been doing pretty good. Anyway, he's offered, and I'm taking him up on this. So what fatty, delicious fried things do you want? And what kind of pie?"

After giving Cam a short list of items that appealed to her, she watched him go back to work. The chill in the wind was beginning to feel ominous.

Her head snapped around, and she looked at Clyde, who appeared unusually serene but was also puffed up like a cotton ball, trying to keep warm. "We gotta get you inside, Clyde. Too frigid for you out here. Why didn't you tell me you were so cold?"

Clyde grumbled deep in this throat but offered no objection. He flew around the porch once more then landed on Audrey's shoulder. "This deserves a millet stick," he grumbled in her ear. "After all, you self-important humans are getting some food."

In about a half hour, Dan returned with a couple of large brown bags that emitted mouthwatering aromas. Overcoming her natural tendencies, Audrey invited him in. He answered with a surprisingly shy smile. "The wife and kids are waiting. But thanks, Audrey."

Then he drove off. Audrey felt guilty as sin as she watched the inevitable dust cloud rise and then settle behind Dan's truck.

She'd been awful, she realized too late. These two men had been working on this house for just over two weeks and she hadn't offered even the most basic hospitality. Introversion was no excuse for rudeness.

Cam opened the two bags on the kitchen table and began setting out containers. Audrey brought out plates, thinking that just because they were eating out of containers, there was no reason not to do it politely.

"Dan bought the whole damn menu," Cam remarked. "I wonder what Maude thought."

A smile creased Audrey's face. "That he was buying for an entire work crew?"

Cam laughed. "You probably got that right."

Maude, owner of the City Café, which everyone called Maude's. A local icon, loved despite her habit of banging dishes on tables and speaking roughly to clientele. Sometimes even ordering for them when they hesitated too long. It was even rumored that when the old sheriff, Nate Tate, had been on a diet and had come into Maude's only for coffee, she had nonetheless slammed a plate of his favorite pie down in front of him and told him not to get scrawny. The whole town had apparently found this amusing.

Audrey surprised herself by remembering so much from her early childhood vacations spent here. That surely was a good thing in spite of her frequent nightmares about the house. Nightmares that made no sense at all.

She sighed, just in time to have Clyde land on her shoulder. "Warm?" she asked him.

"Enough," he answered tartly. He watched intently as she set the table and began to lay out the foam boxes of food. Cam returned from the bathroom, where he had gone to wash up, and eyed the bird.

"Let me guess," he said. "Clyde wants our dinner, too."

"He may think so," Audrey answered. "Nibbles, if anything."

"Selfish," Clyde judged.

"You got that right. Besides, I don't want Gladys to kill me."

Instead of retorting sharply, Clyde remained silent. Great, thought Audrey. The talkative bird was being quiet. Was he sick? "Clyde? You need to go to the vet?"

"I'm fine," he answered sharply. "And you two are boring."

"Ouch," said Audrey.

Cam merely shook his head. "Eat" was his only response.

That was one direction Audrey had no trouble following. There was a club sandwich, which she loved, plenty of steamed broccoli and fries for those who needed more.

Audrey initially thought she wouldn't but proved hungry beyond her own belief.

"This is so good," she remarked. "I'll have to thank Dan for this."

"Hey, we're all suckers for Maude's food."

Including Clyde, it seemed. Audrey fed him small bits, taking care, and the bird gobbled them down. Then, as it was his bedtime, the parrot headed for his bed.

"No argument like you'd have with a kid," Cam remarked.

"None," Audrey answered.

But her thoughts were drifting elsewhere. The curtains over the kitchen window were still open, and late twilight was creeping in.

Audrey suddenly could think of nothing except Paul. Gladys had made it clear that Paul was looking for her. If he located one of her closest friends, he would discover that she had come to Wyoming. Maybe even the more specific location of Conard City. Then what? Finding her would be as easy as plucking a green cherry off the tree out front.

Maybe easier. Uneasiness filled her, driving waking nightmares that might never be erased, or even faded, by the passage of years.

For all she knew, Paul might be out there right now, staring in that window. Waiting for Cam to leave so she would be alone and defenseless. That was important to Paul, separating Audrey from anyone who might see or might defend her.

Well, he'd be able to see that she was alone very soon. Except could Paul tell that Cam was remaining to sleep on the living room floor? Possible.

Then, without realizing it, she cussed.

"What is it?" Cam asked, his voice quiet. Like dark velvet, trying, she realized, not to upset her.

"Paul," she answered finally, hating to reveal her weakness.

She saw him tense.

"Did you see something?" he asked.

Jerkily, she shook her head. "Just a ridiculous feeling."

He stood and went to the windows, where he closed the curtains. Then he came to squat beside Audrey and astonished her by laying an arm across her shoulders. She froze instantly.

"You'll be safe," he murmured quietly. "That's why I'm here, Audrey. To look after you."

Then, unbelievably, she felt a softening deep within her. Almost helplessly she turned her face and let it rest against his shoulder. Closing her eyes. Giving herself up to a snug security she hadn't felt in years.

But it was all a lie, wasn't it? Another man taking advantage of her? Seeing her weakness that made her an easy target? Trust easily taken advantage of, a trust she gave him by leaning into him.

Fear zapped her and she abruptly sat upright, removing all contact from Cam. She was no longer an easy target, no longer anywhere near as trusting. Lately, she'd begun to believe that Clyde was the only being she could trust, mainly because he shot his mouth off without a single inhibition.

Sitting there with her eyes closed, tremors racing throughout her body, she reminded herself of the threat men posed. The threat she apparently had no ability to detect until it was too late.

She heard, rather than saw, Cam straighten. His knees popped a little as he did that. Arthritis. Probably. A very human trait. Not a monster's. But that didn't make her feel any better.

Cam rounded the table. She heard him pull his chair back. It creaked, too, as he sat in it.

"I'm sorry I crossed your boundaries," he said after a minute. "I didn't make you feel very good."

It was true, but there was another side to what had happened: the softening within her. The feeling of cozy security. Incredibly, she had forgotten she could feel that way. She wanted to tell him it was okay because she wanted to feel it again, but the words stuck in her throat.

Slowly, he pushed dessert across the table toward her. "Anything you don't eat that parrot is going to feed on, I guarantee you."

An unsteady laugh managed to emerge from Audrey. "Fruit. Even more of a temptation."

"So he doesn't have a problem with sugar?"

Audrey shook her head and reached for a fork. "You ever seen a bear get into a bee's nest? Lots of calories. I bet we'd get quite a show if we dumped a box of doughnuts outside. Except deer. They want apples."

"Still sweet," Cam pointed out. "Still surprises me with that bird."

"Well, he does prefer his millet."

And just like that, Cam had swung the conversation around to easy and safe. Casual. Audrey felt a shaft of admiration for him.

Then she decided to risk all that and dig deeper. "So how'd you get into construction, Cam? The whole thing I see you doing now. And there's more, right?"

Cam shrugged a shoulder. "I was always handy. Came natural, you could say. I loved working with my hands. Creating things that other people could use. I don't know how to explain it, really. Job, meet Cam. It worked."

"Following your dad, maybe?"

Cam shook his head sharply. "Some things you don't want to admit, Audrey."

"I've got a storage room full. You don't have to answer. Sorry I pried."

Cam sighed. "He wasn't a murderer or something. He was a 24/7 alcoholic, that's all."

Audrey looked down at the pie and suddenly thought it was nauseating. She pushed it aside. "That must have been hell, growing up."

Cam tightened his lips. "Believe it or not, my mother turned it into a good lesson. There was no end to her remarks about how alcohol had turned my father into that man. Then, after she left him, she pointed out more than once that alcohol had cost him his family. His wife. His son."

He shook his head a bit. "I can still remember the way her eyes bored into mine as she said it. Trying to brand it on my brain or soul, I guess."

Audrey pushed her plate to one side of the table and put her chin in her cupped hand. "Your mother sounds magnificent."

"She sure knew where her limits were."

Audrey's stomach plunged. She clearly hadn't known her own limits, unlike Cam's mother. She'd been a weakling.

Disturbed, she pushed her chair back roughly and began to pace the house—at least the small part he'd readied. Weakling. She hadn't even had the strength to press charges against Paul on her own. No, she'd lied for him out of terror. It had taken a prosecutor to push the case against Paul.

One who had forced her for the very first time to look at all the photos of the physical abuse Paul had heaped on her.

Yeah, that had broken the last tie she felt for Paul, but how long had it taken to start feeling free? Nearly six years. Disgusting.

She froze abruptly as she heard an unusual sound from outside. It came again, but she couldn't identify it. "Cam?"

Her voice was barely little more than a croak. Amazingly, he appeared beside her in an eye blink, or so it seemed.

"Hear it?" she whispered.

He stood perfectly still for a few beats until the sound came again. "I want to look around outside. You get yourself back in the bedroom with Clyde."

"Clyde?" she asked blankly, wondering if Cam thought the bird might be threatened.

"Because that damn bird will screech as loud as Gabriel's horn on judgment day if someone gets in. And I'll hear him."

Now *that* made sense. Audrey did as ordered, creeping back to the bedroom. His Highness Clyde awoke instantly. A single yellow eye greeted her.

"What's wrong?" the bird asked in a stage whisper.

"Don't know yet if anything is. Cam's checking around outside."

"That Cam's a good man," Clyde replied, as if his judgment mattered.

Audrey had long since quit wondering about how far down the rabbit hole she had fallen when she met Clyde. Of course he'd make a judgment about Cam. Why the hell not? He was already too smart for his britches, and this just seemed another step.

"What do you think of *me*?" Audrey asked, annoyed but

also trying to forget Cam creeping around the dark out there and the possibility of him getting hurt.

Clyde's answer to her irritable question brought tears to her eyes. "Gladys loves you." As simple as that. Beginning and end. *Gladys loves you.*

Audrey tried not to sniffle and wished for a tissue. Almost as if he read her mind, Clyde flew to the bedside table, then fluttered before her holding a tissue.

"You're too smart," Audrey said, taking the tissue to wipe her face.

"Of course," Clyde answered agreeably.

Then silence fell. Even Clyde seemed to sense the threat in the moment. Cam was out there in the dark, investigating an unusual sound that could be anything at all.

That probably *was* nothing at all. She'd have started to feel ridiculous except that Cam had heard it, too, and had gone outside to check on it.

But such a strange sound. Not like a branch or brush blowing against the siding. Indefinable, which meant nothing at all, really, but might mean anything or everything.

If Audrey wanted one thing for her future, it was to be free of this crippling fear. She plopped down on the edge of the bed and waited impatiently, chewing her lower lip. God, whatever it was, she prayed it didn't threaten Cam in some way.

Clyde returned to his cage, but Audrey could tell he wasn't sleeping. His perch continued to rock in a steady rhythm. She wondered if that soothed him, like rocking a baby in a cradle. Figuring that if she asked, she'd only get some kind of withering response and not the truth.

Sometimes she wondered just how much truth Clyde

told as a rule. Smart mouth, sure. A line for every occasion, it seemed.

A shudder passed through her as she suddenly recalled her strange nightmares about this house. Nightmares without any point.

CAM FOUND NOTHING outside to worry about. A light dusting of snow had coated the world since nightfall. Enough that footprints would surely have been visible as they bared the grass beneath. Grass that had just begun to turn green.

But there were no footprints out there that couldn't be accounted for by a small rodent, a prairie dog or even a rabbit. No human imprints.

That sound had been weird all right, though. A raccoon scratching against the side of the house, maybe. But not very much.

Still, finding nothing, he had to go back inside and tell Audrey exactly that: nothing. He didn't know if that would make her feel better or worse.

He also wondered if there was any way on earth to make her feel safe again. Appalling that one man's abuse could leave Audrey feeling unsafe forever.

But why should that surprise him? She clearly had PTSD from her experience. That could take years to diminish. Or it could vanish relatively quickly. Maybe Audrey had started to recover while Paul was in prison, then *slam!* Her tormenter walked the streets again.

Frankly, he couldn't imagine it. He was also more concerned by Gladys's fear for her niece. He might have dismissed the idea that Paul would come hunting, but Gladys's fear for Audrey had told him all he needed to know about the creep. Gladys believed he would come. Enough for Cam.

He still felt uneasy about the unidentified sound outside but was aware of something equally important: you couldn't stay on high guard all the time. Eventually alertness would fade, would gradually be dismissed. He had to avoid that.

For several minutes he stood still, scanning the area around the house, ears straining for any unusual sound from the night.

Nothing. If the night held any secrets, it refused to share them.

At last he turned to go back into the house. As he passed through the mud porch, he wasn't surprised to see Audrey stirring, with a bird sitting on the back of one chair.

"A welcoming committee," he remarked.

"You must be cold. Anything?"

He shook his head, draping his anorak over a hook before stepping into the kitchen. "Can't sleep?"

"Like I could when you were out there hunting for sounds."

"Well, the night appears safe right now."

She blew a long breath. "For now. Want some cocoa or coffee?"

He chose coffee along with a piece of Maude's pie, left over from dinner. Dutch apple with plenty of cinnamon. Audrey skipped the pie.

"I guess," she said slowly, "that I might be growing paranoid. Some stupid little sound from outside and I'm shaking in my boots."

"You need to remember that I went out to look for a reason for it. You weren't being stupid. Not under these circumstances."

Audrey wrapped her mug in both hands as if to warm them against the cold. *There's no reason he shouldn't reach* across the table and wrap them both in his larger hands. Except that she might bolt like a terrified horse.

Then she put her mug down and rested her hands on the table. Startling her, Cam reached out and laid his hand atop hers.

But she didn't. Her gaze trailed to his, then down to their hands. Other than the slightest quiver, she offered no objection. She didn't yank away. A bud of trust had begun to grow between them. One he needed to cherish carefully, at least until he'd managed to erase Paul from her horizon.

"Tell me about yourself," Audrey said. "None of my business, I know, but…"

"It's your business. Gladys threw me into the middle of your life with orders to keep an eye on you."

Audrey looked at him. "To keep an eye on me. She must not have expected anything awful, if that's the way she described it."

"I honestly don't know exactly what she meant. I got the feeling she was concerned about you being out here on your own, knowing no one. Plus, she'd already hired me to fix this place up. Already here, so to speak."

One corner of her mouth crooked up. "Gladys, all right. Two birds with one stone."

"Hey!" Clyde interjected. "Gladys never threw any stones at me!"

Audrey reached out and smoothed Clyde's ruffling feathers. "Just a figure of speech. No one wants to stone you."

"Better not. They won't have any eyes after that." But then he subsided and appeared to fall asleep.

Audrey returned her attention to Cam. "So you felt this would just be a friendly sort of thing while you worked on the house."

"True," he admitted. "I should have known better. It was Gladys, after all."

"This must be awful for you, then."

He shook his head. "Not really. Not at all, in fact. I'd actually like a chance to get my hands around Paul's neck."

That had apparently been the wrong thing to say. Audrey paled visibly. "What? Audrey?"

She averted her face. Eventually, weak, broken words escaped her. "Paul strangled me. More than once."

Well, hell. He'd put his foot in that one so deeply it might take months to spray off the manure. Finally he decided he had to bull ahead, because there was no way of backing off this one.

"All right," he said. "I'll find a more creative way to deal with that scum."

Slowly, she turned her head back to face him. "I'd like to shoot him."

"Tempting, but too much trouble for you. No, I'll think of something better."

She nodded, relaxing enough to sip her coffee, to take a small piece of apple pie. "Now you," she said. "You probably know all about me from Gladys, but I know nothing about you."

"Not much to tell. I already told you my dad was an alcoholic and my mom who kept the church bake sales full. Dad wanted me to be a plumber, but I wanted construction. Gladys gave me my stake to get started. But there was a break in between."

Audrey lifted her brow. "A break for what?"

"The Army." He shook his head, smiling faintly. "At the time I didn't see any other way out of here, but it turned out to be a good choice in the end. Got a lot of construction work in uniform. Anyway, when I came out, there was Gladys with an offer to get me started. A loan. It all worked out, and I consider myself damn lucky."

"Gladys makes a lot of people feel that way. I'd like to grow up to be like her."

"You may already be on the way."

"Nice thought."

But the earlier tension had given way to a relaxed, almost cozy feeling. When a wind started to blow, even its keening around the corners of the house added to a sense of safety.

Although, truth be known, awareness of how many sounds that wind could cover didn't make Cam feel much better.

Damn. How fast could Paul get here if he'd somehow found out where Audrey had gone?

PAUL COULD COME quite fast, actually. Once he'd found the state, once he realized he could probably locate the name and address of every resident by checking computers at local libraries, he'd started to feel quite smug. Soon he'd be able to prove his love to Audrey again. All he had to do was find out where Gladys owned property. Because he blamed Gladys for getting Audrey all the way up here.

But soon wouldn't be soon enough.

The fates sure seemed to be after him, though. At the height of a mountain pass, he got caught in a blizzard. More than caught. Damn storm dropped over three feet of snow in a couple of hours. The owner of the motel where he'd found a room—the only motel on that hellacious site—had told him it might be a few days. This wasn't the most important road, after all.

Paul considered his own amazing self-control when he caught himself before bashing his fist into a concrete wall.

Instead he bought a few dried-up sandwiches and bags of chips from the motel's front office. The sandwiches tasted as if they dated to the age of the dinosaurs or something.

Then he locked himself in his room and carefully pulled out the folder in which he stored one newspaper article. It wasn't the article that interested him, though.

No, it was the huge photo of Audrey coming out of the courthouse. Looking a bit lost, of course, since she wasn't with him. At least she hadn't testified against him, so he didn't have to forgive her for that. And that lost expression...

She missed him. She didn't know what to do without him. Staring at that photo, grainy as it was, comforted him. She still loved him. Soon they'd be together again.

He could hardly wait.

But first he had to wait out this damn storm.

THAT DAMN STORM caught everyone unaware, as it hadn't been predicted. Up in the mountains, sure, but down here spring was supposed to be tiptoeing in. Overnight the dusting of powder like confectioner's sugar had turned into a couple of feet of snow dry enough to blow around to near whiteout conditions.

Clyde appeared fascinated. This morning he had carried his millet twig out to the porch shelf and cracked the seeds as he watched the weather through the window. Audrey was hardly doing much better. Something about that swirling white cloud out there held her attention. A fascination, like stepping into a new, strange world.

A safe world, because Paul couldn't be out there, not unless he was already an icicle. Because along with the snowfall the temperature had dropped, too.

This morning she'd donned a sweatshirt and jeans, along with slipper socks, and felt comfortable enough in the drafty house. Since Clyde hadn't fluffed up yet, she assumed he was sufficiently warm.

From the living room, the whine of a table saw announced that Cam was already at work. She'd noticed he wasted very little of his time without reason. A worker, through and through.

Eventually she brought Clyde inside.

After a bowl of oatmeal, Audrey brought out her sketching materials. Clyde evinced no interest, which was good, because it left Audrey undisturbed.

Today's sketch would be of this kitchen. Not a perfect, real-life rendering. She didn't go for that. No, she wanted to capture a sense of the age of this room, of the many years it had been in service, used by families large and small. Maybe after the sketch was drawn she'd bring out the small case of watercolors she'd brought with her and add some pigment. Not enough of a palette, but she could mix almost anything she wanted, given enough base colors. And maybe she was getting ready to paint again. The idea pleased her.

Just about the time that Clyde was beginning to exhibit impatience, Cam came from the living room. He headed straight for the sink and downed a tall glass of water, then grabbed a paper towel to dampen and wipe his face. Only then did he turn around and lean back against the counter, smiling at her. "Sorry for all the racket."

"Sounded like necessary racket to me."

Parts of Audrey, parts she'd thought that Paul had killed forever, stirred at the sight of Cam leaning back so casually against the counter. Narrow hips cased in worn denim. A khaki work shirt with the sleeves rolled up, covered now in a faint layer of sawdust. His face, at once hard and open, something she'd never noticed before. How was it possible for him to look as if he could both kill and shelter with the same expression? Make her feel she could safely turn to him despite the stone of his face.

Then there were the laugh lines around his eyes and mouth. Maybe they were what softened the icy terrain.

Regardless, she felt she could trust him, something she hadn't felt near a man in a long time.

But it was no good at all that she felt strong stirrings of sexual attraction. She had been certain that Paul had killed those beyond hope of revival, and she didn't want them back.

Attraction weakened a woman. Made her prey for the unscrupulous, and from what she'd seen and heard in the papers and from her friends, unscrupulous men weren't in any short supply.

But Cam didn't raise those fears in her. Maybe that should scare her more than anything.

In fact, he posed no threat at all to her. Keeping his distance across the kitchen. Paul had never let her get that far from him. And why not?

"He used to burn me." The words slipped out of her unintentionally. Soft as they had been spoken, they sounded loud in the relative silence that was punctuated only by the wind. That was why Paul had never let her get more than a few feet away. Because he wanted to be able to swing an arm without having to reach or move.

Rising, horrified by what she had just revealed, Audrey headed for the bedroom, closing the door behind her. Clyde somehow managed to make it through, then settled in his cage, watching her from unblinking eyes. At this angle he looked much like a bird of prey, eyes focused forward.

Not that Audrey cared. She dropped onto the edge of the bed and stared into space. A dam within her had opened and it refused to stop gushing.

She'd faced those years with Paul only as an emotional landscape of scars, all blurred, but never as physical actions. Buried. She kept it all buried because she had to carry on.

Except Paul was out of prison now, and Gladys thought he was looking for her.

And he would find her. Paul's possessiveness knew no bounds.

Once again she was aware of her time of safety evaporating with Paul's release.

Initially she'd been disturbed but not too worried. She'd moved, she had a different life and he'd probably learned his lesson. Being offered the opportunity to come stay at Gladys's house in Conard County had only added to her sense that the past was at last done.

Because Paul was done.

Except that had been an illusion, a dream of peace more than reality, the illusion shattered by Gladys's phone call that someone was looking for her.

A six-year interruption of hell was all it had turned out to be. Grabbing a pillow, she wrapped her arms tightly around it and buried her face in it.

No escape. None. Not ever.

IN THE KITCHEN, Cam stared out the window at the blizzard he figured was protecting Audrey and probably annoying the hell out of nearly everyone else in the area. Wherever that bastard ex of hers might be, one thing appeared certain for the time being: Paul couldn't possibly be getting any closer, not right now.

Small comfort. He'd seen the expression on Audrey's face as she'd gone to her bedroom. What had brought that on? The fact that she'd said Paul had burned her? The court case had pretty much settled that.

He wanted to go to her, to see if he could do a damn thing to help but figured he might create a bigger problem than the one she was having right now.

Funny, but being a man had never struck him as a problem. It's what he was. Now he had to think about it from an entirely different direction, and he didn't like it.

Maybe to Audrey he represented her abuser. Maybe she had cast him into a class with all the rest of his gender. Maybe Paul was now her standard for a male.

Hell. But there was nothing he could do about that. Not one damn thing.

Then he heard Clyde start singing from the bedroom. A surprisingly beautiful sound from a bird who favored a scratchier human sound. A song of solace?

Cam hoped so, because he sure couldn't go in there and a try to offer any himself. Hell, he had no idea where Audrey had been and where she might intend to go.

He clenched and unclenched his hands, feeling more helpless than he had in his entire life. Then, with no other choice, he returned to work.

The sound of Clyde singing slowly brought Audrey back from the emotional precipice she'd been teetering on. Past and present had mixed until she couldn't tell the difference.

But Clyde's happy-sounding trill was like a lifeline, tugging her back.

She'd escaped Paul, she reminded herself. She could do it again if necessary, but this time from a position of greater strength. She could see through him now, had the measure of the man he was. No more could his phony charm save him. She just felt sorry for the next woman he swayed with his smarm. If he could, given that he had a solid police record now.

But that wasn't her problem. Her problem was staying away from that creep until he gave up. That's all she needed to do. Keep herself safe until he realized he was wasting his time.

And that's what Cam was here for, wasn't it? That's why Gladys had set this up, had sent her up here. Maybe hoping that Paul would never think to look for her here, but also because Cam would be here. She wouldn't be alone.

Although with a man… Audrey sighed. Okay, she wasn't inclined to truly trust a guy again, but Cam seemed a cut above so far, and Gladys trusted him.

Maybe that was all it took. A baby step in the direction of a new life. Her art, stolen from her for so long. Cam, an example of a man who wasn't a beast. After all, to emerge from hiding, she was sooner or later going to have to deal with the men of the universe. In a job, in almost anything.

She looked at Clyde, who was still perched inside his cage. "I'm being a baby."

Clyde didn't agree, but he also didn't disagree.

Sighing, she rose and tossed the pillow toward the head of the bed. "Back to work."

Back to art, which had seldom ever felt like work to her.

The kitchen was empty when she returned. Sounds of hammering reached her from another part of the house.

Clyde, ever curious, followed the sound, then returned to the kitchen.

"You need coffee," he told Audrey.

"Who made you the boss?" she said irritably, even though she knew he was right. It was that kind of day, cold outside, wind keening, drafts inside. Hot beverage. Maybe soup for lunch.

Outside, the whiteout appeared to have deepened. Good. She hoped Paul had gotten stuck somewhere miserable. Maybe even inside his car all alone.

As soon as the thought crossed her mind, she felt shocked at herself. She wasn't the type to wish such ill on people. How much had he managed to change her?

Chapter Nine

Cam had started to measure the living room walls for new drywall. The original builder had been generous with twelve-inch studs rather than the current preference for sixteen. Made the house quieter, as sounds didn't carry as easily. Not to mention it made the house sturdier against the ceaseless prairie winds and frequent severe storms. Some fresh insulation would help, too.

Humming under his breath, occupied with his favorite tasks, he was surprised to hear a car pull up and stop. Strange for anyone to be out and about before the storm hadn't quite finished passing. By the time he reached the front door, a nervous Audrey was there. She must feel it would be impolite not to answer, but at the same time it was clear she didn't want to. Perched right on the top of her head, Clyde looked ready to dive into battle.

"Doesn't that hurt?" Cam wondered about those bird claws as he opened the door.

There stood Gage Dalton, wearing the sheriff's heavy dark green jacket and tan Stetson. "Got a minute?" He eyed the parrot dubiously.

"Clyde," Audrey said, "at ease already." Clyde hopped

down to her shoulder, remaining silent and watchful. "Come in, Sheriff. Coffee?"

"I ain't never turned down a cup of coffee in my life." Gage's crooked smile was charming.

Soon they were all seated at the kitchen table, Audrey wishing she had some other place to invite people to sit, but the way the house was turned over right now, it was a vain wish.

Not that Gage seemed to mind. He'd probably sat at a lot of kitchen tables in his time as sheriff. Few enough folks in this county had room to spare.

Then she remembered an old joke Gladys had told her. "You guys remember the story about the farmer, his wife and the cattle barn?"

Both men shook their heads, which relieved Audrey, because it was as far she could get from grim conversation, and she didn't want any more of that. Not right now.

"Well," she started, "there was a farmer with a large dairy herd he was awfully proud of. Watched them like babies, swearing that the kinder to them he was, the more milk they made."

"Might be true," Cam remarked.

"Might be," Audrey agreed.

"Definitely," Gage said firmly. "Got to know some cattle. They're as emotionally sensitive as dogs."

Audrey smiled. "I'll do that some day."

"But your story," Cam reminded her.

"Oh. Yes. Well, the farmer and his wife lived in this tiny little hut, barely two rooms, just enough to squeeze them both into. The place was ramshackle, with the wind sometimes blowing through the walls. The wife kept thinking since the dairy cows were bringing in enough money, maybe they could fix the house."

Two men nodded, sipping their coffee.

"Anyway, the farmer got busy building. The wife watched his progress every day and started to have visions of a mansion. So much room for them. Even a second story. Maybe more furniture.

"But then came the day the building was finished. The wife could barely breathe from the excitement."

Audrey spread her hands. "Then the farmer moved his herd of cattle into the brand-new barn with its wooden floors and nice windows and…"

"Let me guess," Gage said dryly. "She shot the selfish fool."

Audrey giggled. "Not so awful. No. When the farmer came back to town after selling half his herd for a nice sum, he couldn't find his wife. She wasn't in the house. Then he noticed his cattle were roaming the pasture, and he was certain he hadn't left them there."

"Oh, my God," Cam said, starting to laugh.

Audrey grinned. "You guessed it. He went over to the barn and found his wife had moved in. All the furniture was there, she was cooking on the wood stove and she gave him the biggest smile. All she said was 'Thank you for this beautiful house.'"

Both men laughed. "Good one," Cam said.

Audrey was amused by their reactions to what must be an old joke. She was a little bothered by Gage's suggestion the wife should shoot the guy. But in his job he spent his days dealing with guys. The kind who were rough and tough and pretending to have not an ounce of sympathy or compassion. She might have come right out and asked him if he had talked with Cam, about this situation the day he'd come by. But she thought she saw the faintest of smiles on Gage's face. She didn't want to wipe that away. Too late.

Gage finished half his coffee, then pushed the mug to one side. "Unfortunately, this isn't just a neighborly call. There might be some evidence that Paul Lang stole himself a battered, old, green pickup north of Boulder."

Cam leaned forward. "He might be headed this way?"

"Maybe so. No way to be certain, but I'll keep my ears perked. If he *did* come this way, the snow should have him nailed in the passes. Nothin's moving up there yet. Regardless, that snow is gonna get cleared. And if he's up there, he'll be able to move."

His gaze was somber as he looked at Audrey. "What can you expect from him?"

"You read the record. You know as well as anyone."

Gage shook his head. "I want to know about your experience, not what the prosecutor said. What does it take to set him off?"

Audrey looked down at her hands, twisting her fingers as if they might knot themselves. Anxiety crept into her every muscle, making her feel tight and achy. She didn't want to discuss this, not with anyone. Guilt and shame dogged her even to this day, and no therapist had been able to make her feel that Paul's behavior hadn't been at least some of *her* fault.

"I don't exactly know," she said finally, her voice thin. "I never did, not really. Sometimes it just seemed to come out of the blue, without warning." She shook her head. "I must have done something those times. Other times he always had a reason. And he always apologized. My psychologist said that's standard abusive behavior."

CAM LOOKED AT Gage and saw his own negative reaction reflected there. Audrey was blaming *herself* for an erratic abuser's behavior? God, what defense could there be against that? *He* had a reason. *She* never knew what she did that set him off. It was amazing that Audrey had escaped, given that Paul had made her feel responsible for a lot of her mistreatment.

Cam wasn't totally uneducated about spousal abuse, but this was the first time he had considered it from this angle. *Audrey* felt responsible for at least some of her mistreatment? He'd heard, somewhere in the foggy mists of his memory, that abusers often convinced their victims they were responsible for their own mistreatment. But this felt different somehow. Because Paul took some of the responsibility for his behavior? Because he brought flowers to apologize?

Or was it something else? Maybe something far worse. He had to find a way to educate himself on this topic or he'd never be anything but a heavy who was keeping an eye on Audrey.

And oddly enough for a guy who believed he preferred his bachelor life, he was beginning to want more than just looking after Audrey.

If she'd ever consider such a thing after what she'd been through.

Gage interrupted his train of thought. "Audrey, I need to know the kind of threat Paul is. Would he try to kill you?"

Audrey jerked a little, eyes widening. "No! Oh, no!" She needed to believe that.

"Then what does he want?"

Her answer was little more than a whisper. "Me."

WHEN GAGE TOOK his leave a half hour later, the mood had improved somewhat. Gage was good at that, Cam thought.

How many times had he walked into a situation where people were upset and managed to ease them into a calmer state?

But when Gage walked out into the endlessly swirling snow, Cam grabbed his jacket and followed. The kind of neighborly farewell you'd offer when the weather was better. Not in this kind of mess.

But it wasn't a neighborly farewell Cam was looking for. He stood outside Gage's driver's side door, blowing ice stinging his cheeks, and said, "Okay. You shouldn't even be out in this weather and you know it. What's up?"

Gage had already slid into his Suburban and reached out an arm to close the door, but he nodded. "You need to know. I don't know if Audrey has any idea, but if she does it appears she'd never tell."

Cam's heart started hammering with dread. "So?"

"So she probably doesn't know Paul's record of violence. She wasn't the first, and I'm not only talking women here. He had two years for serious injury in a bar fight. Lucky it didn't get pushed up to manslaughter. A plea deal." Gage shook his head, frowning. "I'm not going to run down his whole rap sheet, but he's had one seriously violent encounter after another since he was fourteen, and too many of them have been pled out."

Gage turned his dark gaze on Cam. "I get that we don't have a lot of money to spend on trials, but I also get that we let too many people walk on plea deals. Ankle monitors are nowhere near the preventative measure that being in a cell is. Anyway, I just wanted to know how she sees this, because you ask me, that man is stuck in the mountains and when he gets down here, he's not looking for a lovey-dovey reunion. My guess is that she has absolutely no real idea just how violent Paul Lang can be."

Gage's Suburban had a snowplow attached to the front, as many of the deputies' vehicles did, useful for helping out ranchers in the back of beyond, useful for getting help to an urgent situation.

As Gage drove slowly away, his engine growling with the added effort, Cam stayed out in the snow, ignoring the way it stung his cheeks.

So Paul Lang had a long record of violence. Not good. Since Audrey was still alive and physically in one piece, it seemed she had escaped the worst of that man's treatment.

On the other hand, it had taken one angry doctor and a fed-up prosecutor to pry her away, to put her ex away. Now she was clearly afraid of him, probably because she figured he blamed *her* for his prison time. Or just because she knew how badly he could batter her.

Or was it something more?

He'd never know how that damn parrot could get so much pleasure out of those tiny millet seeds, but Clyde worked busily at them anyway. Which was where Cam stood: with a few millet seeds of information to crack open in hope of a bit of useful information inside.

But he had a thought that stopped him dead in his tracks halfway to the front door.

Audrey believed that, in his twisted way, Paul loved her. It was even possible.

Damn. Where the hell would that get them?

He resumed striding toward the house, but now the cold didn't come only from the snowstorm. At first, he honestly hadn't expected a death threat. Audrey didn't believe Paul would kill her.

But now Cam did.

When Cam returned to the kitchen, he found Audrey busy with her art at the kitchen table. Clyde, exuding indifference, preened from a position on top of the refrigerator.

"How's it going?" he asked Audrey.

She looked at him, a smile gentling her face. "I'm getting some of my skills back, at any rate."

"That must feel good."

He studied her bent over the table, then had a mental *duh* moment. "Wouldn't that be easier and more comfortable with an easel?"

She favored him with another smile. "I'll get one eventually. A little on the expensive side just now."

He pulled out a chair and sat facing her. "I can make you an easel. A decent one."

"But you're so busy with the house!"

"Not *that* busy. Just tell me what you want it to do and what size you'd prefer. Whatever you need. I'll astonish you with my speed."

The last drew a laugh from her. "Speedy, huh?"

"In my business, there's no dawdling around. Seriously, I'm sure I can make you one by dinnertime." And it would make him feel good, too.

Thirty minutes later, he returned to the living room and the mess his renovations had made there. But he was whistling with Audrey's drawing in his hand. While the winter blew what was probably its last major storm, there was no immediate threat. A few days to relax, to make Audrey her easel and to listen to Clyde.

Although Clyde seemed to have been unusually quiet for the last few days. The sassy bird had silenced his sass. Cam wondered if he should be worried about that.

But Audrey would know better than he whether Clyde was ill. And if he was, what the hell did you do with a sick parrot around here? Could the vet handle it? As if they'd even be able to get to the vet right now.

Cam shook his head. Not now. Leave it to Audrey. She'd know.

He had other things to deal with right now, like an easel and some of the work he'd started in this room. And thoughts of one sexy woman who probably couldn't stand the thought of a man near her.

With a shake of his head and a sigh, Cam turned his attention to the measurements he'd gleaned from Audrey about her perfect easel. Then he loaded a piece of plywood onto his sawhorses and began to work.

AUDREY LOOKED UP at the clock and was startled by how the time had flown. It was nearly four and nobody had done anything about dinner. Although she could hear the sound of a power saw from the living room and knew Cam was busy at work. Why should he think of cooking a meal?

It struck her, not for the first time, how she was willing to label what Cam did as work, but her own painting as something else. A hobby. Not work.

Was it all about a paycheck? Was that the whole difference?

She didn't know, but she lifted her chin a bit as she thought about it. Call it work, call it hobby, it felt like work when it was done. She never felt as if she had wasted time. Certainly not when one of her small paintings sold. She ached a little from forgetting to move, so that the process felt as physical as mental.

Yet some difference niggled at her, trying to parse her

time to deal with the rest of life when other people left that stuff until they drove home after five.

Then she grew annoyed with herself for wasting her time on a question that had no answer she could discover and that only wasted time. She'd had almost the entire day for sketching, and even Clyde had left her alone rather than playing critic in some British voice he occasionally used. *Just be grateful for that.*

Then she headed for the fridge. The weather made her want some warm comfort food for dinner, and she wondered if she had the ingredients. Oh, yes, a huge block of Vermont cheddar and a small package of Italian sausage. Time for mac and cheese, if she had the elbow macaroni, and she did. It was going to be a large casserole indeed, but it might well make two dinners.

Yes. Smiling again, she moved items to the table to work, because this old-fashioned kitchen had no countertop to speak of.

Once upon a time she had enjoyed cooking, had enjoyed experimenting with flavors and seasonings. A creative endeavor if you weren't just following directions. Then Paul.

She closed her eyes, feeling her breathing speed up, her stomach sinking as memories washed over her. He'd killed her desire to cook by criticizing every single thing she'd prepared.

Vivid in her mind was the night he threw a full salad bowl across the kitchen for some reason she could not remember. She just knew her salad had been wrong. And that she'd had to clean up the entire mess, fuming the whole time. Not afraid back then, just angry.

Then the apology...

God, could he be sweet then. Reminding her of the

man she had married. Yeah, he had a temper, but no one was perfect.

Her first big mistake, she thought now. The really big one. Making excuses.

Not even a two-year-old should get away with that kind of behavior.

At last a sigh escaped her and she started grating the big block of cheddar. Just a tingle of her old pride in the work returned. Maybe she could get it back. Like she was getting back her desire to sketch and paint.

Life could turn around, couldn't it?

UP IN A mountain pass, surrounded by growling semis, stuck in a chilly motel room, Paul Lang stewed. What had started out as a desire to see Audrey again, to feel the joy of her love once more, was beginning to change. Little by little, so slowly he didn't know it was happening, anger began to grow in him.

It was *her* fault he was stuck up here. If she'd waited for him like a good wife, he wouldn't be here now.

But even in his increasingly agitated state, he understood that Audrey couldn't cause a snowstorm. She did plenty of other things that annoyed him, but not this one.

He swore and marched through a narrowly shoveled walk to the manager's office. This time the manager didn't even wait for his question.

"They should start plowing tomorrow."

Paul managed a short nod and returned to his room. One more day. Then he'd be on his way to Audrey again. The love of his life.

Even though he'd wondered about that during the six years in prison, he'd settled now. He wondered no more.

She hadn't spoken out against him, not once. She wasn't to blame for that, either.

Just as his anger at this delay grew, so did warm feelings for Audrey. He ignored the fury that was beginning to direct itself toward her. It didn't matter. He wouldn't need to sort that out once he held her in his arms again.

Everything was gonna be good. He paced the small room and thought of holding her in his arms again.

It would all be worth it.

Chapter Ten

The next few days passed quietly. Well, except for the noise Cam made as he worked in the living room. Table saws whined sometimes. A nail gun pounded away. Part of the underfloor needed replacing, and as near as Audrey could tell, that was one of the most difficult parts of the job. Or the most time-consuming, at least.

The snow had melted almost into oblivion, and Dan showed up with a truck bed full of drywall and mud for the room. By the time they unloaded the truck, Audrey had started putting together sandwiches for them.

The cupboard was beginning to look terribly bare and she wondered if her car could get her into town yet. That big pickup of Dan's was another story.

Clyde, looking over her shoulder, demanded some tuna. She ignored him. From what she could see, the road at the end of the drive didn't look terribly clear. At least Cam had cleared the drift down there before dawn this morning.

Staring at the melting snow, she decided she should ask Cam about conditions before she ventured out. In the meantime, she was able to make sandwiches and coffee for all of them.

Including Clyde, it seemed as he demanded another small

piece of tuna. He liked chicken, too, which always bothered Audrey just a bit. Didn't that make him a cannibal?

Oh, hell, he was just a bird. He had a whole different set of rules.

She went to the living room and was amazed to see Cam on stilts mudding the ceiling. Her heart nearly stopped, but she finally managed to say, "Lunch is ready when you guys are."

Stilts? She was half-ready to call off the job despite Gladys. She had to remind herself that Cam must do that all the time. How could he not, given his work?

But she didn't like it at all. Even though she could see that it was vastly more efficient than a ladder.

About twenty minutes later, both men showed up in the kitchen. First order was using the kitchen sink to wash their hands and wipe the white dust from their faces.

When they sat at the table, multiple sandwiches in front of them, both Dan and Cam thanked her with what felt like true appreciation. She smiled and brought the coffeepot to the table, allowing them to fill their own mugs as much as they wanted.

Not bad. She hadn't forgotten everything. She joined them, not wanting to make them feel a need to hurry, and put her easel to one side.

Cam nodded to it. "Still enjoying the easel, Audrey?"

"It's wonderful," she replied honestly. "I've never had such a beautiful easel. I can't believe how you sanded it and polished it for me."

Cam chuckled. "Sure, I wanted your fingers full of splinters."

That brought a giggle from her. It was, she realized, getting easier and easier to laugh with Cam. Losing her fear of men—at least him. That was a good thing, right?

But it was a notion she wasn't comfortable with. Avoiding men seemed like her safest option and had for years now. She knew there were nice men out there but believing it of just anyone threatened her. She didn't want to even try.

But here she was, increasingly comfortable with Cam and starting to become comfortable with Dan, who'd come out here a few times to help and bring supplies.

Alerts in her head had become quieter.

Cam spoke again. "Hear anything from Gladys?"

"She's emailed me a few times. She seems to be happy in assisted living."

"Well, that's good," he said approvingly. "She's always been so darn independent, I wondered about it."

"She's still independent, but now she's got a whole bunch of new friends and a lot of activities to pursue if she wants. It seems to be perfect."

"Happy to hear it."

Then Clyde decided he needed to enter the conversation. "I want to talk to Gladys."

Dan looked astonished. What he'd heard before had been so minor as to be almost ordinary. This was different.

"We're eating lunch," Audrey pointed out.

"*Your* mouth can be full. I can still talk."

Hell, Audrey thought. If she didn't give in to this demand, she'd hear about it for the rest of the day. That was Clyde, as determined and stubborn as a mule.

"Can you wait?" Audrey asked, trying to buy some time. Not wanting Dan to hear Clyde's complete abilities. Gladys had been keeping them under wraps for a long time, for good reason.

"No," Clyde answered flatly. "I can't read your email. I want to talk to Gladys."

Giving up, thinking that if Clyde wanted to out himself there was no way on earth she could prevent it. He'd just let anyone know when he wanted. Short of putting a bag over his head, there was no way to silence that bird. So she reached for her phone and punched in Gladys's number.

"OH, MY SWEET BOY," Gladys said. "It's been so long since I heard your voice."

Clyde cackled. "Which one?"

"Your natural voice. The one you used when we first met. I don't need Humphrey Bogart or Mae West."

"I can do Jimmy Stewart now, too."

"Deliver me." Gladys laughed. "So, what are you up to?"

"Keeping an eye on a houseful of people, including one stranger. Watching a man try to walk like a flamingo on the top of long, skinny legs. Begging for tuna from Audrey. She's stingy."

"Probably best for you," Gladys replied dryly. "So nothing going on except your irritating personality?"

Clyde made a clacking sound with his beak.

"Ha! Didn't like that one, did you, Clyde? Now let me go. It's time for physical therapy. I love you, Clyde."

"Ditto," the bird answered.

AUDREY DISCONNECTED. INSTEAD of speaking to Clyde, she looked at Dan. "Flummoxed?"

"That might be a mild word for it," he answered, still staring at Clyde. "I mean, I've heard of talking parrots, but this one beats all."

"There *is* nothing like Clyde," Audrey said. "And for obvious reasons, I have to ask you not to tell anyone about him."

A situation Clyde caused, which was dangerous for him. Audrey wondered if any of Gladys's warnings had gotten through to that bird. Well, so far he seemed to have accepted her warning about the predatory birds around here. No attempt yet to fly out of the house through the mudroom, and he could have done it successfully.

He seemed to have stopped being extraordinary for now, though. He flew away from the table and perched on the faucet. Audrey was always surprised that the metal wasn't too slippery for him.

Cam eyed her. "So you're stingy with the tuna?"

"And with a few other things," she answered. "That bird has an outsized appetite."

Clyde ignored her. Which was good, because Audrey felt suddenly guilty about how little time he got for really flying. Sometimes he must want to so badly that he ached. Or maybe he didn't care. With Clyde you never knew unless he announced it.

But wasn't that true of anyone?

Instead of wasting any more of her brain on the puzzle of Clyde, she looked at Cam. "I need to get to the grocery. I've about wiped out the pantry. Is it safe enough on the road?"

"In your Suburban? Sure. I don't think you should run into any ice since the sun is still hiding behind the cloud cover and I doubt there's been much traffic." Then he hesitated and asked, "You want some company? I can go with you."

She would have liked that, she realized. She'd have liked it a whole lot. But it didn't seem right. He was here to do a job, and Dan had come to help. Was she going to suggest that Dan ought to leave? She didn't want to do that, either by word or action.

"I'll be fine on my own."

CAM NODDED SLOWLY, thinking of Paul Lang. But from what he'd heard from Gage, Lang would still be stuck in a mountain pass for most of the day.

Then he had a thought. What if Lang hadn't gotten stuck in the mountains or anywhere else for an appreciable amount of time? He might already be in the valley.

Cam stood up. "I'm going with you—it'll make me feel better." He looked at his partner. "You'll be okay, Dan. The bird will keep an eye on you."

A laugh, accompanied by a small amount of coffee, exploded out of Dan. He grabbed a napkin to wipe his mouth and the table in front of him. When the last of his laugh rolled out of him, he spoke.

"I promise to behave for Clyde."

Audrey thought she caught a glint of humor in Clyde's golden eyes. Oh, boy, what did that mean?

Then she looked at Cam and saw a tightness around his eyes that made her a bit uncomfortable. What worried him? Then she remembered Paul.

Oh, God, *Paul*. Did Cam have some reason to think he might be around?

But she didn't know how to ask. Or maybe she was afraid to.

THOUGHTS OF PAUL had given Cam a good case of heartburn, even on top of Audrey's delicious tuna sandwiches.

It had been too easy the past few days to shove Paul to the back of his mind and focus on other things. Way too easy.

Paul had been convicted of violent felonies before Audrey, even if plea deals had saved his butt.

Now, as he drove Audrey to the supermarket in his truck and surveyed the melting snow, he began to think that the normality of life since Audrey had arrived had been a pause in a battle.

Because Paul wasn't the type to just let Audrey go. Even Gage was concerned about that, as was Gladys, so Cam didn't need to feel he was being paranoid about it.

But he'd begun to let his vigilance slip. At absolutely the worst time possible.

Hell. He was working up a good mad at himself, then remembered Audrey was sitting right beside him. He didn't want to have to explain it if he started cussing. Nope.

But Audrey was relaxing, too. He'd felt it and finally saw it. A whole lot less tense than when she'd arrived. He was sure she'd gotten used to him being around, but that wasn't all of it.

No, maybe she'd concluded Paul wasn't coming after her, despite Gladys's phone call. Maybe enough time had passed to make her feel safer.

He understood that. He'd been slipping himself. But no more time for that. Remembering Gage's dispassionate rendition of Paul Lang's priors, he knew that even a little relaxation could be dangerous.

Then there was Audrey. The danger she was in.

At the store he managed to unwind himself enough to be a pleasant companion, especially after he realized that Audrey was looking at him oddly. Dang, his face usually didn't reveal much, but he'd begun to think she was reading him like an open book.

When had that happened?

But grocery shopping turned into a pleasant activity with her, unlike his own dash-and-go trips.

Little by little, Audrey revealed that there was a pent-up chef somewhere inside her. She pored over produce as if it were a dragon's hoard of gold, selecting carefully from a wide variety. She spent a lot of time looking at meat and poultry and side dishes, purchasing basmati rice...

He couldn't even begin to imagine what she was thinking of, but it sure didn't look like anything he was familiar with. Or as if it came from a cookbook. Then she hit the spice aisle. Oh, man.

"I guess I'll have to order some seasonings," she remarked.

He looked at the basket, taking in all the little bottles. "Didn't Gladys leave a lot of these?"

"Too old. Fresh is better."

Apparently so, because hadn't she bought those little green onions? Not just a big, sweet onion, but those ones with the long green leaves. All he knew about those was that he liked them raw.

By the time they left the store, Cam figured the pantry and fridge were going to be full. If Audrey had overlooked something, he couldn't imagine what it might be.

BACK AT THE HOUSE, Dan came out to help cart and carry. Clyde sat on his perch on the porch, fluffed up against the cold.

"Get inside, Clyde," Audrey said impatiently. "God, you must have enough brains to know when you're getting too cold."

Not that he listened immediately. Oh, no, not Clyde. But

before too much longer he flew inside and settled near a heat register.

"I am not a baby," he remarked as he began to preen. "I know when I'm too cold and I'll let you know."

"I'm sure you will," Audrey agreed, pulling a large stalk of celery from a shopping bag.

Satisfied, sitting on the register, Clyde continued to preen. Given how many feathers he had, preening took a lot of time. It was a wonder he had time for anything else, Audrey thought. But clearly he did.

Audey suggested Dan stay with Cam in the living room. Dan thanked her with a smile, then went back to work in the living room, but Cam insisted on helping Audrey put everything away. And with each item, he felt the snow melt seeming to drip icily down his spine. Soon the state of these roads wouldn't slow anyone down.

So all he could do was hope that Paul had no idea where this place was or that Audrey was here. No reason he should.

But there was also no reason to count on that possibility.

"Well, damn," Audrey said.

"What?"

"I need a bigger freezer."

At that he laughed. "You can buy a bigger one, but for right now the mud porch will qualify."

She brightened. "That's a great idea. I should have thought of that."

"You probably weren't raised storing groceries outdoors."

"That's true."

She was pleased to find a few shelves out there that looked as if they might have once been used for the purpose. She couldn't remember if she'd ever seen Gladys use them, but why should she? She was living alone.

"Did you grow up storing groceries outside?"

"Often enough. Mom put the frozen stuff outside most of the winter. She could buy more of it then and cut down on her trips to town."

"Saving pennies."

"Every single one she could."

"Canning?" she asked, remembering all those glimmering jars in Gladys's basement. Had Gladys canned those or inherited them? She needed to ask. So much she didn't know about her aunt.

"Every year."

"I'm starting to feel like a slug in comparison."

Cam laughed. "Don't. You're a painter. Your job."

True enough. Certainly the major goal in her life, and she had to keep getting better if she wanted any better success in the future.

Paul had left a great big hole in her striving, she realized. One hell of a big one. One she now had to make up for.

The sense of being overwhelmed began to touch her, and she yanked herself away from it. That would do no good at all.

Cam started to turn from a shelf toward her and suddenly she noted something she'd noticed only when she had first arrived here. A man's build. And darn, did he have a good one. Broad shoulders, narrow hips, flat butt...

A delicious shiver filled her. No. No. *No!*

She closed her eyes and corralled herself. That was a complication she never again wanted in her life. Never.

Except part of her didn't believe that.

Then she looked out the kitchen window and thought of Paul. A shudder ran through her, colder than the weather outside. Cold as the rapidly melting snow. If Paul had discovered where she was, he might come at any time. She suddenly felt naked.

Hurrying to the window, she drew the café curtains closed.

Turning, she found Cam's eyes on her. They said everything. He knew what had caused her to close those curtains.

She could feel embarrassed color heating her cheeks. She didn't want to look like a wimp to him. Or a fraidy-cat. Not like some damsel in distress.

But wasn't that what Gladys had essentially made her and Cam? A damsel who needed a knight.

He might fill the knight role, but she hoped like hell she didn't fit the damsel role. She wanted to tell Gladys that she could take care of herself. That she didn't need a guardian.

Then, as she dealt with fear and irritation, she began to feel crushed. Flattened. Taking a breath became almost impossible. Everything felt as if it were hitting her like a freight train.

She squeezed her eyes shut, clenched her hands into fists and hardly knew that hot tears had begun to run down her cheeks. Years of self-control, years of recovery seemed to be washing away with those tears, leaving her raw. Wounded.

Then arms closed around her. *No!* Immediately she began to struggle, pushing against a chest as hard as a wall.

"Easy," said a quiet male voice. "Easy. I won't hurt you."

But those arms began to slip away and a new, hard feeling began to rip through her. Cam. It was Cam. She didn't need to fear him. A kernel of surety had grown in her.

But she was beyond all that. Just as he was about to sever all physical contact between them, she took a step forward, pressing her face into his chest and grabbing his shirtsleeves with her hands.

Comfort. Somewhere here, there was comfort. And safety.

Those powerful arms slowly slipped around her again, an easy hug, restraining her not at all. God, it had been so long since she'd had a hug like this.

It felt good. So very good.

Inviting aromas of man and soap filled her nose. She turned her head so that her cheek rested against the wall of his chest and let the tears flow. They wet her face and his shirt. She couldn't stop them.

One of his hands began to caress her back in gentle circles, soothing. Reassuring. A shiver passed through her as anguish began to seep away under his gentle touch. Slowly. Little by little she softened until she was nearly sagging against him.

Then came the pinprick: she was acting like a baby. But before that thought could take over, Cam lifted her, remarking gruffly, "Not too many places to sit in this damn house."

As she began to return to the moment from the hell of the past, he carried her into the bedroom and sat on the bed, holding her in his lap, his arms snugly around her.

"Let it happen," he said quietly. "Just let it happen. It's okay..."

He made her feel as if it *were* okay to give way. For years she'd tried not to, feeling it would be weak. Stand strong, bury most of the feelings, especially those that weren't useful. Don't be a wimp.

But now she felt safe enough to let go. Cam made her feel that way. Or maybe she just couldn't hold it all in anymore. She was in no mood just then to analyze it, but she'd analyze it quite a bit later. That was her nature.

Right now she just let it all flood her, escaping in tears that at times changed to sobs then quieted again. There seemed to be no bottom to the mess that was tearing her apart. No bottom at all.

Like the ugliness that had filled her days with Paul and pursued her ever since. Her therapist had named it PTSS, post-traumatic stress syndrome, but a name affected it not at all. It was a label to stamp on a file folder, a label she might use to excuse herself for whatever.

She didn't need excuses. She needed to cut the chains that shackled her. But even therapy hadn't been able to help her do that. Memories were stamped in the brain in indelible ink. They might grow fuzzier, even distort a little, but something like this? There was no eraser good enough.

Gradually she began to quiet. Lack of energy caused her to completely relax into Cam's embrace. She even got her thoughts back enough to wonder if she was making him uncomfortable. But she felt no strain in his arms, no trembling. Maybe she could stay just a little longer?

Then she felt a light brush against her cheek. Her eyes snapped open, and she found herself staring into two golden eyes.

"There you are," said Clyde in Gladys's voice. "About time. Sheesh."

That *sheesh* always amused Audrey, because she couldn't imagine how Clyde managed to make those sibilants so well. But then he had amazing gifts for imitating sounds. Another question about the vocal abilities of an African gray. She supposed that if she looked into it, she'd find the science behind the amazing mimicry of parrots. But she sure wouldn't find an explanation for Clyde's amazing behavior.

Sniffling, Audrey started to sit up. Cam immediately loosened his hold on her and steadied her until she was sitting on the side of the bed, now with a parrot on her shoulder.

"You okay with him?" Clyde asked right in her ear.

"Fine."

"Okay." Clyde took off and resettled in his palace, swinging on a large perch.

Cam spoke, sounding amused. "Heckuva chaperone you've got there."

Audrey began to wipe her eyes with her flannel shirtsleeve. "Didn't know I needed one."

"Someone else has a different opinion. Right now he's glaring at me." Then Cam twisted and a moment later handed her some tissues.

She took them gratefully, able to dab at her face rather than make it sore by wiping. "Sorry about all that." Her voice sounded thick, a little rough.

"No need," Cam answered. "Sometimes we all need a shoulder. Glad I could be yours."

Through hot, tear-blurred eyes, she looked at Cam and unexpectedly wondered who exactly he was. Because he was too damn nice. Too perfect. No man could be this consistently understanding and gentle.

She averted her face, closed her eyes and pressed a tissue to them, drying the last of her tears. She didn't know much about men in general, thanks to Paul, but maybe in the end Paul was a better representative of a man than Cam was.

Because she'd just cried all over him and he hadn't seemed to mind. Men could barely tolerate that, she'd heard. They wanted to be left alone when it came to depression or sorrow.

As if such feelings made them uncomfortable or irritated. That was how Paul had always reacted, and she hadn't seen anything much different from his friends.

She sighed, drying the last of her face and wondering who

she was sitting beside. He lived a rough life in construction. This response on his part might be phony. Acting out what he thought she wanted rather than his genuine feelings.

And he'd begun to make her feel safe. A bad thing. He might be every bit as bad as Paul.

Feeling sickened, she sought distraction. "Clyde?"

Clyde seemed to feel the same way. He flew the short distance to land on her shoulder, then leaned his head into hers.

Cam rose, a tremor of laughter in his voice. "That bird is jealous." He went back to the living room.

Clyde didn't respond, merely rubbed his head against Audrey. Then the two of them were alone, Audrey so uneasy that tremors kept passing through her. Clyde attempting to soothe her in the best way he could.

What had come over her, Audrey wondered. She'd just begun to feel truly safe with Cam. Had begun to trust him. He'd just offered her kind understanding when she'd fallen apart all over him.

Was something permanently twisted in her own mind now? Or did he merit her distrust because he was a man?

Just thinking that made her wonder about her own sanity. Yet, what had life taught her? At the very least, suspicion was called for. And definitely not trust.

Then she did a really odd thing. "Clyde? What do you think of Cam?"

"He's a man."

As if that answered it all. Maybe it did. Then she tried again. "Why don't you like men?"

"The one who owned me before Gladys. She said he ought to rot in hell."

Audrey could hear Gladys saying that, and she never would have said it lightly. "Why did Gladys think that?"

Clyde's answer was oblique. "I have feelings."

Then Clyde clammed up, a weird metaphor for a bird, and flew back to his perch in his palace and began preening again.

Wisdom from a bird? How likely was that? And why had she asked Clyde anyway? Because any sounding board would do?

Sighing, shaking her head at her thoughts, she made herself return to the kitchen and her art, only to find that Dan was leaving. He hadn't been a bad houseguest at all, if you could call sleeping on the floor being a guest. She was sorry to see him go. He'd been entertaining in a quiet way.

Which left her alone with Cam, a man for whom she was beginning to feel a strong attraction. And suddenly that attraction didn't feel scary at all.

Chapter Eleven

The snow had melted completely off the blacktop and was working its way to bare ground again on the tall, dried grasses and shrubs.

An open area from which to approach the house, except for a few copses of trees—evergreens, cottonwoods and the like. Big enough for concealment but with open areas around.

Cam spent a lot of his free time studying that terrain. If Paul showed up, he'd have a whole bunch of ways to approach the house. But Cam couldn't be there every minute. He'd been trying, but work on his construction projects was starting to develop problems. He needed to go and oversee, at least long enough to get things back in line. And Dan certainly couldn't handle it all by himself. Not when they had more than three projects going, some more difficult than others.

Nor did Cam believe even for a moment that the security cameras he'd installed could protect Audrey well enough. A warning Paul approached and from where, no more. He kept thinking about that with increasing frequency.

But working a single project at a time wasn't cost-effective. Dang, maybe he should drag Audrey along with him.

But he knew she'd refuse. Absolutely. And given her experience with Paul, why the hell *would* she go riding off with Cam?

Or maybe it was high time he just laid it all out for Audrey, show her that police file, discuss Paul's history of violence. Let her know that it wasn't her imagination creating the fears she felt.

Let her know the true situation. This woman didn't need coddling and he felt almost embarrassed for having tried to protect her by letting her know nothing. She wouldn't appreciate that if she knew. *Dunce.*

Frustration had begun to build in him, and now he sensed a distance, even a coldness, radiating from Audrey. What had he done? He'd begun to think they'd gotten past the roughest ground in this misbegotten relationship. Maybe she'd begun to sense he was withholding something.

He hadn't been sent here to be her friend. Gladys had simply ordered him, literally, to keep his eye on her niece. Cam wasn't quite sure how he was supposed to accomplish that without hanging around most of the time.

Frustrated, he used the nail gun more rapidly—always dangerous, but he was past caring. When there was nothing left to nail, he eyed the saw but realized he wasn't ready for any more cutting yet.

He was getting ready to hurl something, he realized as frustration built in him. That was not his typical behavior, it was something he never wanted to do, so what the hell was coming over him?

Yeah, he had a job, another contract, that he was worrying about. Nothing to stop him from getting in his truck and returning to deal with it for several days rather than several hours. Audrey should be all right for several days on her own.

Hell, he couldn't watch over her for years to come. Somehow this Paul needed to be dealt with, and it was best if Audrey could do it herself. Send the guy into flight with his tail tucked between his legs.

Cam rather liked the image of that.

He went outside, needing the fresh air, wanting to take in the area surrounding the house, to make sure nothing important had changed out there.

His phone rang and he answered it, expecting to hear Dan but instead hearing the sheriff. "Hey, man, what's up?"

"Nothing really," Gage answered in his gravelly voice. "Except the passes are clear to all traffic now. This county is as open as a sieve."

"I hear you."

"I'll increase the patrols around Gladys's property, but as usual I'm shorthanded. And what the hell do we know to look for, anyway? Pickups in all conditions run the roads out here. And we're not sure he hasn't replaced the vehicle he's driving."

Cam thanked Gage for the information, but as he stuck his phone back into his jeans pocket, he was still staring at an insurmountable problem that had just gotten even more insurmountable.

This was ridiculous. No one could be sure Paul was coming this way or that he was willing to spend so much time tracking his ex-wife. No one knew anything except that he had stopped in to see Gladys and expressed interest in Audrey's whereabouts.

And so? Maybe he was just curious. Or maybe he just

wanted to spout some anger and leave. Could he really be stupid enough to risk more jail time?

Yeah, Cam thought glumly. He could.

But Paul's mentality was so far from anything Cam could honestly imagine that he had no idea how to predict what this guy would really do.

If the love of Cam's life, assuming he had one, had dumped him, he'd lick his wounds and move on. He certainly wouldn't begin stalking her. And if Paul was really headed this way, the least of it would be stalking. Bad enough, but to come all this way just to see what your ex was up to? Or to get her to take you back?

A bit of a chill ran down his spine. To get Audrey to take him back. How did he intend to do that? Unless she'd been visiting him in prison, he must have gotten the message by now.

But maybe he didn't care. Maybe he was willing to kidnap Audrey and hold her until she agreed to be his wife again.

Cam could hardly believe the paths his mind was following now. Seriously? To force anyone to be his wife seemed like the most pointless thing anyone would want to do. He feared, however, that Audrey was following the same paths to dread.

But then, Paul was a man who'd abused his wife so badly that her hospital records, rather than any testimony from her, had gotten him six years in prison.

Yeah. Someone could do it. Paul could do it, though his reasoning utterly escaped Cam.

He turned around at a sound and saw that Audrey and Clyde had come onto the front porch, Audrey wrapped in a jacket, Clyde in a cloud of feathers. Cam had always liked the way birds could fluff their feathers to hold in their own body heat. Instant jacket.

Although probably not the best. How many times had he seen puffy birds sitting on a sill as close to a window as they could get? Seeking every bit of escaping heat from the house. Every winter. Cam sometimes wondered why they didn't migrate.

Nature's rhythms could be as perplexing as any human's.

One last scan around the acreage, listening for the crunch of snow or frozen ground if anything bigger than a rabbit approached, but he heard only silence out there. Too much? Unusual?

For the first time he was annoyed with himself for not paying closer attention to his environment. Surely he ought to have some idea of how his world sounded.

But he didn't. Frustrated with himself for having considered so much to be a background he could ignore, he walked to the porch and joined the bird and Audrey behind the screening.

"It's melting fast," she remarked.

"Yeah, but the melt seems to have stopped. The remaining snow has a crust that isn't shrinking." He shrugged. "Tomorrow will probably take care of that."

"It's pretty," Audrey remarked. "I was just a kid when I visited Aunt Gladys here and didn't pay much attention. But it *is* pretty. Just odd how it can feel so desolate so close to the Front Street neighborhood."

"Yeah." He settled on one of the chairs. Colder than hell to his butt. "Trees," he answered by way of explanation. "Just enough to create the privacy."

"I guess that would be a good thing under ordinary circumstances."

"These days," he agreed. "But not so long ago people didn't want privacy. They wanted communal protection."

She nodded slowly. "I guess this was the Wild West at one time."

"Yup. And not as long ago as you might think." He hesitated, not wanting to upset Audrey in any way, but honestly facing the need for her to meet some folks. "I was thinking I could take you around to meet some of your neighbors. We could do it here, but I've got the house torn up. Anyway, lots of nice..." His voice trailed away as he saw her vehemently shake her head.

"No," she said. "Please, no."

"Okay," he said. No point in pressing it when it so obviously disturbed her. Now, however, it disturbed him, too.

Wouldn't it make her feel better to know the people around her? People she might have to rely on? People who could come to her aid?

But maybe, after all those years with Paul, she didn't expect help from any direction.

Clyde fluffed a bit more. "Could we *please* go inside?"

Audrey jumped up. "Oh, man," she said, holding out her forearm. Clyde leaped on it immediately.

"You need to speak up sooner," Audrey scolded him.

"Would you have listened?" Clyde actually sighed.

"How the hell can he do that?" Cam wondered as he followed them inside. *"Sigh?"*

"I read up on his vocal construction," Audrey said as she brought Clyde into the warm kitchen. "It's amazing, and yeah, he can even sigh. The truly astonishing part of Clyde is that he's not just mimicking."

Cam couldn't argue that. "No 'Polly wants a cracker'?"

"Spare me," Clyde said.

Audrey cracked a laugh. Then she turned to Cam. "I'm sorry."

He was startled. "For what?"

"For turning down your kind offer to introduce me to people." She looked away. "Might as well admit that I'm a serious introvert. At least now."

He stood perfectly still as he absorbed what she was saying. "I take it not so much before Paul?"

"Maybe not." Then she waved her hand as if to brush away an annoying fly. Brushing away the topic. Brushing away Paul.

Well, he was still cold from his venture outside, because he hadn't bothered with a jacket and flannel wasn't enough. Heading for the coffeepot, he started a fresh one without asking. "Next time I go to check on my projects, you want to ride along? We can get something for lunch that's a bit different."

She was silent for so long that Cam turned to look at her. Her face had paled a bit, but then she nodded. "Yes," she said.

Just one word, but at least it had been an affirmative.

Cam decided he had to be content with that. Then he decided that he couldn't wait much longer to tell her what he feared. What Gage feared.

God, he hated himself. She'd made progress. He'd watched it happen. Now he was going to have to destroy a lot of it.

THE TRIP DOWN the mountain was far worse than the climb. Paul's fingers knotted around the steering wheel until they ached.

"You oughta wait a day," the motel manager had said just a while before Paul set out. "Give the trucks a chance to melt the road more. Besides, a pickup is too light in the tail, and that one's got rear-wheel drive."

Paul guessed all that meant something, but he was in no

mood to listen. Audrey was down there somewhere, and damn it, he was going to find her, whatever it took.

His memories of her had begun to change from the anger he had felt toward her while he rotted in prison. Now he remembered all the good things about her. Some of the great meals she'd cooked. How it felt when she hugged him, kissed him, had sex with him.

All that anger was glossed over by a deepening hunger inside him. Those had been the best years of his life, he thought now. The best. And *she* hadn't put him in prison. Not a word from her in court. If she could have stopped that trial, he was sure she would have. Because she loved him, too.

She'd never spoken a word against him, neither. Never, not to anyone. If she had, one of his buddies would have told him.

Nope, Audrey loved him. She understood he'd never wanted to hurt her. Sometimes he slipped up, but she got it. He always told her he was sorry, the way she did when he didn't like a meal she cooked.

Those buddies of his never got it when they had wives run away. You just had to say you were sorry.

The magic words, his granny used to say.

Yup. And now it was time for Audrey to say she was sorry. Sorry for the big chunk of years that had been cut from his life. Oh, he knew she hadn't done it. No. But she still needed to say she was sorry so much of his life had been wasted.

Satisfied she would do exactly that when she saw him again, when she realized he had come back to her, he nodded to himself then smiled. At that moment the truck fishtailed, just a bit.

Maybe that was what the guy at the motel had meant. Hell, he'd have to drive slower.

AUDREY CHANGED HER mind about going with Cam to check on his business.

"You sure?" he asked. "You wanna be here alone?"

She nodded. "If Paul should show up, I know how to handle him. There's a shotgun in my bedroom. I can use it."

"It'll only be for a few hours." Probably reassuring himself as much as her. She had a *shotgun*?

She shook her head. "I'll be just fine, Cam. Gladys wasn't sure it was Paul who was looking for me, and even if it was, she didn't say anything about this house. That jolted me, but the more I think about it, the more I think he couldn't have found me. Not easily. And I can take care of him if I have to."

He regarded her, clearly annoyed by her decision but unable to argue with her. "I can't kidnap you," he said finally.

"Nope. Whatever Gladys may think, I can take care of myself. What's more, I may have to do it for a lot of years to come. You don't have to twist your life into knots over this."

Cam threw up his hands and went back to the living room. Clyde, perched on her shoulder, remarked, "You're brave. But if Gladys was worried—"

Audrey cut him off. "Gladys doesn't need to worry."

She walked to the sink and pulled back the curtains to look out at a gray day that hovered somewhere between winter and spring.

She hadn't accepted Cam's offer to bring neighbors over. Heard it but hadn't accepted it. This was getting past introversion to something more worrisome, and she didn't want to face it. But she had to.

She was becoming agoraphobic. When she looked at those wide-open spaces out there, she recognized the change. When first she had arrived, they had impressed her and struck her as beautiful. Beyond this acreage, mountains rose, looking purple in the light of a day that couldn't make up its mind. She hadn't even thought about the houses that lay just behind the copses of trees. Just about the beauty of a huge rolling space and mountains.

A Colorado girl, she loved the mountains. They slaked the thirst of her soul. There were places like this where she came from, mountains that gave way to rolling prairie. But this was somehow different.

Now she wondered if all that difference was inside *her*. As if the agoraphobia had already begun.

Regardless, it was there now, and the thought of driving outside for miles with Cam made things inside her clamp with discomfort, maybe even fear.

God, she was lucky to have made it to the grocery store.

"Relax," Clyde said abruptly beside her ear.

"What are you talking about?"

"If you get any tenser, I won't be able to perch here without hurting you. I'll have to go to one of my wood perches."

"God forbid."

Clyde said nothing more, simply took off and headed for the splendor of his bedroom palace.

It was Audrey's turn to huff. Damn bird. Thought he was going to run her life now?

Probably. That sounded like Clyde.

Reaching out, she touched the frigid window glass with her palm. Cold out there. Cold inside her. Her sense of something broken was beginning to grow stronger.

It was more than her introversion. This was far worse

to her way of thinking. Had Paul turned her into an agoraphobe? What else had he permanently changed about her, other than the emotional scars she had learned to live with?

"Sweet Mary," she whispered. In an instant she had a vision of herself as a battered, bloody monster.

She knew how to handle him? Maybe she only thought so. Maybe he had set all kinds of bombs within her. And what if they started blowing up when she saw him again?

Because there was really no doubt that she would. Like a nightmare that kept repeating, Paul would always come back, even if only in the dreams that woke her in the dark, covered with sweat, trembling with terror.

That man was always going to be a part of her.

Even killing him wouldn't change that.

CAM WAS TROUBLED. The next morning, as he set out for the first of his job sites, thoughts of Audrey twisted him into knots.

She'd said she could handle Paul, but how did she propose to do that? Had she really ever done that in the past? And then there was her sudden fear of going out.

He'd glimpsed it on her face, in her eyes. She didn't want to be outside the house or she didn't want to go out with him?

How the hell could he know?

Something had changed, but he couldn't know if this was something recent or something he just hadn't noticed before.

It must be recent. She came out onto the porch and spent time out there with Clyde.

Except, he reminded himself, the porch was screened, protecting her from a whole lot of things.

He pressed harder on the accelerator. Out here in ranchland with almost nothing along the roads, he could drive over eighty without a problem. The staties pretty much ignored infringement unless it looked dangerous.

Cam also knew where every speed trap was. Plenty of small towns claimed they didn't have them, but they sure as hell did.

He didn't like that he was going to have to spend less time than he should at the job site, but the sense that he needed to get back to Audrey as quickly as he could flogged him with urgency.

Thank God for Dan. That man was the best partner he could ever have asked for, and he had no doubt that everything was in good hands. It was just too much for one man to handle for long.

Dan was waiting for him in the trailer near the construction site, talking to a hard hat in front of him.

"If you're sure that cement isn't the right mix," Dan said, "tell them to take it back, and if they got a problem, have 'em call me. Not gonna put up with substandard materials." His eyes lighted on Cam and he said, "Are we, Cam?"

The hard hat turned and shook hands with Cam. "Howdy, boss."

"Great to see you, Bill. And no substandard materials. We built our reputation on good work, not a building that collapses in fifteen or twenty years."

Bill laughed. "That's exactly why I'm in here complaining about that cement. Mix started washing away in the first rain."

Bill departed and Cam bent, stretching his legs from the truck. "We lucked out on that man for a supervisor."

Dan nodded. "He takes as much pride in this work as we do. So how's life as a guardian angel?"

"Your wife must be ready to kill me for making you work so many extra hours."

Dan shrugged one shoulder. "Nella gets it. Sends her best. I think you got a month before she comes hunting you with a weapon."

Cam laughed. Nella was a frontier woman, top to bottom. He could just see her marching toward him in her jeans and floppy-brimmed hat, a shotgun pointed at him. *Gimme my man back*, she'd say.

Stiffness eased, he grabbed a cup of coffee and sat across from Dan, leaning back and putting his boots up on the desk. "What about you? Not fair to ask you to fill in for me."

Dan shook his head. "Fair has nothing to do with it. You need to make sure that SOB doesn't hurt Gladys's niece. I always liked Gladys, so yeah. We can both do her a solid in our different ways. I'll keep these projects up and running so you can make sure nothing happens to Audrey. Seems like a small thing."

It was no small thing and Cam knew it, but he could tell Dan didn't want to make a big deal out of it. His partner was never one to make a big deal out of anything.

Dan spoke. "That parrot still talking?"

"Last I heard." The choice of phrasing made them both laugh.

"And Audrey?"

Cam took his time with that. He sipped his coffee, drummed his fingers on the desk and turned the woman around in his mind. What had he seen? What did that tell him?

"Cam?"

Called back from a meandering trip about everything he'd noticed about Audrey, he still hesitated.

"Hard to say," he said finally. "She not exactly riding in a solitary direction. Still too edgy about Paul getting out of prison, I guess."

"*Too* edgy?" Dan questioned.

"Well, not exactly that. But I still don't know what to make of it. When she arrived, she got a real scare when Gladys called her to tell her some man was looking for her. With time she's started to relax a little. Then…"

He shook his head. "Then this morning she refused to ride along with me, saying she'd be fine on her own, that she knew how to take care of herself. How she'd be able to deal with Paul."

"Dang," Dan exclaimed.

"I guess your thinking is like mine."

"Damn straight. If that woman had been able to handle her ex, then how did it come to him going to prison? What do you think got into her?"

Cam shrugged. "No idea. Nothing's happened that I'm aware of." But Cam was wondering if Audrey were lying to herself about her toughness. About being able to handle Paul. But why would she do that?

Suddenly more concerned, he stood up. "Show me where everything's at. I need to get back to Conard City."

It was probably one of the fastest hikes he'd taken around one of his building sites, but there it was. Conflicting duties. Conflicting responsibilities.

Whatever Audrey might say about being able to handle Paul, Gladys had been sure she couldn't. On this subject, Cam was inclined to believe Gladys's judgment over Audrey's.

He was glad to pull away by late afternoon.

"I CHOSE TO stay here, not to go with Cam," Audrey said. Clyde made a quiet sound of agreement. "I didn't realize..."

She honestly hadn't realized just how strained her nerves were going to get, all alone in this big house. Wondering when Cam would get back, or if he'd even come tonight.

But she hadn't had much to fear living on her own back home. It had never occurred to her how much she had changed. Not even after she'd received the official letter telling her the date on which Paul would be released. But after just a few days she'd begun to feel the crawling fear again. Gladys had immediately taken her in then had begun insisting she leave the state.

Audrey had spent years forcing him into the background and undergoing therapy when she could afford it. Only to realize now, with a sinking stomach, that all her changes could be swept away this easily. Once again she was the Audrey of old, the one who had accepted that love meant physical pain and injury. The one who was afraid when she was alone.

She understood that Cam had to keep an eye on his business. That was a primary concern. And he probably hadn't expected that working on Gladys's house was going to turn into an all-day, every-day kind of job, rather than something he could fit in around his regular routine.

Then came Audrey. She'd changed everything about his life, and while he'd been nice about it, there were probably times he wanted to explode in frustration. What did he owe her, after all? And just how much did he feel he owed to Gladys?

Or maybe he was just that nice of a person. Too nice, maybe.

Audrey hunkered in the kitchen, drinking so much coffee she should have gone into orbital flight. Or rather pouring it, taking two sips, letting it cool, then dumping it down the sink.

And getting another fresh cup.

She could see herself as if from a bit of distance, judge her own behavior, and realized she would have laughed at almost any other time.

Not now, though. Not when she was afraid a threat might be a short distance away. Short enough that he might burst through the door at any minute.

God! Where had all the strength she'd worked on developing gone? Now she felt almost as if Paul had never left. As if he'd spent the last six years brutalizing her and apologizing.

"Wimp," she said aloud. "You damn wimp!"

Then as night settled in, bringing with it all the fears and worries of darkness, she heard a truck approaching the house.

Cam had left the exterior security cameras on for her. She always ignored them, but not today. Not now. She edged over to the little square of kitchen counter and studied the picture for the front approach.

Cam! The relief she felt almost weakened her knees. She grabbed the edge of the counter and drew deep, steadying breaths.

Clyde, who been silent and busy preening his ten bazillion feathers all day, spoke. "Now you can feel better."

God, even the bird had figured out her mood, though why he should care she couldn't imagine. Human and bird. Couldn't get more different. And yet Clyde seemed to have a very strong awareness of her moods. Not that he always paid attention.

Sheesh, she hadn't even thought of making something for

dinner. Surely Cam would be starving. Then she reminded herself that he was a grown man and if he was hungry he knew how to feed himself.

Unlike Paul. As if he were a two-year-old, Paul had always needed her to put food in front of him, whether it was a meal or snacks for a football or basketball game. And beer. Beer always had to be at hand.

She wiped her hands over her eyes then watched the camera as Cam climbed out and headed toward her front porch. She didn't think she'd ever been so glad to see anyone.

She wanted to run to the front door, but embarrassment held her back. She so wanted to appear as if nothing about her day alone had troubled her, but she suspected she was going to fail.

Oh, well. At least she wasn't blubbering on the floor or in a closet.

"Hey," Cam said as he entered the kitchen, bringing some cold air with him. "I hope you haven't eaten already. I found a place on the way back that serves Tex-Mex. As in burritos and tacos?"

"Oh, that sounds wonderful!" It truly did.

"Good. Might have to warm some of it up, though. My truck heater doesn't put out oven temperatures." He slung his shearling jacket over the back of a chair and turned the oven on to a low temperature.

"I can do that," Audrey said, almost automatically.

He eyed her sternly. "Why in the hell should you have to?"

Surprised, she dropped into a chair and watched him bring out white paper–wrapped items and put them on a baking sheet. "Not long," he promised.

"How'd your trip go?" she asked when he joined her at the table.

"Pretty good, actually. Thanks to Dan, everything appears to be in great shape. It's an awful lot to ask of him, though."

Audrey clenched her fists, knowing she had to do the right thing, awful as if felt to her. "My aunt didn't ask you to babysit me. I'm sure you can go back to your business any time you want to."

Cam didn't answer immediately. He went to the stove and pulled out the tray on which he'd warmed the food. "Dig in," he said, setting it in the middle of the table. He added a couple of plates and some flatware, then rejoined her.

"The thing is," he said as he unwrapped a burrito, beans and cheese oozing all over his plate, "Gladys only asked me to look in on you from time to time when I was out this way to work on the house. No babysitting involved."

Audrey looked up from her soft taco. "Then what...?"

"Me," he said, meeting her gaze. "Just me. For now, I just don't think you should be alone for long. Sorry, Clyde, but she also needs someone bigger. Just to be sure. Safe."

Audrey didn't know what to say. She could feel her eyes prickle with unshed tears. "Cam..."

"You can throw me out any time you want."

Then, surprising Audrey—in fact, astonishing her—Clyde took to the air and landed on Cam's shoulder. Cam jerked a little, startled, and twisted his head to look at Clyde. "Well, hello."

Clyde rubbed his head briefly against Cam's face. "He's right, Audrey. You need more than me. He's the bigger man here."

For a second, just a second, the entire room felt as if it

were suspended in a silent vacuum. But then, at the same moment, Cam and Audrey started to laugh.

"What's so funny?" Clyde demanded. "He *is* a bigger man."

Wiping her eyes, this time for a different reason, Audrey spoke, laughter still breaking her voice a bit. "A zany joke, Clyde. That's all. And I don't think I could ever explain it in any way that would make sense."

"Ditto," said Cam. Clyde still perched on his shoulder. "You want some of this, Clyde?"

Clyde leaned forward a few millimeters then said, "Nah. Not my thing."

"I'll get you some millet," Audrey offered. "That *is* your thing."

"Now we're talking." Clyde hopped down from Cam's shoulder and settled at the far edge of the table.

But Audrey's mind was on other things as she went to get the millet stick. Like how much she had acted like a frightened rabbit today. Worse, how sickeningly scared of Paul she had felt.

She eyed Cam across the table as she sat down again and started to work on her soft taco and realized that as much as he was enjoying his supper, he was watching her. Not overtly, but those glances were just enough.

"Quit worrying about me," she said. "I'm okay." Much as she had said to him this morning.

"I'm not worrying about you."

She didn't believe him, but she wasn't about to say so. "Paul's not going to show up here. Even assuming he could find out where I am, why should he? It's a long way to come to tell me he's angry with me. And why should he be angry? I never pressed the charges and I never testified."

"You're right."

Like he believed it. God, she hated herself. Wrecking Cam's life because hers was such a mess. Or might be such a mess. How many times was she going to have to remind herself that Paul was going to be a lifelong threat even if he moved to Kathmandu and took up an esoteric religion?

Because Paul was a threat engraved on her heart and mind. A bogeyman to chase her the rest of her life.

"Hell," she said and put her taco down. It had begun to taste like ashes.

"What?" Cam asked, naturally.

It was probably written all over her face, Audrey thought. She wasn't good at mastering her expressions. Then, what the hell, why not tell him? He was here all the time anyway.

She made herself look straight at him. No hiding by looking down. "I was scared when I was alone. I hate myself for it, I felt like a wimp, but it was awful. And worse, it was ridiculous, because back in Denver I had my own apartment, and I wasn't afraid to be alone there."

"Maybe because Paul was still in prison." He spoke quietly, his tone revealing nothing, not sympathy, not explanation. Unlike too many years since she escaped Paul, unlike too many people, he wasn't even hinting at what she could do or might have done. Just a listening ear.

Which was what she needed right then. Her own brain was throwing up enough stuff to make her scared even of herself.

"And that's another thing," she said, grabbing on to the last vestiges of her courage. "What if he does find me? What if I fall into... What if I don't know how to escape... I can't go through that again."

CAM LEANED BACK in his chair, thinking over what Audrey had just said. That she'd been scared when she was alone was hardly mystifying to him. But this business about not being able to escape Paul. Being worried if he came back that she...what? Might fall under his spell again?

What kind of magic did this guy have, anyway?

Audrey had begun to shiver, her arms wrapped around herself, her gaze distant. One thing for sure, whatever Paul had done to her in the past had just moved sharply into the present.

After a couple of minutes, she said, in a slightly broken voice, "I'm sorry."

"Nothing to be sorry for. You had a stressful day."

"That's a kind way to put it."

"It's just the truth."

But she cried out, "It *shouldn't* have been so stressful!"

That did it. Rightly or wrongly, he tossed down his napkin and went to kneel by her chair, wrapping his arms snugly around her.

If she was having nightmares about men in general, he was about to get a taco dumped on his head. But no such thing happened. She sat stiffly within his embrace, giving in not at all and still shuddering. Tremors ripped through her entire body.

Now what, jerk? he asked himself. She wasn't softening, she wasn't getting any better and his offer of comfort wasn't even penetrating.

Cam wasn't a man who felt helpless or useless very often. He was a take-charge kind of guy, walking into almost any situation and knowing how to handle it. Apparently he suffered from a bit of self-delusion, because he couldn't think of a damn thing to do for this woman.

All he could do was ease her into less stiffness, gently urge her taut body closer to his. Little by little he tugged her closer. And little by little she leaned until she rested against his chest.

The shudders had grown almost violent, but he held her snugly enough to quiet them a bit. To urge her to soften.

Little by little, the shuddering calmed. Then changed into tears. Hot and silent, he knew they were there only because he felt his shirt grow warm and damp.

He began to murmur soothing words and raised his hand to cradle her head. "It's all right, Audrey. It's okay. It'll get better." He hoped like mad that he was telling her the truth.

When she had calmed completely, he rose with her cradled in his arms and sat on the lousy kitchen chair, holding her on his lap. It couldn't have gotten much more uncomfortable. At the first opportunity, he had to get that recliner in the living room back into some kind of function. Right now the whole thing was frozen in position.

To keep Audrey from slipping to the floor, he had to hold her even more tightly, then wanted to cuss himself because *now* he was becoming acutely aware of her womanly shape. Her breasts, surprisingly full, pressed against him. Her hip was perfectly rounded. The part of her bottom that sat on him made contact with a part of him that was trying to get closer, to take over his rational mind and turn him into a… A what? A worse person than Paul?

God! This position wouldn't do. It might not be the sexiest position in which he'd ever held a woman, but it was doing its job anyway.

Gritting his teeth against his rapidly burgeoning desire, he rose and carried Audrey to her bedroom. Yeah, it didn't sound much safer than the kitchen chair, far from it, but at least he could put her down. Could make it possible for him to comfort her at a safe distance.

As he laid her down with the pillow beneath her head, he wished like hell that Clyde would say something to break the moment, to bring sanity back.

But Clyde said not a word, and when Cam looked at him he was pretty sure he saw knowledge in those golden eyes. Then Clyde resumed preening.

What a life, Cam thought. Most of it spent working on those damn feathers. He hoped it felt good. It had to be something like him trying to wash his hair strand by strand. He'd go nuts.

Audrey lay with her eyes closed. Her breathing was too rapid to suggest she had fallen asleep, so Cam figured she just wasn't ready to face the world yet. He wondered if he should touch her lightly, just to tell her she wasn't alone.

But what if she wanted to be alone? He cussed under his breath and reached to lay his hand lightly on Audrey's knee.

She didn't pull away. She didn't start shaking again. Both good signs, he reckoned.

It seemed almost like forever, but Audrey finally stirred. First she sighed, then she rolled over on her side, still slightly crunched. Her eyes remained closed.

"Sorry for the meltdown," she said, her voice a little hoarse and whispery.

"I suspect you've needed that for a while."

"Maybe." She drew up her knees and tucked her hands between her thighs. "Sorry I treated you to the spectacle."

"I was glad to be here."

"Oh, quit being so nice, Cam," she said a bit sharply, opening her eyes and looking at him. "You have a right to be annoyed by all of this. By Gladys's request, by me carrying on like a baby..."

"Stop right there," he said, interrupting her in a harsh voice. "You're not carrying on like a baby. Far from it. This isn't about dirty diapers or hunger. Got it? You got some real problems here, Audrey. You think I'm gonna get upset because you need to let it out? I'm not perfect, but I'm not *that* kind of guy."

"Cam..."

"And we're going to have our first fight here and now if you keep apologizing for your existence. You were married to some monster who twisted you in knots, apart from hurting you physically. Well, those knots ain't gonna go away overnight, and now he's out there again. Guy needs hanging."

A small, uncertain laugh escaped her. "Sounds good to me."

Then, slowly, she rose on an elbow. "I keep having this other thought," she said quietly. "Just a niggle I don't let come to the surface because I'm such a mess."

"What's that?"

"He doesn't need *me*. He could find someone else. He sure attracts women."

"That's not *your* problem."

"Maybe it is. Maybe if I'd had the guts to testify..."

"According to Gage your hospital records did all the testifying necessary. Plus the 9-1-1 calls."

"Oh, God!" She grabbed a pillow and buried her face in it. "Damn it, damn it, damn it."

Cam touched her shoulder. "What?"

She tore the pillow away. "I'm never going to get away

from this, am I? It's all part of a public record! I forgot about that."

God. Helpless as he'd ever been, Cam gave up and lay beside her, gathering her close, as close as she'd let him, which wasn't very close.

Of course not. He'd been the bearer of bad news. It'd be a wonder if she didn't kill the messenger.

"How could I have forgotten that?" she asked angrily.

"Maybe because a lot of people who care about you don't ever bring it up." Unlike him. "Sorry. I wasn't thinking."

"It's not your fault. It's reality. Just because I don't want to remember it doesn't make it any less real. But... I guess I was playing hide-and-seek with myself. Which is never useful."

"But normal. And maybe useful at times." He risked running his hand down her back. "Think what life would be like if we had to carry every single bad thing at the forefront of our minds. We'd all lie around in useless heaps of anger or tears."

That caught her attention, and a watery chuckle escaped her. "Like a graveyard full of restless mounds."

"Well, that's one way of looking at it."

"Or full of vengeance," she said quietly.

Cam's heart skipped. He asked carefully, "Are you thinking about vengeance?"

"Sometimes I do. Instead of sitting in this house waiting for a bomb to explode, I'd really like to get out there and hunt him. Let *him* know what it feels like."

"And if you found him?"

"All bets are off," she said in a voice so angry he hoped he never heard it again. "I don't know what I'd do."

So there was the other scar, Cam thought. With all the

scars this woman bore, she had another one. That bastard had managed to twist her soul.

At that moment, Cam wanted vengeance of his own.

THE FOOD SURVIVED yet another reheat pretty well, and the two of them took another stab at eating. Conversation was minimal—hardly surprising. Clyde emerged from his preoccupation with his feathers and joined them at the table, giving Audrey the side-eye.

"You know," she said, "you really *could* find yourself too heavy to fly."

Gladys's voice answered her. "I've heard that one. Anyway, you don't let me fly much. I won't be trying to escape any hawks."

"He has a point," Cam said, a smile crossing his face.

"And I," continued Clyde, lifting one talon to nibble it briefly, "don't have the weight problems you poor humans do. If I eat too much millet, I eat less of something else."

"Not the best diet," Audrey retorted. Nevertheless, she got him another millet stick. This day had been too rough to worry about anything.

She felt exhausted, hollowed out. But she also felt as if she'd crossed an important line in dealing with Paul and her past. She couldn't have put it into words, but her heart felt lighter now. Not perfect, but definitely lighter.

When they got around to cleaning up the wrappers and putting the few leftover tacos in a plastic container in the fridge, Audrey froze in front of the window. It was dark out there, and she hadn't closed the curtains. But it wasn't the darkness that disturbed her. It was something else that ran up and down her spine, cold tingles.

"He's out there," she said. "I can feel it."

Cam reached up and quickly pulled the curtains closed. "Come away," he said. "Come sit down away from the windows."

Numbly, she did so, then wondered in her whirling mind where that certainty had come from. She didn't think Paul was near enough to see through that window, didn't think he was all that near right now.

But she felt him, as if he were engraved on the very marrow of her bones.

"He's coming," she said, her voice as taut as a violin string. "He's coming." Then she put her face in her hands, not crying, just dealing with an ugly certainty that her marriage to Paul wasn't over. Not by a long shot.

When she looked up again, her hands trembling, she met Cam's gaze. "You must think I'm nuts. How can I know he's coming?"

Cam shook his head slowly. "I don't think you're nuts. Do I think people can sense things beyond the normal? Hell, yeah. My mom did it a lot. Used to make people wary of her, so she just stopped talking about it except at home."

Audrey drew a sharp breath. "She was psychic?"

"She wouldn't have put it that way. Just sometimes she *knew*. Not often. I don't think she liked it very much." He sighed. "Anyway, I told you about the stolen truck, so if you say you feel like Paul is coming, I'm not going to argue with you."

"But how could I know for sure?" That question plagued her even as she felt the truth of her statement to her very core. Paul was coming. How could she know that except through speculation?

"I don't know," Cam answered. "But I wouldn't dismiss it, and isn't that the reason I'm here?"

Then the time came. The horrific time he'd wanted to avoid at all costs but couldn't. "Gage gave me a file about Paul. Needless to say you're a big part of it. What do you want to do?"

"Kill him. Can I see that file, please."

Cam sighed. "Are you sure? His record is bad enough but the stuff about you. The pictures..."

She visibly stiffened. "I lived through it. I can stomach the photos. So is he on the way?"

Cam fisted his hands and it took him nearly a minute to find his voice. He didn't want to tell her this. None of it. Maybe he was a freaking coward and avoiding telling her all this time hadn't been to protect her, but to save him from facing her pain directly. "Yeah, he's coming."

"Oh, God," she breathed and closed her eyes. "Oh God."

"I didn't want to tell you," he admitted. "I tried to avoid it."

Her eyes opened. "Trying to protect me? How the hell could you protect me from Paul until he gets here? I'd have to know then, wouldn't I? You should have told me."

That was true. And maybe it was only tension and everyone else's belief, like Gladys's, that might have taken over, but they sank deep within her to fill her with certainty.

A need to call her aunt began to fill her. To hear her caring voice. To feel Gladys take away some of that worry, just by her caring. That warm voice...

She reached for her phone, and Clyde landed on her shoulder.

"It's about time," he said sounding like Groucho Marx.

"How'd you know?" Audrey asked mildly.

"I read minds. Now dial."

Cam snorted, and Audrey looked over to find him smiling. "It seems contagious," he remarked.

"Yeah," Audrey answered, feeling a bit unnerved. But of course Clyde knew what she was about to do because the only time she'd reached for her phone since arriving here was to call Gladys.

Refusing to give in to a sudden urge to be stubborn, just because of Clyde, she punched Gladys's number and heard her aunt's kind voice pour into her ear.

"Oh, I'm so glad you called," Gladys said. "I was wondering about you and Clyde. Everything is okay?"

Audrey looked at Clyde, who was busy giving her the side-eye again. "Yeah, we're fine. And Cam is going out of his way to keep an eye on me. He's actually living here. Well, sorta. If you can call sleeping on the couch living with me."

"Isn't he a good man? Now, put me on speaker so y'all can hear me, including that sassy bird of mine."

Audrey put the phone down, but just before she hit the speaker button, she looked at Clyde. "Aunt Gladys thinks you're sassy."

If that bird could have grinned, Audrey had no doubt he would have. "I'm also saucy, too," he said as Audrey switched the speaker on.

"I hope you're not driving Audrey crazy."

"Not at all. I'm being quieter than usual, although she probably doesn't realize it, me being new to her."

"The day you become quiet," Gladys retorted, "I'll take you to the bird vet. And I know how you hate that."

"It's demeaning!"

But Gladys ignored him. "Cam, I'm sorry if this is interfering with your work schedule. I didn't imagine you'd have to stay there so much of the time. I wasn't thinking about it."

"It's okay," said Cam. "But this is my choice. I don't feel right about this situation at all."

Gladys fell silent. The crackle and pop of a lousy cell phone connection filled the room. At last she said, "I don't feel right about it, either. That man! I wish I could have him arrested right now."

Sad as she felt, Audrey knew one thing for sure. "He has to do something that he can be arrested for, Aunt Gladys."

"I *know* that. It doesn't mean I can't wish."

Another silence fell around the table, maybe because they were all wishing the same thing.

"Of course," Audrey said finally, "it would be okay if his truck slid over a cliff on these icy roads."

That did it. Cam started to laugh. Gladys's chuckle could be heard over the phone, and after a few seconds, Audrey's laughter joined them. Even Clyde laughed.

"Oh, what an image," Gladys said when she caught her breath. "It would be so fitting. So very fitting for that man. And maybe they wouldn't find him for a week so he could freeze…" Then Gladys caught herself. "I'm going to have to go to confession for this." Then she started laughing again.

After the call ended with a lot of hugs and kisses, many included for Clyde, Audrey looked at the bird. "Gladys is really sorry she had to give you up."

"Of course she is," Clyde agreed. "Anyone would be."

Audrey tsked audibly. Clyde spread a wing then closed it, a mark of disapproval, Audrey presumed.

Then Clyde let out a loud squawk. "I miss Gladys!"

Clyde turned around on his perch, giving Audrey a view of his red tail feathers.

"I'm going to bed," Clyde announced.

Then Clyde did what he wanted, as usual. He winged his way into his palace in the bedroom and began to sing.

"That's probably some kind of hex he's putting on us," Cam remarked. "I should probably do the same and head for the couch."

She didn't want him to find his way to his sleeping bag. She didn't want to sit here alone as she had most of the day. But it was late, awfully late now, and they should all go to bed.

Clyde had been right about that much. But still, she didn't want to be alone again. Clyde talked a blue streak, but he could never be a *real* friend. A human friend.

"Good night," she said to Cam, a forced smile on her face.

"Ah, hell," he said. He shifted on his chair and said, "You don't want to be alone. I don't want to leave you alone. You don't look ready for bed to me."

"But *you* are," she protested.

He shook his head. "Not really. It's been a long day for both of us, but it's funny how that often tends to make us less sleepy. Got any games we can play?"

"Cards?" she suggested. "I seem to remember Aunt Gladys always having a few decks on hand."

"Cards would be good."

Audrey tried to remember where Gladys kept her playing cards with an increasingly unhappy feeling that they were probably in one of the covered furniture pieces in the parlor. Well, of course. They certainly wouldn't be kept in the kitchen.

"Audrey? If you don't mind playing with a used deck, well used, I've got one in my glove box."

Relieved, she smiled. "I don't mind at all."

Which was how she and Cam came to be playing cards at two in the morning while the remaining snow melted.

Chapter Twelve

Morning's light shone all too quickly through the café curtains in the kitchen. It was the first time Audrey noted that this side of the house faced east.

But boy, was that light bright. She squinted against it and rubbed her eyes...

Then sat up abruptly. Where was she? How could she have fallen asleep in the kitchen? There was no place...

But then she noticed she was wrapped in Cam's sleeping bag. *Oh, God.* But for a few seconds before she let shame wash over her, she pressed the material to her face and smelled Cam. Delightful Cam.

Then she wondered how she'd come to be in his sleeping bag and how was he possibly sleeping without it? Wouldn't it have made more sense for him to wake her and urge her to bed?

Clyde zipped into the room and flapped his wings right at her face. "That *man*," he said, "is sleeping in your bed."

"Oh?" It still didn't make sense. A couple of beers? Just two? Could they have knocked her out this much? Man, there was a tale here, and she needed to hear it. Soon.

Clyde hopped around a bit. "Breakfast?" he prodded.

"In a minute. I need to get up, and to do that I have to untangle myself."

Cam's voice answered her. "I'll help you."

She pulled the edge of the sleeping bag up to her chin, as if she needed protection. Maybe she did. Nice as Cam was, he was still a man. "What happened?"

"I honestly don't know." Cam spread his hands. "You fell asleep at the table. I tried to wake you, but you weren't waking up. I mean, Audrey, you were out like a light. So I figured I'd carry you to bed. I don't know what happened, but you were like limp spaghetti and I couldn't get a safe grip on you. My sleeping bag seemed like the only safe solution."

"But…" Perplexed, she didn't know what to say.

"Yeah. I don't understand it either. If you'd drunk a bottle of bourbon, or even half of one…but you didn't. You and I only drank beer."

"That's what I thought. I remember two."

"Well, the second six-pack was pretty much demolished, so somebody drank more than two. Me, probably."

"But it didn't lay you out on the floor."

He smiled. "And maybe you're just not used to alcohol. One way or another, I guess we can chalk this up to weird. Want me to help you up?"

She struggled against the sleeping bag to free herself.

"What the heck were you doing in your sleep?" he wondered. Then he held out his hands. "Come on, I'll get you up. Just keep your feet braced against mine. There you go."

He got her upright, but she was still wrapped in the sleeping bag from her knees down. Clyde hopped onto her shoulder. "I'm hungry."

"I heard you the first time. Just hang on."

"Bats hang. I do not."

But all Audrey noticed was the warmth of Cam's hands holding hers. Strong, large hands, roughened by hard work. She was reluctant to let go.

Audrey leaned on Cam's shoulders as he untangled her feet. At last she was able to step out of the puddle of canvas and set her feet on the linoleum floor. Which was when she realized she was still wearing her sports shoes. Which meant dirty socks.

"God!" she said. "I must stink. Time to dive into the shower again."

"After you feed me," said Clyde.

Audrey sighed. "Yes, Clyde. At your command, Clyde."

Cam spoke. "Feed yourself, Clyde."

An indignant squawk issued from the parrot. "I would, except *she* keeps it sealed!"

"Ah, hell," Audrey sighed.

Cam put his hand on her shoulder. The weight was welcome. "What would happen if you went to shower and I fed the noisy guy? I have before."

Clyde grumbled.

"He'd shut up and eat," Audrey said, offering her first smile of the day. Crooked, but still a smile.

So she told Cam where she kept the bag of parrot food and how to fill his feeding cup and headed for the shower. Somehow she felt as if she were shedding a weight. Clyde? Could he have become a burden?

Nah. It was other weights. Like Paul. A shiver trickled down her spine as she thought of him and how he might be approaching. Beneath the spray of the shower, she closed her eyes and said a little prayer.

Truth was, while she hadn't said anything in court, while she had, honestly, waited for others to speak for her, she knew what she had escaped. If she'd had half a spine, she'd have spoken up for herself a lot earlier even with Paul standing right there. Without lying to medical people who always asked how she'd injured herself. People who would have believed her.

But did she even believe herself? Even now she couldn't answer that question honestly. Hospital X-rays and MRIs, standing as stark proof of all that she had suffered at Paul's hands.

But even then, even hearing a doctor read her record of the entire list of things Paul had done to her, she still had trouble believing it.

Trouble believing that had happened to her. Trouble believing she'd put up with it for so long. Wondering who Audrey really was.

Pressing her hands against the tile wall of the shower, she leaned forward into the spray, as if she wished she could drown herself right there and then. The water began to turn cold and she didn't notice. All these years, all the therapy, didn't answer the burning question: Who the hell was she?

A rap on the door drew her out of her morose thoughts.

"Audrey?" Cam asked loudly enough to be heard over the water. "Are you okay?"

"I'm fine," she answered thickly. "Just fine."

Apparently he didn't like the sound of her voice. She heard the door creak as he opened it. "Need anything? Like help?"

That's when she realized that her thoughts had left her weak. Legs didn't want to hold her. Arms shook. Tears ran down her face as strongly as the water from the showerhead. Cold now. She was getting cold.

She tried to answer that she was okay, but the words

wouldn't come. The next thing she knew, the shower curtain swept back and fluffy old towels wrapped around her. Cradling her. Holding her close and secure.

"It's okay," Cam murmured. "It'll be all right."

Whatever that was, Audrey thought foggily, her mind struggling to emerge from the nightmare she'd been reliving.

"Shh," Cam murmured, carrying her from the bathroom. "It's all okay."

But would it ever be again?

Damn, the tears wouldn't stop rolling down her face. Cam put her on her bed and wrapped another towel around her, this time covering her legs.

So embarrassing, she thought, but the feeling was distant, part of herself so far away that it barely touched her. Gentle hands rubbing her all over with towels. She ought to be embarrassed but couldn't manage it.

Then she was gently tucked beneath the quilt and top sheet of the bed, and a hand patted her hip gingerly. Then she felt the bed springs creak as Cam started to move away.

God, she didn't want him to go!

But Cam had already risen from the bed. "Get dressed when you're ready. I'll throw together some kind of brunch."

Then he was gone, which left Audrey feeling raw and staring at a parrot, who was busy preening again.

"God," she said loudly. A startled Clyde looked at her before resuming his self-maintenance.

Feeling ridiculous, no matter how she looked at it, Audrey slid out from beneath the bedcovers and took the wet towels to the bathroom to hang them on the rack.

Eventually, though, she could smell wonderful aromas from the kitchen. With weary arms, she dressed in jeans and a flannel shirt, leaving Clyde behind in his sanctuary. Not that he'd stay there for long.

"Bath," said Clyde from behind her. It wasn't a demand, but it sure let Audrey know which way the bird wanted to go.

Clyde needed his baths, of course. They were as important to his health as his regular preening. He wasn't being difficult, and considering that she'd just taken her own shower, refusing him his could only be cruel.

"After lunch," she promised him. "When there's hot water again." Something to think about besides the past. Besides Paul. Besides her own inadequacies.

In the kitchen, Cam had thrown together a hash of ham, green peppers, a bit of onion and egg. The toaster still worked, amazingly, after all this time, so he tossed rye bread into it and made four slices.

Not bad for a guy who preferred to hit a diner for breakfast because it was fast, easy and didn't require any cleanup. In his trade, time was a precious commodity, and with a few contracts going at the same time, hours became important even when it was cold.

Except here. He'd slowed down a whole lot on the living room, and Audrey was beginning to worry him maybe more than she should have. Gladys had asked him to keep an eye on her, not become her guard or therapist.

But he couldn't leave her like this. No way. However she tried to appear brave, she was growing more scared by the moment, no doubt in her mind that Paul was somewhere out there, after her. He could see it in the way her eyes had become pinched, in the way she had begun to wrap her arms around herself.

There was no reason he could ease her fear, either. She

knew Paul, but he couldn't say the same. He had to let her judge the degree of danger in this screwed-up situation.

Man, had she been through the wringer this morning. He hadn't been able to do a damn thing to help her, either. He'd gone as far as he dared after her shower…but anyway, he didn't think physical comfort was going to work.

When she came into the kitchen, she looked wrung out. Worn through.

He didn't know what else to do except pour her coffee and give her a hefty plate of breakfast. Somewhere in the handbook of the human body, it said to eat.

She reached for the coffee, her hand trembling a bit. Then she looked at him. "I'm sorry."

Before he could answer, she tucked in to the breakfast before her. A hearty appetite. She would get through this.

PAUL WAS A cusser by nature, but rarely had he cussed as much as he did when his truck slid off a hairpin turn and right down into a ditch. A deep ditch. Deeper than his truck was high.

Hell, was anyone going to see him stuck down here? Not likely. A wind was starting to blow, and with it snow swirled in a nearly impenetrable wall of white. *Whiteout.* "Damn it all to hell!" He kicked a tire that was rapidly becoming buried. Two choices now: ride it out down here or climb up to the highway and hope he could hitch a ride before someone drove over him because they were blinded.

His ears told him, though, that traffic up there was slowing down. Paying attention to road conditions the way he should have. He kicked the tire again. This was all Audrey's fault for making him chase her all the way out here.

Yeah, her fault. He was going to have a few words to say to her about this. And they wasn't gonna be nice words.

Resigning himself to climbing up to the road through the steadily deepening drifts, he decided he needed more clothes, because that wind was freaking *cold*.

That was when he discovered he had to go to the downslope side of his truck, because the passenger side was already too buried to open the door.

He cussed some more, then stopped when he realized he was sucking in frigid air and his lungs were beginning to hurt. When he plowed his way to the far side of the truck, he saw he had to be very, very careful. Damn thing looked almost like it was ready to roll over, and with all that snow pushing on the other side...

This time he cussed silently. Opening the creaky door with care, he leaned in slowly. Gloves. Phone. Balaclava to put over his head and face.

He stared into the cabin, wondering if there was anything else important in there.

Only the pistol in the glove box. Legal in this state, so he didn't have to worry about that being found. Not that it mattered. The ancient rig he was driving was stolen.

God almighty, he thought as he pushed his way up the side of the ditch. He was gonna have a heart attack before he got up to the road.

Wind whipped icy crystals at him, which he didn't feel except around his eyes where the mask didn't cover fully. And around his nostrils, which were close to cracking. Breathe? Ha!

When at last he reached the shoulder of the road, he collapsed onto his hands and knees. That's when he figured nobody was gonna stop for him. The plow had left the snow too high and no room for someone to pull over. These semi trucks might as well have been a train with linked-up boxcars.

He shoulda listened to the motel guy. It wasn't often Paul admitted, even to himself, that he'd made a mistake, but this time he did. *One more day*, the guy had said.

A truck coming by threw a pile of slush at him and most of it indicated it intended to stick and melt on his balaclava. He'd have liked to kill that truck driver. In fact, he was getting to the point of wanting to kill a lot of people and spend the rest of his life in prison rather than deal with this.

Then he remembered Wyoming had the death penalty. So, okay, he wouldn't kill anyone, just think about it.

He covered his face with his hands, elbows and knees on the snow, and wondered just how he was going to get out of this one. Hike down the mountain? How?

"You hurt, son?"

A drawly sort of man's voice spoke, and Paul reluctantly looked up. "Nah," he said, not wanting anyone to interfere with his business. Then he realized he was being stupid again.

"What happened?" The guy towering over him had a nice, thick gray beard and a cowboy hat that was tacked to his head with a stampede string.

"Truck went off the road." Paul waved vaguely.

The older man climbed the snowbank and looked down. "Almost can't see it," he remarked.

Surprise, surprise, Paul thought. "I know. Barely got up here."

"Well, these conditions ain't great for towing you out of there. Not enough room to park myself sideways."

Then he turned back to Paul. "Want a ride, fella? I can get you as far as Whistleblower Creek."

Whistleblower Creek? He wondered about the story behind that but didn't feel like asking, not right now. "Thanks, man. I'm soaked and freezing." Then he added, hard as it was for him to say, "You're saving my life."

"Most like," the man answered. "Terrible to be stuck out here in this weather. Law says I gotta stop. Them big semis would have stopped, too, but I doubt they could without sliding. Come on, find your feet and let's go."

Only when he stood up did Paul realize how cold he'd gotten. His arms and legs didn't want to move right, and he was stumbling like a drunk. His new friend grabbed him by the arm and steadied him along.

"You got too cold," the man said. "I got a thermos of hot chocolate in my truck. Sally always makes me something hot when I gotta go out in bad weather."

Paul was panting again, but through the swirling snow he saw a fairly new blue pickup truck.

"What do you do?" Paul asked through chattering teeth. Information was always useful.

"Undertaker," came the answer.

Oh, God, Paul thought. Maybe the guy was looking for a new client?

Then he shook his own head. Cold was getting to his brain.

"Yup," the guy answered. "Always a need for an undertaker, at least since people stopped keeping the bodies in the living room for the wake."

"Ground," Paul managed just as the guy opened the passenger door of his truck. A broken question that announced his brain was still half frozen. The undertaker understood though.

"Oh, I got cold storage."

Cold storage. This had to be a nightmare. He must be lying almost dead beside the road.

But then hands pushed him up onto a seat in the truck's cab and hot air hit him in the face. So hot it felt like his face was gonna burn up. He struggled to move his hands enough to strip the balaclava off. That only made the heat more painful.

The undertaker got in the truck behind the wheel. "Warm up a bit," he said as he looked over his shoulder at the traffic. "When you stop shaking so bad, I'll give you that hot chocolate."

A couple of minutes later, he eased them into the flow of traffic. Little by little Paul's teeth stopped chattering, and the shudders that ripped through him eased some.

"Good thing you was shaking and rattling," the undertaker said. "Go much past that and you be a lost cause. I'm Uriel Monroe, by the way. Best caskets west of the Rockies."

Interesting introduction, Paul thought. His anger was cooling in light of a friendly rescue. "I'm Paul Campbell," he lied. "Jack of all trades, some better than others."

Uriel slapped his thigh and laughed. "You got any work lined up?"

"Yeah," Paul said, trying to remember the map of Wyoming. "Got a job in Gillette."

"Well, sorry to say, son, I'm not gonna get you anywhere near there."

"Closer is better."

Uriel nodded. "I'll give you the name of a friend of mine. When the road gets better, he'll pull your truck out."

"Thanks." A truck with no license plate and a VIN that could be traced, not to mention a pistol in the glove box.

Uh, no. That truck was gonna stay right there until the state patrol wanted to move it. Or until it turned into a rusted heap. It was already on the way to doing that.

At last Uriel pointed to the thermos on the console between them. "Pour yourself some, son. Sally always likes it when that bottle comes home empty."

"What were you doing up there on that road?" Paul asked, trying to sound pleasant. "Seems kind of an odd place for an undertaker."

Uriel laughed again. "Three people up there need burying. Woulda got out of there before the storm, but they was a gabby bunch and about to spend a whole lot of money. I got a kid who wants to go to college. I gotta do some fixin' up around my place, too. Coupla places the fence is down and the cattle get out."

Paul was amazed. "You're a rancher, too?"

"Cremation is cheaper. So I got a sideline. Or maybe the mortuary was the sideline so I could keep my ranch. Been so long I don't recall."

"And people are cutting every corner?"

"These days. Used to be a funeral had to be a big deal. Never knew whether that was respect for the dead or keeping up with the neighbors, but this was a comfortable job back then. Then everything changed."

Paul couldn't imagine taking care of corpses could be a comfortable job. Maybe the guy got used to it?

"Family business," Uriel said. "Ever since the days of the Wild West. Back in them days, my people used to do a lot of the work in somebody's parlor. Get 'em ready for the ground. Do our best to keep 'em from stinking for a few days." Then Uriel laughed. "Drank a lotta whiskey back then. Poured it on the corpse, too."

Paul shuddered, not from cold. This was too graphic. Whatever else he might do, bodies didn't come into it.

Uriel continued talking. "Too bad you already got a job. I could offer you one."

Work for this guy? No way. Besides, Paul didn't work if he could avoid it. Audrey did the work. Any woman with him was going to do the working. That was all they was good for: paying for everything and lots of sex.

Only prison had made him work. Gave him no choice. But that was it.

"Couple more hours," Uriel said. "My gal will prolly ask you to eat dinner with us. She's a damn fine cook."

Paul thought about it, decided not to answer right away. The less he said, the better off he'd be.

AUDREY SKETCHED ALL AFTERNOON, enjoying the release her art gave her. Thinking about moving along to actually using her watercolors and pens. Wondering if she should order a better set than she'd brought for her escape. More colors. A bigger variety of pens.

She wasn't exactly flush without the galleries that often sold her water color work. But almost the minute she'd heard about Paul's release, she'd begun cutting ties. Almost the same thing he'd made her do when they were together, except this time she was choosing to do it herself.

Squeezing her eyes shut for a few seconds, she drew a steadying breath. *Don't think about that.* Never think about all that beast had forced her to relinquish. She had started to build a new life, and she wasn't going to let him stop her now.

Cam passed by on his way to the sink, covered in white dust. He paused at her shoulder, and she immediately tensed. She didn't like people looking over her shoulder at her work.

But he moved on quickly enough. "That's a great sketch," he remarked as he turned on the water and began to wash his hands. "You paint them up?"

"Depends. Watercolors and ink, mostly."

He nodded and shook his hands before reaching for the dish towel beside the sink. "You sell any?"

Of course it always came down to that. Everything had to pay or it was worthless. "Yeah. A few." Her voice expressed some of her irritation.

"Cool," he said, turning and leaning against the counter. "But it's mostly pleasure for you, I hope."

Now that was the core of it, and at last she smiled. "It satisfies my soul."

He nodded and returned her smile. "That's a good feeling. I hope you never lose it."

Then she emerged from her introversion long enough to ask, "What about you?"

That widened his smile. "Nothing makes me happier than the smell of fresh wood and sawdust. Making stuff with my own two hands. Best thing ever."

"I guess in a way we're alike in that."

"So I'd guess. Can I use the shower later? The other one is going to take more time to fix."

She was startled, wondering how he'd been taking care of himself all this time. Sponge baths at the sink? Like Clyde? But Cam sure didn't smell like a man who hadn't applied any soap or water to himself. "Of course you can use it. I wish you'd asked sooner." But she didn't ask him what he'd been doing in the meantime.

"And the good news is..." He looked around. "Where the hell is that bird?"

Clyde suddenly appeared, all gray except for that bright red tail. "She doesn't like being pestered while she's working. I was on my perch in my cage." He landed on Cam's shoulder and looked at Audrey. She couldn't have said why, but she felt awkward all of a sudden.

Clyde clacked his beak, then brought out Humphrey Bogart. "I need a TV. Not enough to do, and don't tell me I got toys. Booooring."

"Oh, boy," Cam said. "Well, I was looking for you, because I have a surprise."

Clyde inched closer to Cam's face.

"I got the heat fixed in the living room. So as soon as it warms up more, I'm taking down the plastic over the door and you'll have more room."

"Thank God," Clyde said, forgetting Humphrey. "I have wings for a reason, and this part of the house isn't enough room."

"I feel bad about that," Audrey said. Not that she'd had much time to think about it. Her past had been nipping at her heels too much.

Clyde had other matters on his mind, though. He hopped closer to Cam's head and began to rub his feathers against him.

"The best of all men," Clyde announced.

A snort of laughter escaped Cam. "So easy to buy your affection, bird? You'd better remind Audrey that you still love her."

Instead, Clyde flew back to the bedroom.

Cam spoke. "Do you ever want to give him away? Talk about rude."

Audrey smiled, but the truth was, she had grown used to Clyde, rudeness included. At least you never had to wonder where you stood with him as you did with most men.

But eventually she had to slip out of the world she was sketching and back into reality. Dinner. The question that occurred every day and never seemed to have a ready answer.

Clyde returned but flew right past her. *Dissed*, Audrey thought, amused.

Cam was busy taking down plastic, complaining from time to time when Clyde's swooping around got in the way. But he laughed, too. Clyde was a show all by himself.

Rubbing her eyes, rolling her shoulder to relieve the stiffness of being bent over her sketch pad for so long, Audrey headed for the cupboard. They'd bought a lot of staples at the grocery, but now as she stared at boxes and cans, she wondered what to do with them. They'd be useful parts of a grander meal, but not good as stand-alones.

Off to the fridge and freezer. At last she settled on frozen chicken breasts. They'd do with some seasonings.

She put the breasts in some cold water to thaw then gave herself the treat of sitting at the table with an icy glass of ginger ale. Icy. Cold. Oh, yes, even though it was cold outside. The fresh, bubbly soft drink felt good in her mouth as well as tasted good.

Then she felt a blast of heat from the overhead register, more than she was used to. Rising, she hurried to the living room to see if something was wrong.

Cam was wrapping up a length of plastic.

"Did something happen?" she asked. "The heat..."

"I turned it up to get this room heated as fast as possible.

Your feathered friend here doesn't have the sense to wait in the kitchen where he'll stay warm."

She looked at Clyde, swooping around the room. "I guess the space feels too good."

"Must be." Cam watched the bird for a minute. "Some character. He even helped me with some directions." Then a snort escaped Cam. "Directions. From Humphrey Bogart, Jimmy Stewart and Groucho Marx."

"I'm surprised Gladys didn't step in to help." Then Audrey clapped her hand over her mouth to stop a laugh from escaping. She wasn't at all sure that Clyde's help had improved Cam's mood.

"If Gladys had shown up," Cam said dryly, "I'd have had to follow orders."

At that, Audrey let her laugh escape. Cam joined her. Clyde tsked from a new perch on an old curtain rod.

"Maybe you shouldn't have said that," Audrey remarked.

Cam looked at the bird. "Probably not. Now he has ideas."

Clyde tilted his head to one side. "I always have ideas. And I'm getting hungry. All this flying…"

Back in the kitchen, Audrey served him some regular food. "Unless you want a copilot," she told the parrot when he made a sound very like a disapproving sniff. He ate, scattering hulls all over the table.

While Cam went to take a shower, Audrey checked the chicken breasts and decided they were just about thawed enough. So how to season them?

With all she'd bought at the grocery, she ought to be able to come up with something more interesting than baked chicken.

She sat at the kitchen table, put her chin in her hand and decided she was ludicrous. She knew how to make hamburgers and fries, mainly because Paul had preferred that for dinner and, oddly enough, thought Audrey was better at it than fast food places.

So…she'd avoided ground beef and potatoes at the store because of Paul. Now here she was faced with a serious shortcoming. She didn't want Cam to have to figure this out, either. Ridiculous. Since Paul had gone to prison, she'd learned to cook for herself again. But it never involved hamburger.

Ludicrous, she thought again. How long was she going to sit here wondering what to do with that chicken? At last she used her phone to scan the web for recipes. She could follow a recipe.

Naturally, most of the recipes were beyond the ingredients she had in the house, but finally she settled on a simple one and got to work.

The internet, savior to anyone who cared to hunt around. At last she was smiling again and humming as she worked.

Cam reappeared, smelling like soap and shampoo, rubbing his dark hair with one of Gladys's ragged old towels. He'd shaved, and his clean face was even more attractive than before.

She nodded at him and forced her attention back to meal prep. No men. She'd vowed that a long time ago, right after Paul. No men. They couldn't be trusted.

But her body sang, knowing Cam was right behind her, smelling his shower freshness. Thank goodness her hands were now covered with breadcrumbs or she might have turned and reached for him.

Invited him into her personal sanctuary. Risked shattering the peace she'd so carefully built for herself.

But she felt him approach until he wasn't far behind her. Close enough to reach out. Close enough to take her. Close enough to own her, as Paul had.

No! But her heart beat rapidly, her breath sped up, her body began to tingle and ache. Oh, God, she couldn't believe she wanted him. Or wanted him this much. An aching between her thighs began, an ache and then a throb that weakened her knees.

"It's okay," murmured Cam. Then his arms slipped around her waist from behind, drawing her back until she leaned against his hard chest. Now she was close to panting.

"It's okay," he murmured again. "It's all right. I'm just holding you, that's all I'm going to do. I understand. But don't you need some help with that damn dinner?"

She froze. Her throat tightened until her breath caught behind a knot. Then, enough oxygen reached her so she could say, "Are you kidding me?"

"Nope," he answered. "You think I couldn't feel your fear before I touched you? That I couldn't see it? I also get that you want me, maybe as much as I want you, but I'm not going to do that until you're sure. So no, I'm not kidding about dinner."

Standing there, still frozen in his gentle arms, still pressed against his hard chest, she looked at her messy hands and tried to absorb what he was saying.

Where had a man like this come from? Or was he just lying? But his embrace was so gentle, and he didn't attempt to do any more than that.

"Cam..."

"I know. Back off. That's fine. Now, what do you need me to do?"

She closed her eyes. What did she need him to do? Make love to her. Push past all her barriers and make love to her.

But the thought, tempting though it was, made a deep part of her quail. No. Not yet.

She sighed and opened her eyes. "I seasoned the breadcrumbs," she said thickly. "Now I just need to bread the chicken." Her hands were covered in the crumbs. A clear statement of the stage she was at.

He let go of her, his arms slipping away as if he felt her body regaining strength. "Go wash your hands. I'm a master at breading chicken."

AT THE WRONG end of Wyoming, or so Paul thought, the undertaker left him in front of a diner. The last thing Paul wanted was to go home with the guy for dinner and find himself being questioned by a curious wife.

He watched the blue pickup drive away, wishing he could have found a way to steal it. Nah, the cops would be all over looking for it. Hell, for all he knew, stealing a guy's pickup might be the equivalent of stealing his horse in these parts.

Regardless, he needed a new rust bucket, and maybe this was the place to find one. Lots of old trucks and cars in this lot. Maybe some of 'em forgotten by owners who'd found something better.

Paul grinned. Yeah, full of stolen cars and trucks nobody wanted to touch. Ha!

Inside the diner he found wonderful aromas of fried food, a waitress who was a bit too friendly and too few people to account for all the cars outside.

He asked the waitress about it and she shrugged. "Roadhouse up the way. Folks'll come back for them cars when they get done drinkin'."

Well, Paul liked the sound of that. He looked at the Budweiser clock over the bar and saw he had plenty of time to heist one of those cars outside. Plenty. And they were all running, too.

Satisfied, he dug into two hamburgers and two orders of fries. And there'd be more if he wanted it.

Better than anything Audrey had ever cooked. He was gonna have to insist she do a better job, here on out.

Yeah, she'd been lazy, no matter how he insisted she do more work. Always limping around, always with her arm in a sling. He didn't believe she was hurt that bad, but it sure slowed her down. That's the time he most wanted to teach her a lesson, but he couldn't. He couldn't send her back to the hospital so soon.

By accident, of course. He'd never wanted to hurt her that bad. She was his *wife*, damn it. And he was gonna get her back.

Still hungry, he ordered himself another round of food and added a beer this time. To his amazement, this place had paper maps, the old kind that were always a pain to fold up.

He opened one now and started studying it. Maybe he wasn't that far away after all. With a good truck on that state highway... He looked out at the parking lot again. Good truck but not eye-catching. Splattered with rust paint. He saw several.

Before long, he'd picked out three possibilities. He'd have to wait until after dark, though. He didn't want nobody in this diner to see him taking a truck. He doubted any of those guys at the roadhouse would be done drinking early. It'd be eleven or twelve, if not closing time.

Yeah, it was a good plan, at least this far into it.

Satisfied, he made himself more comfortable and ordered another beer. He was gonna take care of this mess, soon. Very soon.

That woman had no right to walk out on him. No right at all.

She needed to understand that.

Chapter Thirteen

Audrey was starting to get the creeps. Aunt Gladys called again, joking with Clyde but mostly expressing uneasiness about Audrey and her ex.

"Six years in prison wasn't long enough," Gladys fumed. "No way in hell. I saw the X-rays. I saw the scans. I saw the—"

Gladys caught herself, but it was too late. The baby Audrey had lost because of one solid punch to her stomach. Audrey tried very hard not to think about who that child might have become. Now there it was again, rising like one of her worst nightmares. A child no one but she cared about. A child who'd never had a chance to grow and develop.

Audrey swallowed hard. Clyde landed on her shoulder.

"You know, Gladys," he said, "I never thought I'd have more compassion than you."

Gladys sighed. "Damn bird is smarter than I am. I wish he could come home."

"Audrey is my home now," Clyde said stoutly. "Now, what's the rest of her day that you want to wreck?"

Audrey objected. "Be quiet, Clyde. You're being offensive."

Clyde subsided to grumbles.

"Anyway," Gladys said, "I've been getting more and more worried about you. I've been thinking...that man found me when he got out of prison. How did he do that? You must have mentioned me, because I can't imagine him learning any other way."

Nor could Audrey. Her stomach sank until it felt like a pit. Slowly she said, "Maybe in the early days." Which meant her danger was even greater.

"When everything was moonlight and roses." Gladys sighed. "Totally possible. But if he could find *me*... Well, there are property records. Oh, honey, take extra care. For me, for yourself."

"And for me," Clyde chimed in.

"Gladys, I'm never alone thanks to Cam. Well, rarely. And he's got this place buttoned up like Fort Knox."

"I'm glad to hear it. Just be watchful, sweetie. Alert."

As if she could be anything else, Audrey thought. A few hours a day while she sketched. The rest of the time fear dogged her heels.

Just because Paul hadn't managed to kill her when they were together, that didn't mean he wouldn't succeed this time. Especially after prison. She'd heard that sometimes made men more violent.

Paul had come close more than once. Like the times he'd strangled her until she nearly passed out. He'd loved doing that, then always apologized and blamed it on something she had done wrong.

It had taken more than a year in therapy to convince her that wasn't true. She wasn't sure she honestly believed it, though. Her therapist had warned her that victims often tried to blame themselves, to tell themselves it wouldn't have happened if they'd done something different.

Maybe that's exactly what she was doing. Regardless, she'd often seen something in Paul's eyes, something that told her he could kill her if he wanted to. After six years in prison, that was probably exactly what he wanted to do to her even though she still clung to the belief, or hope, that he wouldn't.

She went to lay out her sketching materials while Clyde flew around his larger space, clearly enjoying it.

Then she froze. A tingle ran along her spine, stronger than it had been in a long time. She recognized it. It had always meant that Paul was coming home. But out here?

Helplessly, she croaked, "Cam?"

He didn't answer immediately, as he was busy hammering something. "Cam?" she called more loudly.

A moment later he appeared, dust covered, in the kitchen doorway. "What's up?"

She shuddered. "I can feel him. He's not far away now."

CAM HARDLY KNEW what to say about that. He was far from dismissing intuition, especially since he'd seen it save the lives of some of his buddies in battle. And if Audrey had any reason to be intuitive about this, it would be her long association with Paul. She could predict him better than anyone.

And Gladys's call earlier had made him uneasy himself. How *had* Paul found Gladys, anyway? Different last names. They'd never met. Unless Gladys was right, that in the starry first days of marriage, Audrey had given more information than she realized. People *did* like to talk about their families.

Hell. Not that he hadn't expected this, but he'd been honestly hoping that Paul would get lost out there in the wide-open spaces.

The snow was beginning to melt, as if someone had turned a hot blow dryer on it. Soon every road in the state would be passable.

"I wonder if he's hitchhiking or driving."

"Driving," Audrey said with certainty. "Once I heard him talk about boosting cars."

"That's not gonna help much." But that didn't prevent Cam from calling the sheriff and asking Gage about any more stolen vehicles.

Gage sighed. "You ever wish they'd drive their own cherry-red cars and carry all their identification with them... and speed?"

Cam had to laugh. "You wish."

"Well, I'll put out an alert for any older vehicle that's new around here. The new-around-here part is at least relatively easy."

After disconnecting, Cam looked at Audrey, hating himself for killing whatever was left of her innocence. "Ever use a shotgun?"

She stiffened, clearly freezing again. The reality of this situation was obviously becoming too real. "I can't," she said, her voice muffled. She'd shot one, but never at a man.

"Think you could do it if it was loaded with salt?"

"Salt?" Her gaze drifted to him.

"Hurts like hell but usually won't kill. And you don't have to have a great aim."

She turned her eyes down, rubbing her face. Cam didn't like the way she looked right now. It was as if every bit of stress inside her had come crashing down all at once. Tense and paler than he'd ever seen her.

But what could he say? He certainly wasn't about to dismiss her intuition. That would be an awful thing to do.

Presently he said, "You mentioned Gladys had a shotgun. Her dad's?"

"Closet," she answered, her voice muffled.

But shooting was something far beyond anywhere she'd thought she might have to go even though she said she wanted to kill Paul. And he couldn't help feeling guilty because he was helping to bring her there.

He stomped out to his truck and pulled the canvas tarps off two shotguns. But his wouldn't be loaded with salt. No, his load was going to mean business if he couldn't take that creep down with his bare hands. Damn, it was still cold out here, and the metal of the two guns nearly burned.

But first things first. To teach Audrey how to handle that gun just as much as she might need to. To make her feel she wasn't facing her worst nightmare without protection.

When he returned inside, the first thing he noticed was that Clyde didn't flutter by. In fact, the bird seemed to have gone into hiding.

Regretfully, he laid the two shotguns, his and hers, on the table with boxes of ammo, knowing there could be no escaping this.

"Let them warm up awhile," he said. "I'll get us some coffee while we wait."

She was, however, staring at those guns as if they were snakes. This was *not* going to go very well.

"Audrey..." He spoke quietly, knowing he had no words for this situation.

AUDREY LIFTED HER head slowly to look at him. Today he wasn't covered in white dust or even sawdust, although the pleasant scent of the wood clung to him.

Her attraction to him seemed to have broken down all

the barriers she'd tried to build over the years. She didn't want a man, not even briefly. They couldn't be trusted. They were manipulative.

Her brain knew all that, but her body had other ideas. Desire such as she couldn't remember ever having felt rose in her. Her thighs clamped and contradictorily wanted to spread wide. Her heartbeat had become loud in her ears, pounding in time with her growing need. Every skin cell seemed to have become so sensitive that she could feel the brush of her clothes as if it were all amplified.

And her breath sped up, as if the last of the oxygen had been stolen from the room. Along with breathlessness came weakness and a contradictory strength.

As the throbbing between her legs grew, she felt there was only one answer.

Uncertainly, unsteadily, she walked to Cam, dreading rejection when she felt herself opening like a fresh spring bud. Years of building a shell, and it all cracked and fell away.

She wanted. She needed. *Please. Oh, please.*

It seemed to take forever, but she reached Cam in only a few steps. His eyes held hers, steadily but questioningly.

He wasn't going to help her, she realized dimly. This was all going to be in her hands. And she didn't care. Maybe that's what she needed. For it *all* to be her decision.

Slowly, almost fearfully, she slid her arms around his narrow waist. She thought she heard him sigh.

"Cam," she whispered. "Please. Please."

He didn't question her decision. He treated her as a woman who had the right to decide for herself.

In response to her plea, he wrapped her shoulders in his powerful grip and bent his head to kiss her. A deep kiss. One that said he'd always known her, perhaps before time.

One that set off some powerful fireworks throughout her body.

Even as her legs quivered and threatened to buckle, she knew deep in her heart that this was right. Truly right.

She dropped her head against his chest and knotted his flannel shirt in her hands. "Please," she said again.

There was no hesitation in him as he swept her into his arms and carried her to her bed. Dimly she noted that Clyde wasn't there. Thank God. But then the door closed and she knew he wouldn't be coming into the room to comment—or just to watch.

Then every rational thought drifted away as Cam began to undress her, following her clothing with his mouth. A hot mouth. A seemingly hungry mouth. She grabbed and held his head.

"Oh, yes…" she sighed. Heaven was coming to earth, and she couldn't remember if it ever had before. Then she slipped fully into the ecstasy he was creating for her.

Chapter Fourteen

Paul whistled as he drove along the state highway. Lots of big trucks, some carrying cattle, most headed east. Little travel headed west, as he was. Of course, maybe that little ink-spot town didn't get much shipped in or out.

The mortician had taken him well out of his way, but Paul hadn't realized that until he finally got hold of a map at the diner.

It didn't matter. This rattletrap truck was better than the last. Somebody was a weekend mechanic in his own garage, so this baby purred.

The day was warming up some, too. Hard to believe how recently he'd been cussing snow then drove his truck into a ditch. All worked out for the best, he figured.

He sure had a better getaway truck if he needed it.

A hundred more miles, he figured. Then he'd have to find out exactly where Audrey was and how he'd get to her. Thank God for public property records. Thank God Gladys hadn't sold her house. But even then... He grinned.

A hundred miles shouldn't take long. Everyone in the one-stoplight town must know where she was by now. Introducing herself around as Gladys's niece, probably. Shy as she had claimed to be, the woman had sure had a lot of friends when he'd met her. Shy. What a joke.

But this last hundred miles gave him plenty of time to think about how he was going to meet Audrey. Like her long-lost lover, the guy she'd married? Or something darker, something to let her know that she was *his* property and that divorce and jail hadn't changed that?

Probably the last one, he decided. Put the bitch in her place right off the bat. Remind her who was boss. Absolutely.

Besides, it would give him a whole lot of satisfaction to teach her a lesson. A memorable lesson.

And there were so many ways to do it. A knife. His bowie knife had always worked. He'd allowed no other sharp knife in their house, but he was no fool. If that lunatic wife of his took it into her mind for some reason, he didn't want to be missing a part.

But she wouldn't do that. Wouldn't even think of it. She'd known her place and had been grateful for it.

A lot of his friends had envied him, too. The perfect wife. None of them had one. Some of them were even dealing with women who thought they were in charge. But man, did they love hearing Paul's stories. He was always expansive with them, kinda thinking he was a good example and might actually be able to bring a few of them up to snuff.

Occasionally a waitress would slam his beer down in front of him, but he didn't mind. They just hadn't met the right man yet.

Anyway, damn near every night he stopped at a new bar or roadhouse because a motel was handy. Thanks to helping himself to a few wallets back in Denver, he was flush and could afford to sit with a new gaggle of admirers every night, especially when he bought the first round.

This was the life he loved, he realized. All he needed a woman for was laundry, dishes and sex. And a bit of proper cooking.

Maybe he didn't need Audrey at all.

But then he remembered and his mood always darkened. She was *his* property, damn it. *His!*

The next half bottle of beer didn't taste so good, but he remedied that with fries and a burger. Those could always wash away the taste of swill.

Audrey wasn't half-bad at making them herself. Yeah. That was another good reason to drag her back. A burger and fries any time he wanted them.

Good enough.

AUDREY SHIVERED AS cool air touched her naked skin, but that didn't last long. Cam stroked her with his large, warm hands, slightly work-roughened, but that only made them feel better. He followed his hands with his mouth, first plucking at her nipples then licking and sucking on them until she thought she would go out of her mind.

Then he trailed downward, headed for her secrets, and she opened herself, impatient for his touch. Throbbing with need until she felt lightning zinging through her.

With one hand, she reached down and found his head, pushing gently. But he was not to be hurried. Not yet.

Rising, leaving her naked to him, to the world, he began to strip slowly, giving her heavily lidded eyes permission to drink in every line of him. No secrets. He was taking away all the secrets.

The idea thrilled her. So open to one another, and soon

bare skin would touch bare skin in one of life's most delightful experiences.

And she had no doubt that Cam was going to erase her every other miserable memory right now. That he was going to place himself in her mind and wash Paul away.

She hadn't felt like this in years, maybe forever, but she could feel herself opening like a rose, softening all over until she felt she could melt into the bed and become a puddle of desire.

His hands. Oh, God, his hands. They trespassed everywhere, leaving her no secrets of any kind…nor did she want any. Yet as desire slid through her like gentle waves lapping at a shore, she wanted more. She wanted *him*.

She dared as she had never before dared. She didn't need to be a compliant block, and she felt a new freedom growing within her. The right to seek her own pleasure.

Cam's hand gently found her core, leading her to heights she'd never known. But she wasn't yet lost in the sensation. She found his broad shoulders with her hands and urged him up and over her. There she began to explore him with newfound freedom. She was practically gasping, but so was he. He said her name softly, oh, so softly, causing another shiver of delight to pour through her.

She found his small, pointed nipples with her hands and squeezed them. He made nearly the same sounds she had, and delicious hunger grew even stronger. Down over his back, so hard with muscle.

But now he was moving on her, inciting her all the more. She needed, wanted. Any conscious thought was fading away.

She cried out softly as he entered her, a stretching feeling that only excited her more. He belonged there, inside her.

But as he rocked against her, sucking her nipples, he swept her away from reality. Far away.

Out past the stars to a velvety place that wrapped her warmly in her completion, a completion so strong it almost hurt.

Almost immediately he followed her with a groan.

He collapsed on her, their sweaty bodies joined in perfect harmony.

IF PAUL HAD had any idea what was going on, he'd have used that pistol in the glove box. Did everyone around here carry guns in their cars? No matter—it might be very useful to him.

It looked like it was getting more useful by the day. Damn Audrey, she should have waited for him. The way so many wives waited for their men in prison. But Audrey? Oh, no, she'd always been a disobedient bitch.

Then there was that old woman, supposedly her aunt, who'd refused to tell him anything useful. Probably should have killed her, except he didn't want a hunt for him started that early. And not for murder.

Nope, he was gonna get Audrey and train her. But with every passing dusty mile, he got madder at his wife. He shouldn't have to chase her like this. No, she should have greeted him with a chocolate cake and a case of beer. And tons of them orange chips that messed all over his fingers and the arms of his easy chair. That's what she should have done.

Instead she'd run out to the back of beyond.

Well, it'd make her easier to get. Much easier.

He pulled over to check the map again. Getting closer.

This time he didn't bother folding the damn paper, just crumpled it on the floor.

He had a good memory, and he wouldn't forget a damn thing now. Not when he was so close.

AUDREY DIDN'T WANT to get out of bed. She felt so relaxed and so replete that she couldn't remember the last time she'd felt this way, if ever. Cam cradled her as if he were in no rush to leave her side. She passed her hands over him, loving the way he felt. He stroked her in the same way, as if he were making some kind of promise.

But this was no time for promises. She didn't want to think about that. Paul had stolen so much of her and Cam had just given a big chunk of it back to her. Too soon to judge herself and her needs.

But Cam was making her feel beautiful, making her feel genuinely wanted, genuinely sexy. Paul had never made her feel that way, but when she'd met him she hadn't known any better.

Cam had just taught her otherwise.

Dark thoughts that had dimmed her days for so long were gone. Vanished. Swept away.

She smiled easily, happily, for the first time in forever.

But of course Clyde wouldn't take his isolation for long.

"WHEN ARE YOU two going to remember you're not alone on this planet?" That was Gladys's voice, guaranteed to rouse any embarrassment it might.

Except the guarantee didn't work. "It's too early for dinner," Audrey answered.

"My feet are getting cold. I'm all puffed up!"

Audrey and Cam exchanged looks. "Could he be exaggerating?" Cam asked.

"Wouldn't be the first time." Sighing, Audrey reluctantly slipped out of bed and pulled on her clothes. Man, she smelled like lovemaking. Another thing that made her smile.

Cam wasn't far behind her in the dressing department.

Audrey opened the door, and Clyde came swooping in. Indeed, he was puffed up, and he landed right on her shoulder.

"I was polite," he said, more of a crow than words. "Now you gotta take care of me."

Audrey didn't want to think what that might mean. He claimed he was *polite*. Oh, man, paint it on a poster.

At least the bird dropped the subject and began complaining how cold the living room was.

"You've got another place to stay," Audrey pointed out. "The kitchen."

"Boooring."

Nevertheless, an obliging Cam went to the living room to check the thermostat. He came back, shaking his head. "I hate to say it, but Clyde is right. I'll have to check the system before he freezes his toes."

"He *could* go into his Taj Mahal and stay there for a while."

"That's not fair," Clyde groused, Groucho Marx this time.

Cam shrugged. "Agreed, but Clyde's right. Not that the front room is more entertaining, but at least the kitchen is warm."

Audrey had to admit Cam was right. It wasn't like this poor bird could fly anywhere he wanted. It wouldn't be safe.

And not for the first time, she wondered what she had thought she was getting into caring for Clyde despite knowing him from visiting her aunt. Certainly not a little parakeet. Her imagination had failed her. Nearly a yard of mouthy bird. Not sweet little chirps but a demanding voice. Half a dozen of them or more. The most unnerving of them Gladys's.

Oh, man! She looked at Cam, thinking of the hours just past, and wondered how fast he'd run from this demanding, mouthy bird. She was surprised to see a crooked smile on his face.

"I'll go down and take a look," he said. "I must have missed a gap in the duct down there." Then he looked at Clyde. "Stay in here, bird, until I fix it."

"I have a *name*," Clyde said stiffly.

Cam ignored him, going to the living room to get his tool belt and a powerful flashlight. Then he disappeared down into the basement.

"He's rude," Clyde said irritably.

"He'd have to go a long way to be as rude as you."

Clyde mumbled into his beak. Then flew over to sit on Audrey's shoulder. "At least you're warm."

And she'd been a lot warmer just recently. A sigh escaped her, thinking of Cam down in that dank, dark basement, all to keep Clyde's toesies warm. Hell, couldn't he have just stayed in the two rooms that were warm enough for a parrot?

Of course not. That wasn't Clyde's way. She sometimes wondered how Gladys had managed him all these years.

But then, Gladys was a tough bird herself. In the forty years since her husband had died, Gladys had chosen to make her own way through life. No one to help carry the burdens. Just Gladys standing up to the world.

So yeah, she could handle Clyde and probably find him amusing. Audrey had always admired her.

But now there was Clyde, and she wasn't feeling all that fond of Gladys's independence. Although, to be fair, she admitted to herself, she *was* mostly enjoying that sassy bird.

"How long is it going to take him?" Clyde asked.

"I don't know. Fly down and ask him."

Clyde sidled closer to Audrey's face. "It's dark down there. Dark and ugly and it smells funny."

"Since when did you become afraid of the dark?"

"That's my sleeping time," Clyde snapped.

Audrey sighed. "So the dark in the basement really doesn't have anything to do with your refusal to go down there. I get it."

And she did. As a child she had explored out of curiosity. Even though she had never truly liked it.

She supposed she ought to get someone braver than she to recover those many shelves of glistening jams and pickles. A shame to waste all that work that went back as far as her grandma.

Which brought up thoughts of dinner. God, she didn't know what was in the pantry or fridge even though she'd bought it.

Distracted, she told herself. Distracted once again by Paul. God, would that man never stop interfering with her life?

She'd gotten all those years off then *pff*. Why couldn't he go get obsessed with somebody else? Preferably someone who would stand up to him.

Pawing around in the pantry, she found her salvation: two boxes of red beans and rice. A quick search of the fridge found some andouille sausage. Ah, yes.

And even more pleasing was Gladys's apparent love of kitchen gadgets. An automatic rice maker. Yup. She knew how to do all this. And thank God it wasn't hamburgers and fries. She wondered if she'd be able to eat them ever again. Not that it mattered. At least Paul hadn't ruined pizza for her.

Jerk.

The andouille sausage was frozen, so she put it into a bowl of water to thaw. She'd spent a lot of time thawing, mainly because Paul sometimes got a hankering for something different and God forbid it wasn't already in the fridge. Like a whole chicken. She always wondered where that came from.

Just to annoy her, probably. Just to give him an excuse to yell at her and hit her. Well, she'd gotten ahead on that one at least.

Cam returned upstairs. "Apparently one of the braces stretched. Small slit in the duct." He turned to Clyde. "All set, Master Clyde. Give it a half hour to heat up in there. And thanks for being my canary in the coal mine."

Clyde squawked. "I am no canary."

"Thank God," Cam said, turning his attention from the bird. "Oh, man, red beans and rice. A favorite of mine. And is that andouille sausage?"

"Sure is," Audrey answered, feeling a surprising wave of relief. She almost shook her head. Cam wasn't anything like Paul. There was no reason for her to have felt so tense about this. But her thoughts had turned to Paul, hadn't they? Now they were shifting back to Cam, a welcome change.

But once Paul had slipped in, he was not very easy to get rid of. Lingering at the back of her mind like a curse.

Cam came up behind her as she stood at the sink running cold water over the sausage wrapping. He slipped his arms around her waist and sprinkled kisses on her head.

Oh, God, that felt so good!

Clyde started to make a noise from her shoulder, but Cam took care of him.

"Shut up, Clyde. This is none of your business."

To Audrey's amazement, Clyde lifted from her shoulder and flew away. Right then she didn't care where he went. Let him be offended. He'd get over it.

Then Cam turned her and bent to give her a delicious kiss on her lips, which instantly caused desire to drizzle through her. "Later," he whispered. "Oh, yeah."

Then Paul seeped back into her brain, killing the mood.

Cam must have felt it. "Audrey? Are you upset with me?"

She shook her head and pressed her face into his solid shoulder. "Paul," she said weakly. "He won't leave me alone."

"Damn," he swore quietly. "I'm so sorry, Audrey."

"It happens," she said weakly. "All of a sudden he's there."

"Then we'll have to get rid of him," Cam answered, his voice turning to steel. "Somehow, some way, he needs to be erased from your life."

She lifted her head. "Cam... Awful as he is, I don't want anyone to murder him. To go to prison for that. I'd never forgive myself."

"I wasn't thinking about murder. There are other ways, though. Plenty."

Audrey shivered, wondering what other ways he meant. He'd been a soldier once, and she had no idea what he'd learned. Or what he might be capable of.

But she wanted Paul gone for good. She just didn't want anyone else to pay for his crimes.

"Now," he said quietly, "I'm going to take a walk around outside, set the alarms, and then we can spend the evening cuddling and let Clyde run the show."

That brought a weak laugh out of her, but it did sound so good. Sharing that battered old sofa with Cam. His arm around her. Oh, yeah. And Clyde could just shut his beak.

Chapter Fifteen

Paul was fit to be tied. The truck that had seemed so good when he started out was running on rotting tires—two of them blew at the same time, causing him to limp into a gas station that claimed to do tires.

A day to get in tires that would fit that damn truck. And he honestly didn't see one vehicle he might be able to heist. The place was too busy, with cars being worked on, waiting to be worked on and a population of mechanics who seemed to know every car in the place. Plus there were too many owners swigging coffee in the small waiting room.

Hell. Another day. One of the mechanics pointed him to a sleazy motel across the street, but even he had the sense to realize that if he tried to drive off in one of the three cars sitting over there, he'd be headed for trouble.

This was a *neighborly* place. Everyone knew damn near everyone else, including the bastards across the way in the motel. He *hated* neighborly places. Prison had been one of them, and you had to watch your back every single minute. This place was probably no better.

But he knew one thing for sure—drive off in one of them cars and cops would be stopping him by dawn.

At least there was a place to eat. A place where he could

use one of his stolen credit cards. Amazing how few people knew their cards had been stolen for days.

He got his double order of burgers and fries, along with a tall soda. This place didn't have beer, which surprised him. This was *Wyoming*, for Pete's sake. Guns everywhere but no beer?

He kept his mouth shut, though. Drawing any kind of attention would have been idiotic.

Then he heard a guy at the table behind him. "Damn blue laws in this town."

And who the hell had come up with that crazy law, anyway? A man oughta be able to get a drink when he wanted. But from what he'd seen on his trip here, that was probably just this local town. Great place to blow his tires.

When he finally decided to make his way to one of the fleabag rooms with a sack full of yet another dinner, he spent some time thinking about Audrey. His eagerness to find her, to teach her a lesson, was growing in him, along with an increasing rage.

He had that bowie knife. Hadn't intended to use it, only to scare, but he was beginning to have visions of using it on her. Just sparingly. Just to make his point. One she'd never forget. Maybe one she'd see every time she looked in the mirror.

Yeah, that thought made him grin. His mark on her. One she'd never be able to ignore. One that everyone would see: his brand, like a cow.

She sure had it coming. Serving him divorce papers in prison. Making everyone laugh at him, even though he figured most of them had gotten their papers the same way.

But he'd laughed along, swearing he was glad to be done with that bitch.

Ha! Oh, he was far from done with her.

Reaching down, he pleasured himself while he envisioned Audrey's scarred face.

CAM AND AUDREY had taken up the habit of walking lazily around the house in the early morning, when the first pink or gold streamers of sunrise brightened the sky just before dawn. Then they sat on the porch chair to watch the sunrise fully claim the world. In the evening they had begun to do the same thing at sunset. Pleasant times, times that to Audrey had become special. But tonight they did no such thing, and that leeched the peace from Audrey. Even Clyde seemed to have grown nervous, unable to perch in any one place for long.

"What's going on?" she asked finally. "You two are on edge. I can barely stand it. So what's happening?"

"Nothing's happening," Cam answered.

"Then why are you pacing a hole in the kitchen floor and why is Clyde flitting around as if there was a predator overhead?"

"Just getting some exercise," Clyde answered.

Audrey ignored him and continued to stare at Cam. "Well?"

He bit his lower lip and his eyes narrowed, as if he were deep in thought. Then he said, "I figure Paul can't be far away."

At that Audrey sat hard on one of the kitchen chairs. Her vision darkened as memories flashed through her brain, memories that chased her as determinedly as a hellhound. God, couldn't she just forget?

"Audrey?" Suddenly Cam was there, kneeling beside her

chair, wrapping his arms around her in a way that made her feel safe from her past.

Yet he was still a man. Had she trusted him too far? Had she let him get too close?

But she couldn't have torn from his embrace if her life had depended on it. She twisted and raised her arms, digging her fingers into his shoulders, all to keep him near.

"Why?" she asked in a broken whisper. "Why do you think he's here?"

"I didn't say he's here. Just that he's getting close."

"But how can you know?"

"I don't. But when I think about it…" He paused. "Say he found out you're probably up here. Hiding. Say he got information from someone who knows you, who may have heard you mention your aunt Gladys's house. Someone who might casually drop it when they thought they were talking to a friend of yours."

Remembering Paul's charm, she had no trouble believing that he could get that information out of any of her friends. If she'd even told them. Now would be a great time for her unforgiving memory to provide some useful information.

"Gladys isn't related to you by last name in any way?"

Audrey gave a small shake of her head. "My mom's aunt. Nothing close."

"Regardless," Cam said, rubbing her back gently, "I'm thinking this place isn't all that far from Colorado Springs. If he has any idea what direction to head, all he has to do is heist a truck, pickpocket a wallet…"

"He could be here soon," Audrey breathed. "Oh, God! He should *already* be here."

"Maybe. I've yet to take a road trip that didn't involve all kinds of problems. Like getting stuck in the pass because of a blizzard. Or other things. Then when he gets here, well, this is a tight-knit town. He asks too many questions, like where Gladys's house is, and somebody is going to sit up and take notice. Once he gets to these parts, he's gonna have to be damn careful. Maybe he doesn't even know that yet, but he'd better be wary or Gage Dalton is gonna want to know his business."

Audrey drew on her slim memories. "I seem to remember that Gage isn't easy to shake off."

"Or easy to lie to."

"Should we talk to him again?"

Cam nodded slowly. "That might be a good idea."

Audrey didn't really hold out any hope that Gage might be able to help at all, but she needed *something* because the simple truth was she had been doing her damn best to hide herself from Paul and the threat he posed. Yeah, she let the fear emerge from time to time, but mostly she'd been burying her head in the sand.

Why? Because she feared there was no possible escape? Or because she so desperately needed to believe the threat was gone?

Either one didn't much please her. In fact, both made her disappointed in herself. She was stronger than that, wasn't she?

But as she sat there, nearly clinging to Cam's reassuring embrace, she wondered about herself. Wondered why she'd spent so many years putting up with Paul. Knew all the reasons the counselor had helped her understand, but they didn't make her feel any better right now. All that therapy and she still hated herself. *Weakling.*

She shivered and felt Cam's arms tighten around her. Then she felt Clyde's talons dig carefully into her shoulder.

Clyde spoke like Jimmy Cagney. "I can peck his eyes out."

A faint shiver of laughter ran through Audrey.

"That's a good start," Cam agreed. "But I get first dibs."

"Why?" Clyde demanded.

"Gotta soften him up for you."

That did it. Between one second and the next, Audrey laughed. Laughed hard. "You two!"

Clyde started preening. Cam avoided any such display.

While Clyde worked industriously at his feathers, Cam drew her a little closer and said, "You're not alone this time, Audrey. Not alone at all."

That eased most of the tension in her, but she had another thought. "Cam? I don't want you to get hurt."

For once, Clyde stayed out of it, and Cam answered without the chorus. "I won't. But I will teach the SOB a good lesson if he dares to show his face."

Audrey had to admit she liked the sound of that. Angry as Paul had been when he was arrested, the cops hadn't even used their sticks on him. Of course, he was just a wife beater. She had long suspected, because that hadn't been the first call the cops had received about Paul from neighbors, it had been the first time they'd seen all that blood. So it had been the first arrest.

God, she sometimes wondered how she had survived. Her therapist had kept telling her she was brave, gutsy, strong. Instead she felt weak and sometimes hopeless. How could she trust herself?

Content as she was to feel Cam's arms around her, she eased back. She had to grow up all over again. Stand on her own feet, not on Cam's—or, for that matter, Clyde's talons.

Then she remembered the time just past in Cam's arms,

being loved by Cam. Delight and desire both trickled through her, reminding her she wasn't broken. Cam had proved that. She was still a woman with a woman's needs.

A long sigh of happiness escaped her. Her life wasn't over. She still had good things to look forward to, not only the scars Paul had left her with.

She smiled, an easy and comfortable smile. Her heart was lifting, truly lifting, like a balloon filled with helium. It had happened. The last shackle was broken.

Or maybe the next-to-last shackle.

Now there was one thing left to deal with: the monster of her nightmares. The monster who existed only in her mind.

She met Cam's gaze. "He's not a monster."

"Hmm?" He sounded surprised.

"I mean, I've made him worse in my mind than he could ever be in real life. He convinced me he had total control over me, but he didn't. He made me believe it, but it wasn't true."

"I'm not quite sure I understand."

"I just barely understand it myself." Briefly, she rested her head against his shoulder then straightened. "Near the end, I was terrified of him. When the apologies nearly stopped. When there was almost nothing but the brutality. But I didn't need to be that afraid. I should have just hit him over the head with an iron skillet and walked away."

A snort of laughter escaped Cam, but he said, "But you didn't."

"No. Because he apologized just enough that I believed him. I'd been believing those apologies for years by then, so I *wanted* to believe him, even then. Until he had me right where he wanted me. God." She closed her eyes. "I believed him until it was too late. I trusted him."

CAM WATCHED THE emotions roil through her but didn't think it would be a good time to offer an embrace. She had to figure out how to deal with this herself, and interrupting her effort might delay things.

But man, he could hardly believe the blame she was placing on her own shoulders. The creep was responsible for every bit of it. He'd seen the type before, able to manipulate others with smiles and a phony kindness that was so deceptive it could fool anyone. True con man.

He'd never understand where people like that came from. That it must be natural for some to be able to manipulate others easily. He'd never understand how or where it began, but they all seemed to learn as naturally as breathing. And few people could resist it. That was a con man's greatest tool: belief.

And then there were the people they targeted. Good people. People filled with trust who never thought that someone so nice could be scamming them. Couldn't imagine anyone saying "I love you" without meaning it. That this person might propose, for example, without an ounce of caring for you. Or some other shitty thing.

Cam shook his head, realizing he'd probably need to go back to school and take a couple of degrees in psychology before he'd even begin to understand the Pauls of the world.

No point worrying the problem. All he needed to do was make sure Audrey was protected. He didn't need to know why a worm like Paul even existed.

Time was worrying Cam, though. He guessed at how much time it might have taken Paul to find out where Audrey was. How much time it would take him to get here once he did. Snowstorm shutting down the passes didn't exactly make for the biggest obstacle if you had a long-range plan.

Uneasy, Cam left the house around ten, shortly after Audrey headed for bed. "I'm just going to take a stroll," he said as she disappeared into her bedroom. "Won't take long."

"Okay."

He didn't hear that uneasiness in her voice, that faint tremor. She must have made some kind of peace with herself.

But there was still Paul.

Pulling on work boots and his shearling jacket, he set out to take a slow walk. Just to see if he could sense anything, hear anything unusual. He didn't expect to be lucky. But he didn't want to leave anything to chance.

Because no matter how he guessed at Paul's whereabouts, another part of him believed it had been too long. That man was out there, and he wasn't far away.

PAUL WAS INDEED out there. He'd heard from a guy in Casper, who worked for McKay and Shaw Construction Company that the boss was working on renovations of an old family house. Over in Conard County, maybe. Nice money, the guy said.

Well, there weren't a whole lot of houses being refurbished around here, and it was easy to find out exactly where it was in his rusty pickup with a toolbox in the back. An empty toolbox.

All he had to do was claim he'd been hired and needed to get to the place.

No problem.

Paul was careful to stay away from the kinds of guys who would talk about something so boring with anybody else. Workers who seemed to come and go themselves. Migrants of some kind.

People who wanted to remain invisible. And they knew exactly where the house being remodeled was.

He was careful to go out to the house at night, though. Didn't want anyone, any nosy neighbor, to see him about. That was when he learned that Audrey was never alone.

A man was living with her. One she didn't ever leave the house without. Well, of course not. He had her under control, just the way Paul once had.

Just proved the woman needed to be shown the right way to do things. To not get above herself. So she was, in her way, ready for Paul.

But he wasn't ready for her now. She'd been cheating on him with that guy. Cheating on *him*!

Paul's fists clenched until his knuckles ached, and a red fury nearly blinded him. No, he wasn't going to take her back. She was soiled now. Filthy from another man.

Remembering the gun in the glove box of his rusty old truck, his right hand loosened and he could just about feel its butt in his hand.

Yeah, he was going to have to get rid of Audrey. She wasn't fit for him anymore. But he was going to have to get rid of that guy, too. The one who'd touched flesh that belonged to Paul. The one who so owned her she wouldn't leave his sight.

But that upset everything he had planned. He'd expected to come here and find Audrey alone, at least at night. Maybe sometimes during the day. Somebody like this guy wouldn't work on fixing up that house around the clock, seven days a week.

So he had to leave sometimes. To get supplies, yeah? But if he didn't leave, he'd have to be killed.

Sitting in the brush on an increasingly cold night, Paul

stared at the house. He even saw that builder guy walking around outside. What, was he afraid the place was gonna fall down?

The thought almost made Paul snicker aloud. Wouldn't that be a riot? Too bad he couldn't just go over there and give the place a nudge when both were inside.

But he was no fool, and daydreaming wasn't going to get him anywhere with this problem. It appeared now that two people had to die. He couldn't just go get his wife back, and now he didn't even want to.

He didn't want to, but he resigned himself to having to stake out the place for longer. To find out if the two ever separated. Because that would sure make killing them easier.

But if not, he had to come up with a better plan.

Audrey had probably blabbed to this guy, too, so even if he wasn't there when Audrey's murder came down, he'd know enough to point a finger.

Hell's bells. Paul was quick on his feet, a talent that had helped him countless times. But quick on his feet wasn't going to cut it this time. No way.

This called for something more complex than his usual game. Murdering his vics was something he'd never had to do before. Now he had to. A whole different game.

He waited until dawn, able to tell by watching the movement of lights what was going on inside that house.

Then he went to sleep in his truck. For a few hours.

Tomorrow he'd have to watch those two in daylight.

CAM DIDN'T MUCH like the feeling he got as he walked around outside the house. No reason for it that he could tell, but it was still there. Maybe some wolves had come down from the mountains, not that they did it that often. Coyotes, maybe.

There were plenty of creatures, even this close to town, that would grow cautious and watchful at him clomping around out here. The night was their territory, and he was most definitely an invader.

He paused often to stare toward the clumps of trees and brush. The trees were thin enough that he could see the lights of the town, at this time of night mostly the streetlamps. He hadn't paid much attention to them until now. A lot of things hadn't seemed truly important at the outset and now he'd gotten to a dangerous place he'd learned to avoid in the Army. Overlooking the familiar.

He walked on a bit, then paused to eyeball everything. It had always struck him as odd that this large plot of ground hadn't been knitted into the rest of Conard City. Acres of land lying fallow. Pointless. Gladys hadn't even rented it out for grazing. Something ran deep in this land and this family.

Maybe sometime soon he ought to take his butt to the library here and talk to Miss Emma, the supervising librarian. The nickname "Miss Emma" had begun a long time ago, when a twenty-year-old newbie had taken over management of the library. No one knew where the nickname had come from, but it had stuck all these years. When anyone said "Miss Emma," everyone knew who they meant. Sorta like "Maude" standing for the diner.

Cam shook his head, smiling to himself. Well, he needed to see Miss Emma. Her family had been one of the five founding ones in this town, and it was said she'd researched the history down to the finest detail. She would no doubt know what was going on with this spread.

INSIDE, HE FOUND that Audrey had fallen asleep. Not wanting to wake her but also wanting to be close, he stripped silently and slid carefully into the bed behind her. He was touched and no more than a little excited when she turned with a sigh and laid her arm on him. She slept on, and he enjoyed holding her like this, unwilling to fall asleep for fear of losing a single moment with her.

Sometime later, she stirred more and murmured, "Cam?"

"I'm here. Just go back to sleep, darlin'."

A whispery laugh escaped her. "I can tell you don't want to sleep."

He guessed she could. "Ignore me, just go back to sleep."

"I'm awake now."

Clyde grumped from his perch, "So am I now, thank you very much." With a few flaps he left the bedroom and headed for one of his new perches in the living room.

Audrey ignored him and wiggled closer to Cam. He wrapped both his arms around her and thought that he never wanted these moments to end. They would, of course. All she needed from him was protection.

BUT AUDREY WAS feeling quite differently. Cam had carried her to new places. He'd quietly passed all the barriers that had confined her for years. In his care, made safe, she had found a freedom that had escaped her all these years.

But she wasn't being fair to him, she realized. Leaning on him like that, expecting him to care for her and make her feel safe. No, that wasn't right for the long term, but she sure could enjoy this time right now.

Cam's arms closed around her, getting her as close as he could. "Audrey," he murmured.

Sighing happily, she began to run her hands over him.

This time she felt as comfortable as if they were an old couple, but she also felt the powerful tingle of new love. More sighs began to escape her, and her hands followed every inch of him. When she heard him moan as she touched his hardness, she smiled into the darkness, feeling more powerful than she ever had.

But she was not alone in exploration. Cam's hands traced every inch of her, awakening every cell until she felt as if electricity zinged through her entire body, until her hips rocked helplessly against his.

She clung to his shoulders, as if afraid of falling—or afraid that he might move away.

But Cam simply lifted her over him and fused them together.

What started as gentle became forceful and nearly rough. One being in the greatest drive and pleasure of all.

Audrey shattered into a million flaming pieces, and she felt Cam jerk upward, following her into aching peace.

Chapter Sixteen

Paul was growing impatient. He kept watching that damn house, and that guy never left—at least, never left Audrey alone. Paul was also becoming uncomfortably aware that the more he showed up in town to buy something easy to eat, the more people started to notice him and wonder about him.

The hell of small towns.

He was afraid to drive over to some small town in this near wilderness where he'd seem new, for fear he'd miss his opportunity. If he was angry now, he'd only get madder if he had to go away and make this trip all over again at a later time.

More cusswords escaped him, and a nearby raccoon that hung around for his crumbs hurried away. Damn animal was annoying. If Paul didn't keep an eye on it, it'd actually *open* and eat Paul's small food supply.

Didn't that thing have something else to eat? More than once Paul wanted to strangle it, but then he'd see those big teeth and change his mind.

So he spent hours watching and hours daydreaming about what he was gonna do to Audrey. That woman had earned every hell he could inflict on her.

Yeah, those were some pleasant daydreams. They helped, but only a bit. God, didn't this place ever warm up?

He continued to watch, but as the days passed he grew more furious. That woman was cheating on him. Obviously.

And that man dared to touch Paul's property.

Paul's seething grew to higher levels. That man was going to have to go, too. But how?

He cussed some more. He'd wanted to take out Audrey by herself. Living alone like that, no one would notice her being missing, unless she'd made a bunch of new friends. And she didn't look like she was making any here at all, not yet. But that was one of the things Paul had taught her: that he was a threat to any friends she had.

It amazed him that she had started talking to a few after he went to prison. Women Paul had never met when they were married because he didn't allow it. One of whom had known Audrey was going to her aunt's house in Wyoming. It paid to know how to be charming.

But now that man at her house was changing everything. Changing Audrey. Soiling her.

Both of them had to go. The question was a simple *how*. Problem was that question wasn't so simple.

Paul cussed again.

THE MORNING SEEMED chilly to Audrey, but she was feeling too happy to care. Cam. Oh, Cam. He had given her such joy and pleasure last night. Smiling and humming just above a whisper, she buzzed around the kitchen to make something for breakfast.

Clyde, however, had come out of his funk and decided to annoy anyone within hearing. "What's that noise you're making?" he demanded as he perched on the back of a chair.

"I'm singing," she retorted, slamming the cast iron skillet on the stove. She winced as she did so. Cast iron might be nearly indestructible, but the burners might not be.

Clyde squawked. "Now you're making implied threats against me?"

"Then just give me some peace." She brought out a carton of eggs from the refrigerator, deciding to make a scrambled egg omelet. "Do you want some egg?"

"Ack! Now you want to make me a cannibal."

"Sheesh, Clyde. I already thought you were a cannibal. You like *chicken*, after all."

Cam showed up a few minutes later. Once again he'd walked around the outside of the house, but he didn't appear disturbed for any reason. The smile he gave her was apt to melt her heart, though. He'd reached out and crossed all her defenses, and she didn't mind. Not one bit.

Heedless of the eggs, which were sizzling quietly on the stove, he drew her into his arms, making her soften with delight, then released her. "I like your smile," he said. "Should I rescue the eggs?"

Audrey gasped and turned quickly to the stove, afraid she'd scorched them. Relief. They were just about ready. Cam helped by pulling out a couple of plates. "What's with the McBird?"

"I'm pretty sure I offended him."

Cam looked over at Clyde as Audrey scooped eggs onto plates. "I didn't think that was possible."

"Try mentioning that he's a cannibal."

Cam's eyes widened a bit, then laughter burst out of him. "You didn't!"

"I did," she admitted as she carried plates to the table to join the probably cold toast. "He eats chicken."

Clyde remained on the chair back, sending dirty looks to Audrey, who found it surprisingly easy to eat. No bird was going to make it hard to enjoy her breakfast.

Except that she started to feel badly about how she had treated Clyde. There was no excuse to remind him that he ate chicken, a normal part of his diet, as if he were doing something unconscionable. That had been downright nasty.

And Audrey didn't like to be nasty.

Sighing, she finished her eggs and toast, but it was Cam who rose to carry the dishes to the sink. She put her chin in her hand and considered her own behavior. She realized she'd been so busy trying to overcome all the bad things that Paul had forced her to become that she had grown unaware of her own nastiness. Not a happy thought.

CAM WAS RUNNING the water into the sink, waiting for it to get hot, when he caught motion out of the side of his eye. Looking immediately, he recognized a raccoon, a big one, tearing across the grass and brush.

He froze. Raccoons didn't run like that, not as if their butts were on fire. Yeah, they could scatter if found in someone's garbage, but nothing like this. There was a difference between scattering and launching. This raccoon had been *launched*.

Immediately, he scanned the patch of trees to the east of the house, a patch that had been troubling him since he'd learned of Audrey's problem. He'd checked it out several times, but there had been no sign of any threat. It had also been more than a few days since he'd looked out there. Same for a few other clumps of trees and brush scattered about. No reason this one should stand out.

Now brush was moving over there. Just slightly. The animal must have come running out of there. But why?

Paul had finally had enough of that damn raccoon. Stealing his food. Worse, the last couple of days, the animal had dared to rear up on its hind legs and yell at him. Refused to run away when Paul waved an arm at it. The damn thing was waging a war.

And Paul sure as hell didn't like that. It was one thing when the animal was an annoying thief. It was another when that damn thing dared to argue with him.

Paul didn't like not being in control. He hated to be defied. Audrey was down at that house defying him, and now this freaking animal was defying him, too.

His world turned red with rage. So the animal wanted war? It could have its damn war. But with one last shred of sanity, Paul realized he couldn't shoot the thing. The gunshot would warn everybody at the house.

So he pulled out his knife and jabbed it downward, catching the thing on the tail. An uproar ensued. Paul got his face scratched, which caused him to drop the knife. And then the evil animal dashed out across the open land to the house.

Paul calmed himself, panting a bit, then wiped the knife on his jeans. Not much blood. Not much damage. While he regretted that, he was sure that raccoon wouldn't come back, and he'd be content with that for a while.

Besides, he had a much bigger matter to demand his attention. That cheating wife and her apparent lover. That couldn't wait much longer. He was sick of sitting out here in the cold, sick of feeling the seat of his pants growing damp from his body heat against the cold made moisture condense. He knew that because when he was a kid he'd camped a lot. Sick of this whole situation. He'd been patient enough.

Tonight would be the night. All he needed now was a plan to break in and catch them both. Or maybe he could get the man when he strolled around in the late evening. When the world was dark and quiet.

Yeah. And Audrey would be in the house. Locked in by fear when she heard a gunshot.

Audrey was easy enough to scare, and a gun could do it. Fast.

Oh, yeah.

Paul pulled a longneck from the cooler that was nearly full of ice. One of those things that might begin to draw attention when he filled it so often. But this night it wasn't going to matter any longer. By the time those two were missed, Paul would be long gone.

AFTER FINISHING THE DISHES, Cam dried his hands and turned to Audrey. She was already laying out her art stuff.

"I'm gonna go check outside," he said. "I saw a raccoon out there that looked like it might be injured."

She laid down her case of drawing pencils. "I'll go with you. It'd be nice to get out again."

He shook his head. "Rabies. No reason for you to get close and risk a bite. No, I just want to see if it's bad enough to..." He stopped. Did he really want to say that?

"Bad enough to put it out of its misery." She nodded briskly. "You're right, I don't want to be there. But maybe you won't find him."

"Likely not. An injured animal never makes it easy."

Cam left her settling at her table with the easel he'd made for her and headed out the door, pulling on his jacket.

He didn't expect to find the raccoon. Judging by the way that animal had been moving, it wasn't likely to stop for miles.

No, what he wanted to do was check out that stand of trees.

But he'd taken only a few steps in that direction when he stopped himself. Danger.

If that creep Paul was out there, waiting for a chance to get at Audrey, what might he not do to make it easier? What if he managed to kill or disable Cam? Leaving Cam out here unable to protect Audrey. Her hearing the sound of a gunshot, then having to wait for a deputy to answer her emergency call. All alone. That would be enough time for Paul to kill her.

Or if Audrey heard nothing and had no idea that Cam should have been back. It wasn't as if he were as reliable as a clock. She might even get lost in her work, as she often did, and not even notice a passage of time.

Nope. Much as he wanted to know what had happened to that raccoon out there, he wasn't going to risk Audrey. Turning sharply, he went back into the house, knowing what direction to watch more closely.

Then, when he reached the front steps, he pulled out his cell phone and called Gage. As always, the sheriff was readily reachable by phone.

"I think I might have a problem," he told Gage.

"Shoot."

"This is gonna sound nuts."

"Don't mean a thing. Just tell me."

So Cam told him about the raccoon and the feeling he had about why that animal was hightailing it. Then he waited to be brushed off.

Except he wasn't. "I'm going to send some folks out there to check around. It's the copse just east of the house, right?"

"That's the one."

"Okay. We'll have a look-see, might even find a vehicle out that way. You stay with Audrey."

Of course he'd stay with Audrey, Cam thought with the faintest of smiles. That's what he was here to do, although he suspected Gladys had never imagined this kind of threat. Or at least not one of this size. And she'd sure tried hard to get Audrey out of Paul's way.

PAUL DECIDED THAT getting even with that raccoon hadn't been worth it. Hell, all he'd done was get the critter's tail. He'd wanted more than that.

Much as he'd enjoyed the animal's flight, it dawned on him, when he was halfway through his beer, that it might not have been a smart move. If that guy in there had seen that animal running like that…well, even Paul was familiar with how raccoons moved, and they didn't move that fast for long.

Grinding his teeth, cussing between them, he gathered up his camp and carried it toward the pickup. It was only a half mile, but it was long enough with that damn backpack and the ice chest. He oughta dump the ice, but one of his wits persuaded him not to leave that big a trail if anyone came looking.

Not that he expected it. Nah, nobody had seen that animal run. But safer was wiser, or some such thing.

He loaded the truck bed and climbed behind the wheel. Cranky at start-up, but it always had been since he lifted it. It did what he needed and he was heading away down the road just as a police vehicle passed him in the other direction.

A cold sweat ran down his neck and forehead. *Just in time*, he thought. *Just in time*. At least he'd been smart enough not to light a fire out there.

But what made him think the deputy was looking for him, anyway? Over a raccoon? His heartbeat settled down and he laughed at himself.

Sure, the firepower of this entire county looking for someone or something that'd made a raccoon take flight.

He laughed again. Oh, this was getting too easy. Anyone suspicious at that house—namely, the guy who had him so angry—would be focusing on the place he'd just been, not the one he was going to. Would believe him gone, even if he'd been expecting Paul.

Because Paul was smart. He already had a backup location.

A COUPLE HOURS LATER, Gage called Cam, who was in the living room hammering the last of crown molding into place. He put down his hammer and wiped his forehead with the back of his sleeve. It might be cold outside, but it was warm enough in here to take care of a parrot. Fine, but it was not the most comfortable working temperature.

"Well," Gage said, "my people didn't find anything of significance except that someone was out there. Scattered beer bottles, torn food wrappers. Frankly, it looked like some college kids were out there and had the munchies. Nothing to take any further."

"Thanks for looking, Gage," Cam said.

"Oh, we looked, all right. That doesn't mean we're not putting the road on that side of the house on our patrol. If anyone *does* show up, they won't be there for long."

That was real helpful, Cam thought as he disconnected.

Except that if it was Paul, he was going to be around to terrify and torment Audrey for another day if they didn't locate him.

With each passing day, Cam had steadily been moving away from just protecting Audrey to wanting to get rid of this threat. It was the only way she could be truly safe.

And hell, at this point he didn't even know if Paul had made it this far. Seemed an awful long time when he thought about it. But what was Paul's rush? Guy was fresh out of prison. Maybe he just wanted some fun before continuing his pursuit of Audrey.

Which Cam had trouble believing. The guy had started his hunt for her almost from the minute the prison bus had dropped him in Colorado Springs, to judge by that call from Gladys. A call that, by the way, had been the first step in raising Cam's alert level.

So Paul was obsessed. He had to be, after all this time, to still be looking for a wife who'd divorced him six years ago. A wife whose injuries had put him in prison.

Sounded like a major obsession to Cam.

Hell. Well, at least he'd scoped those other stands of trees, too. Figured out what positions might be the best if you wanted to hide until you crept up to the house.

Because of course this guy was gonna creep.

Chapter Seventeen

As the afternoon began to lose its brightest light, the sun sinking behind the mountains, promising a long closure to the day, Cam wondered how to break his concerns to Audrey. Without throwing her back into the terror she'd clearly felt that day when Gladys called and told her about the man seeking to find her.

Damn, the words just kept slipping away until he finally realized he was just going to have to dump the story as it was and give her a shotgun.

He hated to stir this all up for her, but had it ever really settled? Not much, he supposed. How could it when her aunt had sent her up here to be safe? Hidden.

He waited until Audrey finished her day's drawing and his work was at a point where he could stop.

He considered going out to look for the guy, but what if he went to the wrong place? Worse, he'd be leaving Audrey alone, an open target. *Nope. Stay here.*

When Audrey finished putting her supplies away, he sat, reaching out to take her hands in his.

She started to smile, but the smile died as she looked at him. "Oh, God, what's wrong?"

Clyde added his two cents. "He called the sheriff this morning."

In that instant, Cam felt a serious animosity toward that mouthy, noisy, too-talkative bird.

"Why?" Audrey asked, her face paling.

"Because of a raccoon." He gave her a short version, then told her how Gage thought it was kids, that he would keep a patrol along that road.

Audrey didn't look as if she felt any better. Well, the gun sure as hell wasn't going to help that.

Without another word, Cam went to a corner in the living room and pulled out the two shotguns and his pistol. No chances. If they weren't needed, so much the better.

Audrey looked at the gun cases, her eyes widening, but she needed no explanation. "You think it was *him* out there, not kids."

"The raccoon," he said shortly. "Yeah. And maybe the guy had sense to move right after that. He's out there somewhere, Audrey."

She nodded slowly. "I feel it. I've been feeling it when I was washing dishes, feeling like I was watched."

"Why didn't you say something?"

She shook her head, her mouth twisting. "That sounds crazy, doesn't it? The *feeling* that someone is watching you."

"It's not crazy. I wish you'd told me." He paused then, hating himself because he couldn't keep her entirely out of this.

"You remember what I showed you about these?"

She nodded.

"Anyone breaks in here, don't ask questions, just shoot. The worst thing you can do is hesitate. Got it?"

She nodded again, then looked at Cam with reddened eyes. "What about you?"

"If I have anything to say about it, that bastard isn't going to get near this house."

"But why are you sure it's tonight?"

He sighed, nearly hating himself for calling Gage. "Because the sheriff found his hidey-hole this morning." Cam jerked his head slightly, using it to point to the group of trees that had concerned him. "Beer cans, food wrappers. He's gotta be feeling pressured."

"Paul never had much self-control." She looked at the guns again. "Okay, where do you want me?"

As the day darkened, they ate a quick meal of cheese and crackers. Then Audrey went to the bedroom, the only windowless room in the house, and settled herself on a chair with a view of the door.

"You hear a gunshot," Cam said, "you get ready to shoot, okay?"

Like there was any choice. Cam went to the front porch, trying to look as if he were taking a casual check around, as he often did.

But there was nothing casual, and he knew just how to get off this porch without creaking. The advantage of being a builder.

The twilight turned into night and he let himself easily off the porch. No light from the moon through the cloud cover.

But he was as ready as he could be.

PAUL WAS READY, too. Enough of this waiting. He was going to take them both out.

He watched the guy step out onto the porch as he often did in the evening. Nothing unusual. He would have been an easy target just then, but Paul didn't want to risk it. He needed to get closer to be sure he couldn't miss.

So he waited and watched, getting more antsy by the moment. The kitchen light went out, the darkness visible through cracks between the curtains. Then that light from the back of the house turned into a faint glow for him to follow. It was time.

He couldn't wait another minute. First the guy wandering outside, then he'd get inside and hunt Audrey down. She'd be too frightened of him to run.

CAM EASED OUTSIDE to the porch to take another look and felt the bullet slice through his upper arm before he heard the report. He fell at once, figuring playing dead was his best option at the moment. Paul would come to check whether he was dead.

But God, his arm burned—it felt as if a jackhammer were being used on it. He ignored the pain. He had to. But it was his right arm, the one he used to shoot. Deadly moments approached.

PAUL COULDN'T BELIEVE that guy had come out onto the porch. Not a creak of hinges. Who had ever opened a screen door without a creak?

At least he'd caught sight of him. Now he was down, dead. If he'd been screaming or rolling around, Paul wouldn't have known, but the man made not a peep, not a single movement. Done.

Then there was Audrey, the one he really wanted. He swore he could feel his fist sinking into her once again. No half measures this time. Nope.

Not being stupid, he headed for the mudroom. Audrey had to be in the room that was faintly lit as if by a nightlight, the only room that wasn't completely dark, the nearest place. And he had to be fast because of that damn bird he'd seen flapping around on the front porch. If it squawked it might wake her. Then she could try to dodge his bullet. It would be harder.

Paul no longer wanted a fight. He no longer wanted to teach that woman a lesson. He wanted her dead so he could forget about her. So she would never bother him again.

He walked carefully through the kitchen. Dang, the floor creaked, so he moved more slowly. He'd get to her, he thought as he rounded the corner.

CLYDE ANNOUNCED IN his best Jimmy Stewart voice, "Target, twelve o'clock."

Audrey pulled the trigger and sent a hail of salt toward Paul. He squealed.

"Damn, Audrey, you need a better aim," Clyde squawked.

Just as he squawked and Audrey readied another shot, she heard Cam's voice from the front of the house.

"Put down that gun right now," he said. "And my pistol isn't loaded with salt."

Clyde was okay, just not happy about being in the middle of a shooting range. At least he didn't keep scolding.

Cam held a pistol on Paul while he waited for the sheriff. "Damn good shooting, Audrey."

Paul whined. "It burns! Damn it, I need a hospital."

"That'll depend on how generous the sheriff is feeling. You only got a small bit of the load or you wouldn't have been standing."

"Shoot him again," Clyde said, speaking finally.

But shooting a man, even Paul, even with salt, had left Audrey feeling sickened. Calling it self-defense didn't change the fact that she would have fired even with lead shot in the gun.

She wondered how she was going to deal with *this* now. First Paul had battered her into submission, and now he'd added making her try to kill to his list of crimes.

Not that it was the same as what he'd done to her. But hell, even the law didn't think his crimes against her deserved more than six years.

She'd just been judge and jury, and she wanted to throw up.

DAWN HAD COME, pouring golden light through the kitchen windows. Paul had been carted away, complaining, by deputies. Their statements had been taken. Cam's arm had been bandaged by paramedics.

Now they sat alone, and for the first time fear had loosened its claws. Audrey sagged on her chair, face resting on her folded arms, shutting out the world.

Cam got some more coffee. He'd been making it for the cops since they arrived. He put a fresh cup in front of Audrey, but she didn't reach for it. She wouldn't drink it. She hadn't drunk any during this mess. He was starting to seriously worry about her but didn't know what to say that would be helpful.

Ages seemed to pass before Audrey finally spoke. "Thanks for loading me with salt."

"I didn't figure you for a killer, and there's always an aftermath."

She lifted her head. "Still, I pulled that trigger."

"True. And he was about to pull one on you. Self-defense really means something, Audrey. What were you supposed to do? Sit there and let him kill you?"

He saw a softening in her, and now he dared to reach out, to pull her onto his lap and cradle her close.

"I don't fit," she said shakily as tears began to flow.

"You fit on my lap just fine."

Eventually she stopped crying and raised her head. "You're right. I had no other choice."

"None."

A shaky sigh escaped her. "Thanks, Cam. You've been a wonderful help through all this. Really, I can't thank you enough."

Now it was his turn to sigh.

"What?" she asked.

"Okay, I guess I need to throw my heart out there. I want more than thanks from you, Audrey. I want *you*."

She drew a sharp breath, and it seemed to him that her arms gripped him tighter.

"Whenever you think you're ready to trust a man in your life again, just let me know. I'll be waiting."

She wiggled until one arm could wrap around his neck. Dang, the wiggling set him on fire. But then he froze in shock.

Audrey spoke. "I've changed, at least about you. You won't have to wait, Cam. I love you and trust you."

He'd never heard nicer words in his life. Suddenly full of strength and happiness, he rose and carried Audrey to the bed.

"Forever," he said.

Clyde spoke. "Oh, sheesh, you two." Then he flew out to the living room to preen quite contentedly.

And behind him, Audrey and Cam laughed.

* * * * *

COMING SOON!

We really hope you enjoyed reading this book.
If you're looking for more romance
be sure to head to the shops when
new books are available on

Thursday 19th June

To see which titles are coming soon, please visit
millsandboon.co.uk/nextmonth

MILLS & BOON